FIRST CARRIER

BOOK ONE OF THE DISC CHRONICLES

MADELEINE MOZLEY

For David

PART I

FROM THE WILD

CHAPTER ONE

THE CRACKLING OF THORNS UNDER THE CAST IRON POT kept Wren awake. She fidgeted in her blankets and turned on her side, making the dry tumbleweeds, rags, and other miscella- neous debris forming her mattress crinkle and moan. The light from the cooking fire danced on the cave wall. Survivor's hands made shadows against the wall as she poked the fire several feet behind Wren's sleeping nest, and dabbled in the pot as she did every night. Wren thought it was easier to just sleep through the hunger, even though the nightmares that haunted her were little better than the pain in her belly.

"I know you're awake. Come here. I found something good this time," said Survivor.

Wren rolled over slowly, careful not to hurt Biter who was sleeping cradled against her chest. Survivor hunched over the pot, her stirring stick in one hand and a bundle of thorns in the other.

"Come look. How can you try sleeping with this smell?" She shoved the thorns under the pot. They spit and crackled as the fire caught them. Survivor laughed, and her cackling melded with the thorns popping, her laughter burning.

Wren folded down her blankets. A cold gust from the tunnel leading deeper into the cave hit her, and she picked up one of the blankets and draped it over her shoulders. Biter squeaked awake and stuck his pointed nose and big front teeth in her face, searching for warmth. She ran her finger down his nose, between his tiny black eyes against his pink skin, bare except for a few rough hairs here and there, before moving him to the folds of fabric crisscrossing her chest. He burrowed until he disappeared between her cotton dress and patchwork scarf.

Survivor glared at Wren's chest from beneath her cloud of dark hair. "Why don't you just let me cook that thing?"

"You already cooked his brothers. They tasted like snot." Wren cupped her hand around Biter.

Survivor grumbled and went back to stirring.

Wren stood slowly, her sight darkening, and she waited until the familiar lightheaded sensation passed and her vision returned. She stepped over Survivor's sleeping nest and then wound her way between the slanted bench, the basket of shiny trinkets she'd found on her walks in the cave, and the pile of thorns next to Survivor waiting to be used as fuel.

"I'm tired. What's so important?" She leaned over the pot, catching a face full of steam coming up from the bubbling surface. Saliva pooled in the space under her tongue. "Hmm. It does smell good."

There were only a few cups of liquid in the bottom of the pot. A bundle of sage stems and the now empty flour sack lay on the ground nearby. Wren picked up the sack and shook it, and a small teaspoon of mealy powder gathered at the bottom.

"Our flour's gone," she said.

Survivor glanced at her over the edge of the pot. "It'll be worth it."

"What is it?" She watched the thick, tan liquid simmer, entranced.

Survivor put the stirring stick on the ground, and it caked with the dirt on the floor of the cave instantly. "Something delicious."

"But what *is* it?"

"You'll see. It's not ready yet."

She fidgeted and drummed her fingers together. The scar on the back of her right hand—a circle cut through by two slashes—rippled with the motion. Whatever exact meaning the mark had was known only to Survivor; Wren had asked about it only once, and the dead silence she'd received in response had been enough to squelch her curiosity.

Survivor dipped her pinkie into the pot and quickly licked it clean. She thought for a second before saying, "Needs a little something." She bounded over the bench, crawled to her backpack, and began rummaging through the front pocket. She grabbed a tin—a battered rectangle with a strange word engraved on the lid—and skittered back to the fire. Her floppy sleeves were in the way, so she pulled them back and then opened the tin with caution, as if its contents might jump into the air and escape. The tin had been divided into different tiny compartments with thin sheets of scrap metal. Survivor took a pinch of red powder from a corner compartment and sprinkled it in the pot. She quickly closed the tin and shoved it in her bosom.

"Where did you find it, then?" Wren asked. Her stomach flipped when Survivor picked up the stick and stirred again. Even the dirt on the stick mixing with the cooking juices didn't discourage her appetite.

"Oh, far away."

"Far away?" Wren backed up a few inches. "We're not

supposed to go far away. There are things far away. Bad things."

"Yes, but there are also tasty things." Survivor raised her eyebrows and grinned, showing her teeth that were broken and ground down from eating anything she could digest, no matter how inedible. "Tasty things by The Disc."

"The Disc!" Wren shrieked as she fell on her butt and scrambled backward until she was behind the high side of the bench. She peeked over the top. "The Disc isn't safe."

"That's why I went when you were sleeping earlier. You couldn't worry. And now we have dinner. Dinner!" She dipped her spoon in and sipped from it. Her eyes rolled back.

Alma had told Wren about The Disc when she was a child. It had been years ago, but Alma's words charged through Wren's mind afresh.

"The Disc is treacherous," Alma had said as she skewered the big chunks of mottled pink and white rattlesnake flesh Wren handed her. "Monsters live there that will lock you up and make you a slave. Or they'll kill you while other monsters watch."

Survivor seemed to have forgotten the warning.

Wren whispered, "But Alma—"

"Is dead," Survivor cut her off. "Like all the rest of them. It's just us. Stop following her orders like we're still in the forest. Now get your bowl and come here."

Wren swallowed hard. "We don't know that for sure. We didn't see them die."

"You really think that Alma wouldn't have found us by now if they'd survived? We came here just like she told us to. It's been five years. Do you see her anywhere? Or the kids?" She gestured at the empty space.

Wren fell silent. She didn't have the energy, much less the facts, to argue. Crossing her sister never ended in victory for

Wren anyway. They'd quarrel and quarrel, but as food became scarcer and days faded into night entombed in the damp cool of the cave, so faded Wren's desire to be right. It had been replaced by a desire to make it to tomorrow, and if Survivor had a plan for how to do that—which she always did—then Wren obeyed.

"Now, get your bowl," said Survivor, a high-pitched little thrill sneaking into her voice.

Wren tottered over to a faded, green plastic box and retrieved her bowl from inside—a small glass tray only a couple of inches deep, divided in the middle by little grooves.

"Get mine, too. And the plate," Survivor called over her shoulder.

Wren returned to the pot with their dishes. As she watched its contents move, she felt as though it might try to reach out and grab her, the steam and bubbles making it seem like a living, breathing thing. A thing that was watching her back.

Survivor took her own bowl first. It was a tall, red-brown container with a hole in the bottom that they'd plugged with a piece of cork. She poured in a couple of large spoonfuls of the liquid, then took Wren's bowl and did the same. It smelled tasty, a salty tang mingling with the heady spices.

"Now, the best part."

Survivor hadn't been this giddy since they got squirrel and rabbit meat in the forest. She was practically drooling.

Carefully, Survivor dipped her spoon to scrape against the bottom of the pot, searching for something. Her eyes lit up when she felt it, and she gently eased the spoon beneath it. She pulled it up and put it on the plate.

Wren squinted at it, trying to figure out what it was. The tan liquid that had coated it started to seep off, spilling down onto the plate's white plastic.

It was a hand, cut off just above the wrist. Two inches of

bone stuck out of the wrist, and several bits of flesh were missing, having fallen off as it tenderized during cooking. A gold ring was on one of the fingers.

"I forgot! Here!" Survivor removed the ring, tearing off shreds of flesh with it. She held it out to Wren. "For your collection."

Wren retched, spilling bile onto the fire, all she had left in her stomach.

"Idiot! Now I'll have to get more thorns tonight!" Survivor shoved the last bunch of thorns into the fire and blew at it, trying to get the wet parts to relight.

Wren put her bowl on the ground and hobbled back to her sleeping nest, even weaker now than before. The dull ache in her belly turned to a stabbing. She would get no sleep tonight. She settled under the blankets, and Biter squeaked at the adjustment.

The thorns crackled to life and illuminated the cave walls again. Survivor slurped from her bowl. "Don't be a child. You have to eat."

"Not that," Wren whispered.

"Meat is meat. Besides, I'm sure he won't miss it. He shouted a lot when I took it, but I don't know why. He has two." The slurping became chewing, and Survivor's shadow dancing on the wall turned violent with her devouring.

Wren burrowed further under her blankets until a muffled darkness surrounded her.

"What do you mean, you lost her?" Mainstay spat at Caster through his teeth. He spoke over the din of the whistling sandstorm outside and the occasional *plink plinks* of larger rocks hitting the metal slats of the travel dome.

"I mean, she got away. Disappeared in the crags." Caster shoved his long, tangled hair back from his face and sank to his heels in front of the fire pit at the dome's center. He undid the line of buttons stretching down his side and opened his black coat, kicking up a thin layer of dirt as it skimmed the ground. He tented his coat over the fire and let the warmth spread through his sleeves and up his chest. "Finding her in that mess wouldn't be worth the effort. She's just an outlier, starving, probably going to die soon anyway."

Mainstay hissed as Adonis struggled to rewrap the stub of his wrist for the third time that evening. Adonis had tried to tie it too tight and too high up, and as the bandage slipped off, the boy ducked for a blow that very nearly came.

A gust from outside cut beneath the rim of their dome, sending it up a couple of inches before thumping back down. The chill made Caster dare to inch even closer to the fire. The dome was supposed to be set in a trench dug at least a foot deep in the ground, but Adonis hadn't set many up by himself, and the boy had done a piss-poor job on this one. Caster would fix it after Mainstay was done ranting.

Mainstay's grizzled beard wasn't quite enough to cover his double chin. He rubbed at it ferociously. "She was sitting beneath that overhang, crying. I go over to help, and she cuts off my hand with a hatchet. She was a freak. An animal. You think I'm going to just let her get away?"

Caster reached over and grabbed a bitter apple from a sack on the wide, flat rock on which Adonis perched. "I'm sure her large chest didn't have anything to do with your attentiveness, hmm? Adonis said she was practically half-naked. Too bad I was off looking for water or I would've warned you not to give in to your baser drives." He took a bite of the apple, chewing quickly to keep the taste from lingering on his tongue.

Mainstay shifted his attention back to Adonis, his neck blooming red. "You told him *what?*"

Adonis stopped tying the new bandage and looked down. "Nothing. Just that she was pretty, or parts of her were anyway, and I didn't blame you for—"

"Get out of here! Fix the dome!" He slapped Adonis on the side of the head so hard the kid fell off the rock on which he was sitting, sending apples rolling onto the ground. Adonis rebounded quickly and jumped to his feet with the seeming weightlessness of adolescence. He dusted himself off sheepishly and then grabbed a trowel from the stand next to the canvas entrance flap on his way out.

"He's thirteen," said Caster. "Give him a break. He's a boob guy too. It was the first thing he said when I got back—'Did you find the girl with the big rack?' You two have a common weakness." He laughed as he finished his apple.

Mainstay wasn't laughing. He just sat there with his half-tied bandage, not even elevating it as it started to bleed through again while he stared at Caster.

"Why are you out here, pretty boy?" he asked Caster.

It was a trick question. Mainstay wanted a fight.

Caster put his hand on his heart. "You think I'm pretty? Gosh, and here I thought we were just friends." He buttoned his coat and moved toward the exit.

"Stop. Turn," said Mainstay.

Caster did as he was told.

"I asked you a question, Scout."

"I'm out here to do my part and serve the people of The Disc, sir." He made a show of clasping his hands behind his back and standing at attention.

"No, royal bastard. You're out here because you're a bored, rich brat. Everyone knows who your daddy is. You've followed him around like a starry-eyed believer since before your balls dropped, spending his money, eating meat and cheese, fucking women who hoped to impress you with their bodies for a chance at securing their futures. You don't need to be out here. You don't *need* anything. Say you're out here because you're a spoiled little boy playing army. Admit it."

Caster tried to keep the anger from his voice. "No, sir."

"I'm your Soldier and I'm ordering you to tell the truth."

"The truth?" He lost his grip on his temper for just a second. "You're an asshole, sir."

The faint sound of Adonis digging outside, the wind whistling, and the fire popping as it settled to embers filled the dome.

"I'll have to tell Gavel about your attitude," said Mainstay.

"I'm sure you will."

Mainstay eyed him suspiciously, as if trying to decide if he'd just been insulted or not. "Finish this." He brandished his stump.

Caster walked over to the rock on which Mainstay was propping his arm. He shoved the man's arm up off of the rock, above his head, and tied off the bandage with more force than necessary. Mainstay winced, but before he could spit out a complaint, Caster said, "She's an outlier. Her actions aren't surprising. Getting her won't give you two hands again. We need to get to Gavel and report what I saw in Hallund."

"Your non-news is hardly urgent. We'll keep looking for her either when the sandstorm clears or at dawn, whichever comes first." He looked up at Caster, eyes burning. "That's an order, Scout." He said his title with all the bitterness of an atheist addressing God.

Caster stood. "Keep that elevated or you'll pass out." He walked out of the dome.

The frigid wind whipped dirt and tiny pebbles into his face as he secured the snaps of the entrance flap. He then lifted the scarf around his neck until it covered his head, all but a bare slit around his eyes. The thick darkness of the desert settled around him, broken only by the thin halo of light around the vent hole at the dome's peak and the brilliant white pinpoints of stars. He started making wide laps around the dome and pondered his current predicament.

Every time Caster's Body separated, he ended up with Mainstay. Their Head always took the two higher ranking officers—the Arms, who in Caster's Body were an Assassin and a Thief. That left the Soldier, Mainstay, in charge of Caster and Adonis—the Scout and the Grunt. It was getting old. Caster's job was to observe and report, but Mainstay seemed determined to hinder him from even that. And because Mainstay was pushing this issue with the outlier, he'd be stuck out in the Open until they found her. They were supposed to return to The Disc the night after next and were low on rations. Perhaps most alarming of all was that Caster was running out of patience with Mainstay, and there was a whole lot of desert out here perfectly suited for making a body disappear.

Anger came over him. It was as familiar as the pressure of his knife's hilt in his hand, and nearly as dangerous. He shoved out a rough exhale and tried to shed the adrenaline like dead skin, letting it fly into the wind as he shook out his arms.

Adonis jogged up and tried to fall in step next to him, his shorter legs struggling to keep the pace. His balaclava muffled his words and made it sound like he was shouting into a pillow to be heard above the din of the storm. "Fat shithead."

"He's your ranking officer. Watch your mouth."

Adonis kicked a rock hard, sending it flying along the mesa on which they were camped to tumble a hundred feet off the edge. "You can call him an asshole, but I can't call him a shithead?"

"Stop eavesdropping."

He kicked another rock. "Can't you just ask your dad to have him discharged?"

"You're pushing your luck, kid." Caster grabbed him by the back of the neck and shook him side to side. Adonis struggled and managed to free himself, then jumped onto Caster's back. Caster knelt on the ground and threw himself backward to slam Adonis to the dirt, careful to not drop his full weight on the kid with the maneuver. He let Adonis get up, and the kid rushed him, diving straight into a headlock that he should have been expecting. After a few seconds of Caster slowly increasing pressure on his trachea, Adonis tapped his arm and Caster dropped it.

"Got to stop doing what's easy and start thinking ahead," said Caster. "Plan your moves, don't just react." He thumped his arm across his chest twice to show the mock fight was finished.

Adonis thumped his own chest in response.

Caster bent down and felt near the kid's temple where Mainstay had struck him. "Your head okay?"

The kid nodded, making his curly hair bob beneath his hood. "I still think you should have him discharged." He turned his big eyes up, his brow furrowed. "Have you really had meat *and* cheese?"

Caster sighed and squeezed the kid's shoulder before turning to look out along the horizon. It was utterly dark, and for most people, it would have been too easy to forget the shape of the landscape, how the rocks jutted out from the earth in jagged spikes in the distance like broken glass covered in desert dirt and debris. But he could still see them, shapes and outlines and shades of dark and darker that others couldn't see.

"Anything out there?" Adonis asked.

Caster shook his head.

Stones continued to whip him, and the cold wind scalded

his exposed skin. Was this shit what he wanted? Was this where he wanted to be? Absolutely not. But that was the point.

Out here, it was quiet, it was simple. Out here, he followed instead of led. There were no temptations, nothing to distract him from doing his job, and it was a simple job. He needed to know if he could do it well.

As another stone pelted him in the soft part of his thigh, something in the distance caught his attention. A flicker of light, barely there, moved somewhere in the crags to the northeast. He blinked and squinted through a bitter gust. The light disappeared, dropping between two folds of rock.

"We might be home tomorrow after all," he muttered.

Wren and Survivor were up before dawn. Wren hadn't slept at all the previous night while Survivor snored next to her. Actually *snored*. Wren hadn't heard that noise since they were with Alma, and it initially made her jump. She'd rolled over to see Survivor with one hand behind her head, mouth lolling open, her other hand on her swollen stomach.

They'd wound through the complex series of tunnels and pathways below their cave foraging for a couple of hours, and the sandstorm had just recently died down. They now walked among the higher up crags. Wren could tell the storm had passed due to the lack of whistling through the gaps and crevices in the rock around them as they returned to their cave. The air was warmer here, and Wren threw back her hood, letting her dark red hair cascade down her back and breathe. Survivor had a spring to her step that Wren tried hard not to envy.

"At least we found those gray tubers, eh?" Survivor had been trying to strike up conversation all morning, but Wren

wasn't for it. "Your rat thing will enjoy them. I mean, Biter."
She plowed on ahead, sparing an occasional glance back. Wren
suspected it was only to make sure she hadn't fallen into a hole
or gotten her foot stuck in quicksand.

"Maybe this afternoon we could travel to the flatlands and
try to catch some earthworms. Get out of all this rock."
Survivor raised her arms and motioned dramatically at the
sharp tan crags they maneuvered between. At certain points
they didn't have more than a few feet of clearance between
two rock walls, and they approached one of these points now.
Wren referred to it as "Knife Point" because she always
ended up cutting herself on either the wall in front of or
behind her.

"What do you think?" Survivor tried again. "Or maybe we
could hike to the big pool and try to net some cave fish?" She
raised her arms above her head, holding a bundle of thorns
wrapped in thin cloth high up and slid into Knife Point, the last
passage before a stretch of inclined terrain leading to their cave.

Wren pulled her arms tight against her sides—a new tech-
nique she'd been wanting to try—and shuffled in. Her nose was
less than a foot from one jagged wall, while her back nearly
touched the wall behind. She tried turning to the right, facing
Survivor, hoping she might avoid slicing her forehead this time.

"Come on. It's not that big of a deal. I already told you, he
didn't *need* that hand." Survivor dropped the friendly, please-
talk-to-me tone and replaced it with condescension. She looked
straight ahead and slid her feet to the right in a well-practiced
rhythm.

"You went to The Disc," said Wren. "You know we
shouldn't go there."

"I went *close* to The Disc, but I never left the Open." She
glared out of the corner of her eye.

"Then you took—" Wren fought the hot bile in her throat

until it went back down. "You hurt someone. How do you know they aren't angry about it?"

"Oh, I'm sure he's angry about it." She smirked, pulling the left side of her mouth up in a tight arc.

Wren's foot slipped, and she swayed forward. A jagged edge of rock sliced her left cheek open, but not deep. She found her balance again and tried to ignore the stinging. "What if he comes to find you?"

"Find me? As if he could fit his fat ass through these passages. We're safe. I always keep you safe." Survivor reached the end of the passage and stepped onto the ridge leading up to the cave.

On her right was the mountain in which their cave sat, on the other was a sheer drop. Tall, thin pillars of rock jutted up from the abyss at irregular intervals. Survivor stood next to one of the gaps, letting the hot breeze hit her for a minute, then lowered her arms and turned back to watch Wren finish the trek.

After shuffling another couple of feet, Wren emerged next to her. She tore off a piece of her dress and held it to her bleeding cheek. "I'm just afraid of what—" Wren started.

"Shh!" Survivor held up her hand and turned to look over her shoulder toward the cave.

"What is it?"

Survivor yanked her down into a crouch. "Listen."

Bits and pieces of conversation floated down to them from the cave.

"...why it hurts so much. They're just tiny cuts," one voice said.

"...salt content in the rocks...burning...told you to wear gloves," a deeper voice said.

It had been a long time since Wren had heard voices like these. The last time a group of men found her and her siblings, it had ended in fire. But something about the second man's voice this time drew her in instead of sending fear through her chest. It sounded like the trees in which she'd spent her childhood—strong, earthy.

"Men," Survivor whispered. Her nose wrinkled in disgust.

A light appeared in the cave entrance. Survivor shoved her bundle of firewood and Wren's bunch of tubers between two small boulders next to the mountainside. She pulled Wren up and headed for a pair of pillars on their left. They hunkered down, half hidden by a large pillar, half exposed. Wind rushed up the channel that stretched down an unknown distance off the edge of the pathway, catching the fabric Wren held too loosely to her cheek and sending it flying off to ride the breeze. The sun was on the other side of the mountain, casting the abyss in darkness. It could have stretched hundreds of feet to the ground, or just a couple of yards. But even a fall from that height would mean broken bones and a slow, agonizing death. A fresh breeze came up the abyss and blew Wren's wild, red hair up in a whoosh, and Survivor, pressed against Wren's back, yanked up the hood of her shawl and stuffed the crazy hair into it. Wren hugged the pillar in front of them.

Survivor perched as close to the abyss as she could, not caring to look at the cave or whoever was inside it. But Wren peeked around the pillar, daring to get a better view. Survivor was a decade Wren's senior, but the rest of their six siblings, including the three boys, had been several years Wren's junior. She had never seen a grown man clearly—when they'd come searching for her and her family, they'd generally come at night, or she and the others had seen them coming from far off and hidden before they got close. Her curiosity egged her on to squint at the entrance of the cave.

A boy, not a child but not yet a man, exited the cave carrying a strange, flameless torch in one hand while he blew on his other palm, holding it close to his mouth. He had a curly mop of dark hair and wore nice traveling clothes, even knee-high boots with laces.

"Mainstay's going to be pissed that she wasn't here. Should we tell him we found his wedding band?" the boy said.

Wren elbowed Survivor, who grunted in response.

"I suppose he can have it. And I think he's more pissed that he couldn't fit back here himself," called the deeper voice, the owner of which was still hidden just inside the cave.

"Told you. Fat," Survivor whispered in Wren's ear.

Wren sighed.

"There are two sleeping pallets. Why do you think the other one wasn't with her when she attacked? There's obviously someone with her, right? A husband maybe?" the boy said.

Finally, the man came out of the cave, stooped over to fit through the entrance. He stood to his full height, which was tall indeed. His blond hair was wild and wind-swept and reached his shoulders. With a few stiff brushes and pats of his hands, he removed some of the dirt coating his lengthy black coat.

"Not a man. Another woman," the man said. "And they probably just split up for a while."

"Two women in this place? How have they stayed alive?"

"Not sure why their femaleness shocks you, kid. They've survived like all people scraping life out of the Open—they're strong. Have to be." He took a small, cloth bag out of his pocket and tossed it in the cave.

"Strong *flesh eaters*, you mean." The boy stuck his tongue out and shook his head. "Disgusting."

"You're telling me in all your life, in those years you spent out in the Open and with slave traders, you never got hungry enough to consider eating another human?"

"Thinking about it and doing it aren't the same thing," muttered the boy.

The man mussed the boy's hair and grabbed the torch from his hand.

The boy grimaced. "Careful! They still sting." He flexed his hands as if to test the truth of his words.

The man touched something on the torch, and the light at the end disappeared. He tucked it in his belt under his coat and started walking away from the cave, sure-footed on the steep incline, toward where Survivor and Wren were hidden.

"What are you doing?" the boy said. "We're not going to wait for them?"

"Hurry," Survivor whispered, pulling Wren's attention from the men. "I'll climb down, and you come after me. Rest your feet on my shoulders if you have to." Without hesitation, she pressed her hands and feet against the pillar in front of them and the pillar behind them and started descending into the abyss like a spider.

"No!" Wren got on her knees near the edge. "We'll fall. How do we know they'll hurt us, anyway?"

"Do as I say. Now, before they come," Survivor hissed.

Wren stole one last look at the man as he got closer, and her breath caught. An unfamiliar warmth started at her navel and stretched slowly downward.

He was the sun and the forest all in one, rays in his hair and resilience in his gait. As he came closer, she noticed two tiny braids that ran from just behind his temples and met behind his head to keep his hair off of his face. An urge to touch them struck her.

Survivor hissed louder, and Wren finally followed after her. She pushed as firmly against the two pillars as she could manage and then shimmied down until her head sat a solid foot beneath the path, out of sight.

Hurried footsteps thumped against the ground. "The embers of their fire are still warm," said the boy. His voice grew louder as he approached their hiding spot. "Abandoned camp, my ass. If Mainstay finds out—"

"The only way he'd find out is if you told him," replied the man. His voice was as clear as if he were by Wren's side—he'd paused up above. "And you wouldn't do that, because you want to go home too."

Wren started to shake under the strain of holding herself between the pillars. The excitement of seeing new people that had flooded her muscles started to give way to her perpetual exhaustion. Her arms and legs felt like iron growing soft under heat. The shaking started at her hands and feet and made its way past her elbows and knees. Survivor climbed up a few inches and took Wren's feet on her shoulders to hold the brunt of her weight. She was head and shoulders shorter than Wren, but her body was far stronger.

"Do we agree?" the man asked.

A hot gust rushed up the abyss, billowing the women's skirts and tossing sand in their faces. Wren closed her eyes and focused on keeping her arms out, rather than on the increasingly likely fall that would kill them both.

"Agreed."

"Good." The man sniffed twice, as if he had something stuck in his nose.

"Smell something?" the boy asked eagerly.

"Nothing you need to worry about. Let's go. You first so I can watch your back and catch you if you fall again."

"Piss off."

The sound of their movements faded as they entered Knife Point.

"Climb!" Survivor coughed from the darkness.

Wren forced her arms to press harder against the pillars,

heaving herself up inch by inch as Survivor pushed from beneath. When she reached the path, she threw one arm over the ledge, then the other, and strained upward with what was left of the strength in her core.

Survivor groaned softly at the removal of Wren's weight. She crawled up the rest of the way with relative ease, not accepting Wren's help to get up on the ledge. They sat there panting as quietly as possible as the men turned the corner at the end of Knife Point and disappeared from sight. Survivor pointed at the bundles she'd left hidden in the rocks and then jogged off toward the cave. Wren grabbed the bundles and followed.

The cave looked almost the same as they'd left it, except Wren's stash of shiny trinkets had been rummaged through. She was glad they'd taken the ring, though. She hadn't wanted it to begin with. The bag the man had tossed into the cave sat near the fire pit. She went over and picked it up, sticking her nose close to the rough fabric and smelling.

"Don't open that," Survivor called across the cave. She crouched next to her thick sleeping blanket, which she'd laid out lengthwise on the ground. She began piling their clothes and tools on it.

"Why not?" Wren asked.

"Because they're men. Understand?"

Wren hesitated, but when a sweet smell rose out of the top of the bag, she undid the drawstring and looked inside. There were several little round things as well as a couple of dried strips of something dark red and dotted with tiny seeds. Fruits of some kind.

Survivor stopped her work to glare at Wren. "Drop it."

She paused with the fruit touching her lips.

Survivor threw her hands up. "If you die, don't blame me." She went back to packing.

Wren stuffed half of a red strip into her mouth and chewed. Sweetness covered her tongue as she mashed the strip down to a pulp and pushed it into her cheek. The juices of the dried fruit squirted out of the pulp, and her stomach growled audibly. She tightened the drawstring of the bag and tied it to her belt.

"Why are you packing?" she asked around the mass, trying to keep the juices in. "They left."

"Yes, but they know where we live. We can't stay here anymore." Survivor rolled the bundle up and bound it with two pieces of rope.

"But the one in black said he wasn't going to tell anyone."

"The word of a man means nothing. They'll come back."

Wren swallowed a bit of the pulp. "How did they find us?"

"Probably saw my torch when I went out for firewood last night. Stupid. But it was your fault, you and your weak stomach. Pack your things."

"Why do you hate them so much? The one in black seemed..." she trailed off as a heat started at her earlobes and spread to her cheeks. She swallowed the rest of the pulp in one giant gulp. "Good." She went to her sleeping mat and started packing her things, giving Survivor her back so she wouldn't see her flush.

"Listen, and don't make me repeat this again—you can't trust anyone but me. Especially men. Ever," Survivor said, giving "ever" a punch in its soft spot. "Why don't you understand that? Did any of the men you came across in the outlands ever seem 'good' to you?"

No, she supposed they hadn't. Alma certainly hadn't thought so, either. She had taught Wren and her siblings how to hide, and they'd done so successfully for the most part. A couple of times, Alma had taken care of them, usually with her bow, and then dragged them off to bury them somewhere. Wren had never asked where.

The exact reason why men—bounty hunters, Alma called them—had looked for them was a mystery. But after the fire, they'd stopped coming. Maybe they'd lost interest, or maybe Wren and Survivor were too well concealed in their cave. Nobody had ever found them. Until now.

"Besides," Survivor continued, "we're starving here. We couldn't have stayed much longer anyway. Pack up."

Wren dropped the issue, as she always did. Survivor had been on her own for years before finding Alma and the others. The truth was that Survivor knew more than Wren about how to stay alive when everything seemed to want to kill them. So Wren listened.

She'd been listening ever since Survivor showed her how to skin a rabbit and leave the pelt intact when she was twelve years old. She'd started with little incisions around the ankles, then removed the entire skin in one great tug like a magic trick. Survivor knew things like that. Useful things. Alma had taught Wren essential skills: how to build a fire, forage for food and water, patch up a flesh wound. But Survivor knew even more.

Wren had always been drawn to more useless wisdom, like which constellations were visible at what time of year and stories about Pericles, Dr. Jekyll, Buttercup, and all of the other characters Alma told her about. As much as she loved to dream of faraway places and imaginary people, even she had to admit that such fantasies couldn't save her. Not like Survivor could.

Survivor was different from the rest of Wren's siblings. Darker, quiet, always slinking away if one of the children tried to hug her or sit in her lap. Except with Wren. When Survivor woke up in the dark of night panting, sweating through her blanket from nightmares, it was Wren who would lay down next to her. Only then could Survivor fall asleep again.

Once, when they were alone hunting sand diggers at dusk, Wren dared to ask her what her nightmares were about.

Survivor thought about it, stabbed a brown lizard that ran out from the safety of a clump of cacti with a sharp stick, and answered, "Life before you."

And that life had certainly not been easy. Survivor had kept them alive this long, and it would be foolish to doubt her now.

"Where are we going?" Wren asked as she tied off her bedroll.

"After them."

Wren spun around. "What? We have to leave because they know where we live, and you want to follow them?"

"Yes. They're rich, didn't you see that? Rich enough to have a flashlight and just leave a bag of food behind." She nodded at the bag on Wren's belt. "You could use a new scarf. I want that boy's boots." Her eyes went wide, and she rubbed her hands together. "We have to leave and they're to blame. It's only fair that they help us resupply before we look for a new place to hide."

"More hiding? But there's just the two of us. It's been five years since the forest. You really think the hunters are still after us? That they would even recognize us?"

"It's not just them. We need to resupply and then go back underground, somewhere tucked away like this."

"Why? We could find one of the villages Alma told us about. Some small town where we could stay. Other people."

"No." Survivor's voice was clipped and final.

Wren hesitated, but then she whispered, "Is this about The Gentleman?"

Survivor took three massive steps toward Wren and erupted, "How the hell do you know that name?"

Wren shrunk toward the cave floor. "Alma told me."

The only sound for a solid minute was Survivor's heavy breathing.

"Yes. He's still after me," Survivor said at last. "And anyone he finds with me. Always will be."

Wren looked up at her, saw the rare panic in her dark eyes, and stood. She rested her forehead on Survivor's shoulder. "I didn't know. I'm sorry."

"I didn't want you to know." Survivor kissed her once firmly on top of the head. "I'll get the cooking pot. Leave the rat thing here. He'll die in the Open." She turned and headed back to her pack.

Wren stooped over the spot marked with three bright white stones next to her sleeping area and gently dug. She unearthed Biter, who had been resting in the dark, and brushed him off as she held him in one hand. From the bundle nearby, she grabbed a tuber and set it near his face. He munched happily.

She kissed him on the nose, wanting desperately to bring him but suspecting that Survivor was right. Again. His skin was so thin and pale, his body so tiny. He was made for the dark and the damp. She shoved the rest of the tubers close enough for him to smell them before turning away and wiping her tears quickly.

"We don't even know how many are in their group. This is suicide," Wren muttered, more to herself than to her sister.

Survivor ignored her. She tied the cooking pot to the bottom of the pack hanging off her right shoulder.

"They're going to The Disc. We can't go there," Wren said.

Survivor tied her hair back and raised her hood. "Then we better rob them before they reach it." She grinned, showing her broken teeth.

CHAPTER TWO

When Caster returned Mainstay's wedding band
and told him the women were long gone by now, Mainstay had
believed him. They were late to meet the other half of their
Body, and Caster suspected that Mainstay was also starting to
feel hungry for something more substantial than fruit and
protein bars. Those two factors combined seemed to have overwhelmed his impulse to question everything out of Caster's
mouth.

They broke camp and headed in the direction of the Border
Valley, which marked the end of the Open and the beginning
of the land belonging to The Disc and its Principal. While they
were in the Open, they were fair game. But if they were
attacked inside the Border Valley, the opposing party would not
only be trespassing, but declaring war on the economic power-
house of the region. The likelihood of that happening was very
slim. Nobody was stupid enough to attack The Disc. But until
they made it to the Border Valley, they were as vulnerable as
any common travelers.

Caster's Body had spent the last six weeks in the Open on a

scouting mission. Those in the Body most talented with pilfering information—the Thief and the Scout—were tasked with venturing into neighboring territories, although some hardly deserved the status of "territory." They gathered news, eavesdropped, and made trades for especially valuable information. Had a territory found a new resource and was prospering from it? Was their rate of procreation a cause for concern? Were they raising an army? Had they located any lost technology that would be better suited for the forces of The Disc, who would of course never abuse that kind of power? And so the questions went on.

In a couple hours' time, Mainstay's group would meet up with the other half of their Body at King's Rock, which marked the beginning of the Border Valley. There, they'd spend the night and then proceed through the valley to The Disc the following morning. Caster's group had nearly reached King's Rock yesterday, but then the outlier showed up. Mainstay had sent Caster back the way she'd run off while he and Adonis broke camp and followed after him. Now a sense of déjà vu hung in the dry, blistered air as they retraced their footsteps.

Caster couldn't push his legs fast enough to reach King's Rock. When they rejoined the others, his Head would again be in charge, relieving Mainstay of his command over him and Adonis. Mainstay had asked everything short of a foot massage from them in the past week. At one point, when they'd turned in for the night, Mainstay had snored loud enough to drown out the wind hammering against the dome. Adonis sat up from his sleeping bag with his cutlass and pretended to stab him in the mouth repeatedly. Caster nearly blew a rib out trying to contain his laughter.

These periodic scouting parties took six weeks in part because they were on foot. Anyone who was lucky enough to have a horse or, even more miraculous, a working vehicle, would be waving a please-rob-me flag to desperate outliers or, far worse yet, Marauders—people who had turned their backs on society at large, instead forming clans and picking off travelers, vagrants, and merchants as they passed between territories. Firsthand reports of Marauders were tough to find, as victims were either killed immediately or taken. Caster had seen a handful of Marauder scouts over the last couple of years, men looking for targets to report back to their clan's Master. Thankfully, Caster had always spotted them first and told his Body, who in turn found an alternate route. Caster had only once seen a full group of them when he was on a scouting mission of his own. They had been far off, camping on a broad mesa in plain sight, beating drums and shouting. Beasts in human skin.

A need to check their surroundings grabbed hold of him then, and he did a sweep of the horizon, where brilliant blue met pale earth. Nothing ahead but more desert. Mainstay walked ahead of Caster and Adonis, his hand on the butt of the .357 Magnum at his hip and his stump cradled in a sling against his chest. He had the stocky, muscle-turned-to-fat physique of someone who'd been incredibly fit in his youth, but who now plodded rather than strutted. Caster and Adonis walked several yards behind, carrying all of the gear. Poor Adonis was stuck with the dome folded into a great circle on his back, which made him look like a tortoise and walk nearly as slowly as one.

The terrain around them varied between open space dotted with scrub grass with no protection from the burning sun, and rocky zones with weapons-grade cacti and the occasional boulder or other natural shade-providing formation to offer relief from the heat. They were in an open area currently, and Caster was seriously considering throwing off the tattered, sand-colored rags he wore over his black coat, consequences of standing out be damned. Sweat ran into his eyes, and he blinked past the burning.

In the Open, you were either sweating or freezing. The day brought the sun and its oppressive rays, against which the most effective form of protection was light fabric covering as much skin as possible. Fabric that blended into the natural landscape was essential, as it was camouflage against Marauders who would spot an odd color a half-mile away and fly toward it like mosquitos to bare skin, eager to land and drain blood. At night, the cold settled into the air and the dirt, and if a traveler hadn't been hauling a heavier coat or cloak around during the day, they'd regret it then, and it might cost them their life if they couldn't make a fire to boot. Travelers had to have enough clothes on at all times to accommodate both ends of the spectrum, which meant never being comfortable.

Caster was uncomfortable for a reason other than just the heat at present. Since they'd left the crags, a tingling had hovered at the base of his neck. His Scout training had afforded him the ability to know when he was being followed, and he knew without having to look back that someone was behind them in the distance. Mainstay and Adonis were oblivious, and for the time being, he intended to keep them that way. Marauders didn't sneak up—they charged in, blades and blunt objects to the sky. Common thieves were more careful and followed a person's trail until they were vulnerable. Those following Caster's group were neither, and he could smell the salt and ashes on the gusts blowing at his back—the same scents from the cave they'd left that morning. If these women were as daring as he suspected, he couldn't keep their existence a secret for long, and he had to think of a way to get them to back off before then.

King's Rock finally appeared on the horizon. The spines of the crown-shaped formation on top of the precarious looking pile of stones were like a welcoming hand to Caster, who'd grown tired of having to look at Mainstay's wide ass. Three figures were gathered at the base of King's Rock, two setting up a dome and the other with his hand to his brow to shade his eyes as he looked toward Caster's party.

As they approached, a tiny flicker of movement caught Caster's attention near the top of King's Rock. Crouched on his heels was a man, slight and deeply tanned, a white turban wrapped around his head. His yellow eyes seemed to bulge out from his face; Caster could see them clearly even though King's Rock was nearly two hundred feet away and some forty feet high. Those yellow eyes bored into Caster's.

Caster, Mainstay, and Adonis closed the rest of the distance between them and their Head, Gavel. He was tall and weather-worn, with black skin that stood out against the desert backdrop and not a hair atop his head. He had the bearing of a man who could kill you with a flick of his thumb but would rather talk you out of making him do it. Caster had argued with Gavel many times over the years, starting in childhood. He hadn't won yet.

Gavel tugged the tan head covering down from his mouth. "I'm guessing you spotted our company on your way in?" He subtly jerked his head toward King's Rock and the man crouched atop it.

"Marauder scout by the look of him," said Caster. "He's got scars all over his neck. Basic machete in hand. Has he made any move to attack?"

"No, and I don't believe he will. He's most likely watching for travelers leaving the neutral zone, not going into it. The few supplies we have left wouldn't be worth starting a war over. Six gave him a colorful greeting when we arrived an hour ago. The Marauder hasn't said a word."

"Should we move further inward? Out of his line of sight?" asked Mainstay.

"I'd rather keep him where we can see him than move where he can't see us," said Gavel. "He'll likely return to his Master come nightfall. Any news?"

Mainstay opened his mouth to speak, but Gavel spoke first, catching sight of his arm. "There's at least a story to be told."

"An outlier did it, sir," Mainstay said. "She escaped."

"She?" Gavel raised an eyebrow.

Six dropped his trowel by the half-set-up dome and sprinted over to the group, leaving their Thief, Sans, to hold up the dome by himself.

"Lady trouble, eh Mainstay? What *will* your wife say?" Six said.

Six was the youngest Assassin to reach the rank, not yet thirty. He had a strong jaw and a faint old-world Spanish accent that he amped up for the ladies as needed. Out in the Open, his work was generally serving as a fighter like Mainstay, defending against threats such as Marauders and thieves. But every once in a while, he'd get the opportunity to use his true skill as an Assassin to take out threats to the territories that required more subtlety.

He'd once joined a cult in a small town south of The Disc bent on kidnapping adolescents from nearby territories to perform human sacrifices. He quickly sweet-talked his way up to being second-in-command and then killed the leader, making it look like a tragic accident. His first act as leader was to dissolve the cult and scatter the members across the desert. Nobody ever knew he was from The Disc or was acting in its best interest and that of the region. Which, of course, was the point.

"Shut it, Six," said Mainstay.

"Touchy. Wound's still fresh. That's fine, I understand.

Hey, Cast! Donnie!" He clapped them both on the shoulder and took the dome off of Adonis' back. "Oh, crap." He looked down at Adonis. "Does Sans look angry?"

Adonis looked around Six toward Sans. "How can you tell?"

Sans set down the dome, dropping it in the half-completed trench, and headed for them. His features were nondescript—medium toned skin, light brown eyes, and a sweep of brown hair. Everything medium and utterly forgettable. He could have been twenty-five or fifty thanks to the procedures performed on Thieves to make them blend in and impossible to identify. His kanabō was strapped to his back, a massive club-like weapon that he wielded in the Open, though he often concealed most of it under a long cloak. He wore it in plain sight at the moment, and the damage he could inflict with it was incalculable. He strode up and stopped right behind Six, his expression revealing no emotion.

"Little help?" he said.

Six let out a whoosh of air in relief. "Of course, amigo!" He shouldered the dome and followed Sans. Adonis followed close behind, taking out his trowel and trying to keep up.

"We'll sign you up for a prosthetic when we get back. Try to hang in there until then," Gavel said to Mainstay. "Now, is there any news I need to be aware of? Anything in the western territories?"

"No, sir. Nothing to report," Mainstay said.

"Well, not nothing," Caster spoke up.

Mainstay rolled his eyes. "Your naïve suspicions don't count as news, Scout. Learn your place."

"You learn yours, Soldier," said Gavel. "It's his job to be suspicious, and it's yours to use your gun if those suspicions become a reality. Until then, why don't you go help them set up camp?"

Gavel bowed, and with just a second's hesitation, Mainstay bowed back lower before stomping off to the others.

"What is it?" Gavel asked.

"He's not wrong, exactly. All I really have is a gut feeling. I was in a pub on the lower side of Hallund. They have no water, just sour wine and beer. From what I overheard, this has been going on for weeks."

"You're concerned they're desperate and might try to seek refuge in The Disc? Our resources are already strapped thin."

"Maybe. But what bothers me more are the rumors of what happened to their wells. I heard tons of theories, everything from cholera to poison to a bioweapon. The bottom line— someone contaminated their supply."

"How many died?"

"Not sure, and it might not be over yet. After the first few cases showed up, their elders closed off the wells and quarantined the sick to prevent panic and further spread. But who knows how many are carrying the illness with no symptoms yet." He hesitated, then said quietly, "This was intentional sabotage."

"You don't know that for sure."

"Diseases like that haven't been seen in this area for over four years." Caster looked away from Gavel and shuffled his feet a bit.

"You think this is the same sickness that took Reina?" His tone was a millimeter softer.

Caster shrugged. "It's at least similar to rubedo. After years, it just magically shows up?"

"I see your point, but do you have proof?"

"No. And no suspects. Could be a political move or just a local with a grievance who wanted revenge against the entire town."

"Political move is unlikely. Hallund is self-sufficient and

neither growing nor shrinking economically. Their elders have shown no interest in any greater pull for territory. They're neutral. An individual makes more sense, but still, to get their hands on a bioweapon, risking their own exposure, just for some sort of revenge? And what would possibly warrant that kind of revenge? A large portion of their population is women and children. Only a monster would make that move." He trailed off, retreating inward to his thoughts, a place Caster was fairly certain nobody had ever truly seen. "Anything else?"

The tingling on Caster's neck danced around his hairline. He didn't dare look back to pinpoint the women's location, as Gavel would follow his gaze. Gavel was a good leader, an honorable man, but he was sometimes too honorable. He followed authority and procedures. Always. Procedure dictated that if they were attacked or robbed in the Border Valley, they were to take the criminals back to stand trial.

Trials of outliers in The Disc ended one of two ways— death or prison. These women deserved neither. They were desperate, not degenerate. And as much as Caster didn't want to admit it, if the women were found, his lie to Mainstay would come out. Mainstay could go to hell, but Caster would hate to be discharged for something as stupid as protecting some outliers. After three years of keeping his own demons at bay— demons that could have easily gotten him kicked out of Gavel's Body—there was a distinct possibility that he'd soon lose his position because of simple deceit. If Gavel found out, that is.

"No, sir. That's all," said Caster.

Gavel bowed, and Caster returned the gesture. When Gavel left to help the others, Caster did a general survey of their surroundings, as was a Scout's duty when they set up camp. The Marauder at the top of King's Rock continued staring at him, head tilted just slightly to the side. Caster swallowed his disgust and turned toward the direction he'd just come from. Over a hundred feet away, a poof of black hair ducked back behind a sprawling cactus. The Marauder scout wouldn't be able to see the women from his perch, at least not yet. But if they were careless, he'd spy them on their approach. And they were still well outside the neutral zone.

Caster sighed. "Shit."

"That was close," said Survivor.

She set her pack on the ground next to her, a good distance from the cactus behind which she and Wren were hidden. It was a hulking mass of pale green clumps covered in long spines —reaper's horn.

"Get some rest. It will be dark soon. Then we'll move in." She reclined against her pack, using it like a pillow, pulled her hood up to block the sun, and tucked her arms behind her head.

"Our odds were bad with three. Now there are six of them," said Wren between ragged breaths. Survivor slightly regretted not stopping sooner to let her rest.

"Glad to see Alma's math lessons stuck with you."

"Why are we doing this?" Wren sat down in the strip of shade by the cactus and unshouldered her bags. "Shouldn't we be looking for a new place to stay?"

"Of course we'll do that, but we have no idea how long that will take. We need to resupply now that we don't have the food and water from the cave. We need what these assholes have."

Wren opened up the bag of fruit and pulled out a dark, tough-skinned apple. Survivor hated that she was eating the food the stranger had left. There was no way of knowing what he might have done to it. But Wren had been even slower than usual. Her face was gaunt, the skin under her eyes darker now that they were exposed to the light of day. If she didn't eat something, she'd die soon anyway, so Survivor saw it as an acceptable risk in the end.

Wren rolled the apple core away from her and let her head hang back, closing her eyes in the shade. "Wouldn't it be easier if we just found a town that had supplies?"

"Easier has nothing to do with it. Towns aren't safe. People talk in towns, and that talk spreads. Besides, how do you plan on paying for supplies? What can we afford to trade?"

Wren raised her head again and opened her eyes. Her brow got that little vertical line that showed she was thinking. Then she shook her head. "Do we at least have a plan?"

"The plan is to sneak in and steal their stuff while they're sleeping. Simple. Effective."

"It just seems dangerous."

Survivor grunted and sat up. "Finding a safe place to piss is dangerous. Why would this be any different?"

Wren's face lightened another shade. "Okay," was all she had to say.

She was so bedraggled that a firm tone might knock her over. Survivor softened her words a bit. "I'll go in first and make sure they're asleep. I'll signal you if it's all clear. If it's not, I'll meet you back here at this spot. You remember our starling call?"

Wren nodded as she absentmindedly picked at the cactus, wiggling a four-inch spine until it became loose and snapped off, oozing clear fluid from the wound.

"Don't touch that!" Survivor shot up from the ground and took the spine from her. "It'll burn your skin, idiot." She eyed the serrated tip of the spine and realized it was an opportunity. "Move."

She took her hatchet out of the loop on her belt and worked on another spine and then another, tapping them with the back of the hatchet until they snapped off and fell onto a cloth she'd laid beneath.

"Back up and turn around," said Survivor as she wrapped her scarf tightly over her nose and mouth.

Wren obeyed, walking several steps away before turning her back to her sister.

Survivor grabbed a tiny pouch hanging from the side of her pack, the one she'd forbidden Wren from opening. From the pouch, she withdrew a smaller square of cloth, which she unfolded with great caution. She crouched over it to keep the breeze from catching the bright orange powder inside and set to work, dipping the spines into the sticky sap bleeding from the plant. As she coated them in the lanmo powder, the bright orange turned to deep black. The smell through the scarf was potent, like a septic wound, foul and rotten.

She suddenly felt like a child again, when her small hands had fumbled as they tried to coat the big spines evenly, wondering why it even mattered when any amount under the skin would kill. She imagined Reskin watching over her shoulder, and the memory of him slapping a shoddily coated spine out of her hands nearly made her drop the one she now worked on. She took a silent breath and moved on to the next spine. After several minutes, she had a decent collection of spines and a head full of unpleasant memories. She put what was left of the lanmo in its secure pouch, then grabbed a spare pouch and put three spines in it. She loaded the last one into the blowgun tucked beneath her shawl.

She pulled her scarf off of her face and took a big gulp of hot, dusty air. Wren had dropped to a crouch, back still to her. Survivor walked up and found her with her arms crossed on her knees, chin resting there as she watched a darkling beetle trundle along the desert floor toward a discarded blue lizard tail. The beetle climbed awkwardly onto the tail, its girth rocking back and forth as it found its footing before it settled and began to eat.

"Did you make poison?" Wren asked.

"Never know when you'll need it."

The beetle rolled off, keeping hold of the tail so that it rolled with it.

"I can't kill them," Wren whispered. "The men."

"But they'll sure as shit kill you. They'll make you bleed before, too. If they wake up, you have to kill them."

"I don't think I can," said Wren.

Survivor sighed and crouched across from her sister. "I'll go in close to scout it out tonight first. They're sleeping in two shelters, so we'll have to split up to get in and out fast. I can't be right there to save you if something goes wrong. Take your spear. If they wake up, scream good and loud."

Wren nibbled her lower lip, then blurted out, "I'll take the first shelter, the one closest to us."

"Fine by me," said Survivor. She moved back to the shade by the cactus and laid on her side with her head on her pack. It struck her then that the man in black had set his gear inside the first shelter, and Wren's sudden urge to volunteer made sense. Her eyes shot open and she turned to berate her sister's idiocy when she saw Wren staring straight up. Survivor followed her gaze, though she already knew what Wren was looking at.

The gate. High above in the west, seemingly suspended in clear blue far beyond streaks of cloud wisps, was a slightly blurry, gray ring with three needles—antenna, Wren called them—poking out of it, barely visible, like strands of spider-web. A chunk was missing from the ring, and when the sun was in just the right position, it would catch the bits of debris floating nearby, making them shine like water droplets. They hadn't had a good view of it in years, living among the tall crags.

"Why do you watch it?" Survivor asked, annoyed more than curious.

Wren sighed, a deep breath of peace. "It never leaves. Like it's waiting for them to come back through and always will be."

"It's just another dead thing on display. You're going to get a crick in your neck. Now get some sleep."

But Wren kept staring. Survivor rolled her eyes and settled back onto her pack, half-believing her sister had lost what was left of her mind.

———

The Marauder scout left at dusk, as Gavel predicted. Probably headed to a hidden night shelter for warmth and sleep. Caster had stumbled across such an unoccupied shelter before, a lean-to made against a hillside with blankets and water within. The Marauder would likely resume his post in the morning.

Caster's comrades had just fallen asleep after indulging in a hearty swig each from Six's flask of vodka. Caster sat nearby but didn't drink; he'd been sober for three years now. When he was back home and alone, he was sometimes tempted to drink, but it helped when Gavel was around. If he saw Caster drink, or even suspected he might have imbibed, Caster would lose his eyelids. Then Gavel would tell Asha when they got back, and she'd threaten to tear off his arms for it.

Still, it was in these moments in the dark, when sleep was far and unpleasant thoughts close, that the desire to escape his memories found its strength. Thoughts of his mom often came to him at night, and while they were pleasant, they made his chest ache. Without thinking, he would start spinning the small, silver ring on his right pinkie round and round.

He knew that he was supposed to be over it by now, espe-cially in a world where people died prematurely as the rule, not the exception. But he wasn't over it—he was pretty sure the idea of being "over" someone's death insulted the whole institution of life and the seriousness of its end. He would never be over it, and sometimes it was easier to escape it, if only briefly.

Yet, in the stillness of the dome tonight, Caster caught sight of Six's flask tucked into the pocket of his leather vest, which lay discarded on the ground only a few feet away. There couldn't be much in there, maybe one drink—no risk in overdoing it. But also not enough to do a damn bit of good. Besides, he needed his senses now. He might be able to see farther than the others and hear farther still with how sound carried in the Open. But if he drank, was overtired, or even too distracted by good conversation, his Scout senses suffered. They took active focus to use, and he needed his focus currently.

If the outliers were waiting for the best time to sneak up, it was now—an hour after things had quieted down. Part of him thought it would be ideal if the Marauder scout's path happened to cross theirs; the Marauder would eliminate his problem. But that was a thought Caster's father would have had, and he hated himself for thinking it.

He carefully undid the clasps of his sleeping bag and tugged on his boots, trying to avoid waking Gavel and Six. He took his bowie knife from beneath his pillow, mostly because it was scary-looking—it was a tool first, but he hoped the sight of it would be enough to make the outliers hesitant to do anything stupid. He then covered his head with his scarf, tucked his knife under his coat, and slipped out of the entrance flap.

———

Survivor had left not long ago, planning to make several wide circles around the camp to test the waters before she went in closer. As Wren watched and waited in a crouch, she wished

desperately for a fire. Her breath came out in clouds and she
shook with the cold. She pulled her scarf closer around her
mouth and nose.

Above her, the sky shone clear and cloudless like crystal
water somehow not dripping down to Earth. The stars held
their shapes together—Aquarius, hunched over to hide, Pegasus
spreading his wings. She wondered how they never drifted
away from each other, always traveling together across the
current of the sky. She wondered what her constellation would
look like, if one were ever to be named for her. Wondered
which characters or creatures would be her constant companions, or if she'd be off by herself, forever alone.

Her attention was so focused above that she didn't hear the
man creeping up behind her. He grabbed her, one arm around
her waist and the other covering her mouth. She tried to
scream, but only a high-pitched muffle escaped.

"I won't hurt you unless you give me a reason to," he said.

She didn't have to see his face to know it was the man from
the cave. She knew his voice. She struggled to pull his arm
away from her mouth, and he tightened his grip.

"If you scream, my friends will wake up, and your friend
will be found and killed. I assume she's near camp?"

Reluctantly, she nodded. His body heat spread to her back,
and she inadvertently relaxed as her cold muscles warmed.

"You won't scream, then?" he asked.

She shook her head. He took his arm off of her mouth but
kept his grip around her waist.

"If I let you go, will you run?"

The puff of his breath reached her nose; it was warm and
fresh, altogether pleasant, like pine needles crunched underfoot. She felt flustered, her common sense taken to its knees.
She tried to blink past it. This man could hurt her, probably
would once he found out whatever it was he wanted to know.

"No," she whispered. "I won't run."

As his grip went slack, she slipped her hand into a fold of her dress and grabbed the shaft of her short spear. The obsidian head could do real damage if she had the guts to inflict it. She took it from her belt and tried to spin around to face him, no real idea of what she intended to do.

He snatched it from her. With a deft flick of his wrist, he flung it into the darkness somewhere behind her.

"I guess that's my fault," he grumbled. "I didn't make you promise not to attack me."

She didn't move. She was too weak to run and too scared to try. As she fell silent, she was glad for the cover of darkness as well as her hood to conceal her panic. If she could hold out long enough for Survivor to come back, she'd know what to do.

"Were you the one who attacked my group?" he asked. He took out his flashlight and shone it on her face.

The brightness made her recoil, but his hand went to her shoulder and steadied her. She squinted in the light, and her red hair sparkled like embers at the edges of her vision. She knew the dirt on her face did little to conceal her flush.

He lowered the flashlight and cleared his throat.

"No, you're the other one. She would have tried to kill me by now, I'd guess." He let go of her shoulder.

She winced, anticipating a blow.

He held up his empty hand. "I'm not going to hurt you." He took two steps back as if to prove it. "Maybe we should start over." He held the flashlight at his waist, shining the light upward so they could see each other in the darkness. "I'm Caster. What's your name?"

She didn't answer even though she felt a tug in her throat as if her name were trying to crawl up and make itself known to him. Instead, she took in every detail of his face. He was more striking up close than he'd been when she'd first seen him from a distance in the crags. A tall forehead, scruff along his jawline and around his mouth. The two skinny, messy braids in his gold hair made her want to braid her own. She looked into his deep eyes, neither green nor brown but a mix of the two, and forgot what he'd just asked.

He sighed. "All right, then. Why are you following us? What are you after?"

She hesitated.

"Not a talker," he muttered.

She swallowed hard and found her voice. "Supplies."

He tilted his head. "You could have just asked."

"Too dangerous."

"And this isn't?" He raised an eyebrow and stared at her.

She'd never felt vulnerable like this. She wasn't afraid of him anymore, and yet her pulse hammered in her ears.

"I don't have much," he continued. "We're just getting back from a journey. But I'll happily give you what I have if you and your friend will leave without causing trouble."

She looked over her shoulder, squinting in vain through the dark shadows of juniper bushes and leggy tree cholla to catch sight of Survivor. "She won't accept it."

"*You* can, though. And then you can both leave. Without a fight."

"She won't believe you'll let us go. She'll fight anyway."

He shook his head. "She'll lose. Believe me."

Wren shuffled on her feet. "Why didn't you wake them? Your friends?"

"There, more evidence that you can trust me. If I'd told them, they would have arrested you. And if you stay here much longer that's exactly what will happen."

"Why do you want to help me?"

He grew quiet and shrank into his shoulders just slightly. He spoke quietly, more to himself than to her. "Above all, love each other deeply..." He cleared his throat. "Why won't you *let* me help you?" He studied her eyes as if the answer were written on them.

She strained her ears for Survivor's signal. Had they already found her? Could they both get out of here without a struggle? What alarmed her even more than those unknowns was that she wasn't sure she wanted to leave. To leave this taste of a world beyond the Open, beyond dirt and desperation. A place where someone could afford to give what little they had to someone who had nothing, and *wanted* to. Caster's world.

Survivor's starling song floated through the darkness.

"What was that?" he asked, stepping closer.

Wren returned the call without thinking, with a chatter rather than a song. A reflex born of years of training with her sister.

"I'm sorry. She'll be here soon," she said.

"Shit." He took a large hunting knife from the belt underneath his long, black coat and turned off his flashlight. At the sight of his knife, she retreated several steps. He lunged forward and took hold of her hand. "It's just for show. If we can convince her that I'll kill you unless you both leave, she'll go without fighting."

She shook her head. "You don't know her."

"Just play along. I don't want to hurt—" He stopped speaking abruptly and whipped his head around toward something Wren could neither see nor hear. "Stop now!" he yelled. He turned to face an assailant invisible to Wren, pulling her by the hand to stand with him.

Then Wren finally heard it. Rapidly approaching footsteps sending dirt and rocks flying. Out of the darkness, Survivor dove at Caster from a full-on sprint, throwing all of her weight at his waist. He let go of Wren and deftly dodged the attack by backpedaling a half-dozen steps. The clouds covering the moon thinned, and Wren saw her surroundings a bit. Survivor poised on her heels between her and Caster, hatchet raised.

"You're clever, I'll give you that. I bet she almost believed you," Survivor said. The hatchet caught the moonlight as she swayed it back and forth, testing the weight for a throw.

Wren stepped up to Survivor's side and bent to her ear.

"Let him go. He didn't hurt me." She put her hand between Survivor's shoulder blades. "Please."

"Leave. I won't stop you," said Caster. His plea was earnest, but he still held his knife at the ready. "My comrades, however, will. If they find you here," he continued, waving toward the direction of his camp. He took a step toward them.

"Stop there. Throw me your knife," Survivor said.

He chuckled. "No."

"Do you want to die?" she asked.

"You'll still throw your weapon if I give you mine. You'll miss, but then you'll have my best knife. I'm sentimental about this one. Honestly, I don't need it to beat you anyway. It's mostly for cutting rope, skinning animals, all those practical things."

"You're stalling," said Survivor.

"I'm trying to help you see the truth. And you're right—I don't want to die. If I had to guess, I'd say you don't want to either."

Survivor laughed a high, echoing laugh that tossed about in the darkness like a leaf on the breeze. Wren tried to shush her, but Survivor ignored her.

"Please. Go," Caster said. It was clear from his tone it would be the last time he asked.

"You know what," Survivor said, "I'll give you a head start. Run, and we'll see if I can hit you. It's pretty dark. You might get lucky."

"Stop," whispered Wren, stepping in front of her this time. "I'm begging you. Let's leave."

Survivor's grin disappeared. She lowered her hatchet. "Fine. We can go."

Wren smiled and touched her forehead to Survivor's. "Thank you." She turned toward Caster. "We're leaving. Thank you for—"

Something cut through the air and whizzed past Wren's left cheek.

Caster cursed. He lifted his hand holding the knife to examine the cactus spine sticking in the fold of skin between his thumb and pointer finger.

Survivor took her blow gun, a short piece of silver pipe, down from her lips and pocketed it. "Now we can go."

Wren's eyes went wide, darting between her sister and Caster. She sputtered in Survivor's face. "Why? Why would you do that?" She turned back to face Caster. As she started to sprint toward him, she felt Survivor's hand grip the back of her dress to keep her in place, but Wren broke free. She reached him, took his injured hand in both of hers, and looked over the wound.

He bent down toward her, careful to keep his gaze on Survivor a few yards away, still a very real threat. "It's okay," he whispered. "Far from vital. She must have missed." With his good hand, he squeezed her upper arm. "Go."

"Neither of them is going anywhere."

Wren turned toward the voice as a man leapt onto a boulder a few yards to her right, standing several feet above the three of them with his bow drawn. He was as dark as the night around them and far more terrifying.

Caster put himself in between the man and Wren. "Gavel, these women were lost. I frightened them and they defended themselves. Please, let them leave."

"That's not how it works in the Border Valley, Scout. You know that. We have to take them in for questioning." Gavel aimed at Survivor. "Drop the hatchet, woman."

"Kiss my tits, man." Survivor raised her weapon above her head for a throw.

"Stop!" Wren stepped out from behind Caster. "He's been poisoned. If you kill her, he'll die. She knows how to cure him."

"Shut up, Wren. Let him try to kill me. Come on, Dark Wonder, take your shot!" Survivor giggled and feinted from side to side.

Someone, a hooded figure that was more shadow than human, appeared behind Survivor, one arm wrapping around her torso and the other holding something up against her back. Survivor's lips twisted in fury.

"Look, lady," the hooded man said, his voice strange and silky, "how about you just calm down? I'd hate for my stiletto to find your liver. Drop it."

She let loose a string of foul words.

"I don't ask twice," the man at her back said, his tone eerily flat.

She dropped the hatchet, nearly hitting his foot, but he moved it out of the way. The hatchet's blade buried itself in the hard earth instead.

"Don't feel bad," the man said. "I do this for a living. You're impressive for an outlier." He pulled her arms behind her back and snapped strange bindings on them. They sparked and sizzled with a low hum, shining neon blue in the darkness, both fascinating and terrifying in their magic.

Gavel kept his bow taut and aimed at Wren.

"Sir. Please," Caster stretched his arm with the injured hand out in front of her, "she's not a threat."

Wren grabbed his hand and gently moved it so that it rested on his opposite hip, trying to slow the progress of the poison to his heart while minimizing swelling. "Keep it level there," she said to him. Then she called to her sister. "How long does he have?"

Survivor stayed silent.

Wren sprinted to her. "Sister, how long before you can't save him?"

"Save him?" She spat in his direction. "Never."

Wren opened her mouth to speak, but no words came. It was as if the air had been sucked from her lungs. The fate of this stranger suddenly mattered more than her own.

"I think you're right, Scout." Gavel lowered his bow and hopped down from the rock. "This one isn't the problem. Where are the others, Six?"

The hooded man answered, "Sans is checking the perimeter for any more of them. Donnie was still trying to wake Mainstay."

Gavel shook his head. "Of course." He came and loomed over Wren, his broad shoulders seeming to block out half the stars.

"Who are you?"

"Wren," she breathed.

"And your sister?"

"Survivor."

"Where are you from?"

Survivor exploded, "Wren, shut your mouth! Don't tell him anything. He's just a dick—"

Six tugged a bandana over her mouth and tied it. "Hope that's not too tight."

"Where are you from?" Gavel asked again.

"What does that matter?" She pointed at Caster. "He'll die if he doesn't get an antidote."

Gavel looked from her to Caster. "How do you feel?"

Sweat started to drip down his forehead. He gripped his

coat with his injured hand to keep it from falling from his hip. "It's starting to go numb."

Survivor laughed with the fabric between her teeth like a muzzled coyote, and she laughed even harder when Six yanked on the gag.

"You can't make the antidote yourself?" Gavel asked Wren.

Wren shook her head. "Only my sister can. The poison includes an orange powder she has, but that's all I know."

"Will she make it?" He nodded in Survivor's direction.

"I can talk to her, but there's no way you can force her to."

"You sure about that?" Six said. Survivor brought her heel up into his crotch behind her. He shoved her to her knees and grimaced.

"We aren't torturers, but I can't lose my Scout," Gavel said. He shouldered his bow. "Break camp. We leave for The Disc immediately."

"No!" Wren shouted, a gut reaction from deep in her core. Her head filled with darkness and terror and, worst of all, excitement. "We can't go there. We're not supposed to." She backed away from Gavel until she ran into Caster, who put his hand on her back to stop her from fleeing.

"What's wrong?" he asked.

"Not The Disc. Please!" She turned and clung to his coat.

"We leave immediately," Gavel said again. "They might be able to reverse engineer the antidote from a sample of the poison. However, if you," he pointed to Wren, "get your sister to save him before our people do, you both might be shown leniency in court. Bring her."

Wren sank to the ground and wept. Caster knelt down next to her.

"Now, Scout," said Gavel. He turned and motioned to Six, who yanked Survivor to her feet by the neck of her dress and started leading her toward camp.

Caster wrapped his uninjured arm around Wren's shoulders. "I'll tell them you're innocent. Don't worry." He tried to pull her up, but she'd gone dead weight.

"Monsters in The Disc." She put her hand to her mouth, trying to keep the screams inside.

"What?"

She looked over his head, up at the stars. "They watch while other monsters kill you."

The freshly lit lantern hanging from the ceiling of the travel dome released puffs of kerosene smoke, which was nearly as harsh to the senses as seeing Mainstay in nothing but his underwear when Caster and the others came in.

Mainstay sat toward the center of the dome while Caster and Gavel broke down the interior of the structure. Adonis rolled up bed mats and threw supplies into bags. Gavel had ordered Six and Sans to break down the other dome. It all added up to barely controlled chaos.

The outliers sat next to each other on the ground, their backs against the wall of the dome. Survivor was still bound and gagged. Gavel paused in his work to grab another set of e-binds from his pack, which he then tossed to Adonis. The Grunt caught them awkwardly with one hand.

"Put them on her," Gavel said as he nodded toward Wren.

Caster watched as Wren shrunk in on herself when Adonis crossed the dome to kneel next to her. "I told you—she's not the threat here," Caster said softly when Gavel returned to their work.

"Clearly," Gavel replied. "But we follow protocol."

Caster grumbled under his breath. He turned to make sure Adonis wasn't overtightening the e-binds and saw Wren's wide-eyed fear. The e-binds hung heavily from her too-skinny wrists and hummed with their blue charge.

"This is ridiculous," Caster said. "She won't—"

Just then, the blue light from the e-binds glowed brighter and the humming swelled louder and louder. The light turned white hot. *POP!* The light went dark, the humming silent, and the e-binds fell with a dead *thunk* to the dirt at Wren's feet. She'd gone quite pale.

"What the hell?" said Adonis as he unshielded his eyes. He nudged the powerless e-binds with his foot.

"Must be defective," said Gavel. "We'll get them replaced in The Disc. Adonis, find some rope. That'll have to do."

Survivor stood and shouted barely intelligible threats at Gavel around her gag. "Almost killed...defective...bullshit!" She started to rush at Gavel and tried to pull her hands apart as if to throttle him. The e-binds on her wrists responded with a shock proportional in power to her struggle against them—she shrieked and fell back on her ass by Wren.

"We don't have time for this nonsense," said Gavel. "Find some rope, tie her wrists, and then get back to work, Adonis."

Adonis darted over to his own pack, pulled out a short length of rope, and went to work on Wren's wrists. He tied them gently in front of her body. The responsible part of Caster wanted to correct Adonis for doing a shit job, and for tying in front of her rather than behind, but Wren wasn't dangerous, and Gavel was right—there wasn't time.

Caster returned to his work removing the heavy metal pins from the hinges of the main seam of the dome. Before he even lifted his hammer, Mainstay's voice assaulted him.

"Put e-binds on *him*! He lied!"

Caster looked over his shoulder to see Mainstay pointing at him. The Soldier was purple with rage. He sat a few feet from the women, in the middle of his disheveled bedding.

"They were just trying to survive," Caster said between hammer strikes. "Your pride sent us to find them, not your sense of duty."

"The bitch took my hand!" Mainstay glared at Survivor, who jiggled her large chest at him.

"Enough." Gavel's tone was even, with just a touch of exasperated parent to it. He looked between the two men. "This can all wait until we get back." He picked up Mainstay's pants and coat where they sat in a pile on the ground and threw them at him. "For the time being, I suggest you put away your ego, Soldier, and ignore the prisoner. Get dressed. Now."

Survivor winked at Mainstay. He grabbed his wad of clothes and stomped outside, apparently preferring the cold to dressing in front of the woman who'd cannibalized him.

"How do you feel?" Gavel asked Caster.

Caster's vision was starting to blur around the edges, and he could feel a fever setting in. The wound on his hand had turned bright red, sending red trails out from it in a bloody web. "Not right."

Gavel leaned in so only Caster could hear him. "Wren seems to trust you. She'll fix this if she can. Prepare them for travel, and make sure Wren wears her hood. That Marauder scout is likely nearby. If we pass him and he sees her hair..."

Caster nodded, knowing he'd be useless in a fight in his current state. It wouldn't just be him dying if Marauders took interest. He tried to shake the blurring from his eyes as he walked to the women and began to pull them to their feet.

"We were going to get away. Why did you do that? He didn't do anything," Wren said.

It was early morning, and the sun had just appeared,

breathing enough heat from the east to make Wren already crave the night again. Desert scrub dotted the horizon, and wide cracks fractured the ground as if God had pressed his thumb against it.

Wren jogged next to Survivor, who remained silent even though her gag had been removed before they started traveling in the hope that she might share the antidote recipe with Wren. The good deed had not been returned.

Wren let her bound hands hang slack in front of her waist beneath the sand-colored plastic poncho they'd draped over her. Survivor wore a poncho as well, stretching from her neck to the ground. Gavel had made sure their hoods were both pulled up and insisted Wren's hair be tied back beneath it. From a distance, no one would be able to tell that they were women or prisoners, which was the whole idea.

"You always have to be right," grumbled Wren between rhythmic breaths. She was no stranger to long journeys on foot, but she'd never had to endure on so little food and rest. She kept her eyes on the cracked dirt under her feet and focused on keeping oxygen going to her brain.

Survivor stopped jogging, and Wren stopped with her and met her eyes.

Survivor pushed onto the balls of her feet so that their noses were touching. "I *am* always right." She stayed there, her stare boring into Wren, a low growl in her throat.

Six and Sans stopped just behind the women. "We're on a tight schedule, thanks to you," Six said, leaning close to Survivor. He was striking in the light of day, with features nearly as sharp as his blades. "Move it."

Survivor rolled her eyes and started jogging again.

Wren let her pull ahead. She needed time to reclaim her courage. Caster and the other three were at the front of the party. The fat one they called Mainstay led the way, but Wren wondered how long he could maintain this brisk pace. He was rubbing at what was likely a stitch in his side, and he cast occasional sneers over his shoulder at Survivor, who outwardly relished in his misery. The boy, Adonis, trudged behind him, laden with gear and packs. Caster and Gavel were directly in front of the women. Caster's hand had started shaking badly an hour ago; Wren noticed when he'd tucked it into his belt to keep it still. Other than sweat, his expression was blank and impossible to read. Where was fear? Where was hope? Didn't he realize he would likely die soon?

With great effort, Wren caught up to Survivor and stepped in her path, making her slide to a stop and curse.

"What now? Going to tell me I'm heartless?" Survivor said.

Wren took three good breaths before speaking. "Please," she kept her voice low, "I understand why you did it. You couldn't trust him, and he was threatening me. You've always protected me. I don't thank you for that—thank you." She leaned down and rested her head on Survivor's shoulder.

Survivor sighed. "Is that all, sister?"

Wren kissed her on the cheek and then turned to look at Caster. He'd stopped up ahead and was catching his breath with Gavel. He grabbed his unruly hair off of his neck and glanced at the ladies as he tied it back roughly with a bit of black ribbon. He gave a small, pained smile to Wren.

"Oh for shit's sake. Are you serious?" Survivor said.

Wren tried to shake the rush of heat out of her face. "Huh?"

Survivor threw her head back and laughed, tossing her hood off. "I thought you were just curious about him, but you actually *like* the blond one. Good God, I hoped we'd never have to have *that* talk."

"Like him?"

"Listen," Survivor lowered her voice, "I get it. He's the first man you've seen since you grew up, and he's not ugly. It was bound to happen. Now you realize you have urges, but you can learn to take care of them yourself."

"What?"

"Never mind. If we live, I'll explain later. But seriously, don't fall for it. His ass is on the line—of course he'll wink at you. Make you feel special. He's not worth it. None of them are."

Sans walked up and tugged her hood back on.

"Gee, thanks," she said.

"Keep moving," Sans said. It was the first time Wren had heard him speak, and something about his monotone was unnerving, like he had to strain to keep it that way.

"If you're just going to kill me when I get there, I think I'll take my time. And my sister needs rest. She's underfed and exhausted," said Survivor.

Six came up and stood next to Sans. He held some kind of food bar in his hand and lowered it from his mouth. "Move! You heard my friend. He's a lot more polite than I am, but he has a tendency to snap unexpectedly." He took a big bite of the bar and then spoke around it. "You wouldn't want that to happen, would you?"

"Oh, I quake in fear," said Survivor. "Come on," she said to Wren.

They all started jogging again.

"They might show us mercy if you help him. Isn't that a good reason?" said Wren.

Survivor shook her head. "Again, you don't understand them. Mercy isn't on their list of skills, just like it's not on mine."

"Isn't it worth a try?"

"I won't beg for my life. Ever."

"What about for mine?" Wren asked.

Survivor opened her mouth to speak, but Caster's strained shout interrupted her.

"Marauder, due north!" he said.

The men halted and turned sharply to the left, one great line in defensive positions.

About twenty yards away, up on a slight ridge, stood a gangly man. He wore a turban and a shirt that tossed in the breeze around his leathery skin. He walked toward them with purpose, taking big strides. At first, Wren thought he had an unusually long arm, but when it caught the glint of the sun, she realized it was a machete.

Six and Sans drew closer to Wren and Survivor and stepped halfway in front of them. Mainstay drew his huge handgun and took aim with his one hand. He looked over at Gavel.

"Just a warning," Gavel said to him. Then he raised his hand. "Wait. Are you certain you can make that shot?"

Mainstay flashed a glare past Gavel at Survivor, his upper lip tugging into a sneer. Then he turned back to the approaching man, adjusted his grip on his pistol, narrowed his eyes, and fired.

The noise made Wren jump so high that both of her feet came off the ground. She'd seen guns before, but they were usually half-buried in the sand, abandoned long ago to remain silent for eternity.

In the distance, the man's turban flew straight back off his head to the desert floor, where it unraveled and writhed around in the wind like a snake. The sun reflected off his bald head. He didn't stop walking toward them, but he did hold up one hand in deference.

Wren caught snippets of Caster's soft words to Gavel. "Sorry I didn't sense him earlier. The pain...my focus..."

"You're forgiven, Scout," said Gavel. He readjusted by

pulling Caster's arm further up over his shoulders. Caster winced.

Once the man had closed half the distance to them, Gavel called out. "That's close enough!"

The Marauder was the most frightening person Wren had ever seen. Skin and bone, angry scars all over his body, and yellow eyes. He held the machete casually at his side as if it were an extension of himself.

"That doesn't belong to you," he hollered, his voice surprisingly high pitched.

Gavel addressed the Marauder. "Sir, we are well within the neutral zone. Nearly at The Disc's gate. You have no business here."

Caster hunched over and vomited on the dirt.

The yellow-eyed man raised his machete and pointed it at Caster. "He doesn't have much time. Lanmo's effects are obvious even from where I stand. I won't keep you long." He shifted his machete to point at Survivor. "That woman doesn't belong to you. The dark-haired one belongs to him."

"Who belongs to what now?" Six said. He turned as if to ask Sans, whose neck veins were swelling. From her view of Sans' profile, Wren saw the tightness of his jaw, like a cord about to snap. Six punched him lightly on the arm, and Sans looked over. Six modeled deep breathing until Sans nodded and took a shaky breath.

"I'm afraid I don't understand," said Gavel.

The Marauder spoke slowly, as if to a child. "You have something that doesn't belong to you. I'm taking her back to her Master."

"To who?" asked Six.

Survivor whispered so only Wren could hear. "The Gentleman."

The blood left Wren's face at the sight of the terror in her sister's eyes. But once Survivor blinked, the terror was gone, an enraged stare left in its place as she met the Marauder's gaze.

"Look at her hand," said the man. He held up his own hand. On the back was a circle with two lines through the center. "We're part of the same family. Aren't we, Angel?"

Survivor spat her response at him. "I'm not his angel."

"Not since you left," he said. He waved his machete at the group. "Is this your new family?"

"I have no family," said Survivor.

The Marauder looked around, eyes resting on Wren with such intensity that Wren shifted her gaze just past him.

"You two seem close," the Marauder said. "I've been listening to you snap at her for a quarter mile. And that red hair." He whistled. "She'll be popular. Just like Beo. Everyone loves him. All except you. You left him. Left all of us." He took two steps forward, swinging his machete in casual circles.

"I will rip those disgusting eyes out of your rotting skull, Fen!" Survivor screamed.

All of the men tensed and readied their weapons.

Fen giggled. "Seems you have family after all."

"Sir," Gavel called out. "You are wielding a weapon in a neutral zone. We've already fired a warning. I'll say this once— return to your territory immediately. The next shot my marksman takes will be the last."

Fen stopped walking, but it seemed to be more to make Gavel be quiet than out of fear. "I wonder how he'll reward me for finding you. Maybe he'll give me the redhead before he kills her."

Survivor snarled. She started to fight against the e-binds, but then stopped, perhaps remembering what happened last time. Instead, she tried to sprint at Fen, only to be held back by Six.

"This woman is in the custody of the Principal of The

Disc. Leave now. Your refusal to comply will be taken as an act of war," said Gavel.

Fen sighed a great hiss of air. "Master wouldn't want that." He waved at Survivor. "He'll be happy when I tell him. He'll come for you and the redhead. He's always been coming." He turned and started retreating, sliding his machete into the sling hung across his back.

Survivor pulled against Six's grip toward Gavel. "Kill him! Kill him, please!"

Six yanked her away from his superior, but then added, "I've got to agree with the psycho here, boss. That Marauder is a liability. Too big of balls with too small of brain. Mainstay can end him and we'll put him in the ground before we reach home. His Master would never know."

Caster vomited again, great streams of liquid. His knees went soft, and Gavel readjusted his hold on him once more.

"There's no time for this," said Gavel. "The law is clear, and my Scout needs medical attention. Move out!" He started off again, half-dragging Caster in a slow jog.

Survivor turned her request on Mainstay as Six pushed her forward after Gavel. "Please! Shoot him!"

Mainstay took three plodding steps in her direction. He smiled wide as he said, "Get moving, Marauder scum."

Gavel started running, and the others followed suit.

Adonis asked nobody in particular between tired pants, "What the hell was that about?"

"Doesn't matter," Six replied, his breathing more even than the boy's. "We're almost home."

Straight ahead was an enormous wall that curved away from them and looked like a U from their current position. It stretched over thirty feet high, reaching into a dust cloud above. When it caught the sun just right, it reflected light off its silver surface as if intending to blind travelers with its power, its magnificence.

"We're here," Survivor muttered.

Wren's legs froze as if they were locked into vices. She stood rooted to the ground and fought the bile creeping up her throat. A memory overtook her as Alma's face came into her mind, covered in beautiful wrinkles. Her long, silver braid stretched down her back.

There was heat everywhere. Smoke burned in Wren's nostrils, her lungs, her eyes. She dropped to her hands and knees on the forest floor as falling trees crashed and sent heavy vibrations through the ground. Alma appeared out of the billowing smoke with Survivor in tow.

"Take her. Now," she'd said to Survivor, who'd nodded and wrenched Wren to her feet.

"No! Come with us!" Wren had shouted, sputtering on the smoke and ash.

Alma had thrown her arms around her. "Stay safe. Live your life. *Your* life, the way you want to." She backed up and kissed her forehead. Then she was gone, disappeared into the smoke, as Survivor dragged Wren in the opposite direction.

"Hey," Survivor said, blocking Wren's view of the wall. Wren blinked past the memory, fighting to control her breathing. "Nothing left but to keep on."

Survivor nudged her with her shoulder and stayed close by her side, bolstering her up in spite of their bound hands as they approached The Disc.

CHAPTER THREE

IT WAS GETTING INCREASINGLY DIFFICULT FOR CASTER TO stay on his feet. He'd almost blacked out twice in the last hour, but Gavel had caught him each time before he hit the dirt, eventually leaving his arm across Caster's back to be ready if it happened again. Sweat drenched Caster's hair, and he shivered in the heat. They'd slowed to a walk, Caster's toes occasionally dragging along the dirt when his legs buckled.

Gavel had seen Caster endure a lot of dark days. To see this happen to him now somehow felt familiar, and Gavel was tempted to ask God why. But Gavel didn't believe things just happened; people chose them. Caster hadn't chosen all the heartache of his brief twenty-five years, but he'd invited a good bit of it in by his own free will. It was those decisions for which Gavel had no tolerance, those that had driven him to shake Caster by the collar several years prior and drag him, stinking of moonshine and impudent rage, into his Body as a Grunt. The first time he'd ordered Caster to pick up his bags, Caster spat at him and threw a canteen at his groin. So things had gone for the better part of a year, with Gavel pushing Caster back twofold for every act of disrespect, and all the while receiving ridicule from other Heads for not discharging the punk.

After that initial year, things began to improve, and Caster again showed the promise in mind and body for the military that Gavel had seen in him since adolescence. He'd now been a Scout for three years, making better decisions and living on his own, only to get himself poisoned. He'd chosen to break protocol and had been bitten for it. Gavel hoped he would learn from this mistake, but the clumsiness of his steps and the sweat dripping from his chin said he might not get the chance.

"We'll get you into medical as soon as possible," Gavel said for the third time.

"Yes, boss," said Caster.

"This shouldn't have happened," said Gavel, more to himself than to Caster.

"For the record," he said through a wheeze. "I'm sorry I didn't tell you. About the girls, I mean."

"Would you do it again?"

Caster chuckled, but quickly stopped and grimaced as he repositioned his arm from where he'd braced it in his belt. "You have your code. I have mine, old man."

"Stop talking. Focus on your feet."

Caster ignored him. "You know, I really did like being out here, doing this. I've often questioned my decision to serve. But you helped me see the honor in it, the purpose. Thank you. For everything."

"You aren't going to die."

"Pretty sure I am."

"Quiet, Scout."

They walked in silence for a minute.

"If I don't make it to the gate," said Caster, "tell Asha I love her. I know she knows, but—"

"I said quiet. We're getting you to medical. Focus on the

mission." Gavel's eyes narrowed to slits, which was about as close to expressing worry as he ever came.

"Yes, sir."

They stepped into the shadow of the wall, the behemoth of smooth metal and power giving them temporary shelter from the eastern sun. Gavel looked back to see Wren leaning against Survivor, her eyes on the ground and her face gaunt as if she were being led to the executioner. Sans and Six came up behind them and told them to stop and wait.

Gavel propped Caster against the wall, letting it hold most of his weight so that he could stand on his own. He then stepped a few feet over to the scanner in the wall. It was a perfect square of opaque glass one foot across. "Head Keating, returning from a six-week scouting trek with Body 17."

The scanner lit up, turning hot white before projecting a grainy blue hologram of a woman's face in the air in front of Gavel—the gatekeeper. She had a long ponytail tied at the top of her head, and her eyebrows angled sharply, giving her a look of perpetual seriousness.

"Military identification number and seasonal password, please," she said. The hologram flickered when she spoke.

"ID 5792674, password Indigo."

"Barcode, please."

Gavel pulled up his left sleeve and held the sleek, black ID bracelet sitting just above his wrist up to the red light of the scanner. The familiar high-low tone sounded.

"Identity confirmed," said the gatekeeper. "Were there any deaths in your party?"

"No, but we have two that need medical attention, one urgently."

"Understood." The hologram face flickered again as she tried to look around Gavel, and when she couldn't see clearly, she shot up another two feet to look over him. "You have additional party members. Explain."

"They're prisoners. Both female. Outliers."

"Very well. Bring them forward for examination."

"It would save time to process them inside. My Scout needs medical—"

"Bring them forward now, citizen." Her eyebrows shot up another inch, attempting to stab her hairline.

Gavel signaled to Six and Sans. They didn't have time to waste arguing. Six took Survivor by the elbow, leaving Sans to take Wren. A small metal arm shot out of a hidden compartment of the wall next to the scanner. It unfolded and rose up like a viper about to strike, with a tiny needle at the end. Six took a silver card out from under his shirt, where it dangled from a long, thin chain around his neck. He bent down, swiped the card over Survivor's e-binds behind her back, and then returned the card to its place against his chest. Survivor watched him over her shoulder suspiciously all the while. A light on the e-binds flashed green before they went dark and their weight fell off of Survivor's wrists. Six grabbed her left hand. She tried to yank it away.

"Hand, please. Or you will be immediately sanitized," said the gatekeeper.

A neon green laser sight appeared over her heart. Gavel looked up at the patrolman on his knee on top of the wall, pulse rifle tucked tightly against his shoulder.

Survivor tried to bat the light off with her free right hand. "What the hell?"

Six tugged her hand toward the scanner again before Survivor sighed and shoved it onto the needle herself. The needle stuck the middle of her fingertip, leaving the tiniest drop of blood on the surface. She stuck her finger in her mouth.

"Sample shows no transmittable diseases. Low electrolytes and evidence of gingivitis present," said the gatekeeper.

"Gingi-what-is?" Survivor said.

"Bring the other," said the gatekeeper.

The laser sight on Survivor's chest disappeared once Six slapped the e-binds back onto her wrists.

Sans brought Wren forward.

"Don't be nervous, Wren. It's just a *prick*," Survivor said, standing on her tiptoes to be face to face with the gatekeeper's hologram. The gatekeeper didn't meet her gaze, instead rising up another foot.

Sans took Wren's bound hands in his and held them up to the needle. She squeezed her eyes shut as it took the sample from her right thumb. When it was over, she went back to staring at the ground, hunched over in misery.

"No transmittable diseases detected. Extremely low electrolytes. Slight tachycardia. They're cleared for entry. Bring them to holding zone two for further processing. Your men in need of aid are to proceed immediately to medical."

"Thank you," said Gavel.

Internal locks turned, and then with a whoosh of air, a door as wide as three men slid up to allow them inside.

Gavel headed for the entrance with Sans, Six, and their prisoners in tow when Caster collapsed. He seized on the ground, his back arching up as his eyes rolled back.

"Goddamn!" Six exclaimed. "Is this it? Did you let him die, you bitch?" He went to slap Survivor, but Gavel stopped him.

"Get those prisoners to the holding zone. Now!" Gavel dropped to his knees next to Caster, turning him on his side as he let the seizure run its course.

Wren screamed and went for her sister, her hands groping at the front of her dress. "Save him! You did this—save him!"

Survivor didn't respond, instead just ducking out of the

way of Wren's grasp as Six shoved her forward through the gate.

"I'm begging you! Just tell me how to save him!" Wren called, reaching for the back of her hair like she was grasping for the edge of a cliff.

Survivor turned to speak over her shoulder as Six continued to shove her onward. "There's no antidote. He'll be dead in a couple hours."

Wren's outburst apparently cost her what was left of her energy. She sank back into Sans' arms, and he had to carry her through the gate.

"Killed him. Killed us," she mumbled, repeating it over and over.

Caster fell still, strangely still compared to his violent spasms of just a minute ago. Gavel grabbed him around the torso and heaved him up onto his shoulders, draping Caster's dead weight around his neck. He could have called a Quick Cart with his ID bracelet, but he didn't want to wait for it to arrive; the drivers were notoriously unhurried. He broke into a run. The Medical Hub was in the middle of town.

He shouted back at his men. "Radio Asha. Tell her we're coming!"

In the vague, back part of her mind, Wren noticed how strong Sans' arms were around her. Although she passed in and out of consciousness from her perch against his chest, she took in flashes of her surroundings.

There were faces around her, people everywhere. They filled the street. They were so clean, dressed in clean clothes with clean hair and faces. A little girl with white-blond hair carrying a gray stuffed bunny by the ear stared as they walked by, eyes wide with curiosity, before her mother scooped her up and took her away.

Buildings, actual buildings like Alma had told them stories about, made of metal and light stretched high above her. They were big, shiny teeth trying to chomp down on the sky, and in between them were tall poles with glass spheres at their tops, all connected with cords like veins. Darting through the air were bats, or birds, or something else. She couldn't tell, they were so far away and so fast. But they had eyes—two orange lights. Eyes that watched her as she closed her own.

The air changed, now slightly cooler, the severe light of the sun replaced by a dimmer, whiter light. The sounds of the street subsided to a dull hum.

"Two outliers to be processed for trial." Was that Six? It sounded like his accent somewhere up ahead.

"This one looks healthy enough," said a new voice, creaky and tired.

Wren opened her eyes to see a man's wrinkled face with a puffy, white mustache over her. "This one is not so healthy," he said. "Bring her here. Put her on that table."

Sans set her down on cold metal.

"Take that rope off my patient, please," the old man said as he gently tucked a small pillow under her head. Sans pulled a long, skinny knife from his belt and cut the rope around her wrists in one quick slice. Her arms dropped from her abdomen to rest at her sides.

From her back, she took in what she could of her surroundings. It was a small room, just a couple of metal tables and a chair. A basket of prickly pears sat next to a clear jug of water and a stack of silver cups on one of the tables while Wren lay on the other.

The room was crammed with people. Sans and the old man stood on either side of her, speaking softly about readings and numbers that meant nothing to Wren. Survivor sat in the chair just a few feet away as Six held her down with his hands on her shoulders. She snarled and fought. With one good swipe of her foot, she knocked out one of the legs of the chair, sending her to thrash against Six on the strange, smooth green floor.

"Stop it!" the old man bellowed. "I'm trying to help your friend here. Will you please keep your seat? Upright, preferably."

Survivor glared up at him. Six had his knee in between her shoulders and held her arms, still bound at the wrists, behind her back. He gave one of her arms a small tug toward her head. She winced, looked at Wren, and relaxed against his hold. Six put the chair upright, and she rose and sat in it gruffly.

The old man nodded at her once. "Thank you very much." He rummaged in a big, rectangular box by Wren's feet. He filled two tubes from separate bottles, one full of cloudy white fluid, the other with just a tiny amount of orange fluid. As he brought the needle of the white one to the inside of Wren's elbow, she whimpered.

"Get that away from her!" shouted Survivor. Her shout rang in Wren's ears, caught in the close space.

"The man said he's helping her. Put your fangs away," Six said through his teeth. He opened and closed his mouth. "Made my damn ears pop."

Wren looked back up at the old man. "Don't worry, little red." He winked at her. "I've done this a few times."

The white fluid went in, and almost immediately, she was feeling more alert, stronger.

"Now for this one." He injected the orange fluid, and gentle heat spread through her limbs. Her fear let up just slightly, a choking vine pruned back to allow its victim a breath.

She sat up.

"Prepare the prisoners for trial."

She looked around, trying to find whoever had said that. It was a generally pleasant voice, but she couldn't tell if it was male or female, and it seemed to fill the room rather than come from a person.

"She just woke up. Give her a minute, would ya?" the old man said.

"The judge is waiting. Prepare them now. The red-haired one will go first."

"Guess he means you," the old man said to Wren. "Walk slow, all right? I just fixed you; don't want you to break again. Son, help her." The old man put Sans' arm around her waist as she stood.

They walked to a rectangular metal doorway in the back of the room, which slid up as they approached.

"Where are you taking her?" Survivor's shouts again filled the room. Wren looked back to see her sister struggling once more. "Bring her ba—"

The door slid down, cutting off the room and Survivor's demands. Sans led Wren through a tunnel dimly lit on either side with blue lights in the floor. A low humming came from the lights, and a couple of them flickered off and on, making her jump. She had no idea how long they had been walking since her thoughts were everywhere else—with Survivor, with Caster, even with Alma and her ominous warnings of The Disc and its monsters. Her breath was coming harder by the time they reached another doorway, lit around the edges with a thin line of blue.

She stopped.

"What's going to happen?" she asked.

Sans' face was tinted blue by the lights. He looked down at her, the whites of his eyes and his skin glowing. "Tell the truth."

The door slid open to reveal a new room. The overhead

lighting was fluorescent and yellow, hitting her eyes like a hot knife and giving her a headache. Sans led her in slowly.

There were two chairs facing each other, one set on a tall platform. To the left, behind a floor to ceiling net of metal cables covered in tiny barbs, were more chairs. People clamored in and filled the chairs. She recognized a couple of their faces from the street.

A tall, skinny creature—humanlike but far from human— sat in the chair on the platform. His arms and legs were each nearly as long as Wren was tall, with no definable flesh cushioning the frame beneath. His cheekbones looked as if they might pop out of his skin, and his black hair lay flat and slicked back. He didn't look over as Wren approached with Sans.

Sans led her to the chair facing the skinny man and had her sit.

"Thank you, Thief. You're dismissed," the skinny man said. His voice was surprisingly low, and his inflections were off, as he put emphasis on odd parts of words. His small black pupils swelled bigger and then shrank back down as he gave Wren a once-over.

Sans bowed to him and backed away, leaving through the same door through which they'd entered.

The skinny man pressed a small, white button on the arm of his chair.

"Trial 3947-O-U commencing. Solar date: 2 September 2414. Judge Gamma presiding. Prisoner identified as female, approximate age twenty-one years. Ruling to be prison or death, dependent upon truthfulness of answers and severity of crime."

Two curved pieces of metal moved up the front of the arms of Wren's chair and covered her hands, locking them in place and shocking her skin with the cold. The judge stared all around her, his eyes darting from side to side, up and down.

They became still as they landed on her own eyes, his now pinprick pupils motionless, as he asked the first question.

"Do you have any nines?" said Principal Thallium.

He sat bare chested in his boxers on a huge wrought iron bed piled with pillows, a bunch of faded playing cards fanned out in his hands. For a man on the verge of fifty, he carried his age somewhere other than his body. He had a barrel chest covered in hair and well-defined abs. His dark blond goatee was trimmed in perfect symmetry, and a likewise blond ponytail stretched down between his shoulder blades.

Eydis had to admit he was attractive. But eyeing him still didn't quite make up for having to play cards all afternoon, which was a definite possibility. She sat across from him on the bed, fully clothed in a white V-neck shirt and long, shimmering white skirt, with her own cards fanned out.

"Go fish," she replied half-heartedly.

"Oh come on, you have at least one nine."

"I don't. Go fish."

"But I'm down to just these," he snapped the elastic of his boxers, "while you have all your clothes on. It's wrong."

"This happens every time you and I play this game, and yet every time you seem surprised. I feel I shouldn't have taught it to you. Are you requesting that I let you win?"

"No, that would be cheating. Just even up the scales a bit. Start with your top." He put his cards face down on the velvet throw between them before leaning back against a mound of pillows and stretching his arms out over them.

It was still cheating, but Eydis didn't say so. If it would stop him from whining, she would oblige. She reached down and crossed her arms at her waist, grabbing fistfuls of the hem of her shirt. She pulled it over her head in one fluid motion with no ceremony, leaving herself in just her lacey white bra. Waves of waist-length, strawberry blond hair rippled into place down her bare back.

"Much better," he said, addressing her breasts.

"Go fish," she said with the same flat tone as before.

He eyed her as if she'd issued a dare before leaning forward and grabbing a card from the top of the deck.

"Look at that, a nine." He turned the nine of spades toward her. "Still my turn."

Two tones, a high followed by a low, filled the Principal's bedroom. After the tone came the Operator's voice from hidden speakers—a welcome interruption, as far as Eydis was concerned.

"Sir, your son has returned," said the Operator. Theo was his name. Eydis had appointed him recently after the elderly Abigail retired. A young man of seventeen, his voice still held an effeminate edge that made it generally neutral and nonalarming when it sounded through the communication system, surprising residents of the Main House and other government buildings in town.

"You know I'm busy and you interrupt to tell me that?" Thallium rubbed at his brow. "Thank you. That will be all."

"Apologies, sir. He's in the secondary medical ward. He's not well."

"What, did he scrape his knee? Give him two shots of ethanol and a slap on the ass. He'll be over it in an hour." He moved two cards from the right side of his hand to the left.

"Sir, the danger is substantial. He's been poisoned."

He set his cards down and reached over to grab a glass of amber liquor from its precarious perch on an overstuffed silk throw pillow. "My treatment recommendation remains the same, and I'd appreciate it if you'd pass that on to our noble doctor Asha at the clinic." He sipped from his glass. "Tell her I send my love, but if she keeps her teat in his mouth as she is wont to do, he's never going to wean."

The Operator's quiet breathing came over the speakers for a moment. "Tell her that exactly, sir?"

"Oh for fuck's sake. I'll tell her myself. I'll be there in twenty." He downed his drink in one gulp and went for his clothes. First, the red collared shirt draped on a ceiling fan blade; he put the left sleeve on first, concealing the thin, white scars that stretched from wrist to shoulder on that arm. Then the thermal pants on the floor near the door, which were black and made of a material that adjusted to maintain the wearer's temperature at 98.6 degrees in any weather. Eydis had designed them herself.

He spoke as he dressed next to the bed. "Why couldn't he join sanitation or agriculture to rebel? Hell, if he really wanted to teach me a lesson, he should've joined the IPs to stop drunks from shitting in the gutter. That'd be far more effective in taking the Valcin name down two or three notches." He held his hand out to Eydis. "Come along, my dear. Fatherly duty beckons, and if you come with me, we can recommence our game all the sooner."

She took his hand and slid to the edge of the mattress. He started to pull her up and then apparently thought better of it. He grabbed her around the waist, opened her knees with his own, and mauled her. They sank into the mattress as he pressed his lips to her neck. His kisses left wet spots along her skin.

"Sir, there is another matter that needs your attention," the Operator said through the hidden speakers in the room.

He dropped his face to rest against Eydis' chest and sighed heavily. "Good God," he said, his voice muffled against her breasts.

Eydis stood, pushing him back gently. "I'll take care of it. This is why you have an assistant. Go to Caster."

"Your work ethic never ceases to astound." He kissed her cleavage once before removing himself from her and standing. "Follow after me. Don't be long." He grabbed his walking shoes from the mat next to the door before opening it and greeting his two personal Keepers standing in the hallway. "Gentlemen." He closed the door behind him.

Eydis retrieved her shirt from the bedspread and pulled it back over her head and into place. "What is it, Operator?" she asked as she began putting the bed back in order.

"Two outliers were admitted this morning."

"Yes?"

"We analyzed their blood per procedure, and the DNA sequencing the Principal asked us to look for was found in one of them."

Eydis froze in the middle of tugging the bedspread taut. She dropped it and jogged over to the large, metal desk against the opposite wall. "Bring it up on screen."

The glass in a five-foot by six-foot frame on the wall over the desk lit up. A 3D model of a DNA strand spun on the right side of the screen, and the sequencing began scrolling up on the left. Other stats, including hormone and vitamin levels, ran across the bottom, numbers in the equation all adding up to the answer.

Eydis' hands flew to her mouth. "Where is she now?"

"In the middle of her trial. The judge will deliver his sentence soon."

"Tune me into that frequency. I'll send Keepers to pick her up."

"We can't. Not without the Principal's order. The judge's programming—"

"The Principal would order you if he were here. Call his

com device if you want, but patch me into that trial. Immediately."

It had been several weeks since the last outlier trial, and the people had gotten bored. Which was why when Wren headed for the defendant's chair, dozens were jockeying to get a seat in the courtroom before it was filled to capacity. Adonis pushed up onto the balls of his feet to look over the mass at the door and spotted a corner seat far off to the side at the front. He shouldered through the crowd, sperming his way to the corner seat and snagging it out from under a man in a gray jumpsuit who was clearly on break from public waste collection; he reeked of hot rot. He reached down to grab Adonis' shirt front.

Adonis lifted his wrist to him and pulled back his sleeve to show his black ID bracelet. "I'm with the Body that brought in this prisoner. I have to attend this trial for our, uh, records."

The man grumbled, shoved his hands in his jumpsuit pockets, and turned to retreat up the stairs, taking his stink with him.

Adonis adjusted his rear end against the hard seat in victory.

"Liar," said someone near his ear. He jumped and turned to see Sans sitting directly behind him.

"I hate it when you do that."

"I know," said the Thief, who held out Adonis' money pouch, dangling it from his fingertips casually.

"Damn it," said Adonis as he reached back to snatch it from the Thief. "Got me again."

Sans didn't chuckle or smirk, not like Six, who would have taunted Adonis for not being aware of his surroundings. Adonis liked to think that Sans had once had a sense of humor, but that they'd surgically removed it when they changed his face to turn him into a Thief.

"Big turnout," said Adonis.

Sans nodded and looked toward the judge. Adonis turned his attention to the trial. From this angle, he could just see Wren's profile through the security net as she sat across from the judge.

The beats of a trial never changed. The judge asked for basic information, such as name, place of origin, reason for living outside of decent society, etc. Then would come the specific questions related to the outlier's crime, which was typically assault or theft. Finally, there would be a ruling based on their responses.

The rulings weren't very creative, as there were only two outcomes for outliers—imprisonment or death—but that wasn't why people attended the trials. They watched the defendants like they were mythical creatures, unicorns or chupacabras brought into the real world for exhibition. They weren't quite that enchanting to Adonis, as he'd spent most of his life in the Open before Sans picked him up from slave traders a couple years prior.

"Picked him up" didn't quite cover what had happened. Sans had saved him. Adonis once asked Sans why he'd gone to the trouble; he had yet to receive an answer, but Sans had his unfailing loyalty for life nonetheless. So did Gavel, who had welcomed him into their Body. So did Caster, who had taken him under his wing and taught him how to fight. Six could go screw himself.

Even though he'd only been in The Disc for a couple of years, he felt like one of them. A member of society. He liked it that way. But he loved going to the trials because he knew personally how outrageous outliers could be. Something about the sun cooking their brains maybe. If nothing else, they were entertaining to watch.

Their responses to the judge's questioning tended to be interesting, sometimes so naïve that you felt bad for them, and often... colorful? That was it. Colorful. The defendants were usually petrified or indignant, and both made for good fun. Several months back, an older male outlier accused of sexual assault had actually taken a dump and stood up awkwardly in his seat, hands bound to the arms of the chair, and kicked his crap at the judge. It was hilarious, and from behind the security net, perfectly harmless.

Today's judge, Gamma, was the most long-winded of all the judges. His programming called for thorough questioning and an extensive weighing of the facts, and he was utilized for the seemingly non-threatening outliers whose crimes weren't quite black or white. Judge Alpha was the strictest of the three, used in clear cut cases belonging to maniacs and other skeevy criminals. He asked three questions, boom boom boom. Who are you? What did you do? Why did you do it? Then bam, death sentence. Judge Beta's questioning was reserved for middle-of-the-road types, those criminals who had done wrong, they would maybe take it back if they could, but it was clear that they were menaces to society and couldn't be left to run amuck freely. But Judge Gamma's line of questioning was less direct, a meandering path to get to the heart of the accused.

"Who are you?" began Gamma.

"Wren."

"Last name?"

She hesitated and wiggled in the defendant's chair. "Last? That's my only name."

Even Adonis knew his family name—West. Everyone had a family name, often based on where they hailed from, their trade, or some character trait at the core of their familial identity. Had she not known her parents? Did she not remember? The puzzled looks of the crowd in Adonis' immediate vicinity showed they were wondering the same.

"Where did you come from?" Judge Gamma continued.

"The Open."

"Why?"

"What do you mean?"

"Why would you live away from society?"

"I didn't. I was with my family."

"Where are they now?"

"Dead. Except for my sister."

The audience that had been fidgeting, coughing, and whispering, as all crowds do, went still and quiet. They understood that pain, and for just a few seconds, seemed to actually empathize with the outlier on trial. That is, until the next question.

"The woman who assaulted the Principal's son?"

The audience booed and shouted as if a switch had been flipped. Wren cowered under the power of their voices and the hatred they were throwing at her back.

The Judge addressed the crowd, his voice suddenly booming louder. "Silence."

Their attack quieted to a dull rumble.

"Please answer the question," said the Judge.

Wren eked out an answer. Her throat sounded dry. "I...it was a misunderstanding."

"Were you a part of this misunderstanding? Are you liable for her crime?"

"It looks like that's what I'm here for. So that you can decide. Why ask me?"

"I'd like to know your side of things."

"Well, I couldn't stop it from happening. I'm responsible for that, at least."

"What do you think your sentence should be?" he asked.

Wren pursed her lips and thought before speaking. "Are there only the two options you mentioned earlier? Prison or death?"

"That is irrelevant. What do you think your sentence should be?"

The hum of the tube lights high above seemed to grow louder, almost concealing the crowd's whispers of gossip and glee. A group of teenage boys around Adonis' age several chairs down from him elbowed each other and exchanged coins, probably betting on her response to come. Two interior patrolmen in their yellow vests talked in rushed whispers with crossed arms. A mother next to Adonis balanced three toddlers on her knees, looking over their heads with wide eyes.

Wren finally answered. "Kill me."

The crowd sucked in air like a final breath above water.

"Why?" Gamma asked.

"If I'm at fault for not stopping it, then my sister is definitely at fault according to your laws. If the two possible punishments are prison or death, I assume you'll kill her. Is that right?"

Gamma tapped one long finger against the arm of his chair. "Her case will be handled by another judge, but death is the likely outcome, yes."

"The *only* outcome for her," Adonis grumbled, remembering Survivor's wildness, her total lack of remorse. The mom next to him shushed him. Her kids turned to gawk at him— clearly knowing that shush intimately—and he stuck his tongue out at them. Wren's voice, clear and calm, yanked his attention back to the trial.

"If she's dead, I won't be far behind," she said. Then she chewed on her lower lip before adding, "The price is a life for a life. One for one?"

"That is often the case, yes."

"Then I ask that you take my life instead of my sister's."

The crowd went atwitter.

Wren continued, "It's an even trade, isn't it?"

"You would die for her? By your words, she's guilty."

"She's also saved me. Again and again. But that doesn't matter, does it? Not here, anyway." She seemed to fold in on herself, as if she could hide from view if she only made herself small enough.

"Are you not afraid of death?"

"I'm terrified of it." She looked around at the room made of metal and stone, recoiling from the lights overhead. She glanced back at the strangers making their own judgments, but then quickly turned away. "But I'm dead either way. I won't make it without her."

"Why not?"

"I..." She hesitated. "I don't know how."

Gamma drummed the long, thin fingers of his right hand against the arm of his chair, making them dance just behind the red button and the yellow button sitting side by side. He had no nails, and the tips of his fingers thumped dully against the metal. Then his middle and pointer fingers stretched out, one over the red button for death, the other over the yellow for prison. They hovered above them like spider legs on water. He froze, and Adonis began to wonder if he'd shorted out.

"What's he waiting for?" Adonis whispered.

Sans leaned in close behind his ear. "Perhaps he wishes he had a third option."

The suspense in the chamber grew thick and uncomfortable. Someone coughed and the entire audience twitched. Just when an impatient murmur began spreading through the crowd like a sickness, an alto voice flowed through the speakers of the room.

"Judge Gamma."

The judge pulled his hand back from the buttons. "Yes, Eydis?"

"This trial has been postponed. The prisoner is to meet with the Principal before further proceedings."

The crowd didn't bother to whisper this time. They erupted in choruses of *whats* and *whys*, with the bolder spectators throwing in a curse or two. The group of teenage boys near the front tried to throw balled-up garbage they'd snuck in at Wren. Most of the solid stuff caught on the barbs of the net and hung suspended in the air, but some juice from rotten plums and other produce made it through. A little splattered Wren's red hair, and she winced.

Gamma pressed the white button on his chair. "Trial 3947-O-U postponed until further notice. Prisoner released into the custody of the Keepers."

The clasps slid off Wren's hands and disappeared back into the body of the chair. Two Keepers, men wearing gray masks over the bottom halves of their faces, came through a side door. They each took one of her arms and helped her to her feet.

Snippets of the crowd's cries were audible above the general din.

"She's an outlier whore!"

"—killed our prince!"

"Death!"

Adonis was about to make a break for the door to avoid the impending chaos when the crowd turned silent. Gamma stood, all eight feet of his skeletal frame towering over the proceedings. He glared at the left side of the crowd and then turned to the right, scanning every face. He brought his hand down by his knee and snapped. Red nozzles emerged from the ceiling, which would disperse yet-to-be recycled wastewater all over the audience if he snapped again. It had only happened once before that Adonis knew of, and it was rumored the clothes of the crowd at that trial still reeked.

Amidst the silent suspense, the Keepers holding Wren took her out through the far door that would lead to the back exit of the Courthouse.

The crowd mumbled and slowly stood. The show was over. They made their way up the stairs, back to the big set of double doors that led out onto the street. Adonis twisted in his seat to see Sans hadn't moved. He just stared at the garbage hanging on the net, wrestling with thoughts or just zoning out—it was impossible to tell. Adonis squinted at Judge Gamma's still form glaring at the crowd and wondered why an outlier would mean anything to the Principal. He had a feeling that, if Caster woke up, he'd be very interested to know the same thing.

Caster hadn't regained consciousness since his seizure fit at the front gate. He lay on a half-raised hospital bed, sweat covering his face that made his hair stick to the pillow in a slick mess. He'd been stripped of all but his underwear, and thick gel packs were draped over each limb and across his chest. They'd been frozen but were now melted and getting warmer by the minute from his extreme body heat. The wound from the spine on his hand had been wrapped and was inflamed to the point of nearly bursting through the bandages.

Dr. Asha Keating rolled a cart covered in freshly frozen gel packs over to his bed. She brushed a dark curl back from her face before yanking it up into the clip holding the rest of her hair in place.

"Take those off," she said to Gavel, who stood on the opposite side of Caster's bed. "If you refuse to leave, at least make yourself useful."

"Yes, ma'am," he said. He peeled the warm packs from Caster, eliciting a sticky snap every time one came off his skin.

Asha replaced each warm pack with a cold one, and then grabbed the screen of one of the monitors to study it with the intensity of a mad scientist on the verge of a great discovery. She took a pen out of the pocket of her long, green lab coat and snatched the chart hanging from the bedside table to jot down notes.

The quiet in the secondary med ward disturbed Asha. When Six had radioed saying that Caster had been hurt and was being brought to her directly, she'd ordered the other patients and all but one nurse to relocate to the primary ward next door. It was an attempt at keeping Caster's condition on the downlow, but as he'd been seen at the gate by passersby and anyone on the street who happened to glance up as Gavel sprinted past with him splayed across his shoulders, it was a vain attempt. She did it anyway. She wanted to focus on Caster alone.

Now the ward, which was just big enough to squeeze ten beds in—and that was with staff bumping elbows the whole time—felt cavernous. Like a giant metal shoebox with tube lights on the ceiling that flickered every eight seconds—had they always done that? It was infuriating. Blank walls reflected a blurry version of herself moving around in the stillness. She made a mental note to get one of the street kids to make some art she could hang up, something with color. The quiet was the worst part—a terrifying, unnatural heavy hum of nothing, broken only by the beeps of Caster's monitors. She missed the vomiting of pregnant women battling dehydration and the babbling of drunks. The sounds of conditions that were typical, fixable.

Caster's condition was not.

She scribbled notes on his chart as she spoke. "I've never

seen this exact poison. The symptoms are similar to those caused by one I came across in the outlands years ago. Some fucking Marauder concoction. The ingredients used in this one were confiscated from the woman who made it. Bug is trying to come up with an antidote, but it'll take too long."

"She'll do what she can, just as you've done what you can," said Gavel.

She wrote faster, digging the pen into the paper until it tore. "Shit."

"Doctor," Gavel said, and then his voice turned to a whisper, "Honey, you have another patient to see."

She tore herself away from the chart and glanced at Mainstay across the room. He was sitting in a poofy armchair he'd requested be brought in, being waited on for every need by Asha's remaining nurse, who bustled about in her green uniform robe, brow together as though she might be considering requesting a new occupation.

Dr. Keating turned her disgust back to Gavel as her tension went to her jaw. "He can wait a few more goddamn minutes for his shiny new prosthetic. Pretty sure he can still jack off with his non-dominant hand."

"Asha," he said softly, "you've stabilized his temperature well enough." He put a hand on Caster's forehead. "There's nothing else you can do."

She watched her husband wipe sweat from around Caster's eyes with his rough thumb, watched Caster's chest rising and falling too quick, too shallow. She saw in her mind's eye what would happen before the day was out as his stats plummeted and the monitors bleated out their death song.

"Nope. Nuh-uh. This can't be happening. Not going to happen." She amped up the fluids flowing into his IV with one hand and rapped hard on the monitor nearby with the other. "These numbers are off. The connections must be fritzing."

She felt the rage bubbling up from her core. As it spilled over, she hit the monitor full on, cracking the screen in the corner.

Gavel's hand slid into hers. In that moment, she resented him and his composure, his ability to compartmentalize around the clock. Damn robot husband.

"You have enough time to go fit my Soldier for a prosthetic," he said. "I'll be here."

Her jawline softened. "I know you will. Unlike his father."

The Principal had a habit of not being present when someone close to him died, the prime example being Caster's mom, Reina. It was an offense Asha would never forgive.

Reina had arrived in The Disc not long before Asha and Gavel. She worked as a nurse with Ark at the time, but when Asha joined them as a doctor in the med ward and the two women hit it off, Reina began working under her charge. Reina had no living family and was from a small community that had been wiped out by a particularly powerful sandstorm and everyone in it scattered in the wind.

Reina was allowed Disc citizenship for her skills in healing, handed down by her mother. Less than a year later, Asha and Gavel stumbled in after an ordeal of their own. Reina was twenty at the time, Asha only slightly older at twenty-three. The two women bonded immediately over their occupations, their devotion to the care of others in a world desperate for it.

When Asha wasn't with Gavel, she was with Reina. Once a month, they'd splurge together in the market on a tattered paperback and enjoy it together, taking turns reading aloud about people who had to find the killer before they became his next victim or, better still, about the ladies whose biggest problem was deciding whether to wear leather or lace for their lover. They cooked together and enjoyed the little luxuries of The Disc, such as an egg here and a carton of apple juice there.

Reina even lived with Asha and Gavel for two years. Until things began to change.

Reina grew withdrawn and appeared exhausted all the time. For two months, she struggled to keep up with Asha in the med ward. The third time Asha caught her vomiting in the middle of the night, Reina couldn't keep the pregnancy a secret any longer. She refused to reveal the father's identity, only saying the situation was unsafe for her baby. Asha honored her privacy. She delivered Caster on the floor of Reina's bedroom, with Gavel serving as her assistant. The boy was stark blond, clashing with Reina's brown waves, and absolutely beautiful.

When Gavel left the room to get fresh sheets, Reina pulled Asha in close over Caster in her arms. "I can't register his birth with the city. Swear you won't tell Gavel."

Gavel came back in, but the desperation in Reina's eyes held Asha tight as she waited for her answer. Asha nodded. It was the first lie she'd ever told her husband.

Keeping Caster's existence secret was an outrageous risk for Reina to take, one that could easily have resulted in an exorbitant fine at best, separation from her son at the worst. Children—the single greatest resource for the future of the city— were required to be formally educated starting at age four, and their health was closely monitored. An unregistered child was an uncared-for child in the eyes of the system, and such an offense had to be punished.

Caster spent the first few years of his life bouncing between Reina, Asha, and Gavel's care—whoever wasn't working at the time. He was nearly school-aged when Thallium found out about him through dumb bad luck. An Interior Patrolman on the streets scanning faces for known criminals accidentally picked up Caster's little profile in the marketplace and found he wasn't in the system. That was all it took to change everything. One quick scan.

Asha was sitting at the kitchen table when Reina burst into the front door that day, her market bag hanging on her elbow by just one strap, a sack of pinto beans spilling out. She held Caster tightly on her hip, though he'd far outgrown the age when that was easy. Her tan skin had turned pale, her thin lips almost white.

"He knows," she said flatly, as if her spirit had left her.

Caster ran off to watch Gavel doing agility exercises behind the house while Reina sat at the table with her friend and confessed everything.

Thallium sent a messenger to the house that evening. He wanted to meet his son and be in his life. He didn't intend to prosecute Reina—he wanted to marry her.

Reina read the message within the message: both of you come to me peacefully, or I'll take him from you. And so, she became Reina Valcin in name, though never in practice, and Caster met his father, who spoiled Caster from that moment on.

They both moved into the Main House, where Thallium lived with his own father, Principal Valcin—an enigma with a reputation of being severe to those closest to him, a man whom Thallium allowed only minimally into Reina and Caster's lives until he died.

Over time, Caster changed from the sweet kid who loved to snuggle under the stars with his family to a demanding, self-righteous princeling. Especially with his mom.

Night after night, Reina would confide in Asha about her concern for Caster, about what she saw happening within him every day he spent with Thallium. Any time she tried to correct his behavior, he pushed back. Anything she advised him to do, he did the opposite. When he turned fifteen and she could feel him slipping all at once from her life, panic washed over her like a freezing rain. She stopped correcting him out of fear of losing him to Thallium. She knew, if that happened, Caster would lose himself altogether. She loved her son boldly and without condition, praying that her example would at least inspire him to love others in return.

And it did, before the end.

"I'm sure the Principal will be here soon," Gavel said.

There went his unflappable defense of his superior again. It was maddening.

"Caster's not contagious like Reina was," Asha said through her teeth, "but I'm sure something more important has come up that will keep his highness away, even if cowardice isn't to blame this time."

"Asha. Enough, please." Gavel's tone had just a tinge of military to it.

Before she could respond, two Keepers walked in the main door of the ward. The door was diagonal from the foot of Caster's bed, no more than ten feet away, in the center of the exterior wall of the med ward. Gavel had dropped Caster on the bed nearest the door, and they'd yet to move him. The Keepers stood motionless with the door open as they visually scanned the room for threats, letting a gust of dirt and pebbles fly in from outside.

"Sanitation is important here! Mind closing the door?" she shouted.

The bigger Keeper—Asha had forgotten his name—barely glanced at her over the edge of his gray mask. The other Keeper unhooked his mask to show his face. Prady, Caster's long-ago bodyguard. He'd aged since she'd last seen him, and as he saw Caster lying on the bed, he seemed to pale and age all the more. Prady opened his mouth to speak but then closed it again and just kept staring. Finally, he mouthed to Asha, "I'm so sorry." The two Keepers then banged their spears against the concrete floor once. In walked Principal Thallium.

Mainstay, the only one sitting in the room, stood up and faced the door.

Thallium unwound the white scarf from his face and passed the fabric to Prady. He then eyed Caster's bed off to his left, and his features sank for a half second before rebounding to new heights. He saluted Asha with a flourish, hand to his heart. "Doctor. Letting him sleep it off, I see. How motherly of you."

"Gotta be fucking kidding me," Asha muttered. Gavel cleared his throat to cover her words. "Unconsciousness is not sleep, sir," she said, louder this time. "He's going to die. Good thing you got here when you did—a little longer and you might have missed your son's passing." She said the last part through her teeth.

"Honestly, doctor, if you don't control your emotions, they will control you. He'll feel better in the morning."

She silently wished to be a flesh-eating virus or infectious parasite on the man, then allowed herself a deep breath during which she pictured him doubled over in pain before responding. "He won't make it until the morning, likely not even the next half hour. He's been poisoned. Those are medical facts, not emotions, sir."

"And so you administer the antidote. Is that really worth all this fanfare?"

"The antidote will not be finished in time to reverse the damage. Caster is going to—"

"No. That's absurd." The fury in his voice echoed her own outrage at the situation, and recognizing it in him made her stomach flip. As shitty of a parent as he was, he was still Caster's father. He never sported this blatant kind of machismo; it was always much more self-assured than this, more refined. She realized that he was terrified and doing all he could to pretend otherwise. For a brief instant, she felt pity.

"It doesn't help that you have it darker than a tomb in here," he continued, all fear wiped from his countenance, back to the eccentric man's man ready to rally and bless anyone within earshot with his wisdom. "He needs bright light and fresh air. Isn't that basic medicine? Operator, open the windows."

The metal shutters covering the front windows of the medical ward flew up, revealing two rectangular panels of glass on either side of the door looking out onto the busy street. Sunlight streamed in as the civilians walking by slowed or stopped to peer in, catching a glimpse of the Principal visiting his dying son.

Asha glared at the small crowd starting to gather outside. A father lifted his daughter up by the armpits so she could see in while his wife pressed the tip of her nose to the glass, looking from the Principal to Caster's still form.

"My patient needs privacy!" Asha marched over to the Principal with hands raised in annoyance. Thallium grabbed one of her hands in both of his.

"He's my son, and the people should see their prince kicking this poison's ass. Morale, morale, morale, Asha. We've got to keep it up."

She snarled quietly. "They'll be watching your son die in a moment. Let's see what that does to morale." She pressed up onto the balls of her feet toward Thallium's face. "Close. The. Windows." Gavel coughed somewhere behind her. "Please," she added.

The Principal sighed. "Close them, Operator." The shutters fell back into place. Hems and haws of the onlookers were audible as a dull mumbling through the glass and metal.

"Caster is going to die. I'm sorry for your loss. Maybe you want to say goodbye to your son before it's too late. Please excuse me." She took her hand from his. "I have another patient to see." She gave the Principal her back and took several big strides toward Mainstay, whose raised eyebrows over her shoulder at the Principal hinted he'd love a commendation for his injury. He let out a squeal as Asha tested the bend of his elbow a little too enthusiastically.

Thallium yawned a big, showy yawn and then said, "Call me when he's awake. I intend to advise him to reevaluate his life choices and associations to his face. I am his father, after all. Should act like it occasionally, don't you think?"

The door opened again, and Asha turned to see the Principal's assistant enter, the fringe of her thin, cream cloak trailing behind her with the breeze that she seemed to float in on.

Thallium turned to her. "Eydis! Excellent. I was just about to come find you."

She bowed to him. "There's a legal matter that demands your immediate attention, sir. It pertains to your son's assailants."

"Duty calls." He patted Caster on the foot twice and then took a stride toward the door.

"Sir," said Eydis, "I'd like to pay my respects, if you don't mind."

"That's unnecessary. Let's go."

"I'll only be a moment." She bowed her head at Thallium.

"Fine. I'll be outside. Hurry up." He left with his big Keeper right on his tail. A few curious civilians tried to get a glimpse inside before the door whooshed shut.

Prady stayed behind and bowed his head, lips moving in a prayer Asha couldn't hear. Asha went up to him and bowed her head next to his. Then Prady gave her a kiss on the forehead, nodded to Gavel, and after a final glance at Caster, reclasped his mask and followed behind Thallium.

Asha turned back to see Eydis at Caster's side. Asha thought it odd that she would feel compelled to say goodbye, even if it was to a young man she'd known for years—Eydis had always been strange. Strange enough to make Asha's stomach turn a bit sour whenever she saw her, like artificial sweetener or the smell of bleach. She was beautiful, disturbingly beautiful, with human tendencies and expressions. But there was something off about her. She carried herself as if she were always on the outside looking in, standing next to you but really somewhere else entirely.

Caster's heart was hammering, and his chest rose a bit lower with each rapid breath. Eydis bent down and kissed him on the lips, letting her hair shroud his face and the long sleeve of her cloak drape across his arm. She clasped his injured hand.

Then she stood upright and watched, as if she were waiting for him to die. She split her attention between Caster and his heart monitor. A solid thirty seconds passed in silence before Asha broke the awkwardness.

"Isn't the Principal waiting for you?"

She didn't respond. Just when Asha was going to try again, Eydis' laser focus broke into a grand smile. "Thank you for the time with him. I know you'll heal him." She inclined her head, first to Gavel and then to Asha, before leaving. Asha jogged over to the door and locked it behind her.

What was left of her filter was gone as she proclaimed, "Visiting hours are over!"

"Can we please hurry this up?" Mainstay grumbled from his armchair.

"Shut it, Soldier! Or I'll attach a fucking dildo to that wrist!" she said.

Mainstay obeyed.

She went back to Caster. Every irrational part of her wanted to shake him awake and snap him out of it, but she settled for wiping the sweat from his forehead with the damp cloth that had been resting on the bedside table. She put her other hand on his chest. The way it struggled to rise with every breath washed over her, giving her no option but to accept the reality. She hung her head back, damned if she would spend his last moments crying hysterically.

"If you want your men to be able to say goodbye, you'd better radio them now," she said to Gavel. Then she righted her head and looked Caster over slowly. "I'm so sorry, kiddo," she whispered.

Gavel walked around the bed and came up behind her. He wrapped his arms around her waist and kissed the top of her head through her tight, dark curls. "He asked me to say that he loves you. And he knows you love him. You did everything you could." They stood there in silence and let the pain of what was happening embrace them. Smother them.

Then Caster's chest rose in a powerful, great breath. The opposite of a death rattle. Asha shook Gavel off, knocking her skull hard against his chin. She got close to the monitor.

"I'll. Be. Fucked."

"What?" Gavel asked, turning his attention to the numbers on the screen he didn't understand.

Caster's heart rate evened out as his temperature began to fall. In less than five minutes, his temperature had dropped to just above normal. He fidgeted beneath the ice packs and turned his head to the side.

Asha felt his forehead and cheeks with the back of her hand. She took a pen light from her coat pocket. Gently, she opened his left eye and shone the light into it. The hazel color of his iris was now speckled with gold. The specks were vibrant, almost yellow in their intensity.

"That's kind of bright, Ash," Caster said, speaking past the stickiness of his throat.

She dropped the light to the floor and shrieked.

CHAPTER FOUR

THE MAIN STREETS OF THE DISC WERE LAID OUT IN A
grid, making a checkerboard pattern across the whole of the
city. The streets toward the middle of the city were the longest,
as they stretched end to end across the center of the circle. It
was for the street in the very center of The Disc, rather unimag-
inatively named "Diameter," that Eydis and Thallium now
headed, followed by two Keepers.

Diameter was the main thoroughfare of the city, and along
it sat buildings of great importance to the citizens, such as the
Ration Storehouse to the west, and in the middle, the Civilian
Trading Center, which wound all around Diameter in a
wandering square and was the beating heart of the city.

Eydis and Thallium continued their path north toward the
Main Street, but were hampered by the crowd near the
Medical Hub, which was a hundred people strong, fed by the
shoppers coming and going from the Trading Center and the
parents from the upper-class housing district who had just
dropped their children off at the House of Education before
classes started for the day. Those that had seen Thallium visit

his dying son came up to stroke his scarf and whisper their condolences. He touched them each on the face, nodding his thanks. When the crowd became thick enough to block their forward progress, the Keepers held out their spears across their chests, which forced the people to back up and keep a small bubble of space around the Principal. He waved and when they'd reached the end of the crowd and the people looked on at him in sorrow, he bowed and blew a kiss to the whole of them. As he turned around, leaving the mass behind, his face darkened, rage pulling a tight line down the center of his brow.

"Tell me who did this to my son," he said to Eydis.

"An outlier woman called Survivor," Eydis responded out of the side of her mouth as she smiled at a group of women who parted to allow them through.

"Where is she now? Have you seen her?"

"I haven't seen her, but based on the reports of others, she seems unpleasant. She's in a cell awaiting trial."

"No need for the trial. We can swing by the prison and I'll end her myself. Won't take long." He dug his heel into the dirt and tossed up a puff of dust as he picked up the pace and headed in the general direction of the prison.

"Sir, I don't think that would be wise," she said to his back.

He stopped mid-stride. "Excuse me?" He turned toward her and tilted his head slightly to the side. "Perhaps you'll help me understand why I shouldn't kill the subhuman waste that attacked my son." The rage from his brow had moved into the rest of his face, down his arms and to his hands. He flexed and unflexed them at his sides. She knew he was one wrong comment away from violence.

"Of course, sir." She eyed the people on the sidewalks as they neared the end of the bustling part of town. Everyone nodded or bowed at the Principal as they passed his entourage. "But not here."

They'd reached Diameter and turned east, away from the busy city center to cross over into the far end of the seedy underbelly of the street. Everything felt a little dirtier, a little darker, and a whole lot more illegal. The people on the sidewalks here didn't bow. Very few showed their faces at all.

A stretch of bars and shoddily disguised sex parlors greeted them with papered windows and unlit neon signs that would come to life at dusk. It was far less busy here than it would be once the sun went down, but if a passerby were paying attention, they could always hear moans of ecstasy or pain—it was often difficult to tell which.

The underground black market ran beneath their feet, its entrance hidden behind a men's bathroom stall in a tiny smoke shop famous for its evergreen incense. Really, the incense smelled like dirt with a tinge of ammonia, but as the vast majority of people in The Disc had never seen a pine tree, or any tree for that matter, they fell for the false scent, attracted to the magic of the legendary wooden giants.

As they reached the front steps of Screws and Gears, the Principal's preferred den of indecency, Eydis pulled Thallium close.

"I had hoped to wait until we reached the Main House to discuss matters, but as you're intent on killing the outlier on our way back, now will have to do."

She pulled him into the alley between the club and the wall of the gambling hall next door. At the end of the alley, she started to lead him around the corner to the smaller, darker alley behind the club. Thallium stopped and turned to his Keepers, who were diligently following several feet behind.

"Stay close to the entrance, please. We'll only be a moment."

They struck their spears on the ground and did an about face before returning to the opening of the alley to stand watch.

Eydis led Thallium behind Screws and Gears, near the cluster of metal waste drums that emitted a general atmosphere of day-old beer, vanilla perfume, and vomit. She looked from side to side, then turned to him.

"One of the Carriers has returned."

His eyes went wide, and he crossed his arms. "Which one?"

She cupped her hand over his cheek. "The *first* one. Her blood came back positive, and I intervened during her trial on your behalf."

Excitement pulled at the corners of his mouth, but he seemed to push it back. "Does she appear self-aware? Has she used her abilities?"

"Her powers are dormant. For now. The memory wipe did its job. We'll have to restore them."

"And you can do that?"

"*We* can."

His voice echoed through the alley as he whooped in victory, raising his hands in the air to non-existent spectators. He paused with his arms up. "Wait," he got close to her, "is she the one that attacked my son?"

"No, sir. The Carrier is her sister, Wren."

"Excellent!" He took a few deep breaths and held his arms tight by his body, about to explode with pent-up energy. "My dear daddy's work has never been more real than now. Where is she?"

She grinned. "On her way to the Main House with two guards."

He enveloped her, reaching under her cloak and grabbing her butt with both hands as he sucked on her shoulder. "You never fail me," he said against her skin. "I'll execute her sister and then we'll start right away testing her limits. We need to get this project going."

"Sir," she said as she removed his hands from her backside

and sidestepped toward the trash drums. "If done correctly, this will take time. In these matters, it's best to have a happy, willing party rather than a prisoner. I suggest you take your time and earn her trust before we attempt to restore her. That would mean holding off on killing her sister."

He took her wrists, pulled her arms above her head, and shoved her against the wall. He held her arms in place with one hand while he ripped the front of her shirt open with the other. She sighed as he kissed her chest.

"I can't do that," he said in between kisses.

"I only suggest you delay until we've brought Wren to our side, shown her the kind of life she can have apart from her sister." She pulled her arms down out of his grip and took hold of either side of his face. "A loyal servant is easier to work with than a bitter slave, wouldn't you agree?"

He sighed. "I've waited too long for this, and my father died in its pursuit. I've grown impatient. The sooner we see what she can do, the sooner our lives improve. Perhaps she needs a little fear in her to encourage cooperation, a little pain."

Her face went blank, and she fought the urge to move her hands down to his neck. "I've seen her. She's already terrified. Furthermore, you have no idea what she's capable of. She could hurt you back."

He kicked an empty beer bottle on the ground into the wall, which shattered and sent glass soaring upward. Tiny shards landed in her hair and she shook them out. She brought her arms in close to her torso, buoying up her breasts, and approached the Principal as he was letting out a string of profanity. Logic was the wrong tactic here. She had to speak his language, as tiresome as it was.

With a graceful stretch up to her toes, she brought her chest just under his face and whispered into his ear with hot breath. "Great things don't happen in a fleeting instant of brute force.

They are slow, they build with patience and restrained passion, until the perfect moment of triumph." She nibbled his earlobe.

He let out a shuddering breath.

"Promise me you'll be patient." She let her cloak fall to the ground and undid the front clasp of her bra, holding it closed with just her fingers. "Promise me."

"I promise," he said.

She dropped her hands to her sides, letting the clasp fall open. He lunged at her, then hoisted her up by the waist and set her roughly on top of the nearest waste drum. He dropped his pants, hiked up her skirt, and practiced patience as she moaned into his neck.

"K Unit 37 en route to Main House with the prisoner," said the man on Wren's right. He gave her a sideways glance, but when he saw she was watching him, quickly looked away.

A dull voice hummed from the black bracelet he wore, "Copy."

They left through the back entrance of the courthouse. Several men and women wearing long, shiny robes walked past them, casting curious but brief looks before their appointments of the day called them onward.

She and the two men neared the bottom of a short flight of stairs as a group of people came around the side of the building to their right. Many of their faces were familiar. She had seen them scowling at her in the courtroom—a woman with a sharp nose and dark hair, the little girl with a stuffed bunny, a man in overalls. The group formed a long line in front of them and planted their feet. Wren stopped in her tracks, and the men stuck their hands under her armpits.

"Do not stop moving," said the one on her left.

She picked up her feet again but tucked her chin to her chest and let the men maneuver her.

"Clear a path, by order of the Principal's Keepers!" said the man on her right. His words carried through the concrete courtyard.

A whirring noise, like a rapid heartbeat, floated above her. She looked up to see a black orb with two protrusions like wings hovering just above them. Two orange lights were lit on its front, like eyes on an otherwise blank face.

The crowd looked up, spotting the device, and seemed to let out a collective groan. A couple of people toward the center moved to allow a tiny rip in the fabric of the mob, and the two men steered Wren toward it. She didn't meet their faces, instead focusing on their shoes. They weren't much fancier than hers, just simple slippers and sandals, one pair of thin leather boots. The people smelled so clean—she'd only smelled soap a few times in her life, and they reeked of it. As she neared the end of the part in the crowd, the people started to move back together, closing the gap after her. Once she'd left them behind, she didn't dare look back.

The men released their grips under her arms. She realized it hadn't been her they were worried about when they'd taken hold of her, and she walked a little faster. A faint purring was still audible—the black orb floated high above, following the path they took as it stared down with its burning eyes.

After a while, they came to two curved structures reaching out of the dirt like half-buried fangs. They were broad at the bottom and grew narrower at their tops, where they ended in points that angled toward one another to make an open arch-way. The curve on the left was made of red clay, the one on the right made of a thin metal that shimmered with rainbows from certain angles. It was next to the metal curve that they stopped and one of the Keepers spoke into his bracelet.

"K Unit 37 reporting. Standing at monument, waiting for instruction."

As he waited for a response, she looked closer at the arch and found an inscription on it. She hadn't needed to read in years, but Alma had taught her well, and she deciphered the words: *For the future and the progress toward which we strive.* Beneath the inscription, cut even deeper into the metal, was a symbol, a letter she didn't recognize. Nonetheless, the shape, the way the lines slashed and cut together, was somehow familiar, like a piece of a nursery rhyme forgotten over time. As she struggled to place it, the voice sounded again from the Keeper's bracelet.

"Cleared for approach."

"Here," said the Keeper on her left. He pulled a pair of dark glasses with big, round lenses out of his pocket. "Put these on." They put on their own pairs and she followed suit.

"Keep up," the men said together.

They started off again and headed up a flight of stone stairs that disappeared around a bend next to a hillside. As they came left around the bend, she saw what could only have been the Main House, set at the top of the hill, shining in glory.

The silver pyramid, as big as a small mountain, sparkled in the brilliance of midday. Unable to stop her curiosity, Wren moved the glasses down her nose just enough to see over them. Her eyes burned with the intensity of the light the Main House reflected, and she put the glasses back in place as she squinted hard past the green and yellow splotches that now flooded her vision. With the lenses on, the building shone with bearable strength, and it was difficult to look away. Several windows dotted the front of the building, made of the same creamy, rainbow material of the arch, but formed thin enough to see through. Circling the peak of the pyramid were several black dots. The black orb that had followed them since the courthouse zoomed up and joined in the dance above.

Finally, they mounted the last stair and walked toward the entrance of the pyramid. A door opened, but a tight net of the same light that had come from Survivor's e-binds covered it; the men headed for it without hesitation. She tried to pull back, but they urged her forward, not slowing down. She braced herself for pain when the center of the net expanded, leaving enough space for all three of them to pass through. It closed immediately behind them, followed by the door.

The Keepers took position inside the doorway.

"Please wait here in the foyer," one said. Then they went utterly still, statues against the wall, staring straight ahead.

The foyer was a square room set a foot into the ground and filled with strange items on stands beneath glass boxes, with a floor that was covered in red fibers—cloth, maybe—that rose nearly an inch above the sides of Wren's feet as she stepped down into the lower area of the room. She knelt and pressed her hands into the fibers to find they were as luxuriously soft as they looked. Then she wandered between the stands, overwhelmed with fantastical colors and materials and the smell of age and seriousness.

In the first case stood a trio of small rectangles, one white and two black. One side was glass cracked in a spiderweb pattern. Another case held a box of metal pins, all bunched tightly together, shaped to an imprint of someone's face. A long, thick string was attached to the box's side and then coiled into a neat pile. In a smaller, flatter case were laid out coins and bills of various colors and denominations. After a closer look, Wren noticed that a green bill with a curly-haired man on it was dated 1994, and her mouth hung open.

The cases at the back of the foyer held what looked like human limbs—arms, legs, and other shapely pieces—all in a collection together as if someone had been dismantled but only slightly. However, the skin covering them was too perfect, a light brown softness without blemish, as if the sun and wind had never scorched them and they'd been living in that case while the world outside grew old and tired. As Wren drew closer, she noticed they had silver joints just showing on their open ends—not human, but as for what they were, she had no idea.

One case held a head of tarnished metal, crudely modeled to resemble a human, but lacking skin and any trace of emotional expression. She placed her hand on the glass and leaned in to get a better look at the triangular gap where a nose should be. As she did so, its eyes lit up in a flash of yellowy white. She jumped back, hitting her elbow on the corner of the currency display. The eyes dimmed slowly back to black.

"Miraculous," said a voice behind her.

She spun around and came face to face with a woman dressed all in white, with waves of strawberry hair falling past her shoulders.

"Hello," the woman said. "My name is Eydis."

Wren rubbed at her elbow and didn't respond.

Eydis reached out as if to tuck Wren's hair behind her ear, but then pulled her hand back. "I've been told your name is Wren. A lovely name for a lovely girl. We're glad you're here."

"We?" Wren finally found her voice.

"I'd like to take you to see Principal Thallium, our leader. Would that be all right?"

"You aren't the leader?"

Eydis chuckled once, but Wren couldn't see what was amusing about her question. "Please, come with me."

Eydis led her to a room set in one of the front two corners of the pyramid. Two of the walls slanted sharply up, and a massive rug covered in an intricate vining pattern of blue, gold, and red covered the floor. At the rug's center lay a white sheet on which sat covered dishes and platters. A handsome blond man sat in the middle, powerful-looking and somehow familiar. There was something about the angles of his face that she recognized, but she didn't know what specifically. He sat on the far side of the sheet, cross-legged on a big red pillow. He was in the middle of sipping water from a glass when they walked in.

"Phew! Time in that sun will parch you out!" he exclaimed. "Come in! Join me." He motioned toward the other two pillows set at the ends of the sheet.

Eydis bowed to him. "Wren, this is Principal Thallium. The ruler of The Disc." She removed her shoes and sat on his right.

"Fluff and titles. You may call me Thallium. Now, come sit."

Wren pushed her dirty slippers off and set them near Eydis' delicate leather sandals. As she walked across the sheet toward the remaining pillow, her feet stained the fabric with caked-on sand and muck.

"I...I'm sorry," she said, seeing the mess as she sat down.

Thallium shrugged. "Not a problem." He pressed a button on the black bracelet on his wrist.

A tall, narrow compartment in the wall behind him slid open, and out of it walked a person, or something made to look like one. It was five feet tall, with a human-like frame made of shining metal. Its face was less crude than the one in the glass case in the foyer—this one was a smooth mask of white, but somehow overlaid on top was an image of a young man. He had kind eyes and high cheekbones, all of which flickered intermittently like a mirage. He stopped next to Thallium.

"The dirt. Get rid of it," Thallium said.

The young man...person...thing got down on its hands and knees. With one hand, it sucked up the dirt, just breathed it in through its palm in a great inhale. With the other hand, it somehow wet and then dried the stains on the sheet. Thallium spoke over the whirring of its working parts.

"I'm sure this place is quite different from wherever it is you're from."

Wren could only stare at the cleaner, open-mouthed, forgetting to breathe. It scrubbed and scrubbed, its joints squeaking as it changed position to get one particularly troublesome stain from a different angle.

"I'm certain you're curious why I brought you here?" Thallium snapped next to her ear to get her attention.

Wren stared at him, her mouth still hanging open.

Eydis cleared her throat, and Thallium nodded toward her.

"Apologies," he said. "Anyway, I'll explain everything, but I believe in tending to the simple needs of people before expecting them to listen to me. Are you hungry?"

The cleaner finally stood and bowed at Thallium until it was at a 90-degree angle. "Is there anything else I can do for you?" Its voice seemed to match the young face it projected— soft and loyal, but with a hint of an inhuman, metallic echo.

"Remove the food covers," he said.

It did as it was told, removing silver tray covers and serving dish lids and holding them all in a precarious stack in its right hand. As it removed a towel from the top of a bowl near Wren, it smiled at her.

"That's all for now." Thallium shooed the person away.

It left, taking the impossibly high stack of lids with it.

"You've never seen an RS Unit before," Thallium said.

"A what?" Wren replied.

"A Robotic Service Unit. That's one of the earlier models, from the Canis series made in the late 2000s. Don't see many of them these days, but a Scavenger found the CPU of that one in the Open a few towns away. I had it refurbished. I'm a bit nostalgic, as you could probably tell from my little museum. Now, let's eat, and we can get down to business."

The serving dishes before them held more food than Wren had ever seen at one meal. Plump apricots and plums, larger than any she'd foraged in the Open. A bowl towering with green leafy plants. A tray covered in slices of something white, small green circles, and flatbreads. On the center tray was something golden brown in color, with appendages sticking out at one end. Certainly an animal, but colossal compared to the rodents and rabbits she'd grown up eating.

"Chicken leg?" Thallium said. He tore off one of the back appendages, put it on a plate, and handed it to her.

As she caught whiffs of rosemary from the leg, pools of drool formed on both sides of her tongue, and her stomach sent sharp pains from one side of her abdomen to the other.

"You have *meat* here?" she asked, still unsure if the leg sitting on her plate was real.

"Well, we have meat *here*," he said. "My staff raises chickens, but not enough to feed the general populace. I'm afraid if we made them publicly available, the population we've worked so hard to build up would be squandered. Hopefully we'll be able to create this ourselves someday and sell it to the people, but we're not there yet."

"Create it?"

"In a lab. We've tried, like they did before The Fall so that vegetarians could have meat without feeling they were betraying their beliefs. Now vegetarian is *the* diet, thanks to meat's rarity rather than some philosophical, animal-worshipping guilt. Here's to irony." He snickered as he finished piling his plate with slices and bits of mystery food.

Wren held her plate close and tore off a tiny shred of chicken. It filled her mouth with savory warmth, and she devoured the rest of the leg like it might get up and run away.

"That's a good girl," Thallium said. He winked at her, and finally, it clicked. The shape of his jaw, the shade of his hair, even the way he carried himself with an easy grace in his movements—she'd seen it all before in Caster.

"Have some bread, Wren," Eydis said, making Wren start. "It's lovely with a slice of goat cheese and pickles. You may also like the plums—perfectly ripe at this time of the season." Eydis pointed to the items as she named them, then smiled warmly and slid a slice of plum into her mouth.

Thallium burst out laughing and tossed a pickle slice at Eydis. It hit her thigh and fell to the sheet. "You and food. Gets me every time!" He slapped his knee. He must have seen the confusion on Wren's face, because he jerked his thumb toward Eydis. "She's a synthetic—my android assistant."

None of that made sense, and Wren's face must have shown she thought so.

"I'm not human like you. I was made by humans," said Eydis.

"Why?" Wren asked.

Eydis set her plate down and poured herself a glass of water. "To help them." She turned to Thallium. "Sir, while I don't *need* to eat, I've told you a hundred times before that I do so to engage in social ritual. One of my priorities is to make the people around me feel as comfortable as possible."

"Now that, I agree with. I'm always comfortable around you." He teased the end of a square of cheese between his front teeth before biting it.

Wren put a slice of bread and several bits of cheese on her plate while Eydis filled another glass with water and a scoop of tiny clear cubes from a covered bucket. She gave it to Thallium, who set it before Wren. She warily picked up the glass, nearly dropping it as her skin touched the cold. She sniffed it before daring to take a sip.

"Now that we're more comfortable, I want to discuss a few things with you," said Thallium, setting his plate down and wiping his mouth on a cloth napkin. "Did you see the monument as you came in? The two big arches at the bottom of the path?"

Wren nodded.

"You can read?" he asked. "Did you happen to read the writing on them?"

"I didn't read both of them."

"Well, the clay arch stands for our past, and the other arch stands for our future. When you put the inscriptions together, you get: 'For the past and the mistakes we leave there to lie. For the future and the progress toward which we strive.' Do you have any idea what those inscriptions are talking about?"

She shook her head.

"I mentioned The Fall a minute ago—the monument's talking about The Fall of technology that happened 250 years ago. Have you heard of the gate accident?"

She had, thanks to Alma. It was one of the many bedtime stories she'd rotated through. "People wanted to start another world and left in ships through a gate in the sky," she answered Thallium. "The gate broke and closed and made the sun angry when it did. Lots of people on Earth died."

"Actually, after satellites were knocked out and power was lost, *most* of the people on Earth died in the resulting chaos, according to our sparse records. Not only did we lose people, we lost most of the valuable technology men worked centuries to design. The pieces of it that survived couldn't be used without power. The dark age between the accident and the founding of The Disc is what the clay arch stands for—a reminder that we can't fall again. We wouldn't survive it a second time. Now, the future, the metal arch, that's where you come in."

"Me?"

"Odds and ends of lost technology are still out there waiting to be found and brought back to life. We've regained some of it—an RS Unit here and there, flashlights and computers, enough solar power to keep a few government-backed businesses and our own facilities functioning, such as our water recycling plant and, of course, the Main House. Trinkets, all of them, compared to the glory of the height of technology before The Fall, of which our lovely Eydis is a surviving product." He waved at her with a flourish of his hands.

Wren understood the concept of "technology" at large—the space gate was technology, something man made to fulfill a specific purpose. She had a basic understanding of science from Alma, such as what was required for plants to grow, how to care for a broken bone, even which gasses made up the stars. But the things Thallium was talking about were beyond understanding. It wasn't the science she knew; it was a more intimate kind of magic, a magic that terrified her while simultaneously drawing her in to guess at how it worked, to touch it for herself.

"Thanks to Eydis and her researchers," Thallium continued, "we're regaining some of what was lost, but it's a slow process. Painfully slow. I need to improve my people's lives *now*. Which brings me to my point. We took a look at your blood—a standard procedure—and discovered something." He cupped his hand around his mouth and whispered. "You're special."

Alma's voice echoed in Wren's ears from her childhood; she'd called her variations of "special" such as "gifted" and "unique" whenever Wren asked why bounty hunters kept looking for them. But when Wren had pressed for further details, Alma had shut down every time and run off to tend to the campfire or check the perimeter.

"Special how?" Wren asked.

"You can interact with technology in a way non-special people can't."

Eydis added, "You saw how the eyes of the RS Unit outside lit up just because you were near? That's one way you're special."

Wren sucked on her lower lip.

"You also probably noticed that the people out there, my people, are upset," said Thallium. "They're tired, hungry, wanting more from life. You could help bring in a golden age. If you stay, you could bring us into the future bright and shining, a firework in the night!" He shot his arms up, his fingers trembling. "Apologies. I just get so excited!"

"But, why am I special?" she asked

He waved that thought away. "I've found it's best not to question a miracle if it comes along, as they rarely do. Why you're special isn't important, only what you do with it. The other important part is that if you help us, I can help you."

"Help me?"

"You liked the chicken, right? How about chicken with every meal? How about the guarantee of just *having* every meal? A place to live, here, in the protection of the walls of The Disc. Is that the kind of help you'd like?"

At the idea of that level of safety, Wren almost took her first genuine deep breath in ages. But Alma's warning, the smell of smoke, came and went, making her hesitate to jump at the opportunity.

An odd tone sounded in the room. "Sir," said a voice. Wren whipped her eyes around, trying to find where it was coming from.

"Operator, I'm busy," said Thallium.

"Yes, sir, but you said to tell you if your son woke up. He's awake. Dr. Keating reports that the poison seems to have moved through his system."

The mention of poison made Wren sit up straight. Her earlobes warmed, and she wrung the napkin next to her.

He clapped once, the sound a sharp snap. "Did I say it or did I not? He's a Valcin." He raised his glass high and took a sip.

Eydis made a strange noise behind the edge of her water glass, a cross between a contented sigh and a giggle. "Remarkable," she said to herself, as if she were the only one in the room.

Thallium raised an eyebrow at her before getting distracted by the last chicken leg on the platter. "That'll be all, Operator," he said loudly. "Back to the topic at hand."

"The man who brought me here, the one who was poisoned, he's going to live? Is that who you're talking about?" Wren asked.

A grin started at the corner of Thallium's mouth. He reached up and played with the end of the hair on his chin. "Yes, that's right. My son, Caster."

She exhaled and closed her eyes briefly. "Good. That's good." Then she realized what he'd said. "He's your son?"

"I'm his father, yes."

Her eyebrows shot up. The concept of a mother, she knew personally. But not of a father. The only fathers she'd known were the ones from Alma's tales.

"Are you all right?" Thallium asked.

Wren nodded. "I'm glad Caster's okay."

Eydis reached over and squeezed Thallium's hand. He nodded at her.

"You're welcome to visit him," he said, picking up his water glass, "if you stay here, of course."

Wren nibbled on her bread.

"It would be a shame to send you back out there, into no man's land," he continued. "It's amazing you've made it as long as you have, but that kind of luck won't last. Life expectancy out there is, well, let's just say you're a very, very old lady out there. But banishing you would be lenient compared to the more likely outcome of your trial if I were to allow Judge Gamma to declare his ruling. I'd hate to send you back to the defendant's chair." He shook his head and looked down at the rug, sighing heavily.

Wren considered his words. "If I stay, what do I have to do?"

He scratched at his chin as he answered. "Well, you would need to let us see what exactly your gifts are, how much you can help us. Then, help us. Simple, really. Details can be discussed later, but that's the main idea. You'd become one of us, and the people would admire and appreciate your abilities."

"I don't understand. What abilities?"

He patted her hand. "No need to understand everything now. But based on our analysis so far, you might be able to help us provide much needed energy. Who knows, you might even be able to help us get power to the whole Disc! Such potential! Some people would do anything to get it. I think you'll agree that we don't want those gifts to fall into the hands of those who would force or threaten you to use them." He said the last part with a dark edge of certainty. "Here, you'd belong!" He flopped back on his pillow, letting the floor embrace him. "Here," he rolled over on his side to face her, and propped his head up on his hand, "you'd finally have a home."

In that moment, she wanted so badly to just be back in her cave, curled up in a nest of blankets with Biter in her pocket. Even more than that, she wanted the forest, the smell of life and trees greeting her as she woke up to Alma sitting beneath her sleeping branch while singing about bringing home a baby bumblebee. Wren would lead the children again in the hand motions of the song, passing a pretend bumblebee back and forth between her palms.

If Survivor could have heard her thoughts, she'd mock her for dwelling in the past, blaming her weak nature and her sentiment. She'd ridicule her, laugh at her, and then come up with an ideal solution to keep them both out of trouble.

"What would happen to me and my sister if I said no?" she asked finally.

A vein popped out on the side of Thallium's neck, then sank back down like a serpent getting comfortable. Eydis answered for him.

"The Principal has made a great exception to pause your trial, as well as that of your sister. If you were to refuse, we'd have to return you both to trial for a verdict to be declared. Without a trade, such as your help for your freedom, the law is absolute." She folded her hands in her lap, as if there was nothing that could be done about it.

"I have a condition," Wren said.

He raised an eyebrow. "What condition is that?"

"Let my sister go. Then I'll help you."

"Hmm. That would be difficult." He clicked his tongue several times. "The law says outsiders accused of crimes, particularly one as heinous as your sister's, must be tried. She attempted to kill my son, for God's sake. It doesn't take much investigating to know a judge will rule for her execution. That's the law. Unfortunately, she doesn't have anything to offer, unlike you." He tapped against his water glass, thinking. "Maybe there's something I can do," he continued. "I could allow her to stay here, in The Disc, as a citizen. She would have to work off her debt to society. She could have her own place to live, and rations like the rest of my people. She would be assigned a trade, but the money she made would have to be handed over to the government to make amends. Would that meet your condition?"

Wren looked over at Eydis, at the perfect teeth through her

smile that invited her in like a warm bed for a weary traveler. The food splayed out before her beckoned like hands curling inward, telling her to jump on in.

"Yes," she said softly.

"Fantastic!" He leapt to his feet and clapped once. Wren nearly dropped her empty plate. "Eydis, find her some new clothes and set her up in my guest quarters. We'll get started immediately."

"Wren," Eydis said, brushing over Thallium's command. "If you don't mind my asking, were you and your sister all alone in the outlands? You have no other family?"

Eydis' tone had turned serious, almost breathless. Thallium tilted his head and stared at Wren, eager for the answer.

"No. They're dead."

Eydis deflated a bit. "I'm so sorry. How did they die?"

Survivor's voice hissed in Wren's mind: *Don't tell her, you idiot! Don't trust anyone!*

"In a fire," Wren said simply.

Something shifted in Eydis' expression then, her empathy turning to satisfaction as if Wren had just given a secret away. But Wren had no idea what that could be. Survivor's voice again: *Get out of there! Now!*

Wren set down her plate and stood. "I want to see my sister."

Thallium rolled his neck around and back upright while a groan escaped his lips, so quiet Wren barely heard it. "Fine! After you get cleaned up, I'll have some men escort you down to the prison. You can give her the good news of her freedom yourself. Then we'll take a closer look at your DNA, eh?"

He didn't seem to notice her rapid blinking at the term "DNA." In an instant, he was heading out the door, shoeless and without a care, whistling "She'll Be Coming 'Round the Mountain" at top volume.

Eydis reached out to Wren, who pulled her gaze from the door and turned it onto Eydis' golden eyes. They lit up with joy. "Let me show you to your room, little one."

———

Nearly as soon as Eydis had opened the door of Wren's room for her, she'd collapsed and slept, unable to resist the unfamiliar heaviness of her stomach. She slept so hard that not even her nightmares reached her, or if they had, she'd been extended the mercy of forgetting them this time. When she woke, she marveled at how her back wasn't aching. The floor was the most comfortable floor she'd ever slept on. Next to her sat the large bed she'd been offered, but it had been much too soft; she was afraid of sinking into it and suffocating.

The rug beneath her was the closest thing to a bed of grass she'd felt since the forest, and the blankets here were clean, not filled with sand and dust. Gentle light came in through the window on the far wall, which slanted upward on its way to the pyramid peak of the Main House. The sun's intensity was lessened by the glass, and it cast rainbow squiggles on the floor as the beams bounced around on their way inside. She watched the light dance on the walls for a few minutes, soaking in the colors and the rhythm as she enjoyed the folds of a velvet blanket and support of a feather pillow. She flipped onto her back and moved her arms and legs around as if she were underwater. The blankets rippled and dipped, and seemed to move against her skin rather than the other way around.

This room, *her* room, as she kept correcting herself, would have been large enough to house her, Survivor, Alma, and all the children. Their time in the forest had been comfortable, and she did love the feel and smell of bark and soft pine needles. However, things would have been different if they'd been in a place like this. They would have been easier, and Alma deserved easier.

Survivor wasn't here. She would love a place this nice and would've used the bed like people were supposed to. She'd know what she was doing.

The velvet suddenly felt a little less soft, less inviting. She sat up and let the blankets fall from her shoulders. A knock came at the door.

"Miss?" said someone on the other side. "Are you awake?"

She rose to a crouch and peeked around the foot of the bed at the door.

"Miss?" the voice came again. A man's voice. Kind, concerned, which alarmed her most of all.

She stood and tiptoed to the door.

"I'll just leave this here in the hall for you."

Faint footsteps, one normal and one heavy and wooden, retreated down the hallway.

Wren opened the door a crack and saw a man in a striped robe reaching the end of the hall. He had gray hair and walked with a large staff. He turned a corner and disappeared.

In the hall near her door was a package wrapped in burlap and string. She nudged it with her foot and jumped back half a step. Nothing happened. She picked it up, looked both ways down the hall, and then retreated into her room and locked the door behind her.

She set the package down on the floor and crouched next to it. Gently, she pulled the end of the string, undoing the bow keeping it all together. Under the burlap was soft, pale blue cotton. She picked it up and held it out in front of her. It was a dress, long sleeved, with a full-length skirt trimmed in deep red.

There was another soft knock at the door.

Wren lifted the dress up in front of her like a shield.

"I see you found the package," said the same voice from before. "May I come in?"

Something in the voice made her loosen her grip on the dress. His tone was so warm that she found herself disarmed. She crossed to the door and opened it a crack. The gray-haired man stood there with another package. He smiled at her, deepening the lines around his eyes and mouth. "Miss." He bowed his head. "My name is Prady. I've been assigned to serve you."

She opened the door more. "Serve me what?"

He chuckled. "Whatever you need. I thought we might start with fresh clothes." He held out the second package to her.

She let the blue dress fall to the floor and ripped the new package open. Inside was a soft white scarf and a pair of leather slippers that were both sturdy and flexible. She slipped the shoes on, and though they made her toes feel confined compared to her worn out cotton slippers, she appreciated their quality. With the shoes was a heavy cloak, lined on the inside with thick gray wool. The outside was deep red and shiny, the brightest color she'd ever seen.

"Do you like it? Eydis wanted you to have something luxurious. Doesn't get much more luxurious than this."

She rubbed it against her cheek and smiled.

He nodded heartily. "Good. Oh, there's a rag and water in the cabinet here to wash up, as well as some ribbons if you feel like tying back your hair. How about you get changed? We could go see your sister once you're ready?"

Her heart raced with a strange mix of excitement and fear. "How long have I been asleep?"

"Just a few hours, though I wouldn't blame you if you needed to rest a while longer before we go out. In fact, I'd encourage it."

"No. I shouldn't have left her alone for as long as I have."

"Your sister, you mean. Shall we go visit her now then?"

"Yes, please." Hit with a sense of urgency, she reached down, grabbed the hem of her dirty dress, and yanked it up in a whoosh.

Prady spun around. "Miss, you can uh, wait to do that when I leave," he said to the far wall. "I'll go put in a request to get you some underwear."

"Under where?" she asked, still holding her filthy dress halfway up her body.

He took three great strides to the door, leaning on his staff as it thumped dully against the carpet and then thwacked against the stone at the rug's end. He called back, "Just come out when you're decent." He opened the door, stepped out, and closed it behind him in one fluid motion.

"Decent?" Wren whispered.

She walked to the cabinet he'd mentioned and opened the door. As she did, she saw movement on her left and jumped. Something shiny hung on the inside of the cabinet door. She moved in to examine it and saw a woman with tangled red hair, blue eyes, and freckles dotted all over the bridge of her nose. She grabbed a tuft of her hair and looked at it, then realized the woman in the glass was doing the same thing. The last time she'd seen herself was in a dim reflection in the cave pool, and the image had been too shadowy to decipher much at all. So this was her. This was what the world saw.

She got closer to her reflection, looking up her nose and seeing tiny hairs. Her eyelashes were blond, and she blinked rapidly to see how they fanned the air. She showed all of her teeth, short and off-white. Hers didn't look like Survivor's, and she realized that Alma's advice for taking care of her mouth every night had been true. She stuck her tongue out and laughed, then pulled at the corners of her mouth and laughed some more. The skin around her mouth turned slightly pink as she played with it.

She yanked her old dress off, then dipped the rag into the bowl of water provided for her and proceeded to wipe her face, under her arms, and all over her feet. When she tugged on the blue dress, she liked how the scooped neck showed the freckles on her chest. Her hair was its usual untamed self, and she raked her fingers through it a bit before selecting a blue ribbon from the five different color choices hanging on a tiny bar near the mirror. She gathered it together and tied it behind her neck, happy to have it off her face.

Several other shiny odds and ends sat on shelves inside the cabinet. Pale pink creams in little silver tins, tiny brushes of soft hair, a tall dispenser of aloe vera—she recognized that one at least. A row of ten small bottles with labels of various colors caught her eye, and she opened the top of one with the word "Lavender" in purple script on the front. She sniffed it and the power of the scent knocked her back so hard she nearly dropped the bottle. She caught it, just barely, but managed to get oil all over her fingertips in the process. Unwilling to soil her new dress, she wiped it on her hair.

She closed the cabinet before she could get into any more trouble. A knock came at the door as she played with the two strings hanging from her dress just above her hips, flapping them in great circles before letting them hang slack.

"Ma'am, are you ready to go?" Prady asked from the hallway.

She grabbed the cloak and scarf and then yanked the door open. "I saw my teeth!"

He raised his salt and pepper eyebrows. "Well, isn't that nice."

She started down the hall, but he gently stopped her.

"Hold on." He tucked his staff, a thick, carved piece of

yellow wood that was taller than him, under his arm and took hold of the strings at her hips; she felt the dress tighten slightly at her waist as he pulled. "There. All done." He started to smile but then stopped, falling into step next to her, shortening his stride to match hers and leaning on his staff.

"You look happy, but sad at the same time," said Wren. "Like you remembered something."

He glanced sidelong at her. "I do?"

"What are you thinking about?"

He didn't hold the smile back this time. "You remind me of my daughter."

"You have a daughter?"

"Had. She died."

"I'm sorry."

He shook his head as if that could clear his thoughts. "Never mind it, miss."

"People die a lot who shouldn't, don't you think?"

He laughed, a dry sound of surprise more than joy. "Yes, I do."

They walked in silence for a while through corridors of the same white stone that comprised the floor in her bedroom, past other doors like hers. Slits were cut into the walls at regular intervals, letting sunlight in. Glass oil lamps, currently unlit, alternated with the slits.

"We'll be taking the stairs all the way down, miss. Mind your step," said Prady.

They descended a winding stairway behind a door at the end of the hall. The stairs made her slow down. She watched Prady walk just a couple of steps in front of her, putting a foot on one stair, and then the other foot on the stair below it. These weren't like the crags where you had to find your own way up and down with caution, but they weren't natural, either. They made her change her step to fit them exactly.

She held onto the railing on the left and tried to find a rhythm.

She'd only just gotten the hang of it when they reached level ground again. Prady held the door at the bottom of the stairs open for her. She walked into the same cavernous entryway she'd come through earlier. Thallium's collection of relics sat off to her left, across from an open area of floor leading to the front door on her right. There stood three Keepers all dressed in gray and white striped robes. One on either side of the heavy, metal front door, and one pacing along the floor nearby.

Prady lead her over to the pacing man. "Miss Wren, this is Dal."

Dal stopped and faced them. He was massive, towering above even Prady, and his big shoulders were bunched up like he was angry. He looked Wren up and down and muttered something under his breath.

"What was that, Dal? Speak so that your mistress can hear you," commanded Prady.

Dal snapped to attention and struck the end of the long spear he held on the ground. "Hello, mistress."

"Dal and I are normally the Principal's personal Keepers—guards, you could say—but he wants the very best protection for you. Shall we head out?" He reached for her cloak, and she relinquished it to him. "Carry the mistress' cloak until she has need of it."

Dal hesitated, but then raised his free arm for Prady to drape the cloak over. The man looked as if he were carrying a bloody animal pelt, holding it awkwardly in the air instead of tight to his body.

"Off we go," said Prady.

As he spoke, the two men at the door banged their spears on the ground, and the door slid open. A whoosh of hot air came in, carrying the hum of the security net with it. The net opened up long enough for them to pass, and Wren was proud of herself for not hesitating to walk through it this time. She fell in step with Prady, while Dal walked on her other side a little farther behind, still holding tension all over his body that made Wren wonder if she was somehow causing it.

Into the brilliant sunlight they walked. Dirt swirled in the air, though not nearly as thick as it was outside the walls, and the rays of the sun soaked into everything like water into cloth. She could probably press the ground hard enough with her feet to make it seep out onto her new shoes and color them gold. As distinctly uncomfortable as it was outside compared to inside the Main House, Wren's muscles relaxed into the familiarity of the oppressive heat, the crunch of dirt, and the buzz of cicadas. They zigzagged through the path that stretched downward from the house, back onto the same level as the city.

"Remember not to look back, mistress. The glare off the Main House is intense at this time in the afternoon," said Prady.

Wren obeyed, remembering the pain the glare had sent through her eyes that morning. They finally reached the archway that marked the beginning of the path. Wren reached out and touched the metal side as they passed it, but yanked her hand back just before it could burn her, so intense was the heat it had absorbed throughout the day. A handful of people milled around this far end of the city, hoods and scarves pulled up to guard against the brightest time of the day. Wren couldn't see much of the wearers, but their shadowy faces seemed to pause when they turned toward her.

She stepped closer to Prady and spoke softly. "You said you're the best protection. It's dangerous for me here, then."

Dal snorted behind them.

Prady silenced him with a stern glare before speaking.

"Nothing to worry about. You may find the people of The Disc to be a bit distrustful of anyone who's lived outside. Happens to any refugee we take in, at least for a time. But as outsiders settle into lives here, they show the residents that they don't have fangs nor intend to kill them in their sleep. People warm up to them; they'll warm up to you. But as a precaution, you'll never leave the Main House by yourself. Just for now."

She hadn't planned to.

They entered the part of town that held the courthouse— she recognized some of the buildings in shades of silver with wide white stone steps leading to their dramatic doors that stood twice the height of a man. Some people moved between the buildings, wearing the same shining robes they'd been wearing when Wren left the courthouse earlier that day. This time, those who looked at her didn't seem to recognize her from earlier, at least not at first; the brow of nearly every person who took notice of her knit together until a flash of recognition sparked, and the curiosity in their expressions turned to either surprise or outright disgust.

She wrapped the new white scarf around her face and mouth, trying to tuck her hair within it as well. The Disc seemed to rise above her and tuck in tight. She felt it like a great, clawed paw curling up around her, nestling her in the soft part between the pads. The Main House had been so smooth and strong, confident against the earth on which it sat. But here, buildings were tall and slightly jagged, and she wondered how they were standing upright.

"What's in those?" Wren asked Prady, hand to her brow to shade her eyes from the sun as she gazed upward at the tops of the buildings.

"Housing, primarily. For government workers, Keepers and their families, some influential figures."

"Rich people, then?"

"Perhaps compared to some."

It was strangely quiet, not at all what Wren pictured when she thought of a mass of people living close together. Did they keep their noise inside their buildings? Or did they simply not care to make any?

They turned a corner, making a hard left away from the towering buildings, which put the curved city wall on their right. This close, Wren saw it was not metal all the way through, but its interior was primarily mortared stone, several feet thick. She wondered how long it had taken to stack all of those. A lifetime, maybe.

The new street they'd turned down was striking for its lack of luxuries. It seemed a wasteland compared to the housing she'd just come through, with only wide, one-story buildings that didn't seem to hold any people at all. She caught glimpses of ginormous pieces of metal through a couple of windows, pieces as big around as old trees, and sheets of glass.

Prady stretched his arm forward. "Not far now, miss."

She followed his gesture to a building in the distance. Gray and smooth with sharp corners and no visible windows. White, square lettering above a metal-barred doorway read, "Detention Facility."

"Is that..." she trailed off.

"The prison, miss. Yes," said Prady.

She felt sick.

Rock or spit? Survivor had been debating for the last ten minutes which would be more fun to launch at her guard the next time it passed her cell. The little mechanical person, even shorter than her, walked by every so often. It would pause and stare at her with empty light-socket eyes, its creepy lipless mouth set in a hard line, before moving on down the hall. It was impressive as an invention, she supposed, but decided its main purpose was showcasing mankind's ego and lack of creativity.

They'd put her in a room, no more than ten feet square, with only a cot. There were other cells in the same holding area, and though she'd yet to see her prison mates, she'd already heard their complaints and the even less pleasant noises of defecating and self-satisfying.

After standing for the last half hour in front of the criss-crossed bars that buzzed with the threat of a nasty shock, making every face and vulgar gesture she could think of and receiving no reaction from the guard as it passed, it was time to try something new.

She pulled up a mouthful of snot and spit and waited to hock it through the bars when a door at the top of a flight of stairs across from her opened. From her current angle, she couldn't see who it was. She moved the loogie into place toward the front of her mouth, ready to launch it at whoever was coming.

Down into the dark holding area came a woman in a ridiculous blue dress, her shoulders draped in red, a still-white scarf around her mouth and nose. It was difficult to see details through the bright bars, and the dim space beyond them made it impossible to see the woman's face until she had removed her scarf and was just inches from the cell. Survivor spat her ammo on the dirt near the cot.

"What the fuck happened?" she asked.

Wren shrugged and looked at the ground. Her hair was pulled back from her face. The dark brown leather slippers on her feet were new.

Survivor sniffed the air and rubbed at her nose. "You stink. Is that lavender?"

The familiar flush started on Wren's cheeks. "I made us a deal," she muttered.

"You did what? What kind of deal?"

"I met with their ruler. He wanted to talk to me." She sat down on the dirt and crossed her legs. "He said I'm special, like Alma used to say, and asked me to help them. I said I would, and he promised us freedom."

"There are so many things wrong with what you just said I don't know where to start." She crouched down so she could catch her sister's eyes. "The ruler of this hostile community calls you, a filthy outlier, over and says you're *special*. Let me guess, he didn't tell you how you're special?"

Wren swallowed hard. "Not exactly. He said I could help with technology. He mentioned energy. Seemed to know more than Alma, or at least, he told me more than Alma ever did."

"This man claims to know more about you than your mother. Tells you you're special, motherfucking magic. Then he tells you he'd love to let you go, but oh wait, the legal system says he can't. But if you scratch his balls, he'll scratch yours. You say yes, he makes you his doll and dresses you up, and now here you are to tell me how generous he is." She hopped around in her crouch, waving her arms around in mock excitement.

"He said he'd let you go."

"Did he now? Then why am I still in here?"

"He said that you can stay in The Disc and get a job to pay them instead of staying in here."

Rage boiled up inside Survivor. "I won't be a slave. Never again." She stood and crossed her arms.

Wren looked up at her. "You'd rather stay in here than be free?"

Survivor stabbed her hand upward as if it were a sword to gut the world above her. "*That* isn't free. This whole place is a prison. How can't you see it? You get some perfume and a new outfit and you forget everything Alma taught you?"

Wren looked away again. "I didn't forget. But we don't have many options."

"You want options? Tell him to lick dick, say no, bitch slap him! There are some options."

"Not if I want you to live. If I don't do this, Thallium will kill you."

"Let him try."

"No. I won't."

Survivor fell quiet for a moment, caught off guard by her sister's disobedience. She tried to keep some of the outrage from her tone as she continued to argue. "We don't know anything about these people or their all-powerful ruler. If you really are *special*, do you really want them to know more about it than you?"

"What I want doesn't matter right now." Wren stood and turned to leave.

Survivor went to the bars and shouted at her. "We can't stay here. *He* knows I'm here. That *we're* here. He's coming."

Wren stopped. She turned and stared at her sister. "The Gentleman."

Survivor nodded.

Wren fell silent and rubbed at her arms.

God, she was oblivious. But Survivor had to admit that was largely her own damn fault—she'd never told Wren the danger she was in just by being with Survivor, by considering her family. Somehow, it had felt like doing so would give credence to the threat. She didn't want to empower it. Which was bullshit, because it was real regardless. It was that reality that kept rage in Survivor's every muscle, in her every breath—she'd escaped him, but she'd never be free. And now, neither would Wren.

"There's a wall, a locked gate," Wren said softly. "He can't get in. Aren't we safer in here than we would be if we left?"

Survivor got as close to the buzzing bars as she dared. "Listen to my words—he *will* get in. He *will* kill me. After he makes me watch him kill *you*."

Wren turned pale and dropped her hands to hang defeated by her sides.

"Unless we get out of here now before he shows up," continued Survivor.

"I don't...I can't...We..." Wren stuttered. She put her face in her hands.

"The Gentleman and the Open? I know those enemies," said Survivor. "How they work, how to fight them. In here? The rules are different. And different is dangerous."

Wren finally met Survivor's gaze, and in her eyes was pure exhaustion. Survivor realized that Wren couldn't leave this place now, not even if she had the guts to try. She'd die out there before The Gentleman could get a hold of her.

They couldn't leave now. Survivor would have to be patient—a skill she'd long loathed but resorted to in times of desperation. "Be careful, sister," she said quietly. "Don't jump into the devil's bed because it's warmer than the ground, or you'll find you're just another stupid whore."

Wren stood there, not responding, and past the brightness of the bars, Survivor was fairly certain her eyes were shimmering with tears. Good. Maybe she was beginning to understand their situation. She spun around, marched up the stairs, and was gone with the slam of a door.

The guard came back into view and stared at Survivor, unflinching, lifeless. She picked up the biggest pebble she could find and chucked it toward one of the openings in the bars. It hovered in the opening for a second and then flew back, hitting her in the shoulder. The guard moved on.

She laid down on the cot. "Should've tried the spit."

It was far from elegant, this heron. The inside reverse fold that was meant to form pointed feet on which the little paper bird could stand upright had instead ended up as one chunky clubbed foot. The bird fell over straight away. It was this garbage pulp paper from Mantir—perfectly fine for notes, lists, and letters, but for folding? Completely useless. But it was all The Gentleman had to work with currently. They'd need to restock on the finer stuff when they headed further south next month for the cold season.

"Dagnammit!" The Gentleman crumpled the bloated, half-finished crane and threw it over the far edge of his desk. As it arced, it grazed the belly of one of the birds in the flock that hung above his head, sending it flying in itty bitty circles. There were twenty-two of them up there, all different sorts, hung with fishing line and hooks in the canvas top of his tent. He'd only made twenty-two perfect ones in his lifetime, or at least perfect to his reckoning. He held himself to a high standard. Cranes, ducks, owls, and all manner of fowl that he believed were legitimately reminiscent of the faded color photos in the origami instruction book he'd learned from. He closed the book gently, and the pages came together at the bottom of the book to reveal clunky, oversized initials in fluorescent pink—FMH. He stroked them with his thumb and realized how his hands were aching, each knuckle like a rotten tooth. Daggum old age trying to ravage him.

"You there, Amelie?"

The orange sheet separating his office from the great room of the tent parted with the delicate pull of a dark hand.

Sweet Amelie came in and stood just inside the office, eyes intent on the ground a few feet in front of her. "Yes, Father?"

He wrung his hands over the desk, their cracking white skin thinner than the paper he'd just been folding. "Rub these a minute, would you?"

She crossed the dirt floor and knelt by his chair. He gave her his right hand, and she set to work on it, pushing her thumbs in between each joint and making small circles.

He groaned. "My gracious, you do have the magic touch."

She didn't respond, but she rarely did. Little dear. She'd always been shy, ever since she'd joined his family. Now she was all grown up, a beautiful young woman with big round eyes. Demure, quiet as a church mouse.

The canvas of his front door rustled, and arguing voices reached him—Genevieve, of course, and a male. Fen? Quieter than his usual bold self and back two days early from his scheduled post.

"Hush, you two! Get in here already!" he shouted.

Amelie cringed beside him.

Genevieve burst in. She was the spitting image of Amelie but with no hair and a dainty ring of scars just starting to take shape around her left temple.

"Fen's back, Father. I reminded him his punishment hasn't been paid in full yet, but he—"

"—found something." Fen shouldered through the sheet and pushed Genevieve firmly in the small of her back, forcing her to catch herself. She stomped hard on his instep, and he bared his teeth at her.

"Good Lord, you two. Buncha animals." He gave Amelie his other hand, and she started rubbing along his left thumb. "What did you find that justified abandoning your post and starting your ten-day banishment all over again?"

Fen stood a little taller and smiled broad enough to show

the gaps where his upper molars used to be. "It's not what I found, sir. It's who. I found *her*."

The Gentleman forgot his frustration with the garbage paper, the pain in his hands, the juvenile behavior of his second- and third-in-command. A face came back to him from twenty years past, the sunny expression of a child with the eyes of a hunter—her face before she grew up and betrayed him.

Amelie had stopped rubbing his fingers and addressed Fen. "She's alive?" Those round eyes grew even bigger, sparkling with hope.

"Shut up, Mel," said Genevieve.

Amelie quickly quieted and rubbed his hand again.

"Now? She shows herself a decade after leaving? No way. You saw some slave with dark hair." Genevieve rolled her eyes.

Fen turned his jaundiced eyes toward her. They'd gotten worse over the past couple of months. Probably didn't have long now, not that The Gentleman would tell him that. "I've known her since we were kids," said Fen. "It's her."

"Well, good then," spat Genevieve. "Now we can kill her and be done with her memory." She scratched at the scars around her temple.

"I know you want to add to your collection there, Genny bear," The Gentleman said, "but you will not be adding my daughter to it. You hear me?"

Genevieve bit her lower lip hard enough to draw blood. "Yes, Father. But then what do you intend to do with her?"

He ignored her question and addressed Fen, whose head was slightly blistered at the top, his scant clothes stained with sweat. "You must have booked it here from King's Rock. You get any water yet?"

"No, sir. And I ran about a third of the way, to our outpost west of The Disc. Took a buggy for the other fifteen miles."

"Genny, go fill him a canteen," said The Gentleman.

She grudgingly turned and left, smacking into Fen again with her shoulder. He snickered this time.

"Where is she now?" The Gentleman asked.

"Spotted her inside the neutral zone on my way back to King's Rock after a short sleep. She was with a Body returning to The Disc. As a prisoner. And she wasn't alone—had a woman with her. They seemed close."

The Gentleman sucked on his teeth and released his tongue from them with a snap. "Well then, I have a letter to write." He took his hand from Amelie and patted her on the cheek. "Hand me a new sheet of white, sugar. The kind with the flowers."

Amelie stood and headed to a trunk on the right side of the desk. She retrieved a sheet of paper, thick like the pulp paper The Gentleman had been using just earlier, but with a softer surface and dried lavender embedded in it.

He pulled his antique fountain pen from its porcelain cup next to the tidy stack of opened letters from his fellow Clan leaders, in which they traded news and made veiled threats. In the middle of the lavender paper, he wrote his message and then began to fold it into a swan, a simple bird compared to the heron, better for this grade of paper. He finished by gently tugging the head of the swan away from the body and sliding the beak between his fingernails to sharpen it. He held the bird out on his palm to Fen.

"Send this to The Disc with a porter—JJ's young and likes to drive fast, looks nonthreatening. Tell him to take a buggy to the front gate. He'll need to say he has a letter from G for the Principal. They'll take it, and then he can come on home."

Fen stepped up to the desk and took the swan carefully, wiping his grimy hand on his pants before picking it up by its slender neck.

"Then tell Genevieve to pack my things. We'll take six of

our best fighters and leave them just outside the neutral zone. You, Beo, and I will meet with Thallium later this evening."

Fen shook his head as if to check his hearing. "Sir? Beo? Is that a good...Wouldn't you rather take Genevieve?"

"I meant what I said. I want Survivor to see him. Get him, hear me?"

Fen nodded, still holding the swan by its neck out in front of his chest.

"Good. Now get. Daylight's burning."

Fen dashed out.

Amelie watched him leave, still standing near the supply trunk like a bump on a toad. She closed the trunk and sat on it as if her legs wouldn't allow her to stand any longer. Her nose had started to run. The Gentleman took the handkerchief from the pocket of his slacks and handed it to her. She dabbed at her nose, embarrassed.

He reached over and pinched just above her knee. "Cheer up. We're gonna bring her home."

For some reason, his confidence didn't seem to cheer her up at all.

PART II

CIVILIZED

CHAPTER FIVE

"It doesn't make any fucking sense. The hell kind of poison..." Asha continued to talk to herself. She dashed between charts, the medical database at the back of the room, and the monitors still attached to Caster like she was looking for proof of the existence of God.

She threw herself into the desk chair and accessed the database at the back of the med ward. It was just a small desktop computer, rather plain looking with a rectangular, black-framed monitor. The database pooled the wisdom of doctors in The Disc, which had only been founded fifty years prior. During the 200 years between The Fall and the founding of The Disc, medical knowledge had been stored in people's brains, passed down to their children like stories to memorize, lest it be lost forever. This was how Asha had first learned from her parents, who saw healing not as a trade, but as a mission to live and die for.

The gate accident sent ripple effects through the two generations following it: cancers and lung diseases from radiation pouring in through the damaged atmosphere and the bombs that were dropped by desperate nations running out of resources; infections from open wounds with no antibiotics to treat them; mental illnesses and extreme depression for which "talking it out" and prayer were the only medicines available. The worst had been the viruses, at least that was what Asha's parents had told her. Ebola, SARS, even the common flu killed hundreds of thousands.

But now, things weren't quite so bleak. People had wizened up to preventive measures against viruses. Basic antibiotics had been discovered in city ruins and synthesized in The Disc. Today was a frightening time to be a doctor; back then, it was practically a death sentence.

Asha's parents had survived the sicknesses they treated and were so devoted to their mission of healing that they carted her around with them as they traveled from town to town, exposing themselves to all kinds of ailments—physical, emotional, and spiritual. Asha had traveled farther by the time she was sixteen than most people traveled in their lifetime. She'd seen Hallund and its nopales farmers, Ranlock with its mercenaries and its air that smelled of copper and salt. The little villages of Mantir and Non were pleasant in the spring, tucked out of the sun in gorges. She'd met people who lived in tiny houses entirely on their own apart from society, taking it upon themselves to defend their homes from Marauders and any other outliers rather than join a group for protection. She had no idea how big the world was, but it seemed incredibly large when she was limited to the stamina of her feet to see it.

Before The Disc, the last place she'd visited was Kino. She met Gavel there, and it was the last place her parents would ever see. There was one sickness they couldn't heal, and that was the dark heart of man. She wondered if it would ever get further from her, the pain of remembering. The impulse to run to her mother for wisdom and her father for comfort was as strong today as it had been the day she lost them.

At times like this, she would give her right foot to ask them just one question. She envied the doctors who'd lived before The Fall, men and women fed information from infinite sources. Now, there were no medical texts, no case studies, no internet. There was this little desktop, which she backed up daily with a paranoia bordering on obsessive.

Today's search history looked ridiculous: miraculous self-healing, spontaneous recovery, poison magically stops poisoning. They all came back "not found," and she was running out of things to search for. As she was typing in, mostly out of spite, "complete and total lucky fuck," Ark came up behind her.

"Hmm, don't think I've ever entered 'fuck' in there, but who knows, you might get a hit."

She hung her head over the back of the chair and rubbed at her eyes. When she opened them, she saw Ark's wrinkly face smiling down at her. His mustache looked like a giant, fuzzy half-moon from this angle.

"You're upside down, old man," she said.

"No, I think you're upside down, sweetheart. That's why you called me over." He tapped her on the nose gently.

She got up to yank a chair sitting next to the nearest bed over to them, and then sat back down by the computer. He sat in the chair she'd fetched.

"Thanks for coming. I need a sanity check. Bad," she said.

"Your boy seems to be doing better. Stopped by to see him on my way over to you. Begged me to order you to let him go."

She glared at Caster, who was standing next to his bed on the opposite side of the room, shirtless and restless, still tethered to machines all around. He pressed his palms together and lifted them up toward her.

"Sit down! You'll disconnect the heart monitor again!" she shouted.

He ran his hands down his face, smashing his features in frustration, before sitting on the edge of the bed.

"Impatient brat," she muttered.

"I'm glad you don't talk that way to all of your patients," Ark said. "Just the ones you love."

"Yeah, well, he's pushing it right now. The love part, I mean. He should be dead, but all he wants is to get out of here."

"You're disappointed he didn't die? Glad you don't love me."

"I do love you, old man. Disappointed isn't the word I'd use. I'm dumbfounded."

He ticked items off on his fingers as he spoke. "He came in poisoned, his body fought through it, now he's recovering. It's not impossible."

"He came in with a deadly fever, seizing, with a heart rate jumping around on the screen like a goddamn jack rabbit. Then it all stops instantly. He's not just recovered, he's perfect. *Perfect*, Ark. That's not possible."

"Whaddya mean, perfect?"

"I've been his doctor since he was born—I know his entire medical history. Not only that, but he practically grew up in my house. I know he gets hives on his legs when he's stressed and that he was seriously allergic to every kind of nut imaginable."

"He *was* allergic?"

"Yes. I've done a full workup on him since he woke up. He used to have an iron deficiency—that's gone. He used to be 18% body fat—now he's 8% body fat. His heart's stronger than it's ever been. When he was twelve, he broke his arm when he jumped off the roof of my house onto a pile of sand he'd raked together. It didn't heal exactly right and clicked when he rotated it. Now there's no click. I took an X-ray. There's no evidence it's ever been broken."

He pressed his lips together and made his mustache swing from side to side, finally speechless.

"After all this, I put a bowl of peanuts next to his bed."

"When you knew they could close his throat and kill him. Good healing, girl."

"I had a hunch. After he didn't feel his throat swelling, he ate them. All of them. Said he was hungry."

"He has been here since early this morning. You fed 'im yet?"

"Cabbage broth! It's good for you! Fucking impatient men." She stood up and pointed at Caster. "You get solid food when I say you do!"

Caster raised his hands in confusion. She abruptly sat back down and pinched the bridge of her nose. "I need to talk to the ones who did this. Get more information."

"I treated both of those young women a few hours ago."

She leaned in toward him. "What? You're only now telling me this?"

He shrugged. "Didn't seem necessary. What's done to Caster is done. From what I gathered from Six, it was just one of the women that did it. The other was a might bit upset about it, actually."

"What were they like?"

"The one who poisoned him wasn't exactly a peach. Tried to bite my nose when I went to look down her throat. The red head was, well, different. Fidgety, like a baby bird on the ground. Felt sorry for her."

She blew a raspberry. "Sorry my ass. She shouldn't have been with someone like that. It's her fault."

"Sweetheart," he lowered his voice and put his hand on hers, "maybe you ought to be quiet and consider that it's been a while since you were out in the wild. You have no idea what you'd do out there, who you'd stick with if you were desperate enough. Think about it for me?"

"I remember now why I don't have you over here more often. You make me feel like crap." She pretended to glare at him.

"Just some old timey wisdom for you." He winked at her. "Speaking of wisdom, you aren't going to solve this medical mystery today. Send the boy home."

She tapped the mouse button multiple times. "Fine." She stood and pushed her chair under the computer desk. "I hate not knowing what I'm dealing with. Makes me pissy."

"Oh? Hadn't noticed," he said as he pushed his chair back to the nearest bedside.

"Watch it."

Caster spoke as they headed down the main aisle between the beds toward him. "Still keeping me prisoner?"

She hesitated to answer. Ark nudged her in the ribs.

"No. You can leave," she said.

Caster started to stand.

"Wait a second." She took out her pen light and shoved it toward Caster's face as she spread his eye open wide. "Look at this, Ark. Explain this to me!"

Caster froze in an awkward half-stand. "Damn it, Ash!"

Ark leaned in and looked. "Yeah, he's got real pretty eyes."

"Gah, no! Look at his iris, at the change in coloration. Those flecks weren't there before he got sick."

Ark looked closer, almost making a show of it to appease her. "Can you still see, sonny?"

"Of course he can see!" she yelled. "That's not the point. What would cause discoloration like that?"

Ark shrugged. "The poison, maybe. Could explain some of the physical changes."

Asha sighed and released her hold on Caster.

He rubbed at his eye. "Now can I leave?"

"Fine!" She crossed her arms. "There's a fucking mob of mourners on the other side of that door anyway. A fitting punishment for leaving against your doctor's wishes."

Caster lazily wrapped her shoulders in a hug, tugging at the lines leading to the machines. "Thanks, Ash."

"Stop screwing up my equipment. Hold still." She removed the IV from his left arm, the heart monitor from his chest, and the pulse ox from his finger. His hand was still bandaged, and she unwrapped it. The skin underneath was pink and slightly scarred, but the wound was closed, all swelling gone.

"Wouldya look at that," Ark said.

She flapped Caster's hand at the old doctor. "This is not normal. Not normal!" She shook his wrist harder.

"I'll need to take that with me," Caster said.

She dropped his arm and wrangled her frustration back into its shoddy pen.

Caster stretched, putting his hands together behind his back and rolling them up toward his head as he bent over. She saw her best friend's son for an instant, a little tow-headed four-year-old with big gaps in his teeth and a taste for spicy things. Then the flash was gone, and before her stood a grown man with sinewy arms and terrible morning breath.

"If you start feeling weird at all, come find me. Day or night, whatever. Doctor's orders," she said.

He finished stretching and grabbed his white linen shirt from the foot of the bed. "Uh-huh."

As he started to pull it on, she stretched onto her toes, grabbed the neck of the shirt on both sides, and spoke into it. "I'm not kidding. You hear me?"

"Yeah, I hear you," he said from the depths of the fabric.

She released his collar, and he pulled the shirt the rest of the way down. She fetched his belt and knife from the drawer of his bedside table and held them out to him. He took the belt and fastened it to his waist as he kissed her on the cheek, sliding the knife home in its sheath at his hip.

"I'm fine. I just want to eat and get some sleep." He grabbed his coat from a wall hook next to the bed and threw it on as he started for the door.

Something in Asha gnawed at her like mice on wires, and it was going to shock her if she didn't figure out what was going on with this blond brat about to leave her care.

"Come by the house later tonight," she blurted out. "Let me check up on you, and I'll make apple cobbler."

He stopped and nodded, giving her a half-smile as the door of the med ward slid open. A whoosh of air and the pleas from the constant crowd outside blew in. Asha grumbled inwardly about how she'd have to clean up all of the candles, prayer beads, and various trinkets they'd leave behind, only to have her train of thought derailed by a stranger entering the ward.

The door closed behind a woman dressed in finery, with the Principal's two personal Keepers by her sides. Her brilliant red hair shone stark against her pale blue dress. She had high cheekbones and blue eyes that nearly glowed.

Ark jabbed Asha gently in the back with his fist and cleared his throat. She turned to scowl at him, and he nodded between the girl and Caster.

"You must be..." Asha trailed off, closing the distance between her and the girl.

"Wren," the girl squeaked out. She cleared her throat and fiddled with her hands nervously.

"Hiya, red," said Ark.

Wren gave a little wave.

Asha crossed her arms. "I didn't know they dressed outliers

up now after arresting them for attempted murder. Must be a new policy."

Wren shuffled from one foot to the other and opened and closed her mouth like a fish struggling for air.

Caster side-stepped in front of Asha. "Be nice," he mouthed. He turned, forming a wall between her and Wren. "Glad you're okay," he said to the outlier.

"I just wanted to...see you. They said you were getting better," she said.

Asha, tired of having her nose in Caster's back, uncrossed her arms and went to strip the sheets off his bed. Ark walked around to the other side of the bed to help her.

"I'm better," said Caster. "Fine, actually. Looks like your trial went well. I'm glad."

Asha's eyes went wide.

Wren stared up at Caster as if the cogs in her mind had jammed.

"I'm on my way out," said Caster. "After you?"

The girl hesitated. "There are a lot of people out there."

"Then I'd better go say hello, huh?"

She gave a wan smile, then started to turn toward the door.

"See you tonight, Ash. Thanks again!" Caster called, not looking back.

Caster walked out first, then Wren and her Keepers after him, and the sliding door shut. After a few seconds, Ark spoke up.

"That was interesting. Never seen the Principal treat a prisoner that way, giving up two of his own men and everything to show her around."

"Those men aren't showing her around, they're keeping her alive. And she's too stupid to see that she's a prisoner—only reason Thallium would treat an outlier like that is if he wanted something from them. Easier to get it if the person feels like royalty."

Ark wrapped his arms around the pile of sheets and hoisted them up. "Think so?"

She pressed down the foot pedal on the laundry bin in front of the bed, and he dropped the sheets inside. "Thallium needs her, but for what, I can't imagine."

"Hmm," said Ark. "She seems nice enough, though. Odd, but sweet."

"For her sake, I hope there's more to her than 'sweet.' A sweet outlier is still an outlier to these people. When they realize the treatment she's getting, they'll peck at her until there's no meat left on her bones."

She let the lid of the laundry bin slam shut.

Mourners descended upon Caster like locusts even before the door of the med ward had completely closed. Men and women, toddlers and grandparents, all shaking his hand and giving unsolicited embraces. Rich and poor had left gifts in a heap near the doorway, along with lighted soy candles, which were in and of themselves valuable. Caster tiptoed his way through the offerings—beaded clay necklaces, thickly-sweet smelling honeysuckle in great bunches, even sacks of oats and other rations—left as a symbol of hope and prayer for his recovery.

He gently shouldered through the anonymous touches and tear-stained faces to reach the less crowded center of the street. Then he turned and addressed them.

"Thank you for your kind gestures! I beg you, please take up your gifts and return home. They're far too valuable to leave here, and as you can see, with my departure, they've no reason to stay here anymore."

"We thought you were dead, Bastard!" a boy in overalls just a few years younger than Adonis blurted out from the front of the crowd. A man standing behind him squeezed his shoulders. "Ouch, Dad!" the boy said, swiping at his father's hands.

"We're so glad you're well, sir," said an older woman, hunched over from the waist and shaking slightly. Caster wondered how long she'd been standing out in the sun to show support for his recovery.

He stepped up to her and kissed the back of her hand. "Thank you. Please, go home and rest."

She grinned, showing several gaps in her teeth, and started to move away. The crowd began to follow her lead until the kid spoke up again.

"Is it true that an outlier almost killed you?" the boy shouted. His father outright smacked him on the back of the head this time.

The rest of the crowd, at least forty strong, all waited for his answer.

"Outliers fight for every breath in the Open," Caster said finally. "If they feel threatened, they act. I can't blame them for that, and I hope you don't, either."

Their angry grumbling as they finally departed hinted that they did in fact blame outliers for that, particularly the one that had nearly killed Caster.

Once the crowd had finally thinned, Wren and her Keepers emerged from behind them, still tucked back by the door of the med ward.

From a distance, Wren looked entirely different from the woman he'd met in the freezing cold of the desert the night before. Thallium had given her the best of everything, even new shoes, which were a luxury many people in the city could only afford once every few years.

But past the bright colors and clean material, she was still the same unsure person he remembered. She stood at the doorway, shrunken into her shoulders, eyes wide as they passed over the valuables at her feet. Pale blue eyes, he remembered. And coppery hair that now hung gloriously uncovered in the slowly setting sun, drawing him in to study it like flames. He noticed she had freckles all over her chest, across her nose, and under her eyes. And a mole on her neck.

God, she really was beautiful.

He cleared his throat and waved her over. She stepped through the offerings with great care and stopped a couple feet from him.

"There were so many of them. I've never seen so many people in one place." She spoke as if she were talking of ghosts rather than people. "Why didn't they take their things like you asked them to?"

He shrugged. "I suspect some will, before the night's over. Hope so, anyway."

Prady stood on Wren's right, and he removed his mask, although it was unnecessary. Caster knew those piercing eyes. They had watched him his whole childhood. "Sir, I'm so thankful you're well. We were all prepared for the worst." He fell silent, and Caster politely ignored the break in his voice.

Caster shook his hand. "Good to see you, Prady." He turned to Dal, the hulk on Wren's left. "You, not so much."

Dal grunted.

Caster turned back to Prady. "Why are you both with this girl? Don't you have other things to do? Such as protect my father or decorate his doorways by standing in them?"

Dal spoke, struggling to keep his dark, bushy eyebrows from coming together. Though his mouth was hidden behind his mask, Caster knew his lips were curled into a sneer. "She has a room in the Main House, and we're here for her protection."

"Has she? My old room?"

"No, sir." The way he said "sir" negated its use as a term of respect.

"How are things at the old place? Still shiny? I'm assuming you continue to help with the exterior wash every week?"

The bush-brows went together. "I do whatever my Principal says."

"Glad to see you haven't given up your dream of someday wiping his ass. It's a rare privilege. Hold on, you'll get there."

Caster snapped and pointed a finger at Dal, whose grip tightened around his spear. Prady shook his head, and Caster turned his attention back to Wren.

"You look nice," he said quietly.

She turned to look at him then, and those blue eyes cut straight to his core, her look was so focused and intense. Her silence made him wonder if she'd heard him.

"Wren?" he said.

She jumped. "Huh? Oh, yes, I do look nice." She smoothed out the front of her dress, tracing the wandering embroidery. "And I have new shoes!" She paused to waggle a foot at him.

He chuckled. "It's about to get cold, though. You need," he said as he stopped and turned toward Dal, "this." He plucked the cloak from his grip. "Goes with your outfit far better than his." He winked at her and held the cloak open.

She took it over her shoulders and fumbled with the clasp near her neck. Caster came around and reached for it. "May I?" he asked.

She nodded, and he nimbly closed the clasp, revealing the Valcin family crest—a slashed-through V—when the two parts came together. He released it as if it had burned him.

"Sir," said Prady, "I'm sorry to interrupt, but your father is requesting that we return to the Main House."

"Not a problem. It's a good idea for you to head back before dark. Wren and I will be on our way, then." Caster held out his hand to her, unsure if she would take it. But he needed to get some time with her alone, both to learn what had happened while he was unconscious and to show her that the fear etched in her every tentative motion and eye shift wasn't entirely necessary in his hometown. There was goodness here, and given her caustic sister and her life spent starving in a cave, she needed to see some goodness.

She looked at his hand hanging there, considering, and then her hand shot out in a rush to grab it. Hers felt so small in his, slightly cold, and stiff as a board.

"Sir," said Prady, eyeing the hand-holding with polite curiosity, "you misunderstood. The Principal wants all four of us to return to the Main House."

"Hmm," said Caster, buying time to think. He looked up, shielding his eyes from the last few rays of harsh sun before it sank behind the city walls. There it was, a drone, high up as if his father thought he wouldn't be able to spot it.

"Tell me, Prady," he said, eyes tracking the drone's circular holding pattern. "Is your knee still bothering you?"

"I have good days and bad days, sir."

"Can you run?"

Prady sighed. "Not well."

"Good."

Caster spun around, throwing his weight into the motion, and his fist met Dal's nose with enough force to knock him on his ass. He took off down a side street with Wren, her hair flying out of the ribbon holding it as they ran.

Wren was no stranger to running. As she ran with Caster, her muscles stretched and flexed as they settled into the familiar tempo. Yet, she struggled a bit to keep up with him. His legs were much longer than hers, and she pushed her own to match his stride. He'd been bedridden only hours ago, yet now he was flying through town, his hand around hers. That kind of strength fascinated and confounded her.

They wound through tight alleyways, through shadows and occasional patches of sunlight, in between buildings letting off the heat they'd absorbed from the sun. She thought of the cave, of times before the cave where running like this after Survivor had been a regular occurrence. But Survivor wasn't here, and the reason for fleeing wasn't for safety. It was, more or less, for fun.

Fun.

They ran a little while longer before Caster stopped behind a wire fence lined with sheets of black plastic to obscure whatever was behind it. Empty metal bins and packing materials sat in neat piles near the fence. He craned his neck upward like he was watching for something.

For a moment, they both caught their breath and simply stood there, hand in hand. She'd noticed the ring on his little finger when he held his hand out to her before they took off, and she caught another glimpse of it now—silver and delicate, with a small, darker silver stone.

Then it was over, and he dropped her hand and gave her a sheepish smile. "Sorry if I pushed it too far. Just wanted to make sure we lost them and the drone."

She nodded as if she understood.

He started to move along the fence, glancing at the small rectangular signs posted halfway up the fence every so often. Each had a two-digit number on it, and Caster seemed to be searching for one in particular.

She followed close behind. "Where are we?"

"Behind the Trading Center. If you listen carefully," he cupped a hand around his ear as he continued in his search, "you can hear the sound of bargains being shouted and little kids begging for honey sticks."

She stopped and listened. Voices reached her ears, though nothing so detailed as what Caster had said. It was a dull hum, a little like a hive, with an occasional laugh or shout that broke out above the rest.

He stopped at number twenty-one. "Finally!"

"That sounds like a lot of people." She shrank into her scarf.

"That's the idea. We need the cover." He turned to look at her, and he must have seen her reluctance. "I'd like to show you my people, or some of them, anyway. If that's all right?"

She rubbed at her sleeves underneath the cloak and shuffled on her feet.

He backtracked to her. "We're not *all* monsters." He grinned. She noticed for the first time the scars on his face—three short scars, one by his left eye, the other two along his right cheek and jaw, their ridges cutting into the dark blond scruff growing there.

"No, not all of you," she said, her voice sounding weak and breathy and not at all how she wanted it to.

He walked back to the lock on the fence and dropped to a crouch, listening. "Vee," he said softly. "Vee, you there?"

As he continued to listen and whisper, she kicked off her shoes and climbed a stack of faded blue plastic bins a little distance away from him. She perched on the top and tried to see where the voices were coming from over the fence. But all she could see were the tops of colorful tents. She sighed and looked below at the back of Caster's head. She curled her toes around the edge of the bin and tucked her elbows into her lap.

"Don't you think your people will hate me?"

He started at her voice coming from a different place than

he expected it to. He turned and took in the sight of her high up. "Holy hell, you're quiet. I thought I was nimble."

"I've always been quiet. Had to be."

"I guess that would be true in the Open," he said. "And no, I don't think my people will hate you. Not if you're with me. They might be fearful, but not hateful. Those can come off the same at first, unfortunately. Once they see your innocence and how kind you are, how strong, their fear will fade."

Her stomach turned. "I'm not any of those things," she mumbled, shrinking into a ball and wrapping her arms around her knees.

"Hey," he stood and reached up to touch her knee, "are you okay?"

Something about that touch was more intimate than holding hands. It made her lose her balance and burst from her ball like a fledgling, feathers flying and wings flapping in panic. She fell off the bins and bombed headfirst for the hard dirt as the bulky containers tumbled and thudded all around them. He threw himself beneath her, softening her impact.

She scrambled off him and stood, her hands to her mouth, hair tossed around her face.

He stayed down, closed his eyes, and tucked his knees to his abdomen.

"What's going on back there?" grumbled a woman's voice on the other side of the fence. Keys jangled and chains slid over metal as the fence next to them opened. Someone on the other side slid it outward toward them, stopping when it hit Caster's foot.

It was a tiny lady dressed in flowing, pink robes made out of many layers of thin cotton that the breeze tossed around like petals.

Caster tried to smile, but grimaced instead and closed his eyes again.

The lady dropped her keys and doubled over, giggling like water rushing over pebbles.

"I go to the bathroom and nearly miss this," she said. "You tried to kiss her, so she kicked you in your marbles? Sucks for you, prince boy."

"Nice to see you too, Vee." He rolled onto his side and worked his way to a standing position, keeping his legs apart and moving carefully.

"You kick his butt, huh baby doll?" she said to Wren.

Wren shoved her hair out of her face and shook her head fiercely.

"Would you mind if we went through your booth?" he said. "I want to show my friend the market."

"So you take a shortcut and make a move? Your girlfriend's smarter than you. But what else is new. Women outsmart men every day." She stooped down and picked up her keys. "Come on, before it gets busy. Don't want you interrupting my customers." She waved them over and disappeared behind the fence, leaving it cracked open.

Caster swiped Wren's shoes from the ground as he dramatically hobbled over to her. "You ready, *baby doll*?" He held the shoes out to her.

She slipped the shoes back on. "Ready for what?"

"A night on the town."

She thought about Thallium and Eydis, how they might do something to Survivor if they thought Wren had tried to leave. Panic flooded her, and she started to back away from him.

"I can't. I have to get back. I promised," she said. More panic struck when she realized she had no idea which way the Main House was. "Take me to the Main House, please. Before they hurt my sister."

He put his hands up. "Nobody will hurt your sister. Your Keepers know you're with me. Trust me, I'll get the blame for that. So you're stuck with me for now. That is, if you want to be."

Something about the way he declared Survivor safe made her believe it and release some of the tension she realized she'd been carrying in her shoulders. Caster had fought for mercy for her and Survivor. He'd nearly died trying to get it for them. She had to believe his truthfulness now—he'd given her no reason to doubt it.

As for being stuck with Caster? Yes, she wanted that. Very much.

She nodded.

He held the fence open for her. They slipped through and entered the back of Vee's booth, a small space within a closed tent made of thin, gray fabric that was decorated with red lines in dramatic strokes all lined up in an organized fashion—letters or words of another language, perhaps. Wren knew English and a little Spanish from Alma. But this was different. More art than alphabet.

Something sweet with a hint of musk burned from a metal basket hanging in the center of the tent. There were six tables laid out in a three-sided square, covered in soft cloths on which were laid brilliantly colored baubles. They made the trinkets Wren had collected in her basket over the years look like junk.

Vee stood behind one of the back tables, pulling even more shiny things from a box and setting them out. Some of the pieces were small, no larger than a button, while others were the size of a man's head.

"Lock up," she said without moving her eyes from the task at hand.

Caster grabbed the lock and chain from the ground and worked on securing the fence as Wren wandered over to the tables. She'd never seen this many colors in one place and didn't recognize several of them at all. One color stood out among the rest like an old friend in a crowd. She'd never seen this shade of purple in person before, only in her dreams, or sometimes just before she fell asleep when it would creep in around the edges of her vision. She hunkered down in front of the piece at the end of one of the tables, inches from its smooth surface.

Vee stopped laying out more pieces and leaned toward her. "What are you doing?"

She let go of the table and stood slowly. "They're pretty," she whispered.

Vee's expression softened, and she stood a little taller. "Yes, they are."

"What are they?"

"Mostly glass from the outlands. I get some of the Scavengers going out to bring me glass they find. Then I make these."

Wren stared at the same crooked piece of thick glass attached to a leather cord, unable to step away from it. "What are they for?" she asked.

Vee swept her hand over the display slowly. "Jewelry. For wearing. You know, for boys to buy girls they want to impress or for mothers to spoil their daughters."

"Oh."

"I don't change the look of the shards, not like Candi over on the west side." She muttered something in another language —a rapid rhythmed tongue—before continuing. "They've been through a lot. They're fighters. Why reshape them into something else? They're unique." She gently stroked a bright green triangular piece nearby.

Wren reached for the purple stone and barely touched it before pulling her hand back.

Vee giggled at her, letting loose the water to cascade down the rocks again. "You're weird, girly. But you have good taste;

that necklace isn't glass. It's amethyst, and it is really *in* right now. Ready to buy? It'll be gone before the night's out, is my guess."

The murmur of voices outside Vee's tent started to grow, cutting through Wren's singular focus on the necklace.

"Found one you like?" Caster said from behind her.

She ignored him. "I don't know if I should go out there," she said with a tentative gesture toward the people she could sense passing on the other side of the gray fabric and elegant red markings.

He blew air through pursed lips. "Come on. Nothing to be afraid of." He turned to Vee, who stood near Wren watching their exchange with blatant curiosity. "Vee, a pleasure as always." As he leaned in to hug her, Wren thought she heard him say something near her ear. Vee just smiled, showing tiny square teeth, and then shooed them toward the door. "I'm ready to open. Tie back the flap on your way out. Go on."

"You heard the lady," said Caster, holding his hand out to Wren.

Wren stole one last glance at Vee's collection and then put her hand eagerly in his.

"Come back, girly! You're fun to watch, you know?" Vee giggled again before hoisting herself onto a wooden stool behind the tables and beginning to sing a lullaby.

The tent started billowing in the wind with more enthusiasm. Caster tugged a white scarf from his pocket and tied it around his nose and mouth. He made a covering motion to Wren, and she re-wrapped her own scarf, tucking in flyaway pieces of hair. Then he swept open the door flap and tied it back before leading her by the hand into a steadily growing stream of bodies. Their entry went unnoticed in the busyness.

People moved through the street like fallen leaves in a stream, sliding past one another and sometimes bumping together and changing direction. Booths like Vee's lined both sides of the road, some hidden within tents, others out in the elements with little more than a table or other eye-catching display of goods and an eager seller standing by, trying to lure people in.

Some customers hopped from booth to booth, taking pleasure in simply looking, while others moved in on their targeted merchant. The shoppers' clothes fascinated Wren. Not all wore the plain, functional clothes she'd grown up wearing in the outlands. Here there was color and shape, bright outfits that looked as if they'd been lovingly homemade.

Sounds and smells filled the crisp twilight air. Grease and smoke, sage and eucalyptus, friendly shouting, an infant crying, and gruff complaints all danced together around them. Caster and Wren reached a particularly congested area of the crowd and were pushed off to the side, right up against a booth with a sun-bleached sign hanging from a line stretched between two tall oil lamp poles. The sign said, "Toasted and Roasted."

A bearded man in a beanie and dark, round glasses turned the crank of a giant, metal cage over a fire in a raised brick pit. The locusts and other creepy crawling things inside crackled and popped, smelling of cooking oil and spices that made Wren's eyes water. A boy with dirt-smeared cheeks plopped a coin on the table. The man in the beanie took it and then scooped a cup of insects out of the roaster, poured them into a paper cone, and gave them to the boy, who happily crunched down on legs and the bits of sand that clung to them. The bearded man opened his mouth in a friendly smile and lifted his glasses off at seeing Caster. He reached a burly arm over. Caster took it, and they leaned over the table to smack each other on the back.

"Usual?" the bearded man asked.

"Heading to dinner, actually. Next time, man," said Caster.

The man gave him a thumbs-up and then turned to a young family approaching his table.

Caster tucked Wren's arm into his as he cut back into the stream. A shapely brunette woman on the far side of the street held out large metal trays, on top of which were shriveled strips and bunches of various dried fruits. She danced around, displaying the fruits like exotic treasures, while her twin shouted out prices and proclaimed what a deal, deal, deal they had going on prickly pear chips.

A beeping sounded behind them in the crowd, which parted lazily and pressed up against the booths to let a small vehicle pass—a little domed thing on four wheels with an open bed on the back. It held four large crates marked with "DB" on the side. Once it passed, the crowd reformed and picked up the pace right where it had left off.

It was bustling and stressful. And the most exciting place Wren had ever been. An urge to try everything gripped her, but she remembered she didn't have any money or anything to trade. That was what Survivor had said people in communities did—exchanged one thing for another. Even still, just being a part of it all, a part of the living world, was exciting. It was enough.

They neared the end of the booths where the traffic thinned a bit and were able to relax their pace. Up ahead, where the road widened and larger tents and buildings sat on either side, a small circle of people was gathered. A chorus of oohs and ahhs came from the group, which was standing so close together that Wren couldn't see between their shoulders. Caster tried to direct her around them, but she pulled away and leaned toward the crowd. He gave in and she led them now, pulling on his hand like an excited child. They joined the circle.

In the group's center was a man. He wore black sleeves

that ended just past his elbow, connecting to his black cotton vest with two thick cords on either arm. His pants were dyed bright yellow, with a unique pattern of white streaks where the dye had hit certain areas harder than others. He was barefoot, but the skin of his feet was so thick and callused that from a distance, one might think he wore leather shoes. He twirled and tossed around a trio of silver sticks which sent out bright, hot sparks from one end as the crowd watched—he was careful to touch only the unlit ends as he juggled them. The air smelled of sulfur and smoke. As he threw them up into the air one after the other, they went out an instant before they hit the ground in close succession. The crowd clapped.

"And now, resplendent ladies and gentlemen," the man announced with a trill of his R, "It's my pleasure to show you the latest addition to my collection. It's a special gadget I found off near the limestone crater. Please, I beg you, don't venture out there to find another, for it doesn't exist, and the danger posed to you by the vicious, snapping shelled creatures that pop out of hovels in the ground and bite off your big toes would be too great. But not too great for *me*, of course." He tipped his brimmed hat, revealing the dramatic cut of his dark hair, buzzed on both sides with a thick section of hair tousled back over the middle. He smirked at a petite woman in a black dress next to him, leaning slowly toward her before stealing a peck on her cheek.

She rolled her eyes as he continued.

"Here it is—the thing you need, the item you want, the possession that you must possess." He reached into a burlap sack on the ground and rummaged around, building suspense. "Let there be light!"

He took an orb of glass from the sack and raised it a full arm's length above, as if lightning would shoot through his veins and illuminate the sky. The crowd gave a joint groan of disappointment before they started heckling.

"We've seen those before," the petite woman scoffed.

"Doesn't do us any good without *power*, Scavenger," yelled an old man on the outer edge of the crowd. "That's as useful as these pieces of junk all over the city." He looked up at one of the many tall metal poles standing along the edge of the street. At their tops were glass spheres, larger versions of the one the merchant currently advertised.

Several people turned to leave until the merchant urged them otherwise.

"Fair customers, wait, I beg you! First of all," he said, stepping onto a plastic crate next to him, "those lamps really are for show. The idea that they could all be lit across the city in our lifetime is comical. But *my* light bulb, for your personal use, now *that* is feasible!"

"There is no *personal* use of power!" shouted the old man. "It's for government entities and a few sanctioned businesses. That's it. Do you think we're that stupid?"

A flood of yeahs and gesticulations followed his accusation.

"Stupid, no. Ignorant, perhaps. Because," he held the bulb higher, "you most certainly have NOT seen one like *this* before. They stopped making these in the early 21st century— you couldn't have bought one back then, and here and now, I have one! Its antique value alone makes it a collector's dream. But wait, there's more!"

He pulled a small, metal box out of his back pocket, no wider than his palm, with a tiny crank on the side. With all the drama of a man about to do magic, he screwed the bulb into the hole on top of the box.

"Government permission no longer required. Behold, the power!" he exclaimed, flexing his bicep for good measure.

He turned the little crank on the box, and after several

seconds, the bulb flickered to life. It lit up, and those nearby oohed in excitement. He stopped cranking, and the light slowly faded away until it turned off.

"That's it?" the petite woman said.

"Well, I'm still working on it, but just imagine, light at your fingertips. You make your own power! It's the FUTURE!" He gave the crank all he had this time, completing one tiny revolution after another, faster and faster. It glowed bright and strong, then *POP*, *plink!* The bulb went dark.

A breath of silence filled the circle, only to be replaced by snickering and the shuffling of bodies as the group dispersed.

The man stared at the bulb, his hands frozen in their positions on the box. He then gently shook it back and forth, and it jingled with the motion. He gripped the contraption harder, stretched his arm overhead, and prepared to hurl it toward the ground.

"The box might be worth something," Caster said as he approached with Wren. "Don't throw out the functional with the broken, Freddy."

Freddy stopped mid-throw and put on a composed, serious face. "Interested in purchasing, Caster, old buddy?" He shifted his gaze to Wren, eyes flitting about her face and clothes. "Or perhaps the lady? How do you do? I'm Frederick Hawthorn de Bourgh."

She waltzed up to him and snatched the box. Her face fell when she turned the crank slowly and the bulb didn't respond. "How did you do that?"

"Pleasure to meet you, as well. I'm a bit of an inventor. But also a showman, an entrepreneur, and most especially," he tipped his hat, "an astonishing lover. What's your name, blue eyes?" He sidled up next to her.

Caster shoved him hard in the shoulder, knocking him back

several paces. He took the box from Wren and threw it at Frederick.

"You're a Scavenger, Freddy. Let's not get carried away," he said.

"Scavenger is so negative a term," he said as he tucked the contraption back in the burlap sack. He overturned the crate and tossed the bag inside it. "Explorer, trader, master merchant, those are better. I'll thank you to use one of them in the future, your *majesty*." He bowed low to the ground.

"Black market scum peddler?" Caster said. "Maybe that's best."

"Yeah, I'm glad you're back from your trip—I missed the ridicule, truly. Don't come to me the next time you're looking for a new knife or some gadget to zip your pants." He picked up his crate. "Goodbye, my lovely," he said to Wren, removing his hat and pressing it to his chest. "See you, Caster. Hopefully later rather than too soon." He plopped the hat back on, tilted it to the side, and strode off down the street with a hop in his step.

Darkness had settled in subtly like sleep over the eyes of the weary, and with it came the cold of the desert night. Tall torches billowed to life up and down the street behind them as merchants lit them with flint, fighting the darkness as they yammered on about the sale they were having. Up ahead, an area under a wide awning lit up merrily with fires in big metal drums. Whiffs of food cooking drifted toward Caster and Wren.

"Let's keep moving. I smell dinner," Caster said, leading them up the street in the direction of the awning.

He led her into an outdoor pub which proclaimed itself "The Ragged Squirrel" on a pounded tin sign stuck in the ground. As if the name alone didn't cast a vivid enough image, mounted to the top right corner of the sign was a stuffed squirrel—tattered and missing bits and pieces of its limbs—

forever holding a nut near its open mouth. Caster patted the squirrel on the head twice as they passed through an open chain-link fence into the pub.

Several people sat on stools by a long, curving table, which was covered by the awning made of metal sheets. Across from the awning was an open seating area with tall tables built around cylindrical metal drums which functioned as fire pits. A moveable black plastic screen on a metal frame blocked those relaxing in the pub from the wind cutting up the street from the south.

They headed for the woman behind the long table, a round lady with big, soft arms and permanent smile lines. She stood near a hefty, mustached man, who was busy pouring a thick drink for a man in overalls and a white T-shirt hunched over on a stool.

"Are you hungry?" Caster asked Wren as they approached the woman.

Wren shook her head.

"Well, I'm sure glad to see you, hun," the plump lady said to Caster, face alight. "Heard you were on death's door. We were all sick with worry."

Caster tugged his scarf down from his mouth and passed a few coins over the counter. "The rumors were a bit exaggerated, Nita. I'm just fine, as you can see." He spun in place as if to prove it. "And I would love the mixed vegetable plate, please."

Nita laughed. "Sure. How was your trip?" she asked as she wrote down the order and put the money in a metal box on her side of the counter.

"Worth the trouble," he said.

Wren wondered how on Earth he could believe that, and when she glanced over at him, she found he was already looking at her. They both looked away quickly. Her cheeks grew warm.

"What can I get for you, miss?" Nita asked. She studied Wren, eyeing something below her neck. Wren felt there at the clasp with the strange lettering.

"Nothing," Wren replied. "Thank you."

"Nothing? Not even some spiced wine? Cider? Looks to me like you can afford to treat yourself," said Nita, just an edge of suspicion in her tone.

Wren stammered in response. She felt stupid for wearing the red cloak. It was too much, too loud.

"A cider, please," Caster said. He plunked down another coin.

Nita took the coin and dropped it in the box. "Coming up. You look different, hun." She pointed a very round finger at him. "Are you taller? Get a haircut?"

"Haven't shaved in a while. Maybe that's it."

"If you say so. Have a seat here at the bar—Ray, move over!" She prodded at the man in overalls sitting on a stool.

"We'll grab a table," Caster said quickly. "Thanks, Nita."

She looked between him and Wren for an instant, then shrugged. "Suit yourself."

He rapped his knuckles on the counter before turning and looking for an empty table.

They took two tall chairs at a table next to the windscreen. He held his hands up to the fire in the middle of the table, and Wren did the same.

"Welcome home, stranger!" a woman, slender with thin eyebrows, called over from a table nearby where she sat with two other women. She started to stand and come over, an odd smile on her face, as if she were thinking of a shared secret.

Caster waved but didn't encourage her to join them. She

sat back down, making a show of adjusting her overall straps as she did so.

He spoke as he took off his scarf and tucked it inside his black coat. "So I've been waiting to ask. What's your story?"

She slowly undid her own scarf and held it in her lap, lacing it through her hands. "I'm not sure," she answered finally. "You mean which one is my favorite? I like so many. I usually like sad ones the best, but they need to have big moments of happiness."

He smiled behind his hands as he rubbed them together. "I actually meant what's *your* story. Where did you grow up, why have you stayed in the Open, things like that. But this is interesting too. I love books."

"Never read one. I've just heard stories. From my mom."

"Oh yeah? Which ones?"

It was like asking her which stars were her favorites, and she had to think about it for a minute. "There was one about a person who lived underground, but he came out one day to go on an adventure and found a magic ring. Alma, my mom, called it *There and Back Again*."

He grinned, and then spoke slowly, as if remembering something as he went. "This thing devours all other things... kills kings...beats a mountain..."

She waited for him to finish his thought, but he seemed stuck. "What?"

He smacked the table playfully. "Damn. I was hoping to impress you by reciting one of the riddles from the book. The answer was time."

"Well, you failed terribly."

That seemed to catch him off guard, and he laughed out loud. The noise surprised her, and she chuckled under her breath at it. People at the table nearby glanced over, but Caster didn't pay them any attention.

"Regardless, it's a classic," he said. "I know it as *The Hobbit*. I'd say that one's pretty happy overall, actually."

"In the end. But there was sadness along the way. Or at least, fear."

"Pretty common these days. The fear part, I mean. May I ask where your mom is now?"

Survivor's voice screamed in her mind. *Shut up, you idiot, before you tell him everything about us! Information is valuable. Don't give it up to anyone unless you have to.* Wren didn't have to, but she wanted to. Surely, the bare facts couldn't hurt.

"She's dead. Died with my siblings five years ago."

His face fell as if he were reliving the memory with her.

Nita toddled over, breaking the awkward silence that had formed. She put a plate of roasted vegetables in front of Caster—Wren recognized potatoes, at least, though there were also orange bits and something in layered slices. Nita then set a mug of liquid in front of Wren that smelled slightly acidic and spiced with something Wren didn't recognize.

"Use the handle. It's hot." Nita spoke flatly, no smile, and Wren thought there might have been an edge of irritation in her voice. But then she headed back to the bar.

"I'm sorry," Caster said. "About your family, your mom. I lost mine, too."

He cleared his throat and tore into his meal, not talking for a while. Wren sipped at her drink—cider, Caster had called it. At first she drank gingerly, then with more vigor. It was sweet and slightly sour, and the more she drank the less she tasted the sourness. When Caster finally looked up from his plate, she'd slouched into her chair, a grin spreading across her face like honey.

"You sure you're not hungry?" He pointed his fork at the vegetables still on his plate.

"Nope. I'm great." 'Great' came out a little strangely, as if she'd missed a couple letters. She felt warm all over.

"You said you had siblings?" he asked through his final bites.

Survivor screamed in her head again. *Stop talking! Goddammit, Wren.* But it felt good to talk about it. To acknowledge their existence.

"Besides Survivor, six. We weren't really related, not by blood, anyway. But we loved each other like brothers and sisters and brothers." Wait, did she already say brothers? She grew fascinated with the smooth texture of her cloak and traced the section draped over her shoulder with her pinkie.

Caster reached across and grabbed her cup to sniff at the bit of liquid left in the bottom. "*Spiced* cider. Whoops." He put the cup back. "I'm guessing you've never had alcohol before."

"What's alcocall?"

"Yeah, thought so. Don't worry, it was just one drink. It'll pass soon enough. Try to enjoy it."

"I'm enjoying all of this." She gestured with open arms to the pub and the people around and found the courage to wave to the trio of women at the next table over. They didn't wave back, instead furrowing their brows as if she'd done something inappropriate. She reeled herself in then, suddenly aware that she was talking louder than she'd intended.

He laughed quietly and pushed his empty plate aside. Then he looked at her. *Really* looked at her. As he searched her face for something she wasn't sure she wanted him to find, she felt her cheeks flush deeper and turned her full attention to the fire between them. She hated how her body did that, putting her emotions on display. Survivor did, too, and got mad at Wren when it happened, though it wasn't as if she were capable of stopping it.

"You've lived in the Open all your life?" he asked.

She found her courage again and looked back at him. She nodded.

He scratched at the back of his head and sighed deeply. "That must have been difficult. And you must be incredibly strong to have gotten through it."

"Me? No. Not strong. Survivor's strong. Alma was strong. I'm just me."

"Bullshit."

"What?"

"Survivor isn't strong—the woman I saw in the desert was terrified, and she covered it up with bravado and anger. She's resilient, sure. But that's not the strength you have. You're still kind. God." He lowered his voice as he leaned closer to her over the fire. "Do you have any idea how rare that is? To have been through hell and to still give a damn about other people, about right and wrong?"

"But you care."

"Not like you, no. Never have."

"I saw how you treated the crowd that brought you gifts. You're friends with everyone you come across. They love you. You must have given them reasons to."

"Being born to their ruler means they have no choice but to love me. It's socially required."

"But it's not required for you to love them, and you do."

"I *try* to. Don't have many years of experience yet. I've been an asshole most of my life, something I inherited from my father."

She opened her mouth to protest.

He waved his hands as if to sweep her would-be response away. "It's not humility, it's fact. I understand your sister because I was her for a long time. Not caring about others? Being pissed off and cruel like her? It's easier."

"She's not cruel," Wren snapped. It was automatic,

strangely natural coming out of her mouth. She'd told herself the same thing many times over the years. But she hadn't meant it to sound so irritated. Not at Caster.

He raised an eyebrow. "She was treating you like garbage every time I looked over."

"She was just trying to help me understand the danger we were in. Show me she was right to have hurt you."

"Did she convince you?"

"Well, no. But that doesn't mean she was wrong to try."

"She was wrong to belittle you and make you feel more frightened than you already were. That's not strength, and it's sure as hell not love."

"Maybe not to some. But I know her. She's my sister." She looked away, sweeping her fingers quickly through the tips of the flames between them. "You don't see her the way I do."

"Clearly not." He warmed his hands by the fire again.

She tried to shake off the frustration she felt. "You said you lost your mom?"

"Hmm? Oh, yeah. Four years ago. She got sick."

"I'm sorry."

"Me too." He twirled the ring on his pinkie.

She thought he'd say more, but when he didn't, she changed the subject. "And Thallium is your father?"

"Unfortunately, yes."

"Why unfortunately? He seems to care about you."

The trio of women at the nearby table had grown oddly quiet, and the one who had greeted Caster kept looking out of the corner of her eye at them every time she drank from her cup.

Caster lowered his voice to a hoarse whisper even Wren had to strain to hear. "He has nobody's interests at heart but his own. To know what his intentions are, you have to see what he can get out of a situation. Which makes me curious to know what he told you he wants from you."

Hot and foul liquid started to come back up her throat, making her grimace. After letting out a silent mouthful of sour air and shuddering, she answered quietly. "My help, it sounds like. I'm *special*. Something about power and restoring technology. Your city needs energy. I don't really understand it."

He gave a gruff sigh. "I do, at least in theory. It's an insane dream my grandfather had—find lost technology capable of bringing the resources of the old world back. My father adopted it after he died. But why you specifically?"

Wren shrugged and then shook her head slowly. "He said something about taking a closer look at my DNA soon? Whatever that is. But I made a deal that's keeping my sister and me alive, so I'll keep my end of it."

He slapped the table, and it made her jump. "Son of a bitch!" He must have seen the surprise on her face at his exclamation. "Sorry. I figured it was an arrangement like that. Guess I'm mad I was right."

"And that's why you don't want to see him? Your father? That's why you refused to go with Prady to the Main House?"

"That? No. That's something else entirely."

"Then you'll take me back? And come with me." She realized she hadn't asked, instead phrased it as a request, and an embarrassingly desperate one.

He smiled at her, but it was sad. "I don't—" He stopped short, looking over her shoulder. "I think it's time for us to go." He stood quickly and motioned for her to do the same.

As she rose, she realized they had an audience. People at nearby tables stared at them. The young women seemed to be ready to leap at her, faces scrunched up in rage. Men whispered angrily to each other between stealing glances at Wren. But the most hostile of all was the man in overalls at the bar. He glared with red hatred at Wren from his stool, practically spitting as he spoke with the big man behind the bar and Nita, who'd come to join him.

"Follow me, don't look back," whispered Caster close to her ear. He took her hand and started walking toward the exit to the street. To get to the exit, they had to pass the bar, and it was there that Nita and the mustached man intercepted them.

"I have to ask you to leave," said the man standing next to Nita, his burly arms crossed.

"Way ahead of you. Thanks for the food, Nita," said Caster.

Nita stood two feet shorter than the mustached man, but she was far more intimidating, her once-jovial face now dark and bitter. She yelled at Caster loud enough for the whole pub to hear, "Get that outlier whore out of here!"

"Go back to the rotting Open!" shouted the man in overalls as he stood from his stool nearby. He shouted, "She's the outlier who was on trial this morning! Look at her clothes. Just look at them! Goddamn piece of art now." He took hold of the straps of his overalls with both fists, tugging at them like chains. "What makes you better than me?" He threw a short glass toward them. It shattered on the ground, wetting the dirt.

People in the pub started arguing, particularly the trio of women who had been near them. The one that knew Caster shouted, her voice shrill and trembling with outrage. "She nearly killed him, and now he's taking her out to dinner and whispering in her ear? She's deceived him! Get away from him, you murderer!"

An older man stood shakily from his seat and spoke. "I don't believe it was her who hurt Caster. It was the girl she was with. Why shouldn't this one spend time with him if he wants to see her?"

A chorus of retorts flew at the man, with "outlier" being

flung at him as if it were a dart straight into the heart of his argument. He put up his hands and waved them lazily as he sat back down, resigned to sit at his table in silence.

Wren's face turned clammy, and she started to cry softly. Caster pulled her behind him as he turned to the crowd. "I may be your friend, but make no mistake, I am above all your superior. Watch your words, because they can't be taken back!"

Everyone fell quiet.

"I spent the afternoon trying to convince this woman of your goodness! And you have proved me wrong in every way. Shame on you. All of you."

He turned and ushered Wren from the pub, which was now eerily silent, with his hand on the small of her back.

He guided her through the rest of the Trading Center, which ended not far after the pub. Once they were out of the center, he stopped beneath a tall oil lamp pole and bent down to get a good look at her face.

"Feeling sick?" he asked.

"No," she said. She blinked away the tears.

"You sure? Your stomach's okay?"

Halfway through a nod, the same hot liquid from before creeped up her throat. She heaved over and vomited, barely missing him but instead hitting her scarf that had fallen to the ground when she bent at the waist.

"There it is." He patted her back.

She stood and wiped at her mouth with her hand.

"Better now?" he asked.

She nodded, thankful she'd missed his boots.

"Come on."

CHAPTER SIX

CASTER LED WREN THROUGH NARROW STREETS AND abandoned walkways in the dark to a small neighborhood of slipshod houses, glancing behind every so often to make sure she was keeping up. Light poured from the windows of the houses and crept out underneath the front doors to make pools in the dark, casting the neighborhood in a dull glow. The homes here were plopped down without any apparent organization, sitting in clumps, some face-to-face while others sat diagonal from one another with only a sliver of space between their corners. As the population grew, so did the housing. But no plan had been made to accommodate the growth, at least not for the lower class.

The upper class, those who had jobs in an administrative or other capacity for the government, had space aplenty in tall housing buildings near the Main House, which featured the coveted amenity of indoor plumbing. But other than their living arrangements and shinier clothes, the rich were still just getting by like everyone else. Their barely better tasting food was still rationed, they breathed the same dust, clung to the safety of the same walls. They just had a better view of the day-to-day struggle from several stories up.

Middle class only existed as an idea, an identity held by those in the lower class who saw themselves or their occupations as more glamorous than the sanitation workers and farmers. It was a lie. There were rich and poor here, nothing in between. But status was seen as a commodity, even if it was an illusion. People always needed to feel "better than."

The homes of the poor were made of materials rejected by others, the leftovers from businesses or the findings of Resource-Seekers, whose job was to find salvageable material outside the city. Oddly shaped pieces of sheet metal, mud bricks, and stones stacked strategically were common here. Some owners evidently cared about the appearance of their houses—these homes had sheet metal roofs matched to all-boulder bodies, complete with tin and copper whirligigs and wind chimes adorning the eaves. Other houses were patchwork, thrown together from the scraps of the scraps, but serviceable just the same.

Caster checked behind him again. Wren seemed to be doing better, though she still looked a bit peaked. She walked a few steps back, keeping the distance between them constant, as if reverting to an old habit. He slowed his pace to let her come up next to him, but she only slowed hers to match his, following his footprints like stepping stones. He gave up and let her draft.

He led her between two short stone walls on a crooked and uneven dirt path until they came to an opening in the wall on their left. He passed through the break in the stone, and she followed. They came into a courtyard, and the stone walls enclosing it butted up against the backs of four other houses which had been built first.

A stout, circular house made of stones and mud mortar sat in the middle of the courtyard. It had an abrupt roof—two huge pieces of sheet metal meeting at a steep point—and a skinny chimney of old air ducting. The front door was sheet metal too, but cut down to size and fitted with a wooden handle.

Caster had made it himself, and it showed.

"Where are we?" Wren asked, straining to see in the dark. Her voice was airy and tired. It seemed he could sweep his hand back and forth and disperse it like smoke.

"My house," he said. "The Keepers will come looking here soon. I'm rarely home, but they'll figure it out and try to find you here. We'll wait for them."

"Can't we just go to the Main House now?"

"No."

When he reached the door, he retrieved his lighter from his coat pocket and lit the torch sitting in a loop of metal attached to the doorframe. It burned high and hot and lit up the court-yard. He grabbed a key hidden behind a piece of loose mortar and unlocked the door. Then he turned around to see Wren standing farther away from him, looking around as if something might jump her.

"I'm sorry if that was harsh," he said. "I just can't take you back."

"Why not?" she asked.

He wanted to answer her, but he wasn't entirely sure of the answer himself or how to phrase it.

"Prady will be here soon." He went inside.

It was totally dark until he lit the four large, multi-wick candles hanging on each wall. As he lit the candles in clockwise order, they illuminated the sections of the interior one by one. First, there was the wooden chair across from the fireplace on the left side of the great room, then the small kitchen and table on the far side, and the wood-framed bed on the right with a tired mattress, which was barely more comfortable than the ground.

"Bathroom is behind the house, should you feel the need," he said as he knelt near the fireplace. He took big pieces of coal, along with dry grass and tumbleweeds from the oversized tinder box nearby and stacked them strategically on the grate in the fireplace.

Wren stayed by the door with her cloak wrapped tighter around her middle. The cold air snuck its way beneath the door and around its edges through big gaps—Caster had continued to put off fixing his shoddy handiwork from when he'd installed the door and mismeasured. He was hardly home for it to bother him.

He grabbed his lighter again and lit the underside of the fuel on the grate in three different spots. In less than a minute, a full fire was burning, and the room grew brighter.

"You know," he said as he pushed off his knee into a stand, "it's a lot warmer over here."

She hesitated, shuffling her feet on the dirt floor.

He went for the chair across from the fire, took off his belt, and hung it on the back of the chair before sitting. "Or you could at least stand by a wall. They're warm to the touch. Just don't catch a cold."

She took several tentative steps toward the fire and then dropped cross-legged onto the dirt near it.

"You can sit here," he said, patting his chair as he stood.

She rested her chin on her hand and watched the coals turn a darker shade of orange. "I'm used to the floor. I like it."

He sat again. "Never mind, then."

He watched her watching the fire. Her new cloak was covered in dust and, though nobody else would notice, a bit of vomit on the hem. The sourness reached his nostrils. She wiped what was left of her tears away. He felt like shit for not checking her drink earlier and for taking her among the small-minded morons who'd screamed hatred. He'd wanted to slam the overall worker onto the bar on his back and make an example of him. Thinking about it made him itch with anger all over.

"Your house isn't as nice as the Main House," she said suddenly.

"Well, thanks for that. It depends on how you look at it, I guess."

She ran her eyes over the room. "It looks sad no matter how I look at it. Nicer than my cave, though."

He chuffed. "You're too kind." When she laughed in response, he marveled at how round and full it sounded. How it felt right on her compared to the fear and shame she'd shown at the pub earlier. "I'm sorry if those people back there scared you."

The comment extinguished some of the joy on her face, and he was pissed at himself for bringing it up.

"They were so mad," she said, almost like a question she was trying to answer for herself.

"They're always mad at something. At God, at the world they're stuck with, at the truth that they're not superior to people outside of the city. You're something new to be mad at."

"That's sad."

"I was naïve to think they'd accept you because you were with me. I'm sorry you had to deal with that."

"Oh, no. I mean it's sad for them. Being angry all the time."

The light shining on her fair skin and blazing hair made him blink. He rubbed at his eyes. "It *is* sad. They're hard to love sometimes."

"I know the feeling." She retreated into herself then, falling quiet and staring at things he couldn't see.

He got up, heading for the open kitchen. A wide cupboard stretched from floor to ceiling next to a basin and towel, perpendicular to the short countertop and the small food store beneath.

He grabbed a cup sitting next to the basin and opened the cupboard. Inside on a pedestal was a tall plastic drum filled with water. Lines and numbers were stamped on the container —the numbers were ounces and the lines broke the water up into thirty days. The water bobbed just under the five-day line. He opened the spigot at the bottom of the container and filled the cup halfway.

"Here," he said as he went back to the fire. "You're probably dehydrated."

She took the cup, sniffed it, and then downed it in two long gulps. She set the cup aside and pulled her knees up, resting her arms on them and then settling her cheek down on one elbow.

He sat and rested his head against the back of the chair. After a few minutes, her voice roused him.

"I'd only heard of fathers in stories until I came here," she said.

He lifted his head to see she'd turned her back to the fire. She looked up at him, only a couple of feet away.

"You don't know your dad?" he asked.

"I don't have a dad."

He shrugged. "That's better than having one sometimes."

"Why?"

"I have a dad, and I'd rather I didn't."

"Is your dad mean to you?"

"Mean? Not exactly. Not always, anyway. He used to be really great when I was a kid. Taught me how to fight, provided for me and my mom. The three of us ate dinner together and talked about what I'd learned in school that week, the patients my mom was taking care of, how Thallium was having the farmers rotate in a new crop of watermelon that season.

Normal things. Family things. We were happy, or at least I was. I went everywhere with him."

"But now you don't?"

"No. Not for a while now."

They sat quietly for a bit. The fire crackled and popped.

"Was that hers? Your mom's?" Wren asked. She nodded at his right hand and the ring on his pinkie.

He waggled it. "Yes. Hematite for healing. She was a nurse." He cleared his throat and rose to stoke the fire with a handful of dried grass where it wasn't catching properly. "You never did tell me where you're from. Where were you born?"

She didn't answer at first, but then she spoke to his back. "I don't know. I grew up in the forest. My mom found me and my siblings in the desert when we were small. I don't remember anything before then."

"Nothing?"

She shook her head. "Just Alma and the kids."

"I can't imagine having a big family like that. Must have been amazing."

"Yes. But now it's just Survivor and me. Or, it was."

"Was? She's alive. You still have her."

She shook her head. "She doesn't like the deal I made."

"She would have been executed otherwise."

"I think she wished she had been. She doesn't trust Thallium. Even you don't like him. But I don't see a choice other than trusting him. Do you?"

There was a desperation in her tone that made his chest ache. He'd asked himself the same question for the past several years, and the ache had only gone away when he decided. "I think you made the right choice, but no, I don't trust Thallium."

She pursed her lips, chewing on them a bit. Then her words burst forth. "Will you come back with me? Can you stay in the Main House?"

He sighed, opening his mouth to say "no" when the door burst open, falling off the top hinge to dangle like a joint out of socket.

Dal came charging in, mask pulled down, torn pieces of cloth crusted with blood dangling from his nostrils. Dark circles were forming under his eyes, and he glared at Caster with unveiled contempt. Prady walked in behind him, looking the part of the babysitter scorned as he rubbed at his knee.

"It was open, just so you know," Caster said as he stood.

Dal formed some inhuman grunts, probably the native tongue of his people, which made the cloths screwed into his nose blow about.

Prady stepped in between Caster and Dal. "May I talk to you privately?" he asked Caster.

Caster nodded.

"Watch her. *Only* watch," Prady said, slowly and loudly to Dal.

He and Caster walked to the kitchen. Prady tugged his mask down and threw his scarf back to reveal a skinny braid of gray hair and leathery skin that had started to betray his age.

"Please come with us. If you resist, Dal will fight you, and when you kill him, I'll have a whole mess of paperwork to contend with," said Prady.

"You do hate paperwork."

Prady stared him down.

"I don't come when my father calls. You know that."

"Yes, but I'm also getting old, sir. I'm running out of energy for bureaucratic family drama."

"Then you understand why I won't go with you."

Caster glanced at Dal, who only had eyes for him—blood-shot eyes—and a deficiency of emotional maturity that would make this a pain in the ass for everyone involved.

"Do you know Thallium's plans for her?" Caster asked.

"All I know is that he's very interested in her. Eydis wants her in the lab first thing tomorrow."

"What is it about her that he thinks he can use for his research? She's just an outlier."

Caster's gaze fell on her, how tiny she looked next to hulking Dal. She'd been ignorant about something as simple as navigating a crowd, and yet brave enough to exchange her life for someone she cared about. His mom would have loved her.

"She's out of her element here, in the middle of a kind of danger she's not used to," said Caster finally. "Mercy isn't my dad's natural bent; he needs something from her, and I want to know what exactly."

"I can't say I disagree, sir. Perhaps a good way to learn more would be to come with us? Not to please the Principal, but for information."

Caster sighed. "You're too good at your job."

"A cross I bear daily. Let's be off."

With that, Prady tugged his mask back up and turned on his heel. He escorted Wren to the door. "Dal, take point."

After a long grumble and a rather unimaginative middle finger flung at Caster, Dal stomped out before everyone else.

Prady gestured for Wren to walk in front of him as he stared ahead, watching Dal like he was expecting him to lose it. Caster waited until Prady's back was turned before grabbing his belt from the chair. He fastened it around his waist and made sure his knife was hidden beneath his coat.

"I'll take you to the Principal," Prady said to Caster as they ascended the primary staircase in the Main House.

They walked behind Dal and Wren, who'd just reached the landing for the bedroom wing. Dal opened the door for

Wren and then followed her through it. Before it could close, Caster stopped it with his foot and watched Wren head down the hall through the light of the oil lamps. She looked back once and waved awkwardly around Dal's mass to Caster.

"Go with her and get her settled. She's your charge, not me," Caster said to Prady. He nodded toward the hallway.

Prady hesitated.

"I'm sure my father's in his study," said Caster. "I'll go straight there. I'm not here to start something."

"I sincerely hope not. It didn't work out too well for you last time."

"I'm reminded every day." He reached up and scratched at the puckered scar by his eye. "I don't trust Dal with her. Can you honestly say you do?"

Prady sighed deep in his chest, then saluted. "Good day, sir."

Caster returned a lazy salute of his own, and then Prady jog-limped down the hall after Wren.

The Principal's study was attached to his bedroom, which was on the top floor in the apex of the pyramid. Caster wound his way up the rest of the stairs, hating how familiar the cool metal railing felt. He took his hand off of it for the last two flights.

He opened the door at the top of the stairs and came to the secure entryway to the Principal's quarters. It was a rectangular mini-fortress, a sliver of a room with the singular purpose of keeping uninvited people out of the Principal's refuge. Strong bars stretched from floor to ceiling, dividing the room in half. On Caster's side of the bars stood four Keepers, heavily armed, two with blades, one with a crossbow, and another with a pump action shotgun. On the other side of the bars was the door to Thallium's study.

"Name and purpose?" the center one with the shotgun asked.

The Keeper on the end, a young woman with a crossbow hanging from a sling over her shoulder, stepped forward and addressed Caster. "Sorry, sir. He doesn't leave here much, and he was brought in after you left the Main House." She turned to the center guard. "This is the Principal's son, noob."

"The Principal doesn't seem too eager to greet him," spat the center guard.

"Shut your mouth," the woman said, poking him in the chest, "you low slum piece of—"

"That'll be all, Livi," said a third voice.

The Keepers turned around to see the Principal standing on the other side of the bars, and their heads dropped in robotic bows. Thallium's face, shadowed in the checkerboard pattern of the bars, hadn't changed much in the last four years. The same tidy blond hair pulled back, the square chin now covered with a manicured goatee, and cold gambler's eyes with a tinge of madness around the irises.

"Hello, my boy," he said. "Welcome home."

The Keeper with the crossbow, Livi, entered a code on a keypad in the wall, and the bars slid open in the center, leaving space wide enough for one man to go through.

All four Keepers bowed to Caster in unison. He nodded to them before passing through the gap. Thallium had left the heavy cherry wood door cracked open behind him. Caster pushed past it with his shoulder, hit with the memory of the last time he'd entered that room.

Almost four years ago, Caster had barged into the study, intent on killing his father. Thallium told the Keepers to stay back, and then proceeded to wreck Caster, body and mind. When Caster was on the ground, stab wounds in the meat of his thigh and bicep, Thallium stood over him. He took Caster's own bowie knife from where it lay next to him and cut his face, once on the cheek, again on the chin, and finally near his eye, as if he were painting a masterpiece.

"So you don't forget how close to death you came," the Principal had said.

Caster never had.

The study had changed about as much as Thallium himself. He'd swapped the rug out—the new one was far more ornate, with thick red shag and a braided fringe. That was about it.

Thallium sat in one of the dark leather armchairs in the middle of the rug, next to a small glass case of honest-to-God books. His private collection that he read regularly, rather than showpieces he left on display. Caster had read most of them, though it had been years since he'd last had the opportunity. It was the one thing he missed about his father—these myriad magnificent worlds contained by paper.

"Apologies. Those guards are not the brightest, but they're fantastic fighters. Feels like the two traits are becoming mutually exclusive the older I get." Thallium closed a hardback copy of *The Saga of the Volsungs* that had been sitting open on top of the bookcase. "One of your favorites, I believe?" Thallium asked, showing him the cover of the book decked out in ancient Norse runes.

"Was always more of a *Poetic Edda* man," Caster replied.

"That's right! 'The foolish man thinks he will live forever if he keeps away from fighting—'"

"'But old age won't grant him a truce, even if the spears do,'" Caster finished. "Never knew you read *The Havamal*."

"I tried to read all the things you were interested in. No matter how dense or boring." He waved to the seat across from his. "Sit down," said Thallium.

Caster didn't move. "I won't be here long."

Thallium put the book on top of the case. "How are you feeling?"

Caster answered with a blank stare.

"You look good. A lot better than you did earlier."

"Why am I here?"

"Is it so wrong for a father to want to check on how his kid is recovering?" Thallium reached for a glass of ice water sitting next to the book. Condensation dripped down onto his hand and fell to the rug as he took a sip.

"Not for some fathers."

Thallium threw up his hands. "I just wanted to make sure you were doing better."

"I'm fine." He cleared his throat and forced himself to add, "Thanks."

Thallium looked far too happy, which instantly made Caster regret the thanks. "I'm glad."

"I'm sorry if I alarmed your Keepers tonight. Just didn't think it was fair to keep Wren from seeing the city. It's not like she's a prisoner."

"Of course. She's our guest. I'm glad you got to spend some time with her. Girl seems rather fond of you. And are you fond of her? She's lovely, isn't she?"

"I'm more concerned for her well-being. As I'm sure you are. What's your business with her exactly? I don't think standard outlier policy has changed since I've been gone. Shouldn't she be in a prison cell?"

Thallium sighed. "I have no intention of locking her up. In fact, if you'd like to visit her, you'd be welcome any time. I simply desire to help her adjust to life here, find her footing."

"In exchange for..." Caster prompted.

Thallium grabbed his book and sat again, tucking his finger between the pages where a strand of black ribbon held his place. "Who says I want anything in return?"

This was getting tiresome. "You don't clothe, feed, and shelter the family of your enemy without a motive beyond your sense of charity. You've taught me as much. Tell me with a straight face that this isn't about your work with Eydis. Grandpa's insane dream."

Thallium smiled. "The ogre's mantra lives on. He used to call his work *Paradise Regained*. Asshole thought Milton was profound."

"What's Wren's part in it?"

"She's shown potential, a set of traits that's rare to come across. She's a relic of the world before The Fall. We need her. And, just so we're clear, she needs you."

Caster raised an eyebrow. "Why's that?"

"She's distressed. I don't think that's any secret. A friend would help her adjust to this place, make her know she's safe and that the dark part of her life is behind her. She could use a familiar face."

"Then maybe you should reunite her with her sister."

"The psychopath that tried to murder you? Have her here, in my home? Brilliant, son. Really, bravo." He clapped three times.

Caster let out a burst of laughter, releasing the pressure from the dam threatening to break in his gut. "You're afraid of her."

"You always go right for my pride. Try working on my other vices—drinking, rage, flights of fancy." He rose and closed the distance between them. Caster found the red shag filling the spaces between his bare toes oddly macabre. "She assaulted the Principal's son, next in line to rule this oasis. She's lucky to still have blood in her body. I'm not a forgiving man."

Caster stood just a couple of inches taller than Thallium and made sure Thallium knew it as he loomed closer. "Neither am I."

They stared each other down, neither drawing breath until Thallium lightly slapped Caster on the cheek. "Great to see you, my boy. Maybe don't wait for a mortal wounding to come home next time." He started back toward the bookcase, apparently deciding the conversation was over.

"I won't help you deceive her. That's why you want me here, to lull her into a false sense of safety. You want to make her think you care."

"Do you have 'twisting my father's words' down on your list of skills in your military profile? Because you should. Right up at the top."

"That spot's already taken by 'seeing through the lies of delusional narcissists.'"

Thallium rolled right past his slight. "If you're so worried about her, then participate in our work with her. Be her advocate."

"What the hell does that mean?"

"You know, advocate for her. Help her feel more comfortable around here, in the city, in the lab. Keep her safe and—"

"Make sure nobody hangs her by her toes over a bed of nails," Caster mocked in the fatherly tone Thallium had adopted.

"One time I did that to you. One time. Let it go."

"I was nine."

"And it was funny!" He threw his hands up. "It's your choice. Show up, don't show up. Do as you wish. I'd rather have you around, but you've made it clear that you want nothing to do with me. I have to respect that."

"Since when?"

"I've given you nothing but space these past few years. Even you have to admit that. I'm not asking for your involvement for my sake, but you should think about that young girl.

She's not me, and failing to make that distinction would be
petty, even by your standards. She's an innocent girl."

"So was my mom."

Thallium's expression turned instantly withdrawn, a swift
180 from mania to darkness that Caster recognized from his
adolescence. "I don't want to discuss that. You know this. Don't
bring her up again."

"Why? Does it bother you? Is it offensive to discuss her
pain, how she suffered and bled out of her eyeballs while you
hid, searched for the Holy Grail, and screwed your robot
secretary?"

"Get out." There he was, the man Caster knew was at the
core of his father. Fists balled tight, chin as high as his sense of
entitlement. Spitting words instead of speaking them.

"Or what?" A tingle of fury started at the back of Caster's
neck. His grip tightened on the hilt of the knife tucked in the
belt beneath his coat.

"No 'or.' Get out."

Caster flexed his hand around the knife. His mom's voice,
kind and matter-of-fact, rose from his memory and stopped him
—*Hate is for the weak, and you're not weak, my sunshine.*

He eased his grip on the knife. He fought his muscles,
reining in the adrenaline and the anger, and then stomped
through the doorway, yelling, "If you send Dal after me again,
he won't come back!"

Thallium watched his son leave as blood filled the shallow half-
moons he had dug into his palms with his nails. He saw Caster's
mother in the shape of his earlobes, in the way he crossed the
room with intention. In how he could burrow immediately under

Thallium's skin and make him itch. Observations he didn't dare mention aloud, for more reason than one. They were doomed to simply float in his mind every time he saw Caster, specters that couldn't touch him but would whisper in his ear forevermore.

He shook his hands out as he sat in one of the armchairs. Eydis came into the study through the adjoining master bedroom door.

"Do you think it worked?" he said.

She sat in the chair across from his and braided her hair over her shoulder. "I'm certain. He enjoys being the rescuer. Always has. It's simple psychology. He'll come for her."

"If you really want him to be involved, I should have told him to stay away. Rebellious youths do the opposite of what daddy says. I should know." He saluted the portrait of his father hanging on the wall, a man with gaunt cheeks from refusing to eat more than the people he ruled. A façade of humanity when one of his favorite pastimes was punishing his son's disrespect by locking him in a hotbox—a brick cube set in the sun with slits in the bottom to allow bodily fluids out.

"Being the hero will work just fine," Eydis assured him. "His life's pursuit is proving he's better than you. He views you as heartless. Therefore, he'll seek to prove he's not by protecting Wren from you."

He pretended to choke up and held the back of his hand to his forehead. "Yes, I'm the devil, and he's her savior." He sighed and pinched the bridge of his nose. "But are you sure the girl likes *him*? Her temperament is about as dynamic as a cicada's."

She threw the finished braid back over her shoulder. "I suggest you stop underestimating her. Gamma was quite sure. His readings have never proven false during a trial. Everything about her was elevated when the topic of Caster came up, including her rage at her own sister. You saw for yourself her relief at the news of his recovery. She's smitten."

He stood and let his good mood from earlier find him again. People in this world needed a beacon of hope, a magical object to rally behind. Something to worship in fearful reverence. He'd never known the world before The Fall, but this world could be summed up in one word—desperate. People fought and scratched at each other for the simplest of things. He'd been able to take his corner of it and turn it to order. And he intended to do the same for the rest.

How big the rest was remained a mystery. He'd asked Eydis to try to make contact with other places, "Pre-Fall corporate territories," she called them. Her attempts were met with radio static, maybe a few clicks, but still he believed that more people were out there. They'd be desperate, too. Now that he had the magical object, he might not have to resort to bloodier methods to get people's allegiance. Bloody methods were costly and time-consuming. They kept him from enjoying himself, from the kingdom expansion that was long overdue. The expansion his father had died without achieving.

He walked to Eydis and sat on the arm of her chair. She reached out and put her hand on his thigh.

"Wren will need Caster," she said. "She'll need someone to keep her from losing herself during testing."

Thallium liked the way her lips moved when she spoke, all plump around the letters. "You resorted to this before? When working with my father?"

"Not initially. When we first created the Carriers, we treated them as subjects. They had no emotional attachment to anyone. We expected them to muster themselves to give us a miracle, but it's incredible how their human emotions—weariness, loneliness, apathy—interfered with progress. Then we introduced another variable—a caregiver. Someone they could trust and bond with."

"Who ended up biting you in the ass. Big time."

Eydis blinked at him several times, and if he didn't know any better, he'd have thought he'd irritated her. "Regardless of her actions, it worked," she said finally. "Many of the children's abilities materialized."

"You believe Caster will be a 'caregiver' to Wren?"

"Yes, I do."

He gazed at the portrait of his father again, pulled to it by the dead eyes of Valcin senior challenging him to do better. To complete what he couldn't in creating a better future. It was this pursuit that demanded Thallium's father sire a child with an unnamed whore to protect the rule of replacement in a world where people died far more often than they were born. It was what kept him locked in a lab with Eydis for days at a time, not sleeping, leaving Thallium to raise himself and subsequently correcting him for doing it wrong. And it was this pursuit that kept Thallium's father alive long after he should have died from tuberculosis. He'd run after it like a dog on a scent until his lungs gave out. Only to fall short.

"This better work," he said.

"It will."

A knock came at the study door, and Eydis rose and answered it with a lazy, unhurried grace. Livi handed her something and spoke in hushed whispers. Eydis closed the door quickly and returned to the Principal in three great strides, paper in her hand.

"What is it?" he asked, standing and heading to the desk to pour himself something far stronger and more expensive than water, which he intended to take with him and Eydis to the bedroom.

She held out a swan made from floral pulp paper, with a perfectly curved white neck and a sharp beak. "A message."

Thallium restoppered the bottle of deep red Sangre del Sol before taking the swan and unfolding it, starting at the base of the wings. In the center of the paper was written "Screws. 12:30 tonight. Urgent. – G"

Eydis read the message upside down. "That's unexpected."

"I'm sure it's nothing. He's tried to hike the tax in the past by catching my father off guard. Didn't work then. Won't work now. Old man's a greedy little bastard. Get him and two of his men entry passes for our parley. I'll see what he wants."

Thallium balled up the swan and tossed it in the fire behind the desk. His shot fell short and the ball landed on the wrong side of the screen. A sour taste flooded his mouth at the thought of letting Marauders into his city, but he washed it out with a gulp of Sangre del Sol.

As Caster left the Main House and the affluent part of town behind, he left his anger with it. He was constantly amazed by the tangible nature of anger. For him, and he suspected for Thallium, it had always been something as big as his skin, covering all of him. Maybe it came with privilege, a kind of indignance at anything that challenged his position. With Gavel's help over the past few years, he'd practiced shedding that skin on command and leaving it behind.

It was one of many traits that Caster had once let run his life. Along with a love of power and luxuries, and a sense of entitlement that had driven his every choice, from what he ate to who he slept with.

The worst part about those particular traits was how fucking fun they were.

He shoved his hands deeper into the pockets of his black coat as he cut a hard right, taking a shortcut behind the prison toward the poor district in which his home sat. Squatting there in the street dotted with warehouses in the light of a dumpster fire was a small group of kids, young teenagers by their size, right around Adonis' age. They were tossing stones in their midst, and he recognized a game Adonis had told him about—a stupid one where you throw small pebbles straight up in the air and whichever person it hits has to give you one of their pebbles, two if they get hit on the head. The winner was whoever reached ten pebbles first. Bets were made at the beginning of the game, and the pool of goods was kept in the middle of the players. Caster spotted a couple of coins, a scarf, a pair of dangling silver earrings. A girl with a round face threw her stone up. It hit the boy across from her, a kid with a wispy mustache. Everyone cheered as he gave up his last pebble and fell back onto his ass out of the circle.

Caster's mind shot back to his own adolescence when he'd been fifteen and stupid. Good God above, so stupid. Thallium had gifted him with a birthday trip to Ranlock, a colony smartly built to take visitors' money in exchange for entertainment, mind-altering substances, and hired guns.

TEN YEARS EARLIER

The gambling parlor in Ranlock was nearly as packed with people as Caster's pocket was with credits. Caster stood right up against a betting table next to Thallium. The crowd at their backs and all around was ready for the main event of the evening.

The massive table around which they were gathered was for the rats. Racing rats was the most popular spectacle in Ranlock, as the stakes were high and the carnage often brutal. Six rats raced through a maze inset in the table. The paths curved and dipped, went up in transparent tunnels suspended above the table, and occasionally intersected, where rats would often fight to the death upon meeting one another. The dealer —a tall woman whose limbs were covered in a maze of green tattoos—prepared for the next race. It was the race of the night. Only the most elite gamblers were left at the table, the ones who could afford to lose their wagers and wanted the win more for pride than money.

Everyone within Caster's general vicinity knew the weight of his pockets. The three women, each at least ten years his senior, forming a half-circle behind him knew it. The man in the white hat leaning against the table on the far right knew it. So did the pair of hunters at the opposite end of the table, along with their nephew beside them—a guy a couple of years older than Caster. Gray Acosta, the second richest kid in the room behind Caster, a fact which Caster enjoyed reminding him of whenever the opportunity arose. Gray sipped from a clay jug of wine passed to him by his shorter uncle. When Caster raised his own drink in his direction, Gray shuffled through the crowd and came over.

"Heard you having fun from way back at the hold 'em table. Won yourself a new kingdom yet?" Gray asked, his smirk revealing sharp canines. He punched Caster in the arm with more force than necessary for a friendly greeting.

"Having a brilliant time. Buy you guys drinks? Or do you prefer to share cheap wine?"

Gray took a long pull from the wine jug and then sighed with contentment. "Gets me drunk just fine. Have fun with your rats, you and my uncles." He rolled his neck, which made staccato pops, and reached for the cigarette tucked behind his ear. "I'll be playing a game that demands skill. You know where to find me if you realize your gaping need for humility." He dropped the wine jug at Caster's feet, just missing his right foot, and kissed him on the forehead. He called, "Happy birthday, Bastard!" as he walked away.

If Gray had known how badly Caster was losing that night, he would have had a lot more to say. Caster had only won one bet so far during one of the smaller races by dumb luck when his rat jumped over a fight between the top two contenders to take the peanut butter ball at the end of the maze.

The dealer placed the last rat in the starting blocks—clear boxes suspended just outside the table with doors that would be opened when she pushed a button. She waved to the boxes, indicating it was time for the gamblers to take stock of the racers in order to place their bets. The gamblers moved around the table, each allowed a chance to walk the starting line. Caster found his rat—an ugly bruiser with a chunk missing out of his ear. The yellow tag secured around his tail said "Mage." He wrote the name on his betting slip, along with a hefty wager of 5,000 credits.

"Hmm," said Thallium from just behind him.

Caster looked over his shoulder to see his dad peeking at the name he'd written down.

"What?"

Thallium took a long inhale from his licorice root cigarette and then blew the smoke out of the corner of his mouth. "Nothing, my boy. But perhaps since it's your birthday, you should place a bigger bet." He plucked the slip from Caster's hand, struck through the original 5,000 and wrote down 15,000. "One thousand for every year of your life." He addressed the spectators, thumping Caster hard on the chest. "My boy's of age tonight! A cheer for luck, you fine ladies and gentlemen!"

The crowd toasted and hollered, calling, "Bastard! Bastard! Bastard!" Complete strangers Caster came across in his travels with Thallium had heard of The Bastard of the Desert who picked fights with hunters and vagabonds for fun, right after drinking his weight in booze.

Thallium wrote on his own betting slip, then they deposited them in the dealer's open hands as they passed her. Thallium threw an arm around Caster's neck, putting him in a mock headlock as they circled the table, back toward their original spot. "Having fun?" He spoke close to Caster's ear, his licorice breath filling Caster's nose.

Caster grabbed the glass of Yellow Fever offered by one of the women waiting for him in their spot. She balanced it expertly on her ample bosom. "Absolutely." He downed the glass and put it back on her chest, where she immediately filled it up again.

"I'm pleased you came. I know your mom wasn't thrilled with you being gone on your birthday."

Caster cleared his throat and turned his attention to the table. He'd fought with his mom over being here. He didn't want to think about it.

The dealer gave the final call for wagers. The crowd stomped their feet and banged their drinks in a building rhythm as she dramatically reached for the button at the end of the starting block. She bellowed, "¡Buena suerte!" She pressed the button, and the rats shot out.

Mage got off to a good start, dropping down the entrance ramp to the maze like a sack of grain, but once he reached the first turn, he stopped. Just stopped and cleaned his face like he had all the time in the world. Caster yelled at him to go, but he trundled through the maze as if he were on an evening stroll while the rats around him shot through like darts, biting and clawing at their opponents in epic death matches.

It ended with Mage still stuck in the middle of the maze, standing up on his hind legs and looking around as if he were wondering when the race was going to start.

"Shit!" Caster shouted, bumping into the busty lady and knocking the full glass off. Yellow Fever filled her cleavage, and she shimmied toward Caster to offer him the drink.

The dealer went around to collect and hand out the winnings—2,000 to the hunter whose rat had taken third when he'd placed a bet to show, 850 collected from his buddy whose rat had lost a back foot in a fight in the third turn. The man in the white hat quietly pocketed his impressive 4,250 from betting across the board on the rat that came in second. The dealer reached Caster and Thallium. Caster started to empty his pockets, not meeting anyone's eyes as he heard murmurs and chuckles rippling through the spectators. He'd need Thallium to spot him at least 5,000.

Thallium stopped him before he could hand a credit to the dealer. "Poppy, my dear, take his loss out of my winnings, if you'd be so kind." He kissed her hand.

She nodded and rummaged in the collection box strapped around her waist, which threaded through the pin of a grenade that would detonate if anyone tried to steal the box by ripping it from her. The maze on her arms twitched with her muscles as she rapidly moved obsidian marbles from the box to a cloth satchel. Finally, she handed Thallium a hefty bag of credits, and the crowd erupted in applause.

"How much did you bet?" Caster shouted near Thallium's ear over the commotion.

Thallium took a final drag from his cigarette before dropping it and putting it out with his boot. "Just 50,000." He waved to the people. "The rest of tonight's libations are on me!" They hooted their approval, although Caster didn't think one of them knew the word "libations." They adored Thallium, a regular known for his charisma as much as his cash flow. He'd probably spotted each of the gamblers in the room at least once before, usually so that he could take their money later, but they didn't seem to mind that part as much.

"Come here for a minute," he said to Caster above the hubbub over free drinks.

Caster followed him around the table to the end of the maze where the winner was isolated from the others scrounging around outside the closed door, pawing at the plastic divider. The winner was the scrawniest rat of the bunch, his ribs showing through his sides as he devoured the ball of peanut butter. His yellow tag read "Wally."

"You bet on him to win?" Caster asked.

Thallium nodded. "You put your money on the biggest one, the most intimidating. What you should've done is bet on Wally here." He reached in and gave Wally's head a scratch. "He had one overpowering drive, a drive that trumped the weakness in his muscles. The drive to survive. He's starving—he'll run until his tiny nails pop off and he collapses from exhaustion as long as he's running toward food. Your fat one over there doesn't have the proper motivation. He'll lose every time, until he looks like Wally. Then he'll fly through that maze and do whatever you ask him to reach the end."

PRESENT DAY

The excited shouts of the chubby girl as she leapt from the circle of kids brought Caster out of his reverie. She pumped her fists while her friends groaned, then gathered up the goods from the middle of the circle and modeled her new scarf, posing this way and that. The fire in the dumpster nearby had died down a bit, and the kids apparently decided to seek heat elsewhere. They rose together and ran down the alley.

Caster realized he, surprisingly, wasn't cold at all. Nor was he as tired as he expected after only just returning from his travels, not to mention being poisoned the night before. Really, he felt phenomenal. He chalked it up to the buzz of an afternoon spent with a new person, someone who didn't know his past or how much of a piece of shit he really was.

There was something liberating in that. It was like starting fresh. He could be who he wanted to be with Wren. But even as he had that thought, he realized how naïve it was. To be the man he wanted to be, the man his mom had sworn he was, he couldn't be around Thallium. And that was precisely where Wren was going to be for the foreseeable future. He couldn't be part of her life because it would require him to be a part of his father's. And that lifestyle was too easy to slip back into.

Yet, Thallium was clearly using her, and while Caster didn't think Wren was in any immediate danger, the weight of that reality settled over him. He could try to steal Wren away from him, but she wouldn't leave without her sister. And getting Survivor out of prison was an operation he wasn't willing to risk, both because of the consequences of being caught and the fact that it didn't seem worth it for the sake of someone who'd just about killed him. The same someone who had Wren convinced she was worthless and powerless.

Wren would have to decide to leave on her own and abandon her sister. From what Caster had seen, such a thing wasn't possible. She cared too damn much.

Even if she did leave, he couldn't go with her. This was his home, his people, as asinine as they often acted. There was good here, and if there was any chance of protecting that, he had to stick around to clean up whatever fallout came from Thallium's aspiration for power, both literal and figurative.

There was no scenario where he got to simply be near Wren, to sit in awe of her innocence and her kindness long enough for some of it to rub off on him. He would have to be there for her without *being* there, keep an eye on her from a distance. Prady could help with that, maybe even Eydis.

And if Thallium overstepped, Caster would kill him. It would be a long time coming anyway.

Screws and Gears was a sex den dressed in industrial clothing. All the men and women employed there used false names like Clutch, Ball Bearing—BB for short—and Rivet. The owner, Linchpin, was a sixty-year-old woman with a love of lace and white eyeliner. She also possessed a notoriously mean bite. Stories abounded about occasions when she'd seemingly go feral and take chunks out of disrespecting customers. She had her bouncer Crankshaft as her primary weapon now, who was a towering woman covered in lean muscles. She was the only one in Screws that was allowed a weapon while on the premises, and for this purpose she chose a simple metal baton that usually rested in her belt near her hip.

Thallium and his Keepers passed under the club's red neon sign—a cog rotating around a spinning screw—at half past midnight. Crankshaft greeted the three men just inside the door, and the four of them filled the narrow entryway lit by a single torch hanging toward the top of one wall. Just behind Crankshaft was brighter light and the end of the bar that stretched further into the building, out of sight of the entryway. A heavy drumbeat came from inside, accompanied by a funky saxophone melody and the occasional grind of metal on metal.

The bouncer inclined her head to Thallium, and her frizzy white-blond hair fell forward over her shoulders. "Principal, welcome."

Thallium stepped in closer to her so she could hear him

over the music. "Hello, my dear. I'm meeting an associate here. Has he arrived yet? Older man, white hat."

Her lip curled up. "Yes, sir. He and his two men came in not long ago. I sat them at your regular table. I hope that's all right."

"Perfect. You took their weapons?"

"Every one I could find." She nodded to her right at the hanging display on the wall locked behind a large metal cage. The cage was fuller than normal, nearly overflowing with blades and bludgeoning devices ranging from skinny to bulbous, made of bone and metal and God-knows-what else.

"I suppose you'll be wanting ours, as well." The Principal waggled a couple fingers at his Keepers, Prady on his left, Dal on his right. Dal handed his spear over, along with a derisive sneer. Prady shifted his weight to his good leg and held out his staff; Crankshaft hesitated.

"Crank!" a high-pitched voice belonging to someone behind Crankshaft cut through the music. Crankshaft took a step to the side to reveal Linchpin, standing several heads shorter and wearing a cobalt negligee and knee-high black stockings. "No exceptions." She bowed to Thallium, then gave Crankshaft one last stern look before leaving, likely to take her place back on her perch behind the bar.

Crankshaft took Prady's staff reluctantly. Without it, the man's limp would be more apparent, but he didn't seem concerned about the loss. He smiled with grace as Crankshaft secured it in the cage, along with Dal's spear.

"Thank you, my dear," said Thallium as he tried to step around Crankshaft and leave the entryway.

"Apologies, sir," said Crank, holding out a hand with long, elegant fingers in front of his chest. "I'm obliged to lock away your weapons, as well."

"Of course. But I carry none. My Keepers are more than

capable of protecting me, even unarmed as they are. Isn't that right, gentlemen?"

"Yes, sir," said Prady.

Dal gave a grunt.

Thallium opened his vest and did a showy twirl for Crank. After briefly hesitating, she nodded. "Have a nice evening, sir." She stood aside, hands behind her back as she inclined her head to him.

Now free of the tight entryway, Thallium waltzed into the great room. The bar stretched along the wall to his left. Linchpin sat on her typical stool behind it, legs crossed, wiping out tin cups while surveying her patrons. On Thallium's right, across from the bar, was a sunken seating area centered around a square fire pit made of red bricks. The band, if the three men making noise could be called a band, stood on a tiny stage near the seating area. The fire in the pit undulated and sizzled, as did the women and men sitting on couches and chairs made from pallets around it.

Some were whores for hire. Rivet, a compact young woman with a pointed nose, took her hand from a man's thigh as he turned his attention to his drink and waved her fingers at Thallium. He shot her a wink. Others were customers, like the greasy-skinned man with Rivet who seemed like he might eat her as soon as sleep with her. The rest of the patrons were just that—people who were there to have a good time and maybe find someone special, or at least someone who seemed special enough after a few drinks.

BB—a wiry employee with a chiseled stomach and hard jaw—took a timid middle-aged woman sitting near the fire by the hand and headed toward the hall at the back of the building. Thallium and his Keepers followed behind.

At the back of the establishment, past the bar and the seating area, were private rooms. They stretched down a long hallway lit enticingly with red candles between each door. BB opened the second door on the left and held it open for his customer, who dashed inside, as if she were afraid she'd lose her courage if she hesitated. BB pretended not to see Thallium as he closed the door, which, of course, was the courteous thing to do here.

Privacy was paramount. Most of the rooms were reserved for the employees of Screws and their customers for the night, but some rooms were used for secretive business of a less raunchy nature, and Thallium was headed to just such a room at the far end of the hall.

Thallium lifted his hand to knock, thought better of it, and swung the door open jovially. "When was the last time we saw each other? Ranlock? About ten years ago?"

Sitting at a round table facing the door was The Gentleman, a white-haired, stout Marauder Master whose exact age was unknown. Thallium swore he looked the same now as he had over a decade prior. Maybe with one or two more wrinkles, but overall, he was ageless, an eternal old man more caricature than human with his immaculately white panama hat, tan tweed jacket, and purple ascot. On either side of him were his bodyguards, one skinny with yellowed eyes, one tall and broad with red hair chopped close to his head and an inscrutable face covered in wandering scarification.

The Gentleman tapped the tin cup in front of him, which was filled halfway with Linchpin's house vodka that Thallium could smell from the doorway. "I don't put much stock in tracking time. All seems relative when you live for the moment. But last I saw you was in that overstuffed gambling hall with your son, celebrating some birthday, if I recall correctly." He raised his glass as if to drain it, caught a whiff, and then set the cup back down and pushed it to the side. "You won a small fortune at the final rat race, I believe. Did ya' spend it all in one place?"

Thallium ignored the comment and sat across from the Marauders, as did Prady and Dal. "I was surprised to get your message," said the Principal. "What can I do for you? Or are you wanting to renegotiate the terms of our contract?"

"Our contract is just dandy," replied The Gentleman, "but this ain't a social visit, neither. This is about something personal. You have a prisoner that belongs to me, and I aim to get them back." He put his elbows on the table and rested his chin on his folded hands.

"To whom are you referring? I believe I do have a rapist, one or two assailants, and some other odds and ends currently in custody. Which is yours?"

His right eye twitched, but Thallium couldn't interpret the underlying emotion. "A woman. Dark hair. Mark on her hand that looks like that." He jerked a thumb toward the red-headed man's hand. On the back of it was The Gentleman's mark—a circle with two lines slicing through it on opposite sides.

Thallium assumed his poker face, the one that had won him many a game with dangerous men. But none of those men had been as dangerous as The Gentleman. "Hmm. Yes, I believe she was brought in for crimes against The Disc early this morning."

"Is she okay?" asked the redhead, his voice even but hushed, as if he wasn't entirely sure how to use it.

The Gentleman turned his head to gawk at him, eyes wide. "Well now, that's not your concern, is it, Beo? My wishes are your concern and nothing else. My wish for you at this moment is to be silent and look intimidating while I babysit your hide. I'll inform you when that changes." His voice grew quiet, and he seemed to drag each of his next words through mud. "You hear me?"

Beo's features went flat again. His decorative scars possessed more personality than his expression. The yellow-eyed Marauder leaned his chair back and hissed at Beo behind The Gentleman's back.

Thallium slid his reply into the tense space. "I can't give her to you. Not yet, anyway. I need her."

The Gentleman laughed, a wheeze from his throat. "For what? She ain't exactly good company for your city folk. Won't work for you, neither. Not if she's the same stubborn mule she used to be."

"What I need her for is my business." Thallium shrugged. "But when that business is over with, I'll kill her for you myself."

Beo's mask fell once more, and a growl started deep in his chest as he glared at the Principal. Dal and Prady shifted forward in their seats, their shoulders desperate to get in front of Thallium.

The Gentleman sucked on his teeth. "Now, did I say I wanted her dead? Course not. I said I wanted her back. Alive."

Thallium's business casual tone faded. He leaned over the table, close enough to the Marauders that he could smell the unbathed funk emanating from them. "She tried to kill my son. I will end her life for that. This isn't up for discussion."

The Gentleman wheezed out another laugh. "Oh, I'd say everything's up for discussion." He reached into his jacket, and Dal stood fast, sending his chair flying as he prepared to launch himself across the table. Beo leapt to his feet and reached for Dal's throat, eyes burning with indignation.

"Down, boys!" The Gentleman took a copper flask out and brandished it.

Dal and Beo pulled back. Dal looked sidelong at Thallium, who shook his head in response. Dal picked his chair up and sat once more, his foot now tapping against the dirt floor rapidly.

Beo slowly sat as well. The rage in his eyes had been snuffed out instantly.

"And when I say everything is up for discussion," carried on The Gentleman after taking a sip from the flask, "I of course am including our mutual agreement regarding the Border Valley. Maybe it's not as dandy as I thought."

Thallium barely managed to keep his reaction in check. The territory just outside of The Disc belonged to The Gentleman, as far as the Marauder clans were concerned. It had been that way for decades. When Valcin senior started building The Disc, he'd struck a deal with The Gentleman after his Marauders had raided their settlement for the third time—leave us alone and we'll provide you with a tax of supplies and valuables every season. It worked; the raids stopped.

Over time, as The Disc had grown both in economic status and manpower, there had arisen the very tangible possibility of all-out war in the absence of such a peace agreement. To avoid this, Thallium continued to pay the tax every quarter, degrading as it was. He had things in the works currently that he hoped would take care of this disgraceful situation, but in the meantime, he'd have to play politics.

The Border Valley was plotted out as the neutral zone between the outlands and The Disc; any affront therein would result in immediate dissolution of the agreement and, most likely, bloody conflict. If such a conflict were to erupt, even though Thallium would of course win, The Disc would lose countless resources and valuable prestige, wiping out the work he'd put into building the city up as the most desirable destination in the known world. It would be just another settlement, a podunk village with a nice wall. And Thallium's father would elbow Satan in the ribs and say, "I told you he'd fuck it up."

Of course, Thallium couldn't let that happen. His hand went to rest on the outside of his pants pocket, considering diving in for the vial within. He began to wonder how to distract the Marauders long enough to slip it into The Gentleman's flask. The Gentleman interrupted his brainstorming.

"Your daddy and I worked real hard to craft that agreement several decades ago." The Gentleman took off his hat and held it to his chest. "I'd hate to see it in jeopardy because you weren't willing to help out an old friend."

Thallium took a licorice root cigarette out of his vest pocket, and Prady lit it for him with a match from the folds of his robe. A showy stream of spicy smoke came out as Thallium spoke.

"We're more business associates, wouldn't you say?"

The Gentleman waved his hat through the smoke before donning it once more. "Associates, friends. Both are preferable to enemies."

"I don't disagree. But I want you to consider who you're threatening."

"I know exactly who you are. Thallium Valcin, Principal of The Disc, master of this shit-air-breathing paradise and protector of the region. And I know who your son is—the Bastard of the Desert. My man here," he tipped his head toward the skinny Marauder, "told me he wasn't lookin' too good when he saw him this morning. He make it? Because if so, you best know I'm threatening not only you, but him. Bone of your bones."

Thallium dragged on the cigarette through his teeth as the threat hung in the air. Finally, he broke the silence, his voice barely above a whisper.

"Your *slave* only got close enough to see my son because he crossed into the neutral zone bearing his weapon. The sole reason he didn't attack was because he was outmatched. That means, *friend*, that the only affront thus far has been yours."

Thallium flicked his cigarette just past the skinny Marauder's face, sending several sparks to land on his bare skin. The Marauder smirked.

"Regarding your threat," he continued, "the terms of the contract state that it can only be dissolved if there's an assault by one party on the other. There's been no assault, and my son is none of your concern. Caster's only relation to me is by blood, not by choice these days. He has nothing to do with the arrangement between The Disc and your clan."

"Oh, he has everything to do with it," exclaimed The Gentleman as he stood. "I know what it's like to have a child scorn you. The woman you have in custody isn't just some prisoner—I think of her as my daughter." He thumped his palm over his heart. "A disobedient daughter, for certain, but my kin all the same. I will do anything to bring her home, as you would for your son." He leaned over the table and slammed his palm down on it hard. "When you keep my daughter from me, you can be damn sure I'll take your son from you if I get the chance. Last I checked, he likes to come out of the city pretty often. I'm sure I'll get that chance."

Thallium stood, and as he did, the bodyguards all rose to their feet. "You would have war over this woman?" he yelled.

The Gentleman tsked. "Seems as good a reason to go to war as any. I do believe it would be a quick war—I'm sure I could persuade my fellow Masters to call their clans to arms. How long do you think you'd last in your city if you can't let folks in to trade?"

Thallium laughed. "You overstate your organization. Masters aren't known for working together."

"You underestimate our capabilities. Things are changing, Valcin."

"You aren't just animals and murderers anymore?"

"Oh, we're both of those, indubitably. But we also realize the world is changing. Civilizations such as yours are starting to take root all over, and we Masters have started to accept that we can't forever remain lost boys with pointy sticks desperate for something to poke. Someday, we'll have to unite. And if you cross me, that day might just be closer than we thought." A grin broke out, revealing his big, bright teeth.

The vial seemed to pulse in Thallium's pocket, pounding against his thigh to get out. But the window had passed. There was no slipping it anywhere now, not without the risk of infecting himself. The arrangement with The Gentleman would have to stand. At least until Wren's power was realized; Thallium would stomp the Marauder's heart from his chest then.

The Principal found his composure and rested his hands in his pockets. "In the interest of keeping our arrangement intact, you have my word—once I'm finished with the prisoner, I'll hand her over to you. Alive."

"Outstanding." The Gentleman clapped once loudly. "You have until noon exactly two weeks from today. My men will be camped just inside the Border Valley near your front gate. You won't see us, but we'll see you. Everyone that goes in and comes out. If I see something I don't like, or if the clock expires and I still don't have what you've promised, we'll meet again. But this time, it will be when your city has been under siege for six months and you're begging me for mercy while your people starve."

"That won't be necessary."

"Then I look forward to continuing to do business with you." He held out his hand.

Thallium's fingertips grazed the vial a final time as he took his hand from his pocket and shook the Marauder's.

Without another word, The Gentleman headed for the door. The skinny Marauder picked Thallium's cigarette up from the ground and took a long pull from it as he walked around the table. He coughed and twisted his lips in disgust as he put it out on Beo's arm. Beo didn't react. The two Marauders followed their Master out of the room.

Thallium waited for the door to click completely shut before throwing the table over. "Son of a bitch!"

———————

Being back in his kitchen to have breakfast with his wife brought Gavel a peace so deep he could feel it in the floor beneath his feet. The kitchen was the warmest room in the house, small and practical, with cabinets arranged in an L on one side and a recessed fire pit and little round table with three chairs on the other. Asha's cross collection covered the wall space above the fire pit, each unique. Wood, metal, and painted clay, all holding memories of where she and Gavel had picked them up on their travels.

A cobbler sat on the kitchen table, sunken in the middle, slices of apple swimming in the sugary juices like they were drunk and lost. Asha had left it there overnight, untouched. Gavel sat at the table, wiping his bow string with a soft cloth while his wife, who looked particularly fine in just an old T-shirt of his, added a little more water to thin out the oatmeal cooking in the pot hanging over the fire in the alcove behind him. He eyed the ruined dessert and took a break from his work.

"Do you want me to throw it out?"

"No. That would be wasteful," she said, adding a precious bit of sugar from a cloth bag to the pot.

He reached for the pan. "I'll try to eat some of it then."

"No. It's ruined."

He pulled his hand back and closed his mouth before something he'd regret could come out.

She sat next to him at the table, setting two mugs, a glass jar, and a pitcher of hot water down. Roughly, she scooped coarsely ground coffee from the jar into both mugs, and then proceeded to drizzle hot water onto them.

"I'll go by his place this morning, ask him to come to medical," Gavel said.

"Don't. He's on his three-day. It'll be back to training soon enough, and training with you, no less. Leave him alone and let him relax how he wants. He'll come if he feels like it."

He picked up a small chunk of wax from the table and ran it up and down his bowstring. "But he told you he'd come by. It's disrespectful."

"He's not my son, Gavel. He can disrespect all he wants." She stirred the coffee in her cup rapidly, banging all over the interior of the cup.

He set the wax down and reached for her. She slid her hand down her coffee cup and into his.

"You're worried," he said.

She nodded.

"About what exactly? He's recovered. He's home. Are you worried he'll not want to stay in the Body after what happened out there? That he'll want to return to his old way of life?" He had his own concerns about that possibility, but he hadn't wanted to worry her with it until after he'd asked Caster about it. Which he'd intended to do last night.

"Of course not. It's not like a brush with death is unfamiliar to him. I seriously doubt this one will do him in. But something isn't right. He healed better than perfect and I have no idea why. Then when that outlier came by, he seemed, I don't know, different."

"Different how?"

She thought briefly and then shook her head, tossing her curls like springs. "I don't know. Forget I said anything."

He fell quiet and sipped his coffee. He knew her well enough to know she needed to think and wouldn't elaborate until she was ready, which could take minutes to weeks, depending on how much she was processing something.

"Maybe," she started again, "it's just that I haven't seen him that way with any person since before Reina died."

"You mean happy?"

"Not exactly. But he goes years without letting anyone in, and then he gets this look on his face when she walks in the med ward."

"A look?" The corners of his lips turned down as he tried to keep the smile from his face.

"Shut up. I'm not crazy. He looked...concerned."

"That's a bad thing?"

"We don't know anything about her. He could get hurt."

"He'll be fine. Outlier or not, she's not dangerous. I saw the pair of them—the dangerous one's locked up."

"You're probably right." She retreated to her thoughts again, then her words came out in a quiet rush. "He said he'd come last night. I bribed him, and he still didn't come." She pushed the cobbler dish another six inches away. "Is it me?" She said the last part like a secret written down but not intended for reading.

He squeezed her hand before releasing it to rub the wax into the string, running it between his fingers and feeling it warm against his skin.

"He loves you. He's just trying to figure out what he wants, what he's supposed to be doing. It's a frustrating process. Makes us mad."

Caster had been mad for a long time now. Gavel was a patient man, but he felt God tested him most with Caster. Gavel had changed his diapers and rubbed olive oil on his scalp during bouts of cradle cap, but when Thallium entered his life,

Caster had distanced himself from Gavel. Over the years, Gavel came to accept that his role as substitute father had ended. But Asha was now standing in for Reina. He wished he could spare her the rejection of a grown child.

"He'll come around," he said. He hoped he was right.

She tapped her cup in a fast rhythm. "Honey," she started.

He stopped rubbing the string and stared at her. "Uh oh. What is it?"

She got up to stir the food. She spoke toward the pot, sliding her words into the morning as casually as possible. "Do you think it's weird that right after the Principal and his android leave, Caster wakes up and bounds toward recovery?"

Coffee slid down his throat slowly. "His recovery is definitely surprising, but I won't question a good thing."

"That's the prob—" she cut herself off. "Doesn't it seem a little too good to be true? They come in and bam, he's fucking peachy?"

He set his cup down and twisted in his seat to look at her. "What are you implying?"

She hung the large wooden spoon she'd used to stir the oatmeal next to the pot and walked over to him. She bent over and placed her hands on either side of his face.

"What if the Principal is hiding technology that could be saving lives?"

Gavel stood like something had stung him and walked around the table. He took a breath and counted to three before replying. "We've had discussions like this time and again. You always think he's scheming. But the fact remains—he is our Principal. He's my *leader*. I won't dishonor him or his reputation with conjecture."

"And if I got proof? What then?" A glimpse of her fury slipped out.

"I suppose I'd have to ask you what you intended to do with

that proof. Claim the technology for wide use? Convince the city our Principal is the monster you see? It's not treason for him to keep something hidden from his people if he believes there's good reason to do so."

"Good reason? There is no good reason to let people die when they don't have to. He's a psychopath bent on—"

"Enough," he said firmly, barely above a whisper. It was the tone he used to correct his men when they were out of line, and he hated that it had come out of his mouth at his wife. "You're convinced he's a villain because you want him to be. He was terrible to Reina and an irresponsible father—I acknowledge that. But he's our leader, personal life aside."

She paused, and Gavel didn't meet her gaze even as he felt it consume him. When she finally did speak, he realized he'd been holding his breath.

"Your unfailing loyalty has blinded you, my love," she said. "Have you forgotten the consequences of following your leader without question? Have you forgotten Kino?"

He grit his teeth and closed his eyes. "It wasn't following orders that brought those consequences; it was questioning them. I'll never forget that. It's history I don't want to repeat."

And it was a history he carried on his shoulders, an iron weight reminding him of the power of his decisions. Going behind his commander's back—an action utterly counter to his upbringing—had cost Asha the two people she loved most. He wouldn't do it again.

He felt her move closer to him. The urge to reach out and pull her to his chest struck him, but she would likely push him away. He settled for opening his eyes.

She'd stretched up on her toes and gotten right under his face. There was no malice there, just his wife, her eyes heavy from a night of unsettled sleep. The smell of sage oil in her hair made him relax his shoulders. "All I'm asking is that you try to be objective. If he is up to something, your duty is to our people first. Not a title."

The oatmeal bubbled over, sending goop down the sides of the pot. She started toward it, but he stopped her.

"I'll get it," he said.

He grabbed a towel and took the pot from the fire, then set it on the stone floor and scooped out two bowlfuls before returning to the table with the food. She'd sat back down to her coffee and looked as if she'd just lost another night's sleep in one conversation. She was hunched over and staring at the cobbler. A piece of the crust fell into the sunken center of the dessert, floated for a second, and then descended to the soggy bottom.

He set their bowls down and then swept the thick curls back from her neck and sighed against her skin. She turned and kissed him, pressing her lips into his with the familiarity and constancy of the sun rising every day.

"I'm glad you're back," she said next to his cheek. "Let's make the most of your three-day."

He whooped, swept his wife from her chair, and tossed her over his shoulder on his way to the bedroom. She laughed, still giggling under his touch after a quarter century together. It had been a long six weeks.

———

"Get out," Mainstay addressed the guard unit watching the wall of screens in the surveillance room of the prison. The tiny room was illuminated only by the black and white footage. The robot turned, the picture of right angles and straight lines in a mockery of the human form, and walked up to the Soldier.

"What is your directive?" the unit asked. It sounded like it was speaking through a tunnel. Its large eyes, discs of nauseating yellow, stared lifelessly at Mainstay as it issued its programmed inquiry.

"I said, get out, you creepy tin can."

"Directive not recognized. What is your directive?"

Mainstay flicked the unit's right eye. "Directive 636. Principal's orders."

He pushed past the unit with a swipe of his new arm. The unit caught itself on the doorframe and then stepped into the hallway.

The monitors in the surveillance room went all the way to the ceiling. They showed every cell, every path, every latrine. It wasn't a very large prison, as they didn't often take prisoners. Each cell utilized blue laser containment. The Main House used the most power in The Disc, around 50% of what the solar panel fields generated, if the rumors were true. Another 35% was devoted to keeping things like essential equipment, store signage, and ambient lighting in government buildings going. That left 15%, and every bit of it went to the prison's surveillance and containment fields. The building was a power-sucking edifice.

All for outlier scum.

The prisoners they kept were always outliers. If a Disc civilian committed a crime, their punishment was typically some form of community service or a removal of certain luxuries. Someone in prison sucked resources rather than creating them, and everyone in The Disc had to contribute.

If the crime of a citizen were truly terrible, murder or rape or some other form of inexcusable behavior, they were banished, thereby cleansing The Disc of evil and dumping it outside to be dealt with later by those unfortunate enough to leave the walls of the city. The crimes of a select few, those with connections to particularly good mind-altering substances or uncles with deep pockets, would be forgotten like a dream upon waking. Not many were so lucky.

But Thallium and others up the chain thought that banishing criminal outliers didn't solve a problem—they'd be right back like stray cats. Instead of just killing them all, they threw them in here. And the waste drove Mainstay mad.

He scanned the monitors, starting at the top and moving from left to right. They only had a few prisoners. One—a man with a swollen belly—scratched at his face, picking patches of skin off as he walked in circles. Another alternated between punching the concrete of the wall over his cot with shouting obscenities in some kind of masochistic meditation ritual. All of the prisoners were male but one. She stood out.

Survivor stretched in her cell, flat on her back with her feet to the ceiling. She reached up and took hold of her toes as her tattered dress fell down, revealing strong thighs.

Mainstay's wife had refused to share his bed the night before. She didn't believe his version of how it had happened— a woman, more animal than human, viciously attacked him when he tried to help her. He'd lied before. She thought his prosthetic was the wrong skin tone—didn't match his remaining arm. She didn't want it touching her.

He flexed his new hand open and closed. Even though it wasn't his shooting hand, it needed to function just as well. The non-dominant hand was still used to control the weapon, and if his aim was affected, he'd be removed from his Body and assigned a new job. He could end up in the agricultural sector, digging in dirt as hard as concrete with his wife, who possessed an inhuman ability to talk no matter her level of activity.

It would be the outlier's fault.

He zoomed in on her and panned the camera down to get a better look. He hated how they were feeding her, how they'd given her a pillow.

She lowered her legs back to the ground and eyed the camera. Then she got up and walked to the corner of the cell housing it. With enthusiasm, she shimmied and bounced around, putting on a show. Then she leapt several feet in the air.

Mainstay stumbled back from the screen.

She hung from the camera, filling the lens with flashes of ragged fingernail beds until she dropped back to the ground. The camera was now twisted at an angle, the world it observed turned on its side. She went back to stretching, giving the sideways camera a view of her ass for good measure.

"That's the sister, huh? I'm surprised she only took your hand," said the Principal from the doorway.

Mainstay jumped and then fell into an awkward bow.

Thallium closed the door behind him, giving Mainstay a moment to regain his composure.

"You want me to arrange a private meeting?" Thallium asked. He stepped up to the monitors and studied her, this newest addition to his zoo of freaks.

Mainstay tried to calm the pounding in his chest. "Would you?"

Survivor bent over and began biting and tearing at the nail on her big toe.

Thallium stuck his tongue out as if the image were a foul taste. "Unfortunately, I can't. Not yet. I still need her."

"For what?"

The Principal hesitated. "Leverage. I can't sanction her death."

"What if it happened by accident? A prison riot, maybe?" Mainstay's gaze went back to the monitors, taking in the sight of the five men, three of which were quite large and fit.

Thallium sidled up next to him, watching the screens as well. "That would be detrimental. To be clear, she's under my protection." He turned from the screens to face the Soldier. "Is that understood?" Mainstay noticed the dark circles under his eyes and how his hair looked as if he'd slept on it in that ponytail and hadn't combed it since. He stank of cigarettes.

"Yes, sir. Understood," said Mainstay.

Thallium's disposition lightened just a fraction. He reached up and scratched at a smudge on one of the screens with his fingernail. "Based on Gavel's report, I gather you completed your recon of Hallund?"

"Yes, sir." He stood a little straighter, glad he'd shaved that morning. "They've cut off the contaminated water. It won't be long before they come to you for help."

"You confirmed they've quarantined their sick?"

"Yes. The elder in charge of containing the outbreak said they don't want to risk spreading it to other settlements."

"As expected. Too bad. But it doesn't matter now anyway."

"Sir?"

Thallium put a hand on his shoulder. "I know you were expecting your next assignment, but I have to ask you to wait."

"Why? We need to move on to the next settlement, start the—"

"I know what the plan was, but it's changed. It's my job to look at the bigger picture. Something fortuitous has come along, a superior path forward. Take a break. Go back to telling your Head the truth. If I need you, I'll tell you."

"But what about..." Mainstay sputtered.

Thallium smacked himself on the forehead. "The rest of your payment! Of course. Here." He took several brass coins and a small card from the pockets of his tight pants. He dropped the coins into Mainstay's hand, but as he was about to turn over the card, he tugged it back.

"I hope I don't have to remind you not to let this addiction interfere with your work. It's back to your Body as usual in three days, and if your Head finds out, I won't be able to save your job. Not without raising suspicion, which I refuse to do."

Mainstay nodded and held his hand out.

Thallium pressed the card into his palm, and Mainstay read it with fervor. "A 3 a.m. meet time? How am I supposed to meet then without my wife finding out?"

"You're a sneaky man. Be sneaky."

With that, the Principal turned to leave.

"Sir," Mainstay called after him.

Thallium half-turned. "Mmm?"

"About your leverage. If something beyond your control happened?" He looked between Survivor's monitor and the Principal.

Thallium seemed to ponder that, but then said, "Nothing is beyond my control, nor my knowledge. If something happens to her, I will toss you into the Open myself." He turned and left.

The guard unit came back into the room. "Directive 636 accomplished. What is your new directive?" Its right eye flashed off and on.

Mainstay shoved the card into his pocket.

"Directive unconfirmed." The unit crossed the room and took up its requisite position at the monitors, its jointed neck tilted back as it stared at the screens blankly.

Mainstay watched Survivor curling up to sleep on her cot as he addressed the unit. "I have your new directive."

CHAPTER SEVEN

"Miss Wren, I've brought your breakfast. May I come in?" said Prady's voice on the other side of Wren's bedroom door.

She stood from the bed, which she'd bravely tried last night, and quickly crossed the room. She threw the door open. "What is my 'breakfast?'"

Prady's gaze dipped to the covered silver tray balanced on his left hand. "Uh, well, today it's eggs, toast, fruit, and coffee."

"Oh!" she exclaimed. "It's food!"

"Yes, it's food," he said through lips begging to curl into a smile.

He stepped in, staff making the now familiar clack along the floor, and set the tray down on the bed. It sunk just slightly into the plush white comforter. He took the domed cover off, and Wren carefully crawled onto the bed next to it. She looked at the triangular pieces of toast from every angle, holding them up toward the light from the window, and poked the eggs repeatedly until the yellow part broke and spilled its creamy liquid across the plate. The dark liquid in the mug was too hot to drink and scalded the tip of her tongue when she sipped it. She blew on it and tried again, and this time the bitter liquid was just warm. Her nose scrunched up when she tasted it.

"It's not for everyone," chuckled Prady. "If you do try to drink it, go slowly. I'm guessing you've never had caffeine before."

"I thought you said this was called coffee?" she said, trying another sip and having the same negative reaction.

"It's coffee, but it has caffeine in it that makes you wake up."

"I'm already awake." She eyed the drink suspiciously.

"How about you stick with the water for now." He took the mug from her and set it down on the tray.

She turned her attention to the plate and began shoving its contents into her mouth, mixing flavors and liking the way they combined.

"No hurry, miss," said Prady. "It's not going anywhere."

She slowed her pace, but her stomach already felt heavy and strange, like she'd been spinning around in the heat of the day. The sensation lessened a little when she sipped some water. Then something pushed against her abdomen and climbed up her throat, making her grab at her chest in alarm. She opened her mouth to scream, and instead, an echoing reverberation came out. Her hands flew to her mouth as her stomach calmed and she began to feel better.

Prady burst out laughing, but quickly clapped a hand over his mouth and regained his composure. He bowed his head. "My apologies. You just surprised me."

She grabbed at her throat. "What was that?"

"The common term is a 'belch.' You'll be just fine." He picked up his staff and turned to leave, but she stopped him.

"All of this is for me?" Wren asked. "Don't you want some?"

He held his hand up. "No, no. That's yours, miss. Not to worry—I had my own meal this morning."

"Would you stay and sit with me at least? I'm not used to being by myself."

He gave a soft smile and sat gingerly on the foot of the bed, resting his staff on the inside of his elbow. "Of course."

She took smaller bites of food and they sat in silence for a minute or two, but then he started to shift his weight, crossing and uncrossing a foot over a knee. He seemed not to know what to do with himself, and Wren realized he probably wasn't often offered a chance to sit in his job. She searched for a topic, and the first one she came up with was Caster.

"Have you known Caster a long time?" she asked.

He sighed, and Wren couldn't tell if it was out of nostalgia or irritation.

"All his life," he replied.

"Did you used to protect him, too?"

"I used to try. But he never needed, or wanted, my protection."

"Why not?"

"I'm not sure I know."

"Sounds like you do, though. Or have an idea, at least."

He let out an uncomfortable chuckle of air as if she'd caught him in a lie. "He's always been independent. Up until a few years ago, his priority was preparing himself to be the future leader of The Disc, and he wanted to emulate Principal Thallium to that end—show only strength and power, no fear and no regrets."

"But then his mom died," she realized aloud.

He let out a long, sad sigh and lowered his voice. "Yes. She did."

"That can change everything."

"Death absolutely can." Just then, his age peeked through,

and his shoulders hunched under the weight of it. But by the time Wren blinked, it was gone.

"Do you think he would come to see me?" she asked.

"Caster? Would you like for me to ask him?"

She smiled. "Yes. That would be helpful."

He inclined his head to her. "Very good, miss." The black bracelet on his wrist beeped—three fast chirps. He lifted it toward his mouth. "Prady."

"Good morning," came Eydis' voice through the bracelet. "I'd like to show Wren around the lab soon. Bring her to the foyer."

"Right away, ma'am. She's just finishing her breakfast."

Wren stuffed one final bite of toast in her mouth, and when it caught in her throat, she dared to go for a swig of coffee. She swallowed hard and stood. "People really drink that on purpose?"

"I much prefer tea, myself." He waved toward the door. "Shall we?"

They traversed the now familiar path from her bedroom, down the staircase, and into the entryway.

"Over here!" came Eydis' voice from across the room.

They found her standing by another staircase at the back of the artifact collection, wearing a cream jacket with a stiff collar and a pair of bright white pants. Her hair was tied up in a bun, with just a few strands falling out of it. She held a book and pencil in one hand.

As they closed the distance to her, Wren looked over at Prady.

"You'll be here when I get back?" she asked.

He hesitated. "I have some other things to do. Eydis can take you back to your room. She'll call me if I'm needed."

"Good morning, Wren," said Eydis.

Wren didn't respond.

"Humans say *good morning* at this time of day. You should say *good morning* back," said Eydis.

"I know. I just didn't know if the rule was different for androids," said Wren quietly, hugging her arms to her chest.

"Don't think of me as being any different from you, little one. We're more alike than you might think." Eydis tucked Wren's hair behind her ear, just barely stroking her face as she pulled her hand back. "We're going downstairs today. Would it be all right if I showed you a few things?" she asked.

Wren nodded absently, distracted by how smooth and creamy Eydis' skin was. Her lips were a different color than they were yesterday—redder and darker. She was the most beautiful thing Wren had ever seen. The Principal had said she wasn't real, but she looked real.

"Come with me." Eydis went to the stairs and started down them, not looking back.

Wren wavered, turned to Prady, and gave him a wistful look.

He shooed her along. "You'd better go."

She wasn't entirely sure she wanted to, but then she also wasn't entirely sure she had a choice. After a quick wave to Prady, she ran to catch up to Eydis.

The staircase seemed to continue endlessly. Six flights later, they came to level ground. It was cooler down here, almost as cold as the deeper parts of the cave. The lights in the floor glowed blue and emitted no heat like those in the long tunnel Wren had followed to see the judge. A heavy metal door stood closed before them, cast in more blue light from the floor that crawled halfway up its silver face.

Eydis walked up to a square panel in the wall next to the door, perforated all over with tiny circles. "Operator, confirm voice command 278."

"Voice command confirmed—Eydis for entry. Passcode?" came the reply.

"Passcode: Kepler."

"Passcode confirmed. Cleared for entry."

Something behind the door clanked and boomed, the clamor of machinery letting loose its grip. The door slid up, and they stepped inside.

The room was full of silver tables, cabinets and sinks, and numerous machines with blinking lights and whirring parts. Bright white light emanated from long round tubes running across the ceiling, illuminating the worktables. It smelled sharp like vinegar, but with a subtle, underlying tinge of feces.

"Please, please stop pecking my knuckles!" said a voice toward the back of the room, the owner of which was partially hidden from view behind a large wire cage. "No, come back! Miriam!"

The sound of scratching on metal, and then a skitter of nails on the floor. Down the aisle between the worktables ran a mottled black and white bird, its wings flapping as if it were frantically trying to take to the air. It reeled when it got to Eydis and Wren, sending tiny feathers up in a poof of surprise. Eydis tucked her book and pencil under her armpit and then bent down, plucked the bird up, and held its wings against its body.

A lady came down the aisle chasing after the bird. She had long, straight black hair and wore eyeglasses. Her skin was caramel-brown, and she stood tall and lean when she came to a halt in front of Eydis.

"Thanks, Eye. People say chickens are dumb, but Miriam always beelines for the door. I don't know why she's upset with me today. I spent all afternoon with her yesterday." The lady took the bird and held her up close to her face. "Who's a moody bird? You are!"

"Why are you here? Weren't you assigned to field research today?" Eydis asked.

The lady, who looked no older than Wren, tucked the chicken under her arm and stroked the bird's chin. "Yes ma'am, but I don't have any field work to do currently. Plus, I've been making progress—I think we'll have our imitation *Gallus gallus* protein product in consumable form by the end of the year!" She raised and lowered her fist in a big pumping motion.

"Is anyone else with you down here?" Eydis asked.

The lady deflated and went back to stroking the tiny feathers at the top of Miriam's chest. "No, ma'am. It's just me. Is there anything I can help you with today?" She looked back and forth between Eydis and Wren as if searching for clues.

"That won't be necessary," said Eydis. "This is Wren. You may see her down here from time to time. She's helping me with some research for the Principal."

"Nice to meet you, Wren! My name's Whiltierna, but everyone calls me Bug. I work with animals a lot. Including bugs. The other researchers nicknamed me and it kind of stuck. Not that I hate it or anything, but even if I did, there's no avoiding it. Anyway, I don't think I've seen you before. Are you new to The Disc? From Prast? Hallund? No, probably not—you probably grew up here. Though I wouldn't recognize you if you did. I just don't get out much." She gestured with her free hand at the stone walls and ceiling.

"Oh, seriously, Miriam?" She shifted the bird to her right arm and held out her left, which was now marred with thick brown and white droppings. "Excuse me," she said, "but I should go clean this off and put *someone* in her pen." She retreated down the aisle toward the workstation she came from.

"How about we look around? I'll show you a little bit of the future we're working toward," said Eydis.

She led Wren between tables covered in all sorts of equipment and materials—jars of different colored powders with long labels, glassware in various shapes and sizes, strange tools —all of which had purposes that were mysterious to Wren. Eydis paused at a large metal contraption on one of the tables. It looked like an elbow, curved and jointed.

"This is a prototype for a new water pump we're design-ing," said Eydis, pointing to the elbow on the table. "The goal is to pump water faster and run it through the purification system quicker so that people don't have to ration their supply as much. Currently, they're given a month's worth of water at a time, both drinking water and non-purified water, or 'slush water,' to bathe and wash with. It's a sparse supply. We simply can't recycle the water fast enough with our current capabili-ties. Even the non-purified water, while not fit for drinking, has to go through a cleaning process to make it usable."

"You want to get your people more water so they don't go thirsty," said Wren.

"Precisely! We care about the citizens and want to make their lives more comfortable."

"Like the cold squares in the Principal's water. Are you working to get those to the people too?"

Eydis scribbled something in her book. "Hmm? No, ice is not a current project."

"You just said you wanted to make your people comfortable."

"There's a difference between comfort and luxury. We can't afford to give luxuries to the masses."

"Then why are they given to the Principal?"

Eydis cleared her throat. "Because he makes sure the people have water. Understand?"

She didn't. But she nodded anyway.

They wandered through a few more tables, and Wren stopped at one covered in rows of small black discs no bigger than the size of her thumb. She reached out and touched the back of one, and it sprang open and hopped up on several tiny metal hooks like insect legs.

"Don't touch those, please," said Eydis.

"What are they?"

"Shock tablets. A type of defensive weapon used against criminals."

The one Wren had poked started crackling. Tiny strings of light danced between the little metal hooks.

"Do they hurt?"

She heard soft clucking nearby. Eydis turned toward it.

"Let's go see how Bug is doing."

They'd reached the far corner of the room, and it seemed to be Bug's own little kingdom of live things. Various animals were in a wall of glass cages, and a hodgepodge of potted plants in varying shapes and sizes took up nearly every bit of free space. It was all bathed in a warm, purple-blue light from overhead.

Bug sat bent over a worktable, and near her on the ground was Miriam's cage. The bird busied herself scratching about on a bed of dry grass, fenced in all around by wire and a domed roof to keep her from escaping. Bug used a small metal tool to pick up a tiny piece of pale pink flesh from a larger mound of pink stuff. She carefully placed the piece onto a rectangle of glass, and then slid the glass onto a platform illuminated from beneath and peered into a tube positioned above it.

"The makeup of the imitation *Gallus gallus* is remarkably accurate," Bug said, not to anyone in particular.

"*Gallus gallus*?" said Wren.

Bug backed off from the device. "Duh, Bug. Scientific names aren't very well known." She smacked herself on the head a couple of times. "*Gallus gallus* is chicken. Like my Miriam." She looked over at the cage fondly as Miriam bobbed up and down to pick up bits of seed in the grass.

Wren leaned over the dish and sniffed.

"The texture," Bug poked the flesh in the dish with a pencil, "is a little loose. Not that I would really be the best judge of what texture of animal tastes best. Oh," she looked at Wren, "I'm a vegetarian. I love animals. Couldn't eat them if I wanted to. My dream," she hugged her arms to her chest, "is to someday acquire a *Bos taurus* specimen."

Wren blinked a couple of times.

"Right. Scientific names. Tough habit to break. What I should have said is that I want to have a cow someday."

Wren just stared at her.

"I guess most people don't know what those are anyway. They're big animals with white and black hair, hooves, and the most adorable faces you could imagine." She smushed her own cheeks between her hands. "The books I've read say that they smell, but I don't care. I don't judge."

"If you were to summarize what you do here, Bug," Eydis interjected, "it would be working to create renewable, healthy meat alternatives so that people can have protein to keep their bodies strong. Isn't that right?"

Bug moved her hands to her lap and sat up straighter. "For the most part, yes. But I also study plant genealogies, wheat and carrots and all those good things, to see what grows best here. I don't eat to live or live to eat, but food is my life because it ensures life for us. However, if I had to pick my true passion, it's biochemistry."

A quick flash of movement caught Wren's eye from one of the glass cages behind Bug, and she crossed over to it, pulled by her curiosity and a sense that she'd seen movement just like it before. Inside the cage was a sand-colored desert lizard about six inches long.

"You have a sand digger," Wren said.

Bug joined her and leaned closer to look inside. "Is that what you call those? I like that."

"They're everywhere in the Open."

"Yeah, they're very common. Reptiles and insects," she pointed at the other cages, "are the most abundant source of protein we have. I study them, too. I could never let someone eat Zanzibar here—he's a charmer." She tapped the glass, and the sand digger's eyes rolled over lazily, as though he were used to the disturbance of Bug's thumping finger and resented it just a bit.

"Wait a second," Bug said, spinning to face Wren, as if she'd only now gotten a joke. "How do *you* know they're in the Open? Have you been there?"

Wren nodded. "I'm an outli—"

"I'm afraid we're beginning to run behind," Eydis cut Wren off. "Thank you for showing us your work, Bug. We'll be in the inner chamber." She continued writing in her book, not looking up as she said, "Seeing as how you're here, though, I may call on you for assistance from time to time in my work with Wren. Would you be amenable to that?"

Bug squealed a tiny bit and failed to stifle a goofy smile. "A promotion, ma'am?"

Eydis finally stopped writing and studied Bug closely. "If you can swear you'll be discrete, then yes, I'll be sure the addition of this new responsibility is shown in your job profile and rewarded in kind. For today, we're not to be disturbed. Am I clear?"

Bug looked between the two ladies before nodding. "Yes, ma'am. Clear. Thank you, ma'am."

"Wren, this way." Eydis went to another heavy-looking door at the back of the lab.

Wren followed for a few steps but stopped when she

noticed a small cabinet with a glass door in the corner nearby. Inside were tiny, clear bottles with black caps containing dark pink liquid. Their labels were emblazoned with "R6" in big black script.

"What's in there?" Wren asked.

Eydis glanced where Wren was pointing. "Nothing we'll be working with."

Wren gave the cabinet a wide berth—the labels felt like eyes that followed her as she passed.

Eydis touched numbers on a screen by the inner door, which opened with a soft hiss, and they crossed through. The floor was inlaid with more blue lights. Wren couldn't tell how big the space was, but it felt large, so large that the openness and the quiet rang in her ears.

"Operator, lights on," said Eydis.

Small booms echoed as lights high overhead turned on. Those closest to them turned on first, followed by successive lights down the ceiling, until those at the far end of the chamber lit up.

They stood on a walkway of metal grating, which stretched all the way around the chamber, connecting at the far end where it disappeared into a glass-fronted room. Hefty armchairs lined one wall in the space below. Along the adjacent wall sat tables and big plastic boxes behind which were cabinets with glass doors. Opposing the line of chairs was a huge screen mounted high up on the wall. Most striking of all was the rectangular box in the center of the room, just the height and width of a man, with no visible door.

"Welcome to the inner chamber, a place full of history. Now that you're here, it's full of promise again." Eydis stroked the back of Wren's hair. "Let's go below."

She walked down a flight of stairs to their right, and Wren

followed, feeling the dust on the handrails cake onto her sweaty palms.

"What is this place?" she asked.

"Upstairs, we work to make everyone's lives a little easier and help our city run more efficiently. As you saw with Bug, we experiment and tinker until we're successful in creating a new strain of heat-resistant corn or a better way to pump water from the ground. Here," she put her book down on one of the work-tables, "we make all that seem like playing in the mud."

Eydis fell quiet, looking to the ceiling and then closing her eyes. Her deep, contented sigh made it sound like she'd just come home after being gone a long time.

Wren stood there awkwardly. She felt like she was watching something intimate and private, and when it became too much to stand, she quietly meandered toward the box in the middle of the chamber. As she stared at it, at its perfect symmetry and how the entire chamber centered around it, a strange sensation came over her. Not quite fear, but something like it. A gnawing anxiousness that compelled her to touch the glass. It was cold and smooth, and a film of dust came off on her hand as she pulled it back, leaving a clearer spot on the surface.

"An isolation unit," said Eydis close behind her. "One of the tools we use in our work down here."

"I still don't understand," said Wren as she turned around. "What work?"

Eydis smiled like a teacher at her student's endearing igno-rance. "Historically, the inner chamber has been used to make great leaps toward restoring the technology that once ran our world. We lost our research over a decade ago when a disgrun-tled lab assistant sabotaged it, and our work came to a standstill. The focus of this work was isolating a particular genetic marker, or special trait, that very few people have. You have this trait; we just have to wake it up."

"It's sleeping?" Wren asked slowly, feeling foolish as she did.

"In a manner of speaking."

"How do we wake it?"

"By going on a journey."

Wren shook her head. "I thought I have to stay here?"

"Not a physical journey. A journey into your subconscious."

"I don't understand. You've known other people with this trait? You woke them up?"

"We tried. Several times, in fact. But, as I mentioned, we were unable to finish our work. A tragedy really, considering the potential of our participants. Since then, we haven't come across anybody with the genetic marker. Not until you."

"What can I do?"

Eydis beamed and took hold of the sides of her face gently. "I believe there's a power in you. An incredible amount of power that could remake our world for the better."

Wren must have heard her wrong. "Power? In me?" Survivor's cackle bounced around in her head. "That can't be right."

Eydis released her. "Why not? You've already proven yourself to be powerful. You're here, fought your way through fire and the dangers of the Open."

"Not on my own strength."

"Then wouldn't you like to know what your own strength feels like?" Eydis said in a conspiratorial whisper.

An aching "yes" resounded in Wren, so strong it took her breath for an instant. She stepped away from the box toward the nearest chair—an oversized brown thing that looked like it might swallow her. Next to it was a squat table on which sat a curved piece of glass with long strings attached to it. "Will it hurt?"

"Absolutely not. Actually, I think you might enjoy it. Tomorrow, we'll explore your dreams. It's an adventure!"

Eydis' expression was dreamy, filled with supple lines of excitement. Wren tried to return the expression, but as Eydis turned to lead the way back up the stairs, her face fell. As they ascended out of the inner chamber, her stomach turned heavy and twisted. She didn't tell Eydis, but her dreams were never happy; they were dark, slinking things. Exploring them wasn't an adventure she wished to go on.

Sleep didn't come easily in this place. The square walls and rectangular cot made Survivor feel as if she were in nested boxes. The lights in here never turned all the way off—the long bulbs above her still gave out their fake glow, dimmer at night but always on, hovering over her like a sore she couldn't pop. In the connecting corridors, the other prisoners had grown quieter. Even the loudest eventually had to sleep, and with that came relief to her ears, to her muscles wound into knots as the prisoners constantly bitched and hollered for justice, for blood, for whatever they didn't have.

She tucked the old quilt they'd given her up over her head, shutting out the light and the remaining noise in the prison as it relaxed and settled to rest like old bones. Her fist tightened around the piece of concrete she'd chipped out of the decaying wall. It had taken a full day to get it free without breaking it, and half a day more to gently shape it into something sharp enough to do damage. The effort had cost her several finger-nails and made a bloody mess of her hands. She clutched the concrete shard to her chest as Wren had done with Biter not so long ago.

The Gentleman knew where she was. He would come.

The one solace she took was that cities didn't just let
Marauders inside, and the front gate of The Disc had been
several feet thick. She'd taken note of the guards patrolling the
top of the wall and knew that if they had any sense, they
patrolled not only the front gate but the entire perimeter. It
would be challenging for him to get in.

But far from impossible.

She and Wren needed to be gone before then.

As plans upon plans whirled in her head, she found herself
on the edge of sleep, brushing against the veil between reality
and the black on the other side. Blood pulsed in her ears—the
sound of demons whispering—and she pushed past it, one inch
closer to necessary rest.

Dreams came, images she'd started to slowly forget since
Alma took her in many years prior. But she somehow recalled
them again with biting clarity during sleep. A bonfire sent
bitter smoke to the stars above the desert. A white hat with a
stiff brim and a black band around the base floated in a void of
darkness, and in the darkness beneath the hat, brilliant white
teeth flashed as a mouth opened to laugh.

Then the dreams turned far worse. A circle of filthy men
laughed while they threw dice. Beo, a boy with red hair,
screamed and clung to Survivor's legs as he watched them fall
to double sixes before they took him from her. Then it was
night, and it was finally still. Little Beo's hair tickled her nose as
she slept curled around him. Morning came, and he woke with
that unbreakable smile, that display of naïve hope he retained
even once he'd grown into a young man. Her dream jumped
forward in time, and there were the cuts on his forehead—two
thin slices side by side with the sliver of skin between them
removed—the finishing touch of his initiation ceremony. The
Marauders cheered.

Her body wrenched awake as if she were catching herself

from falling, but an alarming sound kept her from jolting upward—unfamiliar voices in her prison cell.

"I don't know anything about killing. But the fat man said it'd cut time off my sentence," said a male voice. It was deep, as if it belonged to someone with a barrel chest.

"Then what are you good for? Just for show?" grumbled another voice. "I'll do it. Pull the blanket back and I'll cut her throat. Quick and easy."

"Why quick?" said a third voice. This one sounded nervous, but with the twinge of excitement of a pubescent kid getting ready to poke a dead body. "This is the first time we're out of our cells in months, and you want it to last a whole sixty seconds? Let's play with her first."

"I'm guessing that's what they locked you up for. Playing without permission," said the deep voice.

"What do you care? Pull the blanket off and let's see what we're working with before you cut her throat."

"Fine," hissed the impatient one.

Survivor tucked her thumb behind the back of the concrete shard. The blanket came off, and she shot up from the cot, jabbing the shard upward toward the closest face. She buried it in the big guy's eye. He was at least 300 pounds, and he reeled back and fell to thrash about on the ground, the concrete still protruding from his eye as he shrieked.

She rolled up to the balls of her feet on the cot as the other two men watched the big guy flail. They were smaller, showing their time in prison with dirty clothes and concave torsos. One had a stubby knife that he brandished at her while the other stared at her body, not once caring to look her in the eye. Behind them, the bars of her cell were down, and the doorway was open. Suddenly, a deafening tone went off in the prison, high and grating like a bird of prey squawking.

"Time's up!" the one with the knife said. He lunged for her, and she leapt off the cot, taking advantage of the bit of spring it gave her. She landed with her knees against his chest and took him to the ground to land with a heavy thud on his back. There was something satisfying about the smack of his skull against the dirt as she grabbed his hair and slammed it three times against the ground, hard, until he stopped moving. The knife she deftly took from his limp hand made the last man think twice about rushing her.

The bird continued to squawk. Just over the din, she could hear the clamor of guards running through the corridors above. Two of them appeared at the top of the stairs, and the man panicked. He went for her, fists going wild. One managed to land against the right side of her face, slamming her jaws together. He then threw his weight forward and his hands out to pin her to the ground, but she got the knife up in time. He fell on it, burying it in his stomach up to the hilt.

"I don't play," she said close to his ear.

His lips twisted with pain before he fell limp onto her chest, blood wetting her dress front in a warm, satisfying spread.

The guards made it to the base of the stairs, and the first went to a panel in the wall across from her cell and swiped the small silver card hanging around his neck against it. The panel opened, and he punched the buttons in a complicated sequence.

The second entered her cell and yanked the guy's corpse off her. He slapped e-binds on her wrists and pushed her down to sit on the cot before taking stock of the carnage around him. She reached up with her bound hands and felt a couple of her bottom teeth, which were now nearly horizontal. With a quick twist, she pulled one out, then the other, and threw them to the ground, adding a mouthful of blood for good measure.

The guard—a young guy based on the blemishes along the

bridge of his nose above his mask—watched all this among the bodies at their feet. He moved between the two still bodies, touched their necks, and gave a quick once-over to the big guy squatting on the ground, wailing, hand hovering near his still impaled eye. "Holy hell," he whispered before leaving to rejoin the other guard in the hall.

Just as Survivor was considering making a run for it, the squawking stopped, and the bars of her cell buzzed back to life. She tugged at her ears in an attempt to stop their ringing.

"What's going on? Why did the alarm sound?" shouted a voice through the guards' black bracelets.

The young one raised his bracelet to his mouth. "Prison riot."

As if he'd been up there just itching to see what had happened, the fat gunfighter called Mainstay plodded down the stairs and joined the men in the hall. "Any deaths?"

"Two dead, one injured," said the guard who'd entered her cell.

Mainstay looked in the cell at Survivor. She was covered in the blood of others, bodies on the ground, both of which seemed to thoroughly disappoint him. His chin jutted out, an outcropping of frustration.

She puckered her bloody lips at him.

He quickly turned away toward the guards. "How was her cell opened? Was there a malfunction? This is unacceptable! The Principal was clear that he does not want her harmed!" He ranted on and on, oblivious to the tall figure descending the stairs in inhuman silence—a skeletal giant out of a children's horror story. It walked up behind Mainstay.

"There was no malfunction of the security system," said the giant.

Mainstay jumped and turned around, peering up at the thing towering over him.

"Are you saying this was deliberate, Judge Gamma?" said Mainstay, regaining his red face. He stretched up on his toes and bellowed, "Someone here disobeyed the Principal's orders? Nobody would dare!"

"I have checked the system log—no malfunction was recorded. There was a shut off ten minutes ago in four cells. The access code belongs to RSU 13."

"One of *you* did this?"

"Not without orders. RSU 13 must have been told to open the cells."

"Impossible. It has to be faulty programming. It needs to be dispositioned. You failed here, judge. It's your job to see to it that prisoners fulfill the sentences imposed on them without incident, and you have failed. Secure this place—lock it down."

"Her sentence given by Principal Thallium was imprisonment, not death," said Gamma.

Mainstay shot his chin out again. "Yes, that's my point exactly. What are you trying to say?"

"The law is final. Nobody is above the law." Gamma stooped lower, searching Mainstay's eyes.

After no more than a few heartbeats of enduring Gamma's scrutiny, Mainstay addressed the guards. "You have work to do. Disposition that defective unit and secure this wing. I'll tell the Principal what happened." He stomped back up the stairs and slammed the door behind him.

Gamma stood as tall as he could in the space, still hunching his shoulders to keep from colliding with the ceiling. He looked toward Survivor, the two bodies at her feet, and the big guy whose wails had turned to hiccuping whimpers. The judge tilted his head and stared.

"Ensure she is cleaned up as well," he said to the nearest guard.

Before she could even stick her tongue out at him, he'd ascended the stairs, taking them three at a time.

Wren sat in a cushy recliner of soft cotton upholstery at the end of the row of big chairs. The huge screen mounted on the opposing wall stared down at her, currently dark. Eydis retrieved the piece of curved glass—a visor, she'd called it—from the side pocket of the recliner and dusted it off with the edge of her jacket. It was black and heavy-looking, stretching into three quarters of a circle.

"This is a VRI, a device designed in the early twenty-first century," said Eydis. "It's old technology, but it has many uses. We refurbished it for our research. It shows the wearer different things, usually whatever they want to see, creating its own sense of reality. You'll put this on, like so." Eydis put the visor on herself. It stretched over each ear and covered her eyes. As she set it in place, three little clicks sounded. She turned from side to side before pressing a small button on the device over the right ear. It clicked again, and she took it off and handed it to Wren. "Take a look."

Wren's hands sank into her lap with the weight of the visor. She examined the inside—its edges were cushioned with black foam, and a rectangle of iridescent glass stretched across the eye area. Foam rings circled the earpieces.

"Let's set you back—it can get heavy if you have to hold your head up." Eydis pulled the handle on the side of the chair, and it reclined. "Rest here and I'll help you put this on." She took the visor back as Wren settled into the chair.

"What will I dream about?" Wren asked.

"That's up to your mind. I'll be watching your dream up there," she pointed at the massive screen, "and I'll talk to you through the headset occasionally. Does that sound easy enough?"

Wren nodded.

"All right. Let's begin." Eydis put the visor in place on Wren.

Everything went dark and quiet, a tangible depth of emptiness that made Wren grip the arms of the recliner tightly.

"Can you hear me?" Eydis' voice came through the parts of the visor resting over Wren's ears.

"Yes."

"Good. Try to relax. I'm going to make the visor interface with your consciousness. This may pinch a bit."

Click, click. Sharp pains like freezing pinches went into Wren's temples. She yelped and started to sit up.

"Calm down, take a deep breath," said Eydis. "You'll start feeling better now."

Warmth spread from her temples and brow into her face and through her limbs. She loosened her grip on the chair's arms as the sensation flooded through her nerves.

"Wren, we're going to get started. I'm going to turn the visor on, and you'll start dreaming. Lose yourself in the dream. Try not to think much at all. Can you do that for me?"

"Mmm, yes," she sighed, relishing in the warmth as it finally hit her toes.

"Off we go."

A rush of color flooded the visor as a burst of wind came through the speakers. Wren's breath caught as a falling sensation overtook her, so strong it made her stomach flip. Dizziness swirled around her temples, accelerated by flashes of white. She nearly yelled out for it to stop when it did just that, cutting off the buzz of sensations like fingers shoved into ears.

Her feet pressed against the forest floor on a cushion of twigs and pine needles turned soft by the passing of time. The perfume of the forest filled her nostrils and soaked into her skin; musty bark, pine, and the faint taste of decay took her mind years into the past. She flexed her toes. The feel of the undergrowth between them slowed the racing of her heart. She turned her gaze up from her feet, taking in the sight of the forest around her and the faint rays of sun pushing through the upper limbs of the pines. The light of dusk turned the glade gray with a tinge of orange before darkness could overtake it.

A towering, aged pine stood close by. She reached out and touched it. It sent a current of life through her, saying "hello again" with the familiar scratch of wood on skin and the relentless stickiness of sap.

"Wren, can you hear me?"

She jumped. Eydis' voice floated somewhere up above, seeming to dance between the limbs and swim through the fading light.

"Can you hear me?" Eydis said again.

A fuzziness expanded over Wren's limbs, threatening to make her muscles fall asleep, as buzzing pulsed in her ears. "What's going on? I thought—where am I?" She fell to her knees and grabbed a fistful of undergrowth.

"You're fine. Listen to my voice. You're still lying down in the lab, and I'm here too, watching what you're seeing. If you fight the two realities, you'll throw off the system. You're in a dream. It's just dreaming."

The disorienting sensations receded slowly. Wren got up, using the tree for support.

"Feeling better?" asked Eydis.

"I think so."

"For the most part, I won't be speaking. I'm here if you get scared or want to talk, but try to let the dream play out. I'm only observing. I just want you to get used to this process. We won't push things too quickly. How does that sound?"

Wren heard a laugh, faint and lilting, from up ahead in the glade. Hanging from a lower limb of a young pine, upside down by the knees, was Mack, one of the youngest children. His chocolate curls danced as he swung back and forth, sending blood to turn his face pink. Kye, with pigtails of dark hair streaked with auburn, jumped below him. She sprinted to his perch, leapt when she thought she had a good angle, and tried to slap his hand. He tucked his stomach and dodged her touch, laughing at her, but she just kept coming. Kye huffed with each good leap and had her lips pursed together in a line of utter determination.

"Mack, hey! Over here!" Wren waved to them.

They stopped and turned toward her, faces brightening with recognition. Kye rushed her and threw her arms around her dirty skirt, with Mack just steps behind after he flipped to the ground. Other familiar faces started to appear as more kids came from between the trees. There was Jace, a boy a few years younger than Wren, who had grown tall and skinny as a sapling. Gully waved as she approached, wearing her usual array of wildflowers in her white-blond tresses. Sweet Pea and Quickstep came up next, the big sister holding her younger brother's hand as he beamed next to her.

Bringing up the back of the bunch was Survivor. She looked satisfied as she threw a pair of dead rabbits over her shoulder, letting them hang down her back. Her blowgun was tucked into her belt, and her hand traced its length. As she got closer to the kids, the familiar look of discomfort spread across her face and tucked her brow together. There, next to her with an outstretched arm to pat her on the back, was Alma.

Her thick, silver braid swayed behind her neck as she walked. Several large strands had escaped and poked out around her hairline in the same controlled chaos she wore every day. Her thin, white coat, tattered at the bottom, fluttered behind her as a breeze blew through the trees. The worn, boxy patchwork dress under it brought out the bright green of her eyes. She broke into a jog, leaving Survivor to watch her depart for the group.

The kids parted so Alma could make her way through. She put her hands on Wren's shoulders and looked her over. Her familiar wrinkles sent ripples of joy through Wren that made her chest squeeze. They hugged tightly. Alma rested her chin on top of her head as she often did. A weightlessness took over Wren, and she felt as though she were floating, relieved of the burden of grief and restored to the period of her life that had been filled with genuine joy.

The sensation didn't last long.

As they backed out of their embrace, the children started to scream. Tendrils of gray smoke stretched along the ground and over tree roots. The tendrils moved toward the center of the glade, reaching up with their tips to stroke the children's feet. Everyone scattered, panicked and skittering through the trees without thinking.

Alma ran this way and that. "Come back! Stay together!" she screamed. But the smoke rose up around her, filling her lungs and making her choke.

Wren tried to go to her, but her legs wouldn't move. She reached down and grabbed at her ankles to urge them upward before falling hard on her butt. Waves of heat carried on the wind surged into the glade from different directions.

Survivor sprinted to Alma with her blowgun at the ready. Alma put her hand to the weapon and pushed it away as she shook her head. She ran for Wren, and Survivor followed.

"Take her. Now," she said to Survivor, who nodded and wrenched Wren to her feet.

"No! Come with us!" Wren shouted, sputtering on the smoke.

Alma threw her arms around her. "Stay safe. Live your life. *Your* life, the way you want to." She kissed her forehead before a plume of smoke billowed between them, swallowing Alma.

Survivor turned and dragged Wren several yards in the opposite direction before Wren stopped and yelled, "I'm going back for her!"

Survivor opened her mouth to protest when smoke enveloped her in a great cloud, heavy like water, cutting off her voice. Wren turned and ran back as she always did in this nightmare—her unconscious mind refused to accept that she'd actually fled with Survivor. The heat was ever present now, oppressive and insulated against her skin by the smoke. The smell of burning wood and undergrowth flooded her nostrils, but more alarming was the scent of singed hair. She opened her mouth to call out, but only swallowed more smoke and ash. Huge cracks and booms echoed through the glade as trees burst from within and fell. A dull red glow grew brighter behind the smokescreen.

Straight above, a ponderosa exploded with an impressive death cry, relinquishing its top to meet the earth for the first time. The trunk fell across her path and sent up a great gust of air to clear the smoke beyond. She scrambled over the trunk—a shower of sparks crackled as her feet met the bark. On the other side of the tree knelt Alma. Her lower body burned as the fire slowly spread to her upper extremities. The dress and coat she wore vaporized, blown away like a ripple of sand across a dune. Her skin puckered and turned from red blisters to black ash in seconds.

Her voice rose above the chaos. "Leave. Don't come back."

The flames licked up her neck and overtook her.

Wren fell to her knees, reaching out toward Alma as she turned to black dust and blew away with two great gusts of wind. Then Wren's own outstretched arm caught fire. Pain shot through her as the fire consumed her, cooking her nerves and her flesh.

Blinding white light replaced the smoke and fire.

Eydis stood above Wren. She held the VRI visor and dabbed at Wren's forehead with a cool cloth. "It's all right. It wasn't real."

Wren turned onto her side in the recliner, curled into a ball, and wept.

CHAPTER EIGHT

EYDIS RELUCTANTLY APPROACHED THE OPEN DOORWAY OF
the Principal's gym. He was blasting horrible music from the
speaker system one of his Scavengers had recovered and
restored. This rap-rock song had been old when she was young,
and never palatable.

She had an update for Thallium on Wren, as well as
another message they'd just received from The Gentleman,
both of which made for an irritating meeting. She'd looked at
the message written inside the swan before carefully refolding
it—a brazen threat from an old self-declared demigod to a
younger one. Thallium hadn't informed her of the nature of
their meeting last week, but he'd come back to the Main House
in a rage. The affairs of men were tiresome things, nauseatingly
irrelevant distractions when there was important work to be
done. She'd have to pass the message along nonetheless and
hope Thallium's resulting tantrum wouldn't affect her work.

She cringed at the distorted guitar riffs and turntable
scratches assaulting her ears as soon as she entered the gym. A
collection of scavenged exercise equipment filled the space, the

most notable of which was an assortment of free weights that Thallium used daily.

He stood shirtless across the room, putting heavy, circular weights onto the bar of the bench press. The muscles of his back rippled each time he bent down and grabbed another one. Sweat dripped from his head and shone in a film on his bare skin. As he turned and straddled the bench, he saw her by the doorway.

He grabbed the little black remote from his waistband and held it aloft. The music grew quieter, and she unclenched her jaw.

"I'm sorry to interrupt," she said.

He waved her over. "I'm not going to stop, anyway." He lay back on the bench and found a comfortable grip on the bar above his head. He unseated the bar and slowly brought it toward his chest. "What is it?" he grunted.

She crossed the tile floor, which was dotted with old sweat that stuck on the bottoms of her bare feet, and stopped near the foot of the bench. "Another message." She held the swan aloft so he could see it.

He pushed the bar back up and said through an exhale, "Read it."

She opened the swan, pretending to discover how it unfolded for the first time. "Time's flying. Keep your word, boy."

He scoffed. "Toss it."

She crumpled the paper and tucked it in the pocket of her black harem pants.

"Progress with Wren?" he asked through a particularly energetic rep.

"Minimal, sir. She's still resisting the process. She's scared." All true, facts she delivered plainly with just an edge of sympathy. After all, he was so close to achieving his father's dream.

She hoped her tone would assuage the urgency he'd expressed for Wren's restoration, an urgency that had ramped up even beyond what she thought reasonable over the past few days. He was fixated on it, and furious. It showed when he brought Eydis to bed with him every night. It was as if he wanted to throttle someone beyond his reach.

Thallium heaved upward and dropped the bar, which crashed into place against the metal holders. "It's been a week! How is it you've gotten nowhere with her?" He sat up and grabbed the towel from the end of the bench and mopped at his face.

She kept her face a mask of calm. "We haven't gotten *nowhere*. I've asked you to be patient, sir. Without a caretaker, we have to do this exceedingly slowly to avoid shocking her system. If you push her too much too quickly, she might not just shut down emotionally, she could die."

He stood and wiped the sweat from his chest and armpits as he walked over to the recumbent bike in the corner of the gym. It sat next to the abandoned exercise ball and pink thigh toner. Nearby was a wall of mirrors behind the racks of free weights. Today wasn't cardio day, but he hopped onto the bike and worked his legs furiously, as if he were running from someone.

"What *do* you know? Have you found out *anything* yet?" he asked.

She picked up a glass bottle of water from its perch on a weight rack and handed it to him. "She's stuck in the same nightmare, with slight variations every time she goes under. I won't know what she can do if we don't get past this. She wakes herself before we've made any true progress in discovering her potential."

"Can't you sedate her more? I'm not running short on drugs. Use them." He guzzled from the bottle.

"If we sedate her more, we'll reach a toxic dosage that could make her heart stop. We could try the opposite and stimulate her with adrenaline, hoping that makes her move past the block in her mind. Again, that would stress her heart, and the sedation and adrenaline together could cause it to stop. All of that aside, we have another problem."

She took a skinny tablet bar from the depths of her pants pocket and pressed the power button on the end. The bar split in two lengthwise. She pulled the two halves of the bar apart and a tablet screen glowed to life between them. She scrolled through a set of files on the touch screen, selected one, and played it.

Wren was in a forest as it burned, huddled with children. White hands—the claws of unseen beasts—shot through the wall of smoke all around them and pulled children into the haze. Wren held her spear out to defend a little girl with dark pigtails gripping her hand. A claw reached out and grabbed the girl's foot, yanking her to the ground. Wren stabbed the puckered white flesh of the hand, whose unseen owner bellowed out in anger. Through the smoke appeared a white beast seven feet tall, with hunched shoulders and bulging green eyes.

Eydis paused the footage.

"There." She pointed at the beast's left shoulder and zoomed in.

On the front of the shoulder, just an inch out from the collarbone, was a mark—a capital V with the right half extended upward, cut through with another slash. The Valcin crest.

Thallium stopped pedaling.

"How is that possible? You said your assistant erased the Carriers' memories before she took them. That's why we have to restore Wren's abilities in the first place."

"Perhaps she didn't wipe Wren's memory thoroughly

enough. It's possible she's just seen the symbol since arriving and internalized it by chance. But it's also possible she's beginning to remember her past here, and we don't want her remembering the wrong things. She needs to focus on her abilities and, as I've said before, that is best done with a caretaker, someone to ground her during testing. If Caster would go into VR with her, then I believe she could restore her abilities. Once he comes, I'm sure the restoration will follow."

He stood and took the screen from her, staring at the frozen frame. Then he closed the screen, collapsing it into the bar again before tossing it to her. "Let her out of the Main House."

She slipped the tablet back into her pocket. "Sir?"

"Give her some space, but watch her. See where she goes. If I'm right, she'll go to my son. He's clearly determined to stay away, but he won't be able to any longer if *she* goes to *him*, and we'll finally have her caretaker. Nothing distracts a girl from her troubles like a boy, anyway. It's double duty. Two birds."

"It is surprising that he's kept his distance this long, but he's angry with you. If you just give him more time, he'll come on his own. We won't have to risk sending her out into the city by herself."

He took his towel back to the weight bench and mopped his sweat from the leather surface. "What are you afraid of? Think the people will kill her?"

A flippant joke about a very real threat. But he didn't view his people as dangerous. He saw humanity as lower than himself and, while it was an incorrect designation, she understood his reluctance to identify as one of them. They were a bumbling mob. But they were also emotional and imprudent, as all humans were, and therefore dangerous.

"It's not wholly unlikely that they'd try," she replied.

"We don't have that kind of time. I need her restored now.

Send Prady with her to keep her safe. He's respected out there."

She lowered her tone and grabbed his bicep. "I must protest."

"Oh, you must?" He pushed her down onto the weight bench and straddled her. "Then it's a good thing I'm the Principal. You, sweet thing," he grabbed a ten-pound dumbbell from the floor by the bench and held it just above her throat, "do as I say. When I want your opinion, you'll know. Right now, I want your obedience, or do I need to fiddle with your programming?" He pressed one end of the weight into her throat, and she swallowed against it.

"I understand, sir," she said.

"Good." The weight clattered on the floor when he dropped it and put his lips to hers. He kissed her hungrily and then pulled back and stared at her. "Let her out. Today."

She stared just past his right ear at the white ceiling above. "Of course. Will that be all, sir?"

"For now." He got off of her, grabbed his towel, and tossed the water bottle up in the air a few times, making a game of catching it in various ways as he left the gym.

She pushed her hair back and rose from the bench. She looked in the mirrors behind the weights, at the skin on her neck that was now reddened with the force of Thallium's touch. The dumbbell was still on the floor. She picked it up, spun once, and chucked it at a mirror, shattering it. Fragmented reflections of her stared up from the broken pieces.

She pressed the com button on her black ID bracelet. "Prady?"

"Yes, ma'am," his voice replied. "What can I do for you?"

"Take Wren out of the Main House. She needs fresh air. Let her go wherever she pleases, but go with her. Keep her safe."

"Understood."

She let her arms fall limply to her sides. She was patient, but moments such as these reminded her of the importance of her vision. As she strode to the door, pieces of glass crunched beneath her bare feet, and little spots of blood marked her path.

Being outside did little to improve Survivor's mood, especially since they'd fenced her in with garbage. The yard they'd thrown up behind the prison was fifty feet across, just enough space to allow her to walk in an endless circle, which she'd done every day to keep herself from losing her mind being in her cell. But the laps had their own way of driving her mad. The walls enclosing the space were made with plastic crates and big, mangled pieces of metal, debris from the outlands piled up for a makeshift wall that was twice her height.

The primary benefit of her time in that circle of waste meant that she could plan her escape. Which of course was what she'd been doing for the past several days. Walking in the yard, examining each section of wall as she slowly passed it, watching how the guards consistently positioned themselves out of the sun.

Her planning was done. She and Wren would leave today, together. Hide somewhere until nightfall and then climb over the wall. The Gentleman was close—she could feel him like she could feel a monsoon coming. Deep in her bones. She had to put as much distance between them and The Disc as possible. Now.

She sat with Wren on plastic chairs under a big tattered umbrella. Wren's old watchdog stood close behind, and Survivor's requisite trio of guards stood farther back, pinning themselves against the wall to keep in the sliver of shade it offered.

Survivor hadn't seen Wren in a week, and the fact that Wren had been the one to request Survivor be allowed outdoors had done little to make up for her sister's absence. They were finally together again, and Wren was silent. Survivor had expected her to gush about all she'd seen and done, maybe talk about that man in the black coat she was clearly attracted to. But instead, she was even quieter than she'd been when they were starving and had no energy to speak, much less for the arguments their conversations were prone to turn into. What concerned Survivor the most were the dark circles under her eyes, the way she stared out at nothing with unbreaking intensity.

After an unbearably long silence, Survivor asked, "What's wrong? Are they hurting you?"

Wren blinked hard, snapped out of her trance, and immediately changed the subject. "Here." She took a bundle out of the pocket of her white skirt. She opened the wrapping to reveal a short stack of brown wafers. "Have one."

Survivor sniffed at them. "What are they?"

Wren took one and bit off a piece. "They're called cookies. They have fruit in them."

Survivor wrinkled her nose. "I won't eat from my enemy's palm unless the alternative is death."

"My palm is your enemy's?"

"You know what I mean."

Wren folded the cloth over the remaining cookies and put them back in her pocket. "How have you been?"

"Oh, you know, just loving my new place. Complete with gruel and little shitstains who try to murder you in your sleep."

Wren reached for her sister. "What happened?" Wren's hand clasped her knee. The panic in her eyes was a rabbit darting around in a cage, and it kept further explanation from Survivor's lips. There was no point in telling her what had happened, not when they'd be gone soon anyway.

"Just a figure of speech." She pushed Wren's hand off her leg.

That seemed to relax her a bit, and she settled into her chair again. "I'm trying to improve things for you. You can come outside. Isn't that better?"

"Sure. Sun and the smell of the herd of people in this city make all the difference. I'm practically free." She adjusted her hands, making the e-binds on her wrists hum as they kept her arms from moving too far apart.

"You could have been free," mumbled Wren. "You chose this instead."

"When the alternative is slavery in shinier packaging, you're damn right I chose this instead."

Wren pulled her legs up into the chair and stared off again. Survivor regretted the sharpness of her tone a bit as she watched her sister retreat into herself because of it.

"Why haven't I seen you more?" Survivor asked, gentler now. "Are they keeping you locked up too?"

"No. Not exactly."

"What the hell does that mean?"

"I've been busy." She pulled her hair back and lifted it off her neck, fanning it up and down to cool some of the sweat there. Her temple was swollen and red, broken skin barely healed over.

Survivor leapt up and scrutinized Wren's head, poking at the skin of her temples. "What are they doing to you?"

Wren dropped her hair so it covered her injuries again. "I'm letting them run tests on me."

"Run tests?" Survivor scoffed. "You mean cut you up and see what's inside. If they do get what they want out of you, do you really think they'll let you live? That they'll say, 'Great, now we know. You're free to go. Take care!'?" She kicked her chair over.

Wren's guard closed the distance to them in an instant and stood between the women with his staff held out in a defensive posture.

"It's fine, Prady," Wren said as she got up and walked around him. She stood next to Survivor. "She's just frustrated. Right, sister?"

Survivor hissed at him.

"Can you stand over there?" Wren asked him, pointing to one of the three Keepers patrolling the makeshift fence.

He hesitated.

She pushed down on the staff in his hands until he'd lowered it. "I'm safe. She's kept me safe for years—she's not going to hurt me."

He repositioned his staff as a walking stick. "I won't be far." He finally strode off to the fence.

Wren picked up Survivor's chair from its side and then sat back down in her own.

Survivor watched Prady to make sure he moved well out of earshot. "Good of them to provide you with a guard dog, but he looks a little old. They should probably just put him down."

"He's nice. I like him."

Survivor grunted in response. "What have they found in their tests?"

"Nothing very useful yet. Eydis—the Principal's assistant—says that what they've found shows potential, though. She thinks I'm powerful. She calls the process my *restoration*."

"Last time I checked, you weren't broken."

Wren hesitated, but then whispered, "Do you ever miss Alma?"

Survivor reached up to hang her hands from one of the thin metal rods holding the umbrella open. "Sometimes. Why?"

"I miss her. A lot."

Survivor tugged hard until the rod came free with a sharp *ping*. She hid the thin piece of metal between her hands before turning to see Wren looking back curiously. As casually as possible, Survivor wandered around the chair and crouched in front of Wren, careful to tuck her hands and the metal into her lap to hide them better as she leaned toward her sister. "You miss her more than usual?"

Wren nodded. "During the tests, I dream about her. Over and over. About the kids and the forest. The fire."

Survivor kissed her on the nose. "She wouldn't want us to be here. It's my fault—I should've been more careful. I screwed us by attacking that group. I'm...sorry." *Sorry* came out like a hard shit, unnaturally and with great effort.

Wren's mouth fell open. "What did you say?"

"I'm not gonna repeat it."

Wren rested her forehead on hers. "I love you."

"I know." She raised her hands over Wren's head and rested them behind her neck, letting the e-binds buzz close to Wren's ears. "That's why I have to do this."

Survivor stood, hoisting Wren up and spinning her around so that the e-binds moved to the front of Wren's neck. She jabbed the metal rod against Wren's throat, barely scratching the skin.

Prady was the first guard to move. He sprinted for them, urgency throwing away his limp like unwanted baggage. The three other Keepers followed his lead.

"Stop! I will kill her!" Survivor called out.

The guards stopped, Prady a few yards away, the others farther.

Wren tugged at Survivor's elbows. "What are you doing?"

Survivor whispered close to her ear. "Getting us out of here. Move with me." They slowly began sidestepping toward the wall of trash.

"Let her go. If you do, I swear that we'll forget this happened. You'll just go back to your cell," Prady said. He took small steps forward.

Spittle sprayed from Survivor's mouth as she shouted, "Maybe you didn't hear me before, old man. Stop walking!"

He did.

"Do what he says," Wren whispered. "If you get caught, you'll be in worse trouble."

"I won't get caught. We're leaving."

"We should stay. What is there for us out there, anyway?"

"It's not in here. And *he* knows I'm here. That's more than enough."

Prady held his staff at the ready, clutching the bottom quarter of it with both hands a forearm's length apart as he again started toward them.

"You've got nowhere to go," he said.

Survivor grinned. "Sure I do."

She let Wren go and gently pushed her to the ground a few feet away, then sprinted for the wall, drawing the attention of the three guards as Prady rushed to Wren's side. The guard closest to Survivor tried to cut her off. He stepped in front of her path and raised his arms up. He didn't draw the blade on his hip, a mistake he wouldn't have long to regret. She barreled into him, taking him to the ground. He reached for his sword under her grasp, but too late. She jammed the piece of metal from the umbrella into his throat. It stuck in his trachea as blood bubbled up and spilled down his neck in rivulets, choking him.

A second guard came up behind her before she could stand. He tried to grab her under the armpits. Before he could, she took the sword from the dead guard's hip and spun around. With one knee planted firmly on the ground, she absorbed the impact of the guard's weight as he impaled himself, the blade disappearing into his upper abdomen.

The final perimeter guard seemed to have learned to be careful from the fate of her two comrades. She stopped several feet away with the butt of her rifle—a type of weapon Survivor had shot only once before, many years ago—held tight against her shoulder.

Survivor pushed out of her stance, dumping the dead guard on the ground. Blood radiated out from his gut, a blotch of crimson spreading through the white and gray cloth of his robe. The mask covering his mouth flopped up to cover one of his still-open eyes instead. Once she got him on his back, she pulled the sword from his core. It came out with a sick, wet sucking sound. She held the hilt with her bound hands down by her right side as she stepped over his body. Small rocks bit with their heat into the soles of her feet as she slowly walked toward the guard with the rifle. Her blade dripped red onto the earth.

The guard looked down the sight of her rifle and exhaled slowly as she pulled the trigger. A blue burst of energy—glowing and sizzling—hit the ground just inches from Survivor's feet. She stopped and examined the scorched dirt. "That's neat."

Survivor again sprinted for the wall, intent on retrieving a big, flat piece of metal she'd spotted several days ago and noted for just this occasion. The guard shot after her. Several near hits zoomed past her shoulders and head, and one near her hand made her drop her sword. She scrambled up the debris and picked up the metal sheet. With it, she blocked the guard's shots to her upper body as she ran along the top of the wall.

The pulses hit her makeshift shield, jerking her arms as they bit into the metal and melted holes in it.

Survivor wound her way along the wall, her shield losing its structural integrity with every hit, until she was perpendicular to the guard. With a great push of her legs, she leapt from the wall and flew through the air toward her. The guard rapid-fired, hitting the shield Survivor held in front of her face and torso and scoring a couple shots on Survivor's legs. Survivor threw the sheet away at the last instant before landing on top of the guard's shoulders like a hawk grabbing a rodent. The guard moved to use the butt of her rifle as a club, but Survivor was too fast. She whipped her e-binds over the front of the guard's neck, threw her weight back, and took the guard to the ground. A loud snap came from the guard's neck as Survivor tugged hard to one side. Her limp body settled on the dirt as Survivor pulled herself out from under it.

Two wounds on Survivor's legs—one above her left knee, the other in the meat of her right calf— smoked and stung. They'd nearly reached the bone. The smell of cooking flesh and singed hair accompanied the pain shooting up her legs.

"You're hurt," Prady called over. He stood in front of Wren several yards away.

"What, this?" Survivor lifted her left leg and poked at the wound above her knee. The flesh, bright pink toward the center and blackened around the edges, pushed back at her touch. "This is nothing. You don't know hurt."

"Surrender and you'll live. I give you my word," he said.

She bent down and picked up the rifle, tugging the strap off the guard's shoulder and down her arm, which flopped back to the ground as the strap released it.

She looked the rifle up and down, examining its parts. "What have I told you about the value of a man's words, Wren?"

"Run!" Wren screamed at Prady.

Survivor raised the rifle and fired. Pulsing bursts flew all around Prady, sporadic and unpredictable. She tucked the rifle tight against her shoulder as the guard had done, and her shots hit closer to their mark. Prady ran away from Wren, giving Survivor practice at leading a target.

He pivoted and ran toward her, spinning his staff in front of him to catch any pulses that happened to fly at his torso. Her shots grew more unfocused, losing what little grouping she'd achieved. As he neared, she stopped firing.

She eyed the rifle, muttered "Fuck this," and hurled the gun at him.

He batted it away with his staff, which was now thoroughly covered in scorch marks, then swung the staff overhead in a well-practiced spin before bringing it down toward her head. She rolled to the side before he could land his strike, and the staff bounced off the ground. He drew his body into a defensive posture, placing his hands at the base of the staff and waiting for her to move. He glanced back at Wren.

"Did she hit you?" he called out.

Survivor picked up a rock from the ground while he was focused on Wren. It barely fit into her closed fist. "Your concern is precious. But she's not yours to worry about. She's mine."

She feinted throwing the rock at Wren. Prady dashed in that direction, and she threw the rock at his bum knee. He shouted as his leg went out from under him, and he fell to the ground in a heap.

Survivor shuffled over to him, really starting to feel the pain in her legs now. Prady was trying to breathe through the agony and use his staff to help him to a crouch. She kicked the staff out, and he fell to the dirt again.

"Noticed you have a bit of trouble with that knee. Well,

now you have a lot of trouble with it. For the record, I wouldn't have thrown that at her. She's my sister." She plucked up the small silver card hanging on a chain around his neck and swiped it over her wrists. A light on the e-binds turned green, and they fell off and went dark as their power faded. She then stomped hard on the black bracelet on his wrist—it bent inward, digging into his skin, and Survivor hoped that would be enough to keep him from using it to communicate. She kicked a puff of dirt in his face for good measure and then went to Wren.

"We're leaving." Survivor took hold of Wren's arm and pulled her into a run.

Wren turned pale when she looked at Prady crumpled on the ground as they passed him. Once they reached the fence, Survivor picked up the sword she'd dropped earlier and pushed Wren ahead of her. Survivor tried to ignore the now throbbing pain of her wounds as they scrabbled up the wall of trash. Wren nearly fell when her foot slipped on the smooth side of a metal drum toward the top, but Survivor caught her backside with her hand and heaved upward. The wounds throbbed more with the effort. They finally got to the top of the fence and dropped down to the ground on the other side, and Survivor choked back her whimper with the force of the impact on her legs.

Nobody was around—the yard area was behind the prison, and no citizens were nearby. Survivor pulled them against the wall of the prison.

"Which way is out?" she asked.

"It's far west, the opposite side of the city," said Wren, her voice subdued. "We can't get there without being seen."

"We just need to get partway there. Find somewhere to lie low until nightfall. You know the layout of the city?"

"Not really. It's huge," said Wren.

"We'll stick close to the wall. Can't get lost that way."

"They have watchers posted on the wall. They'll see us."

"Hmm. We'll improvise, then." She started to move, but Wren stopped her.

"Back there—why didn't you kill him?"

"He seemed to care what happened to you. Besides," she took the sword in the folds of her skirt and wiped off the blood and dirt, "last time I tried killing someone you liked, it made you sad." She moved her grip from Wren's arm to her hand.

Wren squeezed her hand back, a bemused smile forming on her face. "A second apology."

"I didn't say sorry, did I?" She turned to glance around the corner of the building. "This is our chance. I'll find us a new home, somewhere safe, where they can't poke at you anymore. You believe me?"

Wren didn't answer.

"What is it?"

"I just..." Wren trailed off.

Survivor got eye to eye with her. "We can't stay. They don't care about you. I do."

The bridge of freckles along Wren's nose wrinkled a bit as she sniffed back tears. "I know you do."

They took off along the edge of the prison, Survivor leading in a westerly direction as she tried to let adrenaline distract her from the pain flooding her legs.

"Here, let me show you," Six said. He picked up a handful of dirt from the floor underneath the white plastic table and then dropped it onto the table's surface. His ID bracelet slid down to rest just above his wrist as he spread the dirt into a thin layer and dragged his finger through it.

The women, one on either side of him, scooted closer until their hips pressed up against him.

"That's supposed to be a person?" the one on his right asked. Her brown hair fell to her chin in a neat bob, just above the first of the rings pierced into her neck and laced together with red ribbon.

"A stick figure, Clara. I never said I was an artist," Six said.

"You're supposed to be quite the artist behind closed doors." The woman on his left traced his ear with a fingertip and tucked his dark hair behind it.

"Moxi, please, not now. We're in public." He indicated the bar around him with a jut of his jaw.

There were several other patrons at the Ragged Squirrel, as it was just past noon. Six sat at a table with the ladies, with a view of the street. A few people passed by on their lunch breaks. The women with him sipped at bright red drinks. Prickly pear nectar and vodka, referred to affectionately as a "Crimson Itch," was popular among the ladies, particularly the kind of ladies Six spent time with.

"Now," he said, turning his attention to his stick figure drawn in the dirt, "every Body has six parts."

"I think there's a few more than that," Moxi said, her voice perforated by chain smoking and the desert heat. She less than subtly angled her leather-clad bust toward him and flipped her straight, black hair over to the other side to reveal the shaved half of her head.

"The image of the Body is used to denote authority from top to bottom," he continued. "The higher-ranking members are the Head and the Arms. And the lower-ranking members are the Torso and the Legs. I'm the Right Arm."

"What did you say your job was again?" Clara asked.

"Assassin. I kill people, love."

"Now that you've told us, how will you get us to keep quiet?" Moxi asked. She reached for the zipper of his jacket.

"It's no secret around here. And, madam, I'm on duty."

"You're on lunch," she corrected.

"Precisely."

"So we would have plenty of time," Clara said. She reached to untie the tan scarf wrapped around his neck and tucked neatly into his cracking leather jacket.

"No," he took her hand and kissed it, "no, we wouldn't. Not nearly enough time." He put his scarf back in order and then finished off the short glass of clear alcohol in front of him.

The women exchanged a glance of alarm, as if their clothing was about to burst off and they didn't know how to stop it. They started to paw at him desperately, but something in the street caught his eye and he stood before they could subdue him.

The two outliers walked in front of the pub. The wild dark-haired one, with what looked to be blood on her dress, limped along. Behind her followed Wren, who seemed as if she might throw up at any second. Her hair was haphazardly stuffed beneath her scarf, poking out in places, waving hello to those she passed. Even more than that, her fine clothes were about as subtle as a strobe light after dark. Everyone knew that an outlier had been taken into the Main House, and those outraged outnumbered those unperturbed by several thousand. Word had spread through every corner of the city, and anybody paying attention had heard of the red-haired woman and her unstable sister, who hadn't been as lucky and was rumored to be locked up.

"Hey!" called Nita. "Hey, you! What are you doing back on my street? You're not welcome here!"

She grabbed a hefty kitchen knife from under the counter

and came out from behind the bar. The people close enough to hear her looked up from their drinks or paused in mid-stride.

"Not good." Six bounded over the table, ruining his stick figure drawing and kicking dirt into the ladies' faces.

People started to flood out of the Squirrel and nearby businesses, drawn by Nita's voice. Most were oblivious spectators looking for some entertainment with gaped mouths and necks strained to see over the crowd, but others were eager to come to the matron pub owner's aid and were undoubtedly armed. They closed in around the outliers. The woman who'd poisoned Caster yanked Wren behind her and pulled a sword from the folds of her dress.

"We have to go back," Wren whispered.

The knot of people grew tighter around them. She recognized Nita toward the front of the circle, and the big bartender just behind her.

"Pretty sure they don't want to let us go anywhere," said Survivor. "Back off! If you get any closer, I'll cut off whatever limbs I can reach."

The knot loosened a bit, but not enough for them to pass through.

"Whoa! Everyone, calm down." Wren recognized the voice from the depths of the crowd—Six's lilting accent. "What is this, a cock fight? Come on!" Six emerged from the mob and stood near Wren and Survivor.

Survivor spat at him.

"I guess you remember me. That'll save time." He turned his back to them and faced the crowd. "Please just go about your business. I'm sure the Keepers are on their way as we speak. I'll go ahead and start escorting these ladies back to wherever it is they should be. No need to get testy, am I right?"

"These are the scum that hurt the Principal's son. And one of 'em had him buying her dinner!" shouted Nita so all could hear. "This is what outliers do—kill and mutilate, and if you're not careful, they invade your very hearts and homes!"

The mob responded with scattered "yeas."

"I'll ask you one more time to go back to your meals and shopping," said Six. "These women are protected by the legal process of our fine city here. If you attack them, you're the criminal. I'm taking them back now. No need for violence."

His plea for peace had the opposite effect; the mob cursed at him and brandished their weapons.

"You're no better than them!" shouted Nita.

"Whose side are you on?" came another man's call.

"Traitor!" a shrill voice declared above the rest.

Survivor muttered so only Wren could hear. "We need to move." She raised her sword as if she were preparing to hack into Six's back like a block of wood. Wren stepped in front of her and Survivor stopped mid-swing.

The crowd fell silent.

Six turned around, throwing knives between his fingers, ready to release. "I thought it felt a little like imminent death. Hell of a way to thank me, lady."

Survivor spat at him again, and he sighed.

Wren held her hands up at her sister. "Listen, please. We're outnumbered and outmatched. Even if we could escape, we have nothing. I know you hate it here, but I just think this is where we have to be right now."

"*I* hate it here?" Survivor said. "*We* hate it here. They're torturing you, and these people want to kill you." She waved her sword toward the crowd, which backed up a half-step. "Don't say it's just me."

"They're not all bad. They're afraid of what they don't understand. I'm the same way."

"No! NOT the same, not like them! Don't even think that!"

Wren shook her head. "Is it so bad to belong somewhere? What are you scared of?"

Survivor lowered her blade. "These people don't scare me. They're cattle, nothing more. But *he* is coming, and we have to leave before he gets here. This is our chance."

"To go where? The Open? There's nothing for us there. Our family is gone. This place you hate is all we have. Outside, we're nothing. But in here, we're strong."

Survivor glared at her. "I'm already strong."

"Oh, come on! Aren't you tired of barely making it every day? Running from a boogeyman? Don't you think we're safer in here than we've ever been out there?"

"Nowhere is safe! After all this time, you still don't understand that. There is no safe, there is no happy, there is no motherfucking hope. There is living and dying." Her blood-spattered neck bloomed red with rage. "You're a naïve and ungrateful child. I kept you alive!"

"By making me wish I were dead!" After the words were out, her hand shot to her mouth as if she could pull them back in.

Survivor's expression turned hard and cold. "This is a waste of time. It's my job to keep you safe. I promised. I have to, even if you don't want me to."

She grabbed at Wren's wrist, but Wren wrenched it free and took a step back toward the crowd.

"No!" she shouted. She met Survivor's gaze, fighting past the shaking in her limbs. "Not this time."

A man, not much younger than Wren, started sneaking up behind Survivor as she looked Wren up and down. Survivor then closed her eyes and let her head fall back. The sun shone on her cheeks, and the blood stains there glistened.

"So be it." She spun on her heel and sliced horizontally, just barely missing the gut of the boy trying to ambush her. The people shrieked, and those closest looked to Six for protection, any complaint they'd had about him just minutes before now forgotten. Survivor turned her attention to him. She jumped to bring her blade down on his head, and he pulled back to throw the small knives from between his fingers in response.

Before he could release his throw, something fell from above and hit Survivor's back. She dropped instantly, barely avoiding landing on her own sword, and convulsed on the ground. Wren lunged for her, but Six stopped her before she could lay a hand on her sister.

"Don't. You'll get shocked," he said.

Between Survivor's shoulder blades, attached with metal hooks embedded in her skin, was a shock tablet. After a long minute of fighting it, Survivor finally fell motionless. The tablet turned dark.

Wren threw herself down next to her. She turned Survivor's head to the side, pushed her hair out of her face, and wiped the drool from her chin.

"I'm sorry. I'm so, so sorry," Wren cried, even though she wasn't sure what she was apologizing for.

Survivor coughed, clearing the saliva from her throat. She glared up at Wren. "Fuck off. You're not my sister. She died when we passed through the front gate of this place."

Whistles blew beyond the throng of bodies surrounding them, and then four Keepers burst through. Two of them cleared the people from the street, and a third bound Survivor's hands while the fourth kept his gun trained on her. The one who'd bound her hands dragged her to her knees. She went deadweight, and the one with the gun helped pull her up. They carried her between them. Her feet dragged on the ground as they took her back in the direction of the prison.

Wren's legs felt nailed to the ground. The knot of people slowly began to reform now that the Keepers had left with the dangerous outlier, leaving Wren on her own. Six put his hand on her shoulder, making her jump.

"Time to go." He helped her up and moved them quickly through and away from the crowd. As he passed Nita, he tossed a coin, which landed squarely on her forehead.

"Ma'am, shall I send more men to pick Wren up?" the Operator's voice came through the speaker inside the observation booth.

On the screen atop the console in front of Eydis was live footage from a drone above Diameter. A man wearing a black ID bracelet guided Wren away from the group of people trying again to converge on her. Eydis took a freeze frame of his face with the drone and ran it through their database. After a quick search, his photo came up, staring at her with chocolate eyes and a smirk—Six, the Assassin for Body 17.

"No," said Eydis. "He's part of Caster's Body. He'll take care of her. Keep a drone in her vicinity, but don't interfere."

"Understood."

She rolled her chair closer to the console and pressed a button on the edge of the screen. The footage whirred backward, hiccupping over the bump in the video when the drone had released a shock tablet. She stopped the footage. Wren's sister held her sword high above, with her arms and head thrown back so that the drone had a good, clear view of her face. Eydis paused it there and rolled up a small dial on the screen to zoom in.

She stared at the image for a long while, wondering how this could be possible, and even more, how she'd missed it. Only Wren's scan had come back positive; Eydis had barely glanced at Survivor's test results since they held nothing out of the ordinary. She hadn't even given the ID photo they'd entered of her into the system a close look. This woman was supposed to be dead, and yet here she was all grown up, finally come home. With a new name that fit her better than she realized.

Eydis stood from her chair, leaving Survivor's frozen face to hang on the screen. She walked to the door in the back wall of the observation booth, and when the keypad prompted her for the code, she slowly punched in "8142020." The light on the keypad flashed green, and the door opened. Inside was a small room filled with filing cabinets. She went to the black four-drawer cabinet on her right and opened the top drawer, then flipped through the manila folders with slightly shaky anticipation.

At the very back of the drawer was a folder with a black label reading "Pre-Carrier" stretched diagonally across the cover and a shorter, bright red stamp beneath it—E.A.I.

She took the file back to her seat and opened it. A thick bunch of lab notes, medical charts, and X-rays were inside. She glanced through them, and the red E.A.I stamp accosted her on every page. Toward the back, behind the papers and charts, were three photos paper-clipped together. One was the equivalent of a mug shot—the front and side profiles of a young girl with a bushy, black ponytail and cuts and bruises on her face. The second photo was of the same girl sitting cross-legged in the isolation unit in the middle of the lab. Her bruises were gone, and she was studying the nose of the pink teddy bear in her lap with the barest of smiles. The last photo was an overhead shot of the girl on an exam table, her head lolled to the side. A bump with several stitches across it marred her fore-head. Scratches covered her arms and neck. Her little hands lay face up by her sides, and dried blood was caked under her fingernails.

Eydis flipped the picture over to see "Vande—2393" written in her own flowing handwriting. She tossed it and the file onto the console. Papers spilled out and slid across the console in a stream. Survivor's face remained frozen on the screen.

This was the beginning of Eydis' work after The Fall—this wild woman standing in the street, back from the dead.

Eydis' thoughts flew back hundreds of years to that great flash of light in the sky. It had been noon, but the flash had still been visible. The gate hung in space like a ring marrying this world to one beyond, and after a ship of colonists went through, the ring snapped. A burst of energy shot out of it, and the sun in turn licked Earth, scorching it with its tongue, initiating the chaos that would cause the people left on it to fight for their lives. It was a fight most would lose.

Many years later, Eydis met Valcin, and they began their work together on the Carriers as a way to protect and power the resources and technology they were recovering from the ashes. Their initial attempt would not succeed, but as Eydis studied Survivor's grimace on screen twenty years after she'd last seen it, she found herself delighted that it had refused to be discarded.

And she determined to make good use of it.

Sweat ran down Adonis' face in rivulets. It dripped from his scalp and had turned his already mussed-up hair into a sticky, lopsided mess. His thin white shirt was pasted to his skinny torso. He bent over and rested his hands on his knees, huffing and puffing.

"I don't...get why I...get stuck with...this job," he heaved.

Caster stood a few feet across from him, drinking water from a canteen. He wiped his face with the bottom of his gray tunic and threw the canteen to Sans, who sat on the edge of the pit near a rack of weapons. Sans sighed softly and took a drink from the canteen.

They were in the third zone of the training area for all the Bodies in The Disc. This area, referred to as The Pits, was in the southwest quadrant of The Disc, near the entrance in case the city was attacked. Patrolling outside the walls took the vast majority of their time and attention, but Bodies were for defense of the city above all. It was a noble job, sure, but as of yet, no group outside of The Disc was large enough, organized enough, or foolish enough to attack the city. So they just kept training for the theoretical threat.

There were twenty pits, each fifteen feet square and three feet deep. There was a symbolism to the digging of the pits established by Caster's grandfather decades prior, much of it having to do with camaraderie and the simple act of building character through manual labor. Now the pits were just maintained, but if a new Body were to be formed, they'd be required to dig their own pit.

Currently, there were twenty Bodies functioning in The Disc, with four out on patrol at any one time. Now that Body 17 was home, it was back to training and general conditioning, which wasn't feasible when they were on patrol. On patrol, their time was consumed with travel, scouting, or setting up and tearing down camp. They squeezed in light conditioning if they had the time or the energy, but that was rare. Their training back in The Disc would last until their next patrol mission, which would likely be in a month or so. Caster's theory was that the military leaders wanted to give their men enough time to rest and bulk up, but not so much time at home that they grew lazy and forgot the danger they'd be facing on the outside.

Each pit held weapon racks, stools, and a table, and each Body in training was also provided with an extra ration of water to share. Caster and Adonis sparred in the open space across from the weapon racks where Sans sat, swinging his kanabō in tight circles just above the ground, more out of habit than for practice. It was an outrageous weapon—six feet long and made of heavy, dense wood, covered in short metal spikes—and it was Sans' joy, if Sans were to ever express joy. It was a unique weapon, not ideal for a Thief meant to be invisible. Whenever he had to venture into a city when they were on patrol, he wore it across his back, concealed under his cloak except for a foot of the handle. Subtle, it was not, but it had belonged to Sans since before he arrived in The Disc, and he'd refused to give it up when he became a Thief. Nobody had been bold enough to insist.

The first time Caster had met Sans, he'd doubted a man of his average build could wield it. Caster would have had trouble with it, and he was a good bit bigger than Sans. That thought disappeared the first time he'd sparred with Sans and seen close up how the Thief danced with it.

"Why can't Mainstay or Six spar with you?" Adonis asked Caster. He pushed off his knees to a stand.

"Because," Caster started, drawing a fresh line in the dirt between them with the point of his thin, rubber shoes, "Mainstay thinks he's in great shape and exempt from training, or at least that's what I have to assume from him no-showing. As for Six, he doesn't need to build muscle mass. You do."

"I'm just a Grunt. It doesn't matter how big I am. Come on, please!" He hunched over.

"You have the job of a pack animal. The difference between you and a pack animal is that the animal is strong."

"But. But—"

"What? Want to bitch some more? Or do you want to beat me?" Caster took his stance and held his arms at the ready.

Adonis was fairly new to The Disc, having lived there for just under two years. Gavel and Sans found him with nomadic slavers in the Open, up for sale at auction. He'd been the youngest slave at eleven. The kid had been with their Body ever since. He was incredibly strong minded—had to be to get through his childhood and still retain a sense of humor—but his body needed discipline. Everyone in the Body taught him, but Caster and Sans in particular shared the task.

Caster's teacher when he was even younger than Adonis had been Thallium, and although Caster didn't employ his father's more brutal methods, he did push Adonis with similar fervor.

Thallium had personally trained Caster four times a week in two-hour sessions, with Caster working independently on his off days. Thallium taught without mercy, treating his eight-year-old son as he'd treat a man his own age, just as Thallium's father before had taught him. Every mistake earned Caster a lash to the back of his bare legs. Every victory bought him a modicum of respect. It was the only habit that Thallium seemed to have willingly inherited from his father's way of life.

As far as Caster knew, Thallium hated his father, so much in fact that he'd barred him from Caster's life almost entirely. Caster only had vague memories of his grandfather as this spooky specter floating between rooms, or returning dusty and windbeaten from working among his people to let his eyes pass over Caster playing near the entryway of the Main House as if he were a tumbleweed that had been blown inside by accident. Thallium had only short, crisp sentences for the man and would stand between him and Caster whenever they happened to be in the same room until he died when Caster was nine. But Thallium admitted that his combat skills were unmatched, and therefore carried on the regimen with Caster that Valcin had used with him.

Caster's martial arts training was a mix of Krav Maga, wrestling, and Western boxing. He sparred with full grown men, fighters who knew what they were doing—the only type of opponent Thallium allowed. Thallium was largely about power moves, but Caster, being a child, utilized speed and adaptability, possessing a talent for improvisation that surprised Thallium a time or two.

With mastery of Caster's body came the introduction of weapons, starting with guns—they trumped other weapons every time, Thallium had said. But even though Valcin had gifted Thallium a fair collection of antique handguns and had ammo manufactured for them, Caster noticed Thallium didn't use them himself often. After Caster got fairly decent with handguns, he moved on to knives, which Thallium expressed much more passion for. When Thallium felt Caster had mastered knife fighting at thirteen, he gave him his own bowie knife; seven and a half inches, stainless steel, black non-slip handle. A relic over three hundred years old. He'd told him the legend of Jim Bowie and the sandbar fight—the man was shot, stabbed, and still managed to defeat his opponents and live to tell of it later. Someone to look up to, Thallium had said.

After knives, Caster got decent with the staff and spear, the most common weapons he'd be facing. Now, he could pick up any weapon and use it well enough in a fight—when motivation was high and his life was on the line, whatever was handy would do. But his real love was martial arts, then his bowie.

Adonis, on the other hand, had no experience with weapons. He'd been entrusted with a cutlass, but it was out of necessity rather than out of reward for his mastery of any fighting skills. In the Open, you had to have a weapon, whether you were an expert with it or not. Caster gave the panting, sweat-drenched Adonis a once over. He'd have to work further with him on sword training soon, assuming the kid didn't melt into a puddle before then.

Adonis shook his head hard to toss sweat off. After one last breath, he stepped up to the line and took a similar but lazier starting stance to Caster's.

The feel of his muscles, hot and flexible, brought Caster comfort. It was routine, it was cleansing, and it was distracting. He was beginning to worry about Wren. He'd only seen her twice over the past week, and he'd refused to go beyond the entryway in the Main House when he did. They were quick visits, mainly because Wren spent most of her time in the lab. Eydis kept her on a tight schedule, as if there were a deadline to meet in whatever work they were doing together. Both times, Thallium had shown up and encouraged Caster to join Wren in the lab. Something about the way he asked—too eagerly, almost desperately—caused Caster to decline. Caster had last seen that level of fanaticism a year before his mom died, when Thallium's interest in Eydis' work deepened into obsession. It was disturbing, and Caster refused to be a part of it. He also had his own responsibilities to his Body, and he wouldn't use his position to shirk them, especially when Gavel would berate him for it.

Prady called his ID bracelet at the same hour every morning with an update on how Wren was doing. Prady wasn't allowed in the inner chamber where Wren and Eydis worked together all day, but he was with her for the small amount of time she was out of the lab. She seemed well enough, but she was tired. Always so tired, staring off into space for minutes at a time. Yesterday, Prady had started resorting to outright guilting Caster: "I know she'd love to see you more," he'd said.

Caster wished he could get her out of that place, away from whatever Eydis and Thallium were working on with her. He wondered if he could find her a little town to lie low in, and if he could even manage to sneak her out in the first place. He wanted to try, but it all felt so futile.

"Can we please take a break at least?" Adonis asked.

Caster shook his head and refocused. "How about we work on something else. Tying knots? Another thing you're terrible at."

As if on cue, Sans grabbed a coil of rope from where it hung on the end of a weapon rack and tossed it to Caster.

"I'm not that bad at it. And besides, we always use e-binds," said Adonis.

"Not always," said Caster. "The way you tied Wren up when we were in the Open was abysmal. Lucky for you, she wasn't a threat. But someday, you'll have to tie up someone who wants to hurt you. Tell you what," said Caster, tugging the ends of the rope to test its strength. "If I can't get out of your knots, then we can be done for the day. You can go home."

Adonis perked up. "For real?"

"For real. But if I can get out, then we keep training. With no complaints this time."

"Deal." Adonis yanked the rope from him.

Caster held his hands together behind his back, keeping his elbows apart. Adonis went to work tying the rope around his wrists. When he finally finished, he walked around Caster with his arms crossed smugly.

"Get out of that. I dare you."

Caster couldn't keep the grin from his face. He tested the strength of the knots, and to the kid's credit, he had done a fairly good job. But in just thirty seconds, Caster had straightened his arms and used the bit of extra space to pull his right wrist free. He took the rope from his left wrist and held the knotted mass together in front of himself.

Adonis dropped his arms. "Again? Seriously?"

Caster tossed the rope back to Sans. "Let's continue. Take your mark."

Adonis started to complain, but then seemed to remember their deal and quickly shut his mouth. He opened his stance and nodded.

"Begin," said Caster.

Caster didn't move, instead letting Adonis charge him like he always did. He stepped back on his left foot, turned sideways, and grabbed Adonis around the neck in a choke hold. Adonis kicked and tried to wriggle out of the grab, but it was futile. Caster gently forced Adonis down to his knees and just as Adonis' eyes began to roll back, he let him go. Adonis coughed on the ground and tried to catch his breath.

The slightest of chuckles, no more than a throaty heh, came from Sans on the sidelines.

"It's not funny!" heaved Adonis from the dirt.

"It's kind of funny," said Caster. "You keep doing the same thing again and again. Are you expecting different results every time? A plus B always equals C."

"Heh," said Sans, louder than before.

Caster laughed at Sans' reaction, which was the equivalent of a good belly laugh for the Thief. He then faced Adonis and thumped his arm across his chest twice. Adonis returned the gesture with a sarcastic flourish before turning on Sans.

"What's so funny? I don't think you could do much better," Adonis said. After the words were out, he immediately took a few steps back, widening the already large space between himself and Sans, who wasn't chuckling anymore.

The Thief jumped down from the edge of the pit and took

off his overshirt, staring with cold eyes at the boy, who seemed to be trying to determine if he were fast enough to run past him and out of The Pits. Sans then hefted his kanabō, which elicited a squeak from Adonis, but Sans just moved it to the safety of the weapon rack. He cracked his knuckles as he stepped out onto the dirt and drew a line in it across from Caster.

Adonis' exhale came out as a gust of relief.

Caster took position across the line from his superior, eager for a true challenge, but before Adonis could start the match, Six jogged up and jumped down into Pit 17.

Wren trailed behind him, and she looked as if she'd just watched someone die. When she saw Caster, her eyes welled up, and he fought the urge to wrap his arms around her after he helped her into the pit.

"What happened?" he asked.

"She was walking down Diameter with her sister," said Six. "Some people recognized them, and I had to jump in."

"Are you injured? Why isn't Prady with you?" Caster asked Wren.

She swallowed hard. "My sister fought him. He's hurt."

"Your sister? Why would she do that if they let her out?"

"They didn't let her out. We—she—escaped. I went with her. I tried to stop her, but she wouldn't listen. She killed guards."

"The Principal's Keepers?" Six asked. "Damn. Yeah, she's not going back to prison. More like a short walk to the execu—"

Caster punched him hard in the chest.

Six rubbed at his pec. "How about I give you two some privacy? Seems to be a good idea." He walked off to where Sans and Adonis stood by the weapon racks, less than subtly watching the two talk.

Caster ran his hand over his forehead to keep the sweat in

his eyebrows from finding its way into his eyes. "Six isn't wrong. Survivor was already shown more grace than any other criminal outlier. I'm not sure my dad can give anymore—it looks bad. The people won't like it."

"He's going to kill her?"

"I don't know. Possibly. But you at least won't be allowed to see her again. She won't be allowed to see anyone."

"Just like that? After all I've gone through to keep her safe?"

"Some people can't be saved. She chose not to let you."

She looked as if the ground had been taken out from under her. Caster couldn't stop himself then. He wrapped one arm around her shoulders, and she leaned into him.

Six and Sans kindly looked away at the display of intimacy, but Adonis ogled as if Caster had just dipped her and kissed her. With a quick glance around, it was clear that the other Bodies in the adjoining pits sympathized with Adonis. Women and men had stopped sparring and fine-tuning weapons to gape at the Bastard and the outlier embracing.

Caster ignored them. He felt his thin long-sleeved shirt sticking to her cheek. "Sorry about the sweat," he whispered to the top of her head.

She chuckled and then backed out of his arm. "I'm used to sweat. Just not so much of it at once." She wiped at her cheek with the sleeve of her tunic.

"Listen," he started, keeping his voice low. "I don't think you should go back to the Main House."

She blinked at him. "I have to."

"No, you don't. You were doing it to keep Survivor safe. But what happens to her is out of your control now."

"That was why I agreed to it, but now...there are other reasons. To work with Eydis, I mean."

"What other reasons?"

She started to blush. "She's helping me find something inside of myself. I...I want to see what it is."

Damn his father and Eydis. They had her *wanting* to let them use her. It was brilliant and sickening. Whatever time he'd stupidly thought he had to mull over getting Wren out of The Disc was now gone. "Trust me, you need to get out of here. Let me help you."

"Out? Out where?"

"Back to the Open. I'll find a place for you. Somewhere with other people. Just not here."

"Even if I wanted to, I can't just leave Survivor."

"She's already left you! Can't you see that? She's resented your choice from the start, and now she's killing people instead of thinking about what's best for you."

"And what *is* best for me? I guess you know the answer to that?"

"No. It's just...you have to leave. Prady's told me how exhausted you are, that you hardly speak to him anymore. You have to get away from what they're doing to you."

"And also away from food, shelter—"

"No, I'll make sure you have those things—"

"Away from you," she said softly.

That kicked him in the gut. "It's not what I want."

Her expression tightened as if she were trying to keep something hidden behind it, but then her words suddenly came out in a rush. "If I went, would you come with me?"

His shoulders sank. Part of him wanted to say yes, absolutely. But it was impossible. "It's not up to me. I have to stay for my people. I belong here."

"I've forgotten what that feels like." She gave him a wan smile and fell quiet. After a long pause, she said, "They can do whatever they want to me. Survivor's all I have left, and if they kill her, there's no reason for me to keep fighting. She's *my* people—I belong with her."

She pulled away from him as her face fell. Then she spun on her heel and heaved herself out of the pit with one surprisingly powerful shove. Without a look back, she jogged away, hair bouncing from side to side until she covered it with her scarf. She left The Pits, turned east, and ran out of sight.

The Bodies in nearby pits started oohing and snickering. From their point of view, it would look like Caster had been rejected, which he technically had been. But he'd done it first. And watching the light leave her face, hearing her give up, was utterly devastating. He hated himself for causing it.

"Don't you guys have some muscles to rip? Get back to work!" Six yelled. The onlookers grumbled and resumed their training. Six walked up to Caster, who hadn't moved since the exchange. "Dude, what the hell did you say to her?"

"Leave it," said Caster. He headed for a towel hanging on a rack. He needed to get out of here, clear his head.

Six followed him. "Don't get pissed."

"I said leave it, Six."

"Look, let's just go get her. I'm sure she hasn't gotten far yet."

Caster snatched a short staff from the rack and got in Six's face.

"You know how this ends, man. You sure?" Six said. He reached for a butterfly knife on his belt.

Caster threw the staff to the ground and backed up a couple of steps. He took a starting position.

"You struggle to beat me on a good day when you're focused. You really want to do this now?" Six asked.

Caster just waited.

"Fine."

Six removed his belt and held it out. Adonis ran over and

took it, heavy with knives and other miscellaneous instruments of death, and retreated to the sidelines with Sans. Six widened his stance a bit and nodded once to Caster.

Caster ran toward him, going straight for his legs, since those were Six's primary weapons when he didn't have knives. It was an impetuous move, which is probably why it surprised Six enough that he reacted a little too slowly and barely shifted his weight in time to sidestep the blow. Caster regretted his rash attack when Six's dropkick hit the full of his back and sent him to his knees. But Caster leapt quickly to his feet and charged again. He threw strike after strike like an idiot, blinded by his emotions, as Six just danced around defensively. The primary contact made was Six's occasional block of a strike when he didn't dodge it completely.

Caster started getting frustrated. He shouted, anger at the fight and himself coming out in a great burst from his vocal cords. His movements sped up, and surprise lit Six's face. Caster started landing strikes, including a couple of shots to his core.

Six turned from defense to offense, getting in close to limit Caster's movements before catching him in a grab. He took him to the ground, pulled him into an armbar, and urged Caster to submit with each tug of his arm. Caster fought, and the cartilage in his shoulder started to pop like corn.

"Dude, stop fighting it. You're going to break your arm!" said Six.

Caster kept pulling and tugging until *SNAP!* His shoulder pulled out of joint, and his arm broke at the elbow. Six let him go and rolled away, face pale.

Adonis and Sans ran over. Adonis knelt next to Caster as he sat up, his arm dangling like a hook from a line, and examined the damage with a vacant expression.

Six stood and rambled to Sans. "Why didn't he just submit?

Gavel's going to kill me. Shit, no, Thallium's going to *actually* kill me! It's not like I meant it." He turned back to Caster. "I'm so sorry, man!"

The tendons and bones started to twist and move in Caster's arm, and he cried out in pain. Like a three-dimensional puzzle, he felt his humerus turn against itself near his elbow until it snapped back into place. His shoulder slid up and into socket as if pulled together by magnetic force as the muscles on top twisted back together. In seconds that felt like an eternity, the pain stopped, and he fell silent.

He rose to his feet, turning his arm over one way and then the other, and finally lifted it up as if to high five someone. It was perfect.

His three friends stared at him.

Six cleared his throat. "Um, what the hell just happened?"

Caster laced his fingers together behind his neck and pulled down, trying to make himself focus.

"You okay?" Six said.

Six started to reach out to him when Caster snapped out of it and leapt up to grab his bowie knife from a rack. He tucked it into his belt before leaping out of Pit 17 and breaking into a sprint. He didn't feel his feet as he ran; they seemed to barely touch the ground as the world streaked by. He ran up Diameter, dodging people and curious looks, and only slowed once he reached the Trading Center.

A few shops were open at lunchtime, but more food stands and bars than anything else. However, one man was always open for business. Caster spotted Freddy standing near one of the fruit twins, who sat on her counter in the shade of an overhang with her legs crossed. Freddy held a white ball covered in dimples out to the fruit girl, who feigned interest and took the ball from him.

"No, I swear," he said. "People used to hit these at each

other with metal sticks. A shot to the head was five points, six if you struck when they weren't looking. Many brave athletes lost their lives."

Caster jogged up. "Freddy."

"Ah!" said Freddy, taking the ball from the girl's hand and shoving it toward Caster's face. "This is a gem, a vintage symbol of virility. Twenty-five coins, and that's the returning customer price."

"Not interested." Caster steered him away from the fruit girl, who turned her attention to biting her nails.

"Then to what do I owe the pleasure of your visit?" He pocketed the ball and crossed his arms over his open snakeskin shirt.

Caster hesitated. The skin under his ring itched and burned, and he told himself it was the sweat trapped beneath. "Would a case of Yellow Fever be enough to kill a person?"

"A case? All imbibed in one sitting? Yes, my good man. That would do the job soundly."

"Do you have access to a case?"

Freddy chortled. "Do I have access? You're a riot." He held out his open hand. "Seventy-five, plus fifteen percent for my discretion. Seeing as how you're being so cryptic and all."

"Fine." Caster dug around in the pouch tied to his belt and paid the man.

"My old friend," said Freddy, tucking the coins inside his shirt before Caster could change his mind, "where would you like that delivered?"

PART III

CARRIER RESTORED

CHAPTER NINE

THE BUILDING WAS SMALL AND DUSTY, THE SIZE OF A
large closet and nearly as dark. Machines dotted the edges of
the room. Two robots that looked just like the one that had
cleaned up after Wren in the Main House stood motionless
against the wall on top of square platforms, light streaking from
their feet up the sides of their legs and all the way to their blank
faces. Parts, either spares or recycled pieces, sat on shelves,
organized and labeled: CPUs, arms, legs, and eyes with trailing
mechanical retinas. One robot, less dusty than the others, hung
from the wall by two nails under its elbows, head slouched over
to the right onto its boxy chest as if it were a puppet that might
leap into motion if someone pulled the strings.

Two new Keepers had found Wren after she left the The
Pits, and she'd asked to see Judge Gamma. She'd expected them
to take her to the courthouse, but instead they'd gone to this
tiny building near the prison that they referred to as a "charging
station."

Gamma sat in a folding chair with his back hunched in a
great question mark over his legs. He was like a spider curled in

on itself, its size hidden and only to be revealed when necessary. His right arm hung free of his tangle of limbs to dangle to
the floor. A thin gray cord stretched from a hole in the wall to
his wrist, where the other end connected to a small opening
just above his hand.

Wren stood across from him. Even sitting, he was taller
than her. She looked up at the black centers of his eyes. They
were smaller now, little specks compared to the fathomless
wells they'd been during her trial.

"Why are you in this place?" she asked.

"This is where I stay when I need to rest. Energy." He
lifted his wrist from the floor, gently tugging at the line holding
him to the wall.

"My sister just committed a crime. You weren't at her
trial?"

"Judge Beta was presiding today."

"Do you know what her sentence was?"

"Yes. Solitary confinement."

Relief flooded her. She was alive. "For how long?"

"Indefinitely."

Her relief dissipated. Alone. Forever in a cage. Would
Survivor blame Wren for it? Would she have preferred death?
"Can you do anything to change her punishment? Can you ask
the other judge to change it?"

"The law is final," said Gamma. "Once a ruling is made, it
cannot be unmade. Your sister chose her path and received
what she deserved. The equation has been balanced."

He made it sound so black and white. She supposed it was.
But mercy came more naturally to her. "Is Prady okay?"

Gamma's pupils widened as he spoke. "Retrieve evidence
from Trial 3965-O-U."

His eyes darted rapidly from side to side, faster and faster
until they turned into blurs of black and white. Then they

turned entirely white and lit up from behind. He projected a
hologram in the air between them. Prady lay in a hospital bed
with his leg suspended in a low sling. His face contorted in pain
while Asha felt around his knee. The hologram changed,
showing the faces of the Keepers Survivor had killed, forever
fixed in pain and fear. One of them still had his mouth open, as
if he'd left things unsaid before he died.

"That's enough," she whispered.

The hologram faded away. "Judge Beta's protocol was over-
ridden during the trial—he would have ruled death, but
protocol 89 allows the Principal to decide the sentence."

"You mean, the Principal saved my sister?"

"He showed leniency. The price would have been blood for
blood," said Gamma. "It is always blood for blood."

"Always? You believe that?"

"That is the law."

"But everyone makes mistakes, even good people."

"They choose to make mistakes. There are no good people."

That hit hard, as if Survivor were speaking through
Gamma, her life's philosophy in his voice.

"Can I see my sister?"

"No. She must remain isolated. Her first parole hearing is
in six months. She may be allowed visitors then, depending on
the outcome of the hearing."

Her shoulders drooped as the weight of the sentence
descended on her. She'd hardly been away from Survivor for
the past decade—six months was incomprehensible. When
Survivor was freed—*if* she were freed—she would hate Wren.
Promise aside, there was no way she could love her after what
had happened. Wren had chosen the city, and Survivor would
never forgive her betrayal.

She sat across from Gamma, her will to stay standing
leaving her.

He leaned closer, the spider uncurling. "You are unusual. You are not like the rest."

They sat together, not talking, resting in the silence. He took in power through his wrist as her own strength poured out. The spare parts stared on from their shelves, resigned to their lack of purpose and the dust that clung to them.

Cold consumed Caster's left side, but his right side was still slightly warm, though growing chillier as wetness spread under him. A drumming, the beat of an unheard song, pounded in his head. Or was it the sound of water sloshing back and forth? He couldn't tell. The pounding crept out and circled his temples, then finally reached around to his forehead and sinuses. It was dark. He tried to open his eyes, but they refused. That was fine —he wanted them shut anyway.

Something tasted foul—acetone, bile, and habanero. It slithered around in his mouth and then settled on his tongue, which felt as if it were covered in fur. He opened his eyes, catching a glimpse of a bare back a foot from his face. There were angel wings tattooed on it, or were they butterfly wings? The world spun. He squinted his eyes tighter, let out several exhales of acid breath, and the spinning slowed until it stopped. The hard surety of the ground gave his body relief, and he let his muscles relax into it as if it were clay he only had to allow himself to sink into. He pressed his palms to the ground, into the clay, molding himself to it as he started to fall back asleep.

A crash assaulted his ears. His body jerked, and the room went back to spinning. Then a voice called out to him like roll call in the barracks.

"You have GOT to be kidding me!"

His limbs jerked again. The pulse in his ears pounded

louder, trying to drown out the voice. It was time to sleep. Good
God, it was time to sleep.

Bottles clinked together as if ushered into a herd by a
broom. Someone sniffed.

"He could get the best booze money can buy and he drinks
acid made in a bathtub by some low slum wannabe chemist.
Fantastic." Footsteps came closer, and he was vaguely aware of
someone standing over him. "Ooh, and he picked himself up a
treat to complement the booze."

Glass shattered, then an arm slapped him as the girl next to
him flailed awake. She grumbled something at the intruder. He
caught the words "bitch" and "need coffee." A hand stroked his
chest, and he slapped at it.

"Sweetie, throw on that collection of strings you consider
clothes and get out," said a voice he recognized. "Your dreams
of becoming a princess are officially over. I suggest you shoot
for something more attainable, like self-respect."

Shuffling noises. Curses from the girl. A slamming door.

"Get up."

Asha. Right at his ear. Loud as hell.

His ceiling greeted him as he rolled over and opened his
eyes. He started to lift his head, but hot liquid rose up his throat
as his stomach lurched. He let his head drop back down, where
it thumped against the dirt floor.

A drizzle of water fell onto his mouth and nose. He threw
himself into a sitting position and coughed out the liquid.
Vomit crept back up his throat, and there was no stopping it
this time. A hand thrust out a metal wastebasket to him. He
grabbed it and proceeded to fill it with the meager contents of
his stomach. After he finished, he turned to see Asha opening a
window. Sunlight streamed in, and if he could have, he
would've sprinted from it.

"Really? We're back here on the floor where I've found

you scores of times before, with enough empties to make a stained-glass window." She left the window to stand over him. "Why?"

He set down the wastebasket.

She uprighted the chair lying on its side nearby. "Sit."

He tried to comply, but standing was difficult. His legs felt like a cross between wet fibers and stiff boards. She stepped behind him and helped him into the chair, and he was vaguely aware of her examining him; she poked and groomed, and he did his best to keep his eyes from closing.

She opened a duffle bag that sat on the floor, took out a bag of saline, and hooked it to the back of his chair. He felt a small pinch as she stuck the needle in near his elbow, and then cool fluid flowed into his arm. She gave the bag a few firm squeezes before rummaging in her duffle some more for a plastic cup and an egg. She cracked the egg into the cup and then dribbled honey on top, followed by a dollop of thick, bright green wasabi. She poured just a splash of water over it all and handed it to him.

"Drink."

He drank. It slid down his throat in one great globule. "God, I hate that."

"I could have brought a less disgusting remedy."

"Then why didn't you?"

"I can't beat you up. This was the next best option. Totally worth the two weeks of sugar that egg cost me."

She sat on the hearth nearby. The small landfill of bottles lay between them, some still dripping cloudy yellow liquid onto the dirt.

"Is this all you've done for the last two days?" she asked.

"No. I ate too."

She spotted the greasy paper cone with a few red crumbs in it on the kitchen counter. "Spicy locusts, by the look of it. Great combo with moonshine. And the young lady, let us not forget. Are you in love? What was her name?"

"Aileen? Artemis? Something with an 'A.'" He smacked his lips together. "Could you get me some water?"

She rose and went for the tub in the cabinet, where she filled a cup and brought it back to him. He swished the water around, washing the fur off his tongue and the vomit from his taste buds.

"You have no idea how difficult it was to convince Gavel to let me help look for you. I said you probably wouldn't be home. You're never home, but I'd check just in case. And of course you wouldn't be partying. You're not the punk you used to be. He bought it. I hate lying to my husband."

"You know me too well."

She squeezed the bag of saline again, then sat on her heels in front of him and nodded toward the bottles. "Was it worth it?"

"Never is."

He smelled his own sweat, a combination of salt and stale alcohol seeping from his pores. When he'd started screwing around the day before yesterday, he'd been concerned that he'd like it as much as he remembered liking it, rather than about the physical consequences to come. Truly, he hadn't liked it, and that would have probably been a more pleasant surprise if he weren't actively fighting down vomit.

She grabbed his chin. "I thought we were done with this. You'd grown past it."

"I'm sorry."

She stood and tugged at her hair as she sighed. "Gavel's going to have a fit if he finds out. He'll throw you out of the Body, you selfish asshat!"

"I didn't do it to hurt you. Or Gavel."

"Why *did* you do it?"

"As an experiment. You're right, something's wrong with me."

"What happened?"

"Something impossible." He flexed his magically healed arm, almost wishing it would be spontaneously broken again.

"So you believe me now? Imagine that."

"Never mind."

"No, sorry." She took a breath and made herself sit on the edge of his bed across from him, butt barely on the mattress, no doubt praying it was a spot uncontaminated by his evening activities. "What exactly is happening?"

"I can heal."

She rolled her eyes. "Already knew that. You should have died in that med ward—a fact that continues to confound me."

"This was different. Six broke my arm and it," he searched for the words, "fixed itself."

She considered that as she crossed her legs at the knee. "You're not screwing with me?"

He shook his head.

"Okay then. Still doesn't explain why you drank a case of what equates to insecticide."

"To test my theory. You wouldn't have been willing to risk killing me." Though right at that moment, under her livid scrutiny, he wasn't so sure.

"And you were willing to kill *yourself*, you little shit?"

"It's not like I stabbed myself in the chest. After not feeling anything after the first two bottles, I was confident I'd pull through if I kept going."

"Oh, you were confident. Phew! Then by all means, fuck science and fuck the people who care about you. Get wasted!" She stood and started pacing in a huff. "Look, I understand that you're confused by this. It's driving me insane that I can't figure out how it's happening. But *where* this ability came from concerns me even more than the ability itself."

"Where? Sounds like you have a theory."

"You're not going to like it—I suspect your father."

"How the hell would he be capable of doing this to save me? He doesn't even know what to take if he has a headache. Has servants to tell him."

"But he has an android. And she's the head of his researchers. She has around three hundred years of knowledge stored up—she was alive before The Fall. Do we really know what she's capable of?"

"You think Thallium used her to save me?"

She shrugged. "He's a dick, but he's still your father. He didn't want you to die. He was fucking distraught in the med ward, though he'd never admit it."

"Okay, but what about these other side effects—whatever was done didn't just heal me the one time. It changed me."

"Fundamentally, yes, it did. I have no idea why or how, and I intend to find out. However, there's a more pressing matter to deal with." She stopped in her tracks and faced him. The way she crossed her arms and glared reminded him of his childhood. "You obviously didn't drink a metric ton of swill booze just to experiment with your new gift of healing. That doesn't explain little miss sunshine on your floor or why you didn't stop drinking when you figured your hypothesis was correct. Something else is bothering you."

He let out a tired, shaky breath. "I'm worthless, Ash. Absolutely worthless."

"Well, that's bullshit."

He raked his hands through his damp hair, growing irritated with the needle in his arm as it tugged against his skin. "No, it's not. I tried to get Wren to leave the city, told her I'd help her. She's choosing to stay and continue working with Thallium and Eydis."

"Working with them how?"

"As a test subject. They're using her somehow to reclaim lost technology."

"Not this delusion again."

"Yes. And I can't stop it. Thallium wants me involved. I don't know why, just that it would play into his mission somehow. Getting involved is a risk I haven't been willing to take. And now Wren's going to end up another innocent person that I'm powerless to save."

"Another?"

He realized his slip up. He hadn't meant to talk about his mom. Asha often tried to coax him into discussing their memories of all going to the market together, where Caster would spontaneously pick up his feet to hang between their arms as they were walking, nearly pulling them over several times, or memories of the rhyming game they played until it drove Asha up the wall. But he'd always managed to evade, and she'd respected his need to. However, as Asha continued to stare him down, he knew there was no way out this time.

"I mean Mom," he said.

Her gruff façade broke instantly, and seeing the pity in her face nearly brought forth a sob from him, something he knew had been wanting to get out for years.

"Oh, honey," she said, "what happened to Reina wasn't your fault. You couldn't save her. Neither could I. And as much as I hate the man, it wasn't Thallium's fault, either." She knelt in front of him. "I think what you feel so shitty about is that you took her for granted when she was still here. Long before she got sick. Which is something she fully forgave you for."

"That wasn't up to her. As far as I'm concerned, there's no forgiveness for that."

"You have to forgive yourself if you want to be the man she knew you to be. Have to. But as far as Wren's concerned, you have nothing to hate yourself for. Wren's still here. The opportunity to be there for her is still here. And she doesn't need a hero—just you. So be with her." She paused. "Not like you were there for Aileen Artemis what's-her-name, please."

"Yes, I'm a whore. Don't need the reminder."

"Philandering may be your norm, but it would seem like it's different with Wren."

"What makes you say that?"

She blew a raspberry, and he caught a drip of her spit on his cheek. "I was in the med ward when she came to see you. It was like you were both staring at the sun. Nauseating, truly." She stood and walked around to the now nearly empty bag of saline on the back of the chair. She pinched off the flow and gently removed the needle from his arm. As she covered it with a small piece of cloth and tape, she said carefully, "Her sister nearly killed you, and your people ascribe that crime to Wren by association. Is she worth the trouble?"

He pondered that for a minute before he stood, fighting the shakiness of his legs and the gong sounding in his ear canal. "She's everything I'm not. Yeah, she's worth it."

"Where are you going?" she asked.

"To get her out of there." He looked around, spotted his knife on the bed, and went for it.

She dashed ahead to stand in between him and the front door. "You're a fool. Between the Keepers, the security system, and Thallium himself, you're going to just waltz out with his prisoner?"

"I'll say I'm there to take her for a walk. She just won't come back."

"He'll find her again. You know he's capable."

"Then I'll stop him."

"How? By fighting him? Brilliant. Didn't go so well last time, I recall. Besides, how does that look to the people if their beloved Principal's son attacks him *and* tries to leave with an outlier? They'll call for your banishment. And fair or not, according to the law, they'd be right to do so. Are you going to abandon them like that? Let them continue following Thallium in their short-sighted stupor until he dies, and someone worse comes in and demands their loyalty?"

"If their loyalty is so easily swayed by stupid prejudices, then they deserve Thallium and whoever would come after him."

"You're absolutely right. It's what they deserve. But they can do better under *you*. You just have to have the grace to love them in spite of their nature."

"You act like I'll be better than Thallium, that I'm somehow morally superior. But at my core, I'm just like him. It doesn't matter how many scouting trips I go on or how long I stay sober. He's in my blood, and I fucking hate myself for it."

The room grew warmer as the sun rose higher, flooding the window with more heat. The pounding in his head was racing his heart to see which was faster.

She crossed from the front door to the trunk at the foot of his bed and opened it. "Can't change who your family is, honey. You might as well accept that. Just like we can't change the people we care about. What we can control is our own actions." She pulled a clean white shirt and khaki jeans out of the trunk and laid them on the mattress. "You can leave the city with Wren and abandon your people, or stay and look out for Wren by joining Thallium in his work. I don't see any half-measures."

"And what if I can't stop him?"

"I'd bet you and Wren can together. And me, of course."

"You? Forming a rebel group, Ash?" He smirked.

"Is that funny to you?"

He stopped smiling.

"Somehow," she continued, "he's responsible for whatever happened to you, and he's clearly got plans for Wren that she'd rather not be a part of." She rubbed at her neck. "I told Gavel my concerns, but he won't listen. Which means *we* have to look into things. And you should start by going to see Wren."

It had started to get uncomfortable in the house. The walls absorbed heat and the roof kept it all in like a lid on a pot. The heat of four summers ago, the smell of aspirin and sweat and blood, poured from his memory into the present as if someone had opened a valve.

FOUR YEARS EARLIER

Caster's mom sat propped up in her little twin bed, three pillows tucked in all the right places to lessen the pain. It was the hottest day in recent history, and he did what he could to keep her cool. He squeezed in next to her on the bed, careful not to touch her too much and pass on his body heat, and fanned her with a damp cloth. The mask covering his nose and mouth and the goggles he wore made him feel like some alien thing, and as much as he hated them, they were Asha's requirement for him to see his mom. Rubedo didn't appreciate that he was taking care of a loved one—it would happily, and easily, infect him just the same.

He waited. Asha had said it would be soon.

"What's on your mind, sunshine?" his mom whispered, casual and relaxed, as if she'd have plenty of time to ask it again and again.

"I don't know who I am without you." It was a selfish thought, but she didn't say so.

She angled herself to face him and stopped his fanning with her limp hand. "You're who you choose to be. It's not up to anyone but you. And I know you'll choose well. 'Above all, love each other deeply.' Start there, then remember that your job as a leader isn't to be served, but to serve. That's what Thallium never understood." She took the ring from her thumb—a silver band with a small hematite stone in the center. It had been her mother's, who had died before Caster was born. She slid the ring onto his pinkie. "My heirloom for you. When you feel yourself drifting, see it and know that *I know* your heart. I knew you before you were born. Trust me."

He wept. "This can't be the end."

"No, my sunshine," she said through a wince as she shifted her body to lay flat on her back again, "it isn't the end. I'm leaving, but it's just a change in location. I get to see what's after this place." She closed her shining hazel eyes, and bloody tears escaped. "Just a change in location."

PRESENT DAY

Random images stuck in Caster's head from her death, wedged in his mind like goatheads. He'd wiped the red drips from her cheeks with the damp cloth. She'd told him she liked how scruffy he was getting, that he looked like a Viking, her own personal Tyr. Would he sing a war song to her? Her eyes went in and out of focus, her words became more erratic, until she finally didn't hurt anymore. He was the only witness to her last breath—a wet exhale around the blood in her throat.

She'd loved him absolutely and unconditionally. And he'd been too late to do the same for her.

Asha's hand on his elbow startled him. "What are you going to do, kiddo?" she asked softly.

He moved around her to the bed and yanked the clean shirt on. "Go home."

Thallium drummed his hands against the console in the observation booth. He flipped switches off and on, turned knobs all the way to the left and the right, and poked every button. As he slid a toggle down, the lights in the main chamber dimmed. Eydis' voice came over the communication system, spilling through the speakers in the booth.

"Do you need my assistance with something, sir?"

He pushed the toggle back up, and the chamber grew brighter. When he peered through the glass front of the booth at Eydis below, she paused in her work settling Wren into a recliner and tinkering with a VRI headset to look up at him.

He pressed the big blue button labeled *PA* and held it down as he spoke. "Just getting reacquainted with everything. Carry on."

She went back to work. If he didn't know better, he would have sworn she'd glared at him. He wished she were able to show emotion, real emotion—not a calculated impersonation, but unbridled and unpredictable. He imagined an angry Eydis, all flushed and full of adrenaline, and squirmed from the waist down.

Wren was pale, almost pasty. Going the patient route wasn't going to be fast enough. Time was running out. But he'd come today to observe and, if possible, speed things up. When he allowed himself to look beyond the immediate threat of The Gentleman, to see the bigger picture of Wren's potential in his hands, a thrill shot through him. He could show her to the surrounding territories, and when they saw what she could do, he'd get their fealty in exchange for her power. No blood. No mess. No waste. And if they refused the gift of her power, they'd instead feel its wrath. Assuming, of course, that Eydis' analyses were accurate. And they always were.

He dropped into the rolling chair behind the console and put his feet up. This was where Eydis was spending her days lately and, regrettably, most of her nights. He couldn't complain. He'd told her to restore Wren, and she was following orders as she should. But his bed was terribly big for one person. He'd considered going down to Screws and Gears, but he'd restrained himself. There were advantages to being with Eydis. Her body, for one, but also her lack of sentimentality and desire to use his position for her own personal aspirations. The latter two qualities were rare indeed.

"Wren, we're about ready to get started," said Eydis. Her voice floated again through the speakers. "Can I get you anything? Are you feeling all right?"

"I'm fine," Wren said.

"You don't seem fine. What's wrong?"

"I'm tired. That's all. Leave me alone." The little lady had some spunk. Who knew?

A triple beep came through the intercom. Thallium sat up and looked at one of the small screens embedded in the console. The weird girl from the lab looked back at him through the video feed.

"Oh, sir, sorry to disturb you. It's me, Bug. Is Eydis there? Not that I can't talk to you, but she's usually the one I talk to about lab-related things."

"What is it?" he asked.

She cleared her throat and straightened her glasses. "Your son's here. He says he's come to see Wren. Should I let—"

Caster gently pushed his way in front of her and got excessively close to the camera. His nose hair filled the screen. "Hello, Father. Am I interrupting?"

Thallium tried to keep the satisfaction from his face. "Gracing us with your presence at last?" And not a moment too soon.

"You, not so much. However, Wren could use some advice on dealing with your puerile tendencies. And general assholeishness." He ducked out of the camera's field of vision, but his voice was still audible. "Bug, open the door, please."

Bug must have been farther away from the camera; Thallium heard her indistinct mumbling, but nothing specific. Caster's voice grew fainter, as if he'd walked away from the door. After a minute, he was back with Bug, and each of their faces filled half of the screen as she leaned in toward the keypad to enter the code.

"Don't look!" she snapped.

He rolled his eyes.

A few seconds later, the door slid open. Caster strode in, took a quick look around, and started down the stairs when he spotted Wren. Bug came back on the video screen.

"Sir, please don't fire me. This job's my life. I'm pretty sure I'd spontaneously combust and die in the sun now, anyway, or else break out in heat stroke that—"

"Get back to work." He pressed a button and the screen went dark.

Caster stepped off the last stair, and Wren got up from the recliner to meet him halfway across the floor. It seemed her skin had turned a little brighter, her expression changing to one whose faith had become sight.

Thallium looked down at Eydis to find she was already

looking back at him with her scientific it-was-only-a-matter-of-time eyes. He squirmed again. He'd been right to wait for her these past couple of weeks. It would be that much sweeter when he got her alone after all this was over.

Caster sat hooked up to a VRI of his own. Eydis connected his headset to Wren's with a cord as Wren closed her eyes and tried to prepare herself for the nightmare she'd relived dozens of times now.

"Hey," Caster said.

She turned toward him. He sat in the recliner next to hers, a cracked leather monstrosity, with his VRI visor propped up on his forehead.

"I'm sorry I took so long getting here. Should have come with you the first time you asked."

"Why didn't you?" she said.

"Because I was afraid of coming back, allowing myself to get caught up in my father's business. I was a coward."

He leaned forward and pushed sideways against the floor with his boots, scooting and thumping his chair toward hers until their big arms were touching. He held his hand out.

She put her hand on his and he curled their fingers together. The feel of his hand, as cracked and leathery as his recliner, was like her sanity returning, so long had she been living inside the shadowy parts of her own mind. She flexed her hand, and he squeezed back.

"Maybe we should wear these the next time we go out on the town." He adjusted the visor so that it was crooked on his forehead. "What do you think? Is it a good look for me?" He pulled up a corner of his mouth in a sneer and crossed his eyes.

She shook her head and stuck her tongue out.

"You'll be able to interface now," said Eydis. She wound one last piece of tape over the cord connecting their headsets. The cord slithered across the tops of the recliners with each end connected to the ports on the temples of the visors.

"If you don't mind," she said to Wren, "please try thinking of somewhere other than the forest, like you've done in our last couple of sessions."

"Where?"

"The first place that comes to your mind. Don't force it. I just want to prime your mind to look somewhere we haven't gone yet."

Wren stared at the ceiling, tracing the exposed ventilation ducts' routes above, as she let her mind wander until it came to a starting place.

"Ready," she said.

Eydis smiled. "You can lower your visors now. I'm going to go upstairs to answer any questions the Principal has during the session." She leaned down to Wren's ear. "Good luck."

She went for the staircase on the opposite side of the lab as the ominous screen above them turned from black to white.

Wren angled toward Caster, nestling her cheek into the fabric of the chair. "Thanks."

He nodded. "Let's get this over with." He wriggled in the recliner, as if it needed adjustment in specific places. "Take it easy on me, all right? You're the experienced one here."

"I'll try."

He chuckled as he lowered his visor over his eyes, and the double snap sounded as the visor pierced his temples. He thrashed in his chair and cursed. "Wasn't expecting that," he said sheepishly.

"You get used to it."

She lowered her visor, and it pierced afresh her tender skin, just barely healed from the salve Eydis rubbed on it between sessions. She winced. Caster's thumb rubbed the top of her hand, and she relaxed.

"Test, test. Can you both hear me?" Eydis said through the speakers of the visors.

They said they could, and then the rush of pixels came, the burst of wind like they were passing through a storm at night. The wind continued as they found themselves at the entrance to the cave in the crags where she'd seen him for the first time. A hot breeze carrying the taste of salt blew between the pillars on their left. The cave entrance was dark except for a dim orange glow emanating from inside.

"Wow," said Caster, extending the word to multiple sylla-bles. He reached down and grabbed a fistful of dirt, letting it fall through his fingers. "How is this possible? I mean...this may not be our world, but it feels real enough to be a world of its own. You could live here, you know? It's that convincing."

"Eydis said some people did used to live in this world. A long time ago. But I don't think you'll want to stay in my version of it."

He brushed his hand against his pants and looked around slowly, still taking it all in. Then he turned his attention toward the cave and the light flickering there. "Right, we're here on a mission. Where to?"

She looked behind them where Knife Point should have been and saw only a haze of blackness. The only other option was climbing down between the crags, descending into yet more darkness. The light in the cave entrance grew brighter for an instant before settling back to the dull glow of embers.

"Forward," she said.

They started walking. Dirt and small stones crunched underfoot, and the hot wind slicing between the crags started to dry out Wren's lips.

"I didn't expect this to feel so real," he said again.

A whiff of something foul rode the next breeze, coming from the cave—rancid flesh with a hint of fresher death, like the innards of a body that had made their way outside only recently. Cracking and sucking sounds grew louder as they approached the entrance.

He pulled her behind him and pressed up against the passage wall, just out of view of whatever was making the horrific noises.

"I definitely didn't think the smells would be so real," he coughed. He spat as if he'd caught some of it in his mouth.

"What do you think it is?" she said.

"Well, there's something in that smell I recognize. Death—decay. But as for the sounds..." he trailed off. "No idea. But this is your dream. What do *you* think it is?"

More sucking, like slurping mud.

"Something big," she replied.

She stepped out from behind him and started creeping toward the entrance. He stopped her.

"Are you sure? You don't have to do this. I can get you—" he stopped short and searched for the word, perhaps remembering their conversation wasn't private. "More options."

"It's just a dream." She said it like a mantra. "And I have to do this for Survivor. You know I do."

He studied her as he sighed. "It's your decision."

"You're with me, right?"

He nodded once. "The whole way."

She continued onward, and he followed. As she reached the entrance, she put her back against the edge and peered inside. The fringe of a low fire was visible. Something sitting out of sight cast a shadow—a gigantic shadow with sharp edges —on the far wall. She slid down the opening to a crouch and switched to breathing through her mouth to avoid choking on the stench that grew so strong it made it hard to think of anything else.

She went inside with Caster following close behind. The feel of his presence was tangible, comforting. Her steps forward fell surer because of it.

Silence. No more crunching. The shadow on the wall disappeared, leaving a pure wall of orange to dance on the rock. Whatever they'd heard before had vanished.

"Good God," said Caster.

On the ground all around them were human corpses in varying stages of decay. They lay in different positions, a few propped against the wall, waiting for a rescuer that never came. Most were missing limbs, others the entire contents of their torsos—cleaned out as if a huge spoon had been taken to their abdomens. Some were down to bones and stringy bits, either due to decomposition or because something had removed all the juicy stuff. It was hard to tell which.

Wren wrapped her scarf around her nose and mouth, but it did little good. She tried to breathe less, but then she felt dizzy on top of sick.

"This is the kind of stuff you dream about?" said Caster.

"Does that surprise you?"

"I just didn't think you were so," he hesitated, "dark."

"What do you dream about?"

He removed a fleshless femur from where it stuck out of the ground, like a toothpick that had been discarded. "I don't think I do."

"That must be nice," she said, taking the femur from him and tossing it aside.

"Look." He pointed to the back of the cave, where a flash of white disappeared around the bend into the tight passageway that led deeper into the rock. He went ahead of Wren, picking a path through the carnage that would result in the least amount of filth on their shoes. They made it to the fire when she stopped.

"Wait," she said.

The mud bench near the fire was broken, the top portion broken in half. On it lay a skeleton wearing a dress that drooped in between its ribs. Its hand was tucked underneath its skull as if it were resting. Wren picked her way over the decay, trying not to think about how something had just squished under her heel like an uncooked sausage. She got close to the skeleton's teeth and saw that they were darkened, with chips and sharp edges. They looked an awful lot like Survivor's teeth.

She recoiled and nearly tripped on a leg. Caster caught her and came up beside her.

"Let's keep moving," he said.

They skirted around the bench and came upon Wren's basket, the one in which she kept her trinkets. It lay overturned and had spilled out not trinkets, but syringes, scalpels, and pills. She moved in for a closer look and found a pacifier—her youngest siblings had had similar ones long ago when they were toddlers. This one was white with a tiny bumblebee on it, its wings little half-spheres far too small for its bulbous body. She reached to pick it up. When she opened her hand to look at it, she instead found the same symbol she'd been seeing in every session—an extended V cut through with a slash—burned into her palm. She shrieked.

He knelt next to her. "What happened?"

She opened her hand again. No burn.

"I'm fine," she said.

"I'm surprised your yell didn't get that thing's attention, whatever the hell we're following." He stood and wandered around the fire, leaving her to stare at her palm. Less than a minute later, he dashed back to her. "You know what? I think we should go. We can try another day, maybe in a happier, less blood-and-guts setting. What do you think?"

He didn't give her a chance to tell him that there were no happier settings, instead taking her elbow and picking his way to the exit as if he'd been spooked.

She planted her feet. "What is it? What did you see?"

He groaned and reluctantly pointed to the side of the fire the thing had been sitting on.

She headed for a large stone that probably served as the creature's seat. Nearby, as if dropped in alarm, was a hand. The flesh of the two primary fingers was stripped, and the rest of it was dripping with saliva. She tilted her head as she examined it, and then reached down to hold her left hand next to it. Minus the missing flesh, the two were identical, down to the trio of freckles between the thumbs and pointer fingers.

A section of red hair poked out from behind the large rock. She followed it, knowing what she'd find but still needing to see for herself; confirming her fear would be better than anticipating it. Behind the rock lay her own body, still recognizable, but with the left hand removed and chunks of flesh torn away here and there. It was as if the creature was taste testing, trying to decide where to start.

"We're stopping now," Caster said to the roof of the cave. "End the session."

Eydis didn't respond.

"Do you hear me? Wake us up!"

"No," said Wren. She went over to him and jerked her thumb over her shoulder. "That's what it wants. That's why it's trying to scare me away."

"And what is 'it'?"

"Something that doesn't want me here. All the other times too, it's been the same thing. Something attacks me. I get scared and don't make any progress. Not this time. I can't be afraid this time." She steeled herself. "I need to do this."

He looked toward the passageway. "You have one intense unconscious mind. This is the first and last time we come here. You hear that, *Daddy dearest?* She's not doing this again."

Thallium's voice bounced around inside the cave. "Then I suppose you had better make this time count." A click ended the transmission.

Wren pulled at Caster's arm. "Come on."

They reached the passage at the back of the cave. It was more a series of tight switchbacks of ragged stone than a passageway. Although it wasn't as sharp as the crags of Knife Point, one wrong move could still result in a deep cut. She dove in, leaving the dim glow of the fire behind and abandoning herself to darkness and the feel of passing between two mismatched puzzle pieces.

"Wait. I can't see," he said, sounding genuinely surprised. He stood half in and half out of the passage.

"We'll make it. I can tell you how to get through."

He edged the rest of the way in, and his voice echoed against the stone. "That humongous thing fit through here?" He hugged the first corner and exhaled so that he could inch around it and into the next straight section of the path.

"It's a dream," her voice echoed back. "Doesn't have to make sense. Besides, I didn't see the thing. Did you? How do you know how big it is, smart guy?" She glided between the stone, moving her arms above her and out to the side in rhythm with the turns and twists.

"Well, excuse me, miss expert," he grunted. "I guess you have an attitude in your dreams, *and* the laws of physics don't apply."

"You're seeing what others don't get to see, I guess. The

things I stuff down...It's just easier to hide it out there, outside my mind. Oh, it's kind of low here."

But it was too late. Caster cursed as a smack filled the darkness. "Ow."

"Sorry."

They went further in, and she did a better job of keeping him from hurting himself or getting stuck. The air grew increasingly damp, and the temperature dropped steadily. Condensation dripped down the passage walls just before they reached the end. She popped out through the final corner, and he followed, exhaling again in order to clear the outcropping.

The feel of this place versus the tight passageway was jarring. Although it was still dark, the sensation of openness pressed against Wren's ears. There was little movement of the air, and it was cool and aged like death suspended.

She stooped to the ground to the right of the passage exit and reached out. The bundle of thorns and tinder she and Survivor kept there was missing. Just as she was about to tell Caster they were going in blind, orbs of different colored light shimmered to life and grew brighter and brighter high above. They rippled as if made of fluid and lit up the surface of the wide, shallow cave pool in a rainbow of blue, orange, yellow, white, gray, and green.

"Wild guess—that didn't used to happen here?" said Caster. His face was cast in the blue light closest to them.

"Definitely not."

They were just a few feet back from the edge of the pool. Wren walked to it and looked all around, expecting to see something that told them what to do next.

"Wonder where our scary friend went?" said Caster.

"This is the end of the cave. I don't—"

Something caught her eye across the water. In the middle of the pool, just beneath the water line, glowed something purple. Her heart beat faster, and she found her feet taking her into the water before she realized what she was doing.

"What is it?" Caster asked.

She just pointed.

"Let me check it out," he said.

"I'll be fine. It's not deep, just knee-high. Be right back."

She took another step into the water, scattering tiny, white cave fish and sending ripples out from her foot. As she was about to head in further, a set of ripples came back toward her from far out. The ground trembled. Her hair rose on her arms.

A beast rose out of the water in front of the purple light for which she was heading, obscuring it. The beast stretched up to the roof of the chamber and hunched forward, too tall for the space, and the lights from the orbs shone down in colorful splotches on its head. Its skin was translucent white, much like the cave fish that swam for shelter, and it hung from its lanky limbs in ribbons. Hooked fangs poked this way and that out of its mouth, and several pieces of flesh were impaled on them. Its eyes were globes of emerald, and they fixed on Wren.

"Go!" Caster shouted. "I'll distract it."

He picked up a few of the stones, large and smooth like dinner plates, near the edge of the water and began hurling them at the monster, spinning once to gain momentum before letting them fly. They soared at the thing's back, and it turned its attention on him. It moved through the pool, which sent water to spill out over the edges.

Wren gave the creature a wide berth and waded deeper in. Caster shouted and taunted it as he bent down for another armful of stones. The creature reached a gangly arm out toward him, and he aimed his stones toward it instead. Wren closed half the distance to the purple orb. It seemed to beckon her onward from under the water, calling her name without words or sound. She was about to lunge for it when she saw a stinger emerging from the creature's spine and moving upward like a curved needle. It aimed for Caster, who was too focused on the thing's hand to see it.

"No!" she screamed. "Don't hurt him!" She felt herself losing control of the dream, her fear beating back her desire to awaken her abilities with a stick.

"I'm going to give you a little push, Wren," came Thallium's voice across the water, as if he were standing on the bank next to Caster.

Eydis' voice followed for just an instant. "Sir, please don't —" before cutting off.

Wren felt a rush of energy and clarity. It rippled through her body and mind and forced her to catch her breath as if she'd just nearly fallen to her death. Her muscles freed themselves from her fear, and she shoved her way through the pool, fighting with the fabric of her dress weighed down by the water as she angled straight for the creature.

"I'll keep it busy! Don't stop!" Caster called from shore.

The stinger reared up, preparing to strike at Caster.

Wren reached the creature. "You want me!"

The stinger slowly receded, and the creature moved toward her instead. Great sprays of water shot up as it walked.

Wren took several steps back, and nearly fell when her feet tangled together. She hadn't thought through what she'd do if she managed to get its attention.

Another rush of energy, this time so strong it took Wren's breath entirely. She finally gasped, and her whole body felt like it would jump out of her skin if it could.

"Wren, we're having problems with the adrenaline dosage," Eydis said, an edge of panic in her voice. Was that anger, too? "Try to relax. I'm going to end the session."

"No, we'll not be ending the session. Keep going. You're nearly there," said Thallium, as if he were addressing a child.

The monster hulked over Wren, shutting out the light as it encircled its arms above her and its ribbons of flesh hung down in curtains. Caster's shouts turned to a dull murmur in the distance. The glow of the thing's deep green eyes filled the space enclosing her, and she fought the urge to gag from the smell of death pouring from its mouth. The thing leaned down further, nearly grazing her face with its fangs. She leaned back and let the water dripping from the creature fall on her face as she met its stare.

Her hands started to shake uncontrollably. "I've lived with you in my mind for long enough. You want to keep me in fear, but I'm done. I'd rather die than be afraid anymore." She took a steadying breath. "Leave me."

The monster let out a roar that seemed to grate out of its gullet. Once it stopped, a quiet fell between them, as if the creature were waiting for Wren to admit her bluff. In the silence of the pause, Caster's voice rang out clear even through the limbs of the beast hovering over her.

"End the session!" he shouted. "Thallium, tell Eydis to end it now!"

"No!" Wren replied, not sure if he could hear her with the creature between them. "I'm fine!" She lowered her voice and stood on her tiptoes, getting right up against the creature's foul mouth. "We're done."

The beast released a vibration from its throat, a moan of relent. It started to shrink in size, slowly at first but then faster and faster. The fangs receded, and the stench faded from the air until a human form was left in its wake.

There in the water, hunched over on her knees, was Alma.

She hung her head as if praying by the grave of a loved one. Her white coat hung in tattered ribbons into the water and her silver hair was gathered in sopping ropes around her face.

Wren dropped to her knees next to her, taking in the wrinkles around her mouth, the curve of her cheekbones. Tears prickled Wren's eyes even though she knew none of this was real. She threw her arms around Alma—she sure felt real.

When Alma didn't hug her back, Wren released her and said slowly, "Why are you here?"

Alma's face remained downcast as Caster started trudging through the pool toward them.

"Alma?" Wren craned her neck to try to see her eyes. "Ma?"

Alma's head shot up; it was as if she saw the face of the devil. "No going back. Can't escape again." She clutched at Wren, taking fistfuls of the front of her dress. "Don't wake it. Leave now."

"Don't wake what?"

"The past. It's in you." She glared at the purple orb several feet away before kissing Wren's forehead. "Leave. Don't return."

She let go of Wren and fell backward into the water. Caster ran the rest of the distance to them and thrust his hands under the surface, trying to pull her out. But she was gone, like she'd just kept sinking right through the floor of the pool and into the earth.

"Who was that?" he asked.

Her response came out wistfully, begging for this part of the dream to be real. "My mom."

She stared at the purple glow with newfound hesitation. Instead of beckoning to her like an old friend, it seemed to order her onward, a master sick of waiting for its slave to be compliant.

Caster reached down to help her up. "What did she say?"

She didn't answer at first, so transfixed by the purple orb that swelled beneath the water.

"That I need to get out of here," she whispered.

The water started to rise, the pool filling up from an unseen source. Soon, it rose past their waists, and it didn't look as though it was going to stop anytime soon.

"This should be interesting. I can't swim. You?" he said.

She shook her head.

The water kept rising and began tossing them this way and that, as if they were in a poorly carried bowl of water.

"Eydis, this session is over. End it now," he called out.

Wren started to sink as the water grew higher than her, and he held her around the waist to keep her head above it.

"Eydis, now!" he shouted.

Only Thallium replied. "We're not done. We'll stop after you get the orb."

"Where's Eydis?" shouted Caster. "Don't you do this, Dad. She's done enough. End the session!" Wren felt him turn weightless beside her as his feet came off the ground.

"Get the orb." A click sounded.

"Dad?"

No answer.

"Son of a bitch!" Caster slapped the water and tried to keep them afloat by kicking. Wren kicked too, and they bobbed awkwardly, their mouths and noses occasionally dropping into the water to make them sputter and cough.

"I have to find it," she said.

"We can't."

She looked across the water, trying to see any hint of purple beneath its surface. Then, just a couple of yards away, she saw it shimmering. It was impossible to tell how far below the surface it was, but it was there.

"I'll be right back," she said.

He held her midsection tighter. "No. The session will end, even if we have to drown to get out of here. We'll wake up."

"Then they'll make me do this again tomorrow. And the

next day. I don't want to come back. I can at least try to get the orb before I drown."

"No, I won't let them. You're finished. It's over."

The light under the water drew her gaze. She swore she could feel warmth emanating from it, swirling around her toes. Her heart raced at the thought of taking hold of it with both hands.

"Wren?" Caster's voice made her face him.

Water dripped from his soaked hair and nose, and the heat of his rhythmic breath hit the cold skin of her face as he worked to keep them afloat. It was a dream, but the pressure of her side tucked up against his, his arm tight around her waist, felt real and right. She wondered if this was what dreams were supposed to do rather than terrify you—make you feel powerful, confident. Invincible.

She somehow knew that's what the orb could offer her. Beyond a shadow of a doubt, she knew it would make her stronger, turn her from victim to victor. The thought was both elating and terrifying. The desire for that power took hold of her. She wanted to know what it felt like to have it, just once. That would be enough.

But she had to go and get it first.

"Wren?" Caster said again.

She leaned in close to his face and kissed him on the cheek. "I need to do this."

She wrenched out of his grip and got a good, deep breath before she sank into the water, ignoring his muffled pleas from above. Everything turned blurry: her vision, the feel of the water as it pushed and shoved her body around, her awareness of her limbs. She took a couple of seconds to gather her bearings and then moved toward the light. It seemed impossible to find a rhythm in her sweeping arm and kicking leg motions, as if she were upside down with no hope of righting herself. The fact that she couldn't breathe started to creep into her thoughts, and she fought to keep her lungs closed. She wasn't going to make it.

One last rush of energy overtook her, this time creating an intense pressure on her chest, and sending a clutching pain through it and down her arms. She thrashed her legs harder, gaining speed and getting closer to the orb. There was no way she could hold her breath much longer; she put one hand over her mouth and nose as if that would keep the water out. With great effort, she reached out her other hand and closed it around the orb. A tingling immediately spread up her arm. The orb melted and disappeared into her skin, shooting purple light through her arm and to the rest of her body.

Her limbs crystallized, turning her into a human amethyst stone. Then the crystal shattered, revealing new limbs. Her arms shone white and pointed into blade-like wings as her hair floated above her in a halo of brilliant white fire. She pulsed with light and energy and felt as if she could cut through the water, the air, even the rock around her. Just when she felt she might burst from the intensity, everything turned dark.

A few clicks sounded around her temples, and then the darkness turned to sickly artificial light as her visor was removed. Sharp pain shot through her chest, and she fought for breath in the midst of it as Caster and Eydis stood over her.

She forced out three scratchy words. "My chest hurts."

"Thank God," breathed Caster. He brushed sweaty strands of hair back from her forehead.

Eydis glared up at Thallium in the observation booth. He blew her a kiss, and she turned her attention to Wren. "I'm afraid I broke some of your ribs bringing you back. That's the pain you're feeling."

"Bringing her back?" Caster said. He growled quietly, "What the hell happened?"

Eydis lowered her voice to match his. "Our Principal took control of the session. The adrenaline he administered caused a cardiac incident."

Rage twisted Caster's features. "He stopped her heart?"

Thallium's voice came over the PA system. "And now she's been restored, son." He beamed down at them from the booth as he poured something dark and thick from an ornate bottle into a short glass. "It was a risk worth taking."

Caster turned to look squarely up at Thallium in the booth. "You risked her *life!*" he shouted. "You and your fucking greed nearly killed her!" He started to stomp toward the staircase that led up to the booth, but Wren stopped him.

"Don't. It's done," she wheezed. "I'm fine."

"You heard her, son. She's fine. Can you drop your righteous outrage now, or will I have to ask you to leave?" His glass was already empty.

Caster stood there, silent, considering.

Eydis broke the silence. "We don't *know* that she's restored. There was an increase in her brain activity readings, but we can't know for certain yet."

"How do we find out?" asked Wren.

Eydis looked over her face with a small smile, studying, as if trapped in a memory nobody else could see. "We test you."

CHAPTER TEN

It was nearly impossible for Adonis to keep from jangling the six coins in the front pocket of his shirt. He stood in line at the counter near the kitchen of the Ration Storehouse, stuck behind an elderly woman picking up an order of toffee that she insisted was shy by an ounce—could you please weigh it again? Adonis grumbled and jangled the coins. He, Six, Sans, and Caster had a tradition of pooling their money together every other week to get some potato cakes with a side of green chile sauce. Caster had ditched them tonight, but Six and Sans were still up for the purchase.

They always made him fetch the order, and although he pretended to complain about being treated like their errand boy, he loved picking up the cakes. The guys were usually a couple of drinks and a poker game into the night back at Six's place by the time he returned, so they didn't notice the tiny teeth marks around the edges of the cakes where he nibbled just enough off to make running the errand worthwhile. He imagined the oily smell and the crunch of the potatoes and the burn of the spicy chile and wished the kitchen attendant would just put two more pieces of freaking toffee on the lady's pile already.

The Ration Storehouse was, as the name implied, the place where citizens of The Disc picked up their portion of food for the week. Citizens were assigned a day of the week to get their food so as to avoid a ridiculous line and a whole lot of pushing and shoving. Rations were dealt out to either individuals or families. An individual's week of rations contained supplies for two meals a day and a sack of some kind of grain that could be boiled and eaten for breakfast. People didn't have many choices in what they were given, but they could usually choose between two different vegetables, or substitute extra butter instead of salt, etc. Meat was never given out. They'd need to kill the rats in their houses or settle for the insects that were roasted in the Trading Center if they were after that kind of protein.

Currently, a few people were there to pick up their rations, but most came in the morning or right after work rather than at seven in the evening. When people went out on a Friday night in The Disc, they went to a bar. Or some other skeevy place the likes of which Six tried to keep Adonis away from even though he sometimes went to those places himself. Hypocrite.

The other people in the Storehouse at the moment, mostly older folks and small families, were seated for dinner. In addition to being the pickup site for weekly rations, the Storehouse was also the only real restaurant in The Disc. There were bars that served a dish or two, and plenty of vendors selling edible things. But the Storehouse served legitimate meals, sometimes even with dessert. To those who could afford it, that is.

Just off from the kitchen pickup counter and the space dedicated to the lines that formed there like life-sucking leeches were a few tables and chairs. The space wasn't fancy, but that didn't keep some from paying that bit extra in taxes to spoil themselves on food made to order and a waiter to bring it to them once a week.

Adonis looked out over the three occupied tables. A couple with a crying baby, what were probably middle-aged brothers out with their elderly parents, and Mainstay and his wife. Adonis lifted his scarf to cover his face. Usually when Mainstay was out with Bambi and he saw Adonis, he'd make him come over and poke fun of him for his wife's general amusement and to make himself feel big.

Adonis suspected that Mainstay had never fully gotten over being demoted from the Head of his own Body to a Soldier in Gavel's—he'd botched a rescue mission of some kind around five years ago. At least, that's what Six had said. Apparently, Mainstay's reaction to the demotion was to become a full-fledged super douche. In spite of it all, Adonis kind of felt bad for the guy. Kind of.

Bambi sat across from Mainstay, talking at him rapidly. She was a whopping four feet, eight inches tall, with a short blond bob and bangs cut straight across and the skin of a person who worked long days outside. Tonight, she wore pink barrettes and bright blue eye shadow. Must be date night. Most of her food was still on her plate as she talked—apparently without pausing for breath—at Mainstay, who ripped through his mushroom steak as if finishing it would shut her up.

Finally, the old lady left with her toffee, and Adonis stepped up to the counter. A layer of grease and grit coated the steel surface, but that hardly deterred anyone. Folks breathed, ate, and dreamed of dirt, no matter how high the walls of The Disc reached.

"I'm here to pick up an order. The name is," he took the slip of paper out of his shirt pocket with the handful of coins and read it, "Miso Pretty." He cursed and crushed the paper in his hand. Six got him. Again. He had to start remembering to check the names beforehand.

"Hold on," said the kitchen attendant, a chubby kid about the same age as Adonis, who was probably learning his future life's trade. He popped his head in the swinging door of the kitchen.

"Order for Miso Pretty?" he yelled, louder than necessary.

He returned to the counter, fighting back laughter. "They're just about to come out of the oil. Should only be a couple more minutes. You can stand to the side and I'll get them when they're ready."

"Thanks," said Adonis.

He stood next to the counter and shuffled back and forth on his feet. It seemed Bambi still hadn't paused to breathe, but her roll was gone—how had she not choked on it? Mainstay's jowls jiggled as he guzzled what looked like apple cider, probably pretending it was something stronger.

A cook in an apron came out of the kitchen and put a delicate glass on the counter for pickup. It held a chocolate parfait, something Adonis had only tasted once, with several fluorescent pink sandwich cookies sticking out of the top around its edge. The cook rang the bell and went back through the swinging door as a waiter came up to take it. Just as the waiter turned with the dessert in hand toward the dining room, the cook burst back into the pickup area. He stopped the waiter and slipped him a piece of paper, small and folded, and then whispered something. The waiter nodded before departing. The cook slapped his chest a couple of times like he was trying to get his heartbeat back to normal and disappeared into the kitchen.

Adonis watched the waiter, half-heartedly thinking of ways he could steal the silky chocolate dessert without getting caught. Sans could do it, but he wouldn't, and he wasn't here anyway. The waiter took the dessert to Mainstay's table and put it next to Bambi's plate. She oohed and ahhed and smelled the cookies like cigars as the waiter slipped the piece of paper to Mainstay beneath the table. Mainstay wiped his mouth as he took and read it. Bambi remained transfixed by the parfait. The waiter left, and Bambi indulged in a cookie. Mainstay started to stand, but Bambi stopped him with a look and two words. He pointed at his empty cider glass, jerked his head toward the hallway leading to the bathrooms, and pushed the parfait dish closer to her. She shrugged and started in on the pudding as he turned in the direction of the bathrooms.

"Miso? Your order's up," said the kitchen attendant.

Adonis turned to see a brown paper bag with the top folded over on the counter. "Can you hold that for me? For just a minute?"

"Yeah. But if someone else pays me for it, it's theirs."

Adonis looked back at Mainstay's table, occupied only by Bambi, who was nose-deep in pudding, and waited for Mainstay to reappear. He didn't.

"Fine." He slammed the coins down on the counter, grabbed the bag, and speed-walked toward the other side of the Storehouse and the bathroom hallway.

A voice called after him from the counter, something about sauce, but Adonis didn't stop.

Mainstay had been acting weird ever since they got back from their last scouting mission. He rarely showed up to train, and when he did, he was monosyllabic and pissier than usual. He had dark patches under his eyes and the focus of a man nearing retirement—half-assed and grumbling—although nobody in The Disc ever retired, and Mainstay was no exception. Gavel had called him out on his crap a few times, making him carry water and clean weapons, but that was as far as he went to investigate the matter. Gavel had always been the type of leader to stay out of his men's personal business, with the notable exception of Caster. It seemed that Gavel and the other guys all blamed Mainstay's behavior on him being down a hand. But Adonis thought it was more than that, and Mainstay's shiftiness tonight pushed his curiosity to its limit.

He tugged the scarf up higher, right below his eyes, in case Mainstay came barreling down the hall and saw him. He turned the corner into the hallway leading to the bathrooms and saw nobody. There were two doors on the left, the men's and ladies' rooms, and a door at the end of the hall that opened to an alley and a loading dock. As Adonis put his hand to the bathroom door, he had no idea what he was expecting to find on the other side. He'd probably find Mainstay taking a long, painful piss or a dump. Something in his mind urged him to investigate anyway, like a poke in the back of his brain, and he pushed the door open.

There were three stalls and a sink on the right, and a urinal trough inset in the ground on the left. He ducked down to check for feet in the stalls but saw none. Had he possibly just not seen Mainstay leave? Had he gone into the ladies' room? The smell of urine stains and someone's dinner after its long journey out mixed with the smell of the hot potatoes and tainted the snack. If Six knew where he was with their investment, he'd hang him upside down from the top of the outer wall. He turned to leave, but the sound of Mainstay's voice stopped him.

"I don't understand."

The voice came through the half-open window set high up in the wall shared with the alley.

"I'm unsure of how to say it any clearer," came the response.

Adonis tucked the edge of the potato bag between his teeth and lifted the tall metal trash can next to the sink with both hands. It wasn't heavy, but it was half his height and cumbersome. He tried to keep it from scraping the ground, paranoid the men in the alley would hear it and investigate.

He set the can down beneath the window and climbed on top of it. It shifted beneath his weight, rocking on its edges until he stood astride it evenly. He moved the potato bag from his teeth and held it in his hand, careful not to rustle the paper as he stretched up and looked out the small, rectangular window. A thin piece of glass opened outward just enough for him to see into the alley. The half-light of dusk cast the scene in eerie yellow.

Mainstay stood on the loading dock, facing a man whose back was to Adonis.

"Sir, I thought I did the job well," Mainstay said, an irritated edge to his voice. "We've been learning a great deal from Hallund. You said so yourself. Now, because of some girl, you're firing me? Again?"

"See, you do understand. You disobeyed my orders. Again. Just like the fire in the forest, you took it a step too far," the other man said. Adonis still couldn't see his face. "The evidence shows it was you. The RSU's logs say you commanded it to open the prisoner doors. You hired the prisoners to kill her—the one left alive traded that confession for a synthetic eye. And you ordered the disposition of a perfectly functioning RSU to cover your ass, an order which of course stood out to maintenance, who flagged the request and contacted me. Is that enough insubordination for you?"

"Sir," Mainstay started, careful and slow with his reply. "I thought that I'd be offering you the gift of plausible deniability. You would keep your leverage and I'd get my revenge. Win-win."

The man lowered his voice, but the intensity of his words made the half-whispers terrifying. "Your win-win nearly cost me everything. You're lucky I don't kill you where you stand and leave you for your wife to stumble over on her way home." The man turned to leave, giving Adonis a clear view of his face. Adonis recognized the Principal's sharp profile from the posters around town proclaiming his mission for The Disc to lead the world in hope and advancement for a better future. He quickly tucked his scarf back around his mouth as he started to walk away.

"But I—wait, please!" Mainstay called out. He dashed over to the Principal, which was quite a feat for a man with Mainstay's fat belly and short legs.

Thallium stopped and turned back. "Excuse me?"

"We had an arrangement. It seems unfair to end it. I was expecting..." he trailed off.

"Really? This again? You have a problem." Thallium shook his head. "Get your vice yourself. Our business arrangement is over." He turned on his heel.

Mainstay spoke in a burst of words, as if he'd tried to hold them back but failed. "Then maybe Caster would like to hear about the work I've done for you."

The Principal rushed back toward him. "Watch yourself."

"I'd rather not tell him, sir," he said, the "sir" clashing with the blackmail. "But he already suspects something unusual about Hallund. He hates me as it is, and you, if the rumors are true. I think he'd believe the truth."

Thallium's form went stock-still. Adonis swore he could see the rage building in him, and apparently, Mainstay did too, because he squeaked out a final plea.

"Just one last meet, please."

Thallium remained silent, and Mainstay started when he finally spoke. "He gets a shipment in later this week. He prefers the 3 a.m. meet time. I'll tell him to be there on Friday."

"Thank you, sir! I swear, you won't hear from me again. I

won't cause you any trouble." Were those tears or sweat beads on his face? "Same place?"

"Yes. The southeast quadrant, same spot as last time near the wall. I'll tell him to expect you." He turned again to leave.

"Thank you," Mainstay breathed into the air as Thallium left the alley.

Mainstay opened the back door of the Storehouse and reentered, but Adonis stayed atop the trash can as he tried to process what he'd just seen. Then the bathroom door started to open. Adonis panicked and threw his weight too far to one side, knocking the trashcan over as he grabbed hold of the window ledge. He nearly smashed the potatoes in the bag clenched between his hand and the windowsill with his elbow, but just missed it.

The door partially opened, but Mainstay was still on the other side. "I told you, I need to go!" he said to someone in the hall.

"You haven't gone yet? What were you doing for God knows how long? Hiding here, in the dark, rather than sitting with your *wife?*" It was Bambi. Her whiney tone was unforgettable to anyone who'd heard it before.

Adonis nearly let go of the window ledge but realized the trash can was on its side beneath him—he'd make too much noise dropping now. He tried to pull himself up to see if he could squeeze through the window, but found his biceps weren't up to the task. Damn Caster for being right. He hung there like a rabbit in a snare, waiting for the inevitable.

"Fine! Because me needing to shit makes you feel neglected, we can leave. How about that?" Mainstay yelled.

The bathroom door swung closed and then the alley door slammed. Two sets of footsteps crunched along the gravel in the alley and grew fainter until they were gone.

Adonis' arms gave out, and he fell hard on the trash can.

His feet went sideways, which made the can rocket out from under him. He landed on the square of his back on the cracked and stained linoleum, sending the bag of potato cakes flying. They landed all over the floor with glorious thuds and splatters.

He rolled onto his side, swept the cakes back into the bag, along with hair, dirt, and other substances he didn't want to think about, and hobbled out of the bathroom. He left the Storehouse and ran back to Six's place, a square little stucco house in the nicest part of the family housing district. Adonis reeled to think about how much Six paid for the neighborhood alone. He burst through the door and slammed it closed by shoving his back against it.

Six's place was stylish, a total bachelor pad. He had *two* bedrooms. But the real luxury was the indoor bathroom, separated from the open living and kitchen area by a door. Shiny black pots filled with cacti sat on the windowsill in the living area, along with an impressive library of ten books and an authentic black leather couch draped in a gigantic, deep purple wool throw that Adonis knew had come from Dearborn and cost a fortune. It had adorned what Adonis guessed was an uncountable number of women on cold nights.

Six and Sans sat at the kitchen table across from each other, holding playing cards to their foreheads. Based on the five empty shot glasses in front of Six and total lack of glasses in front of Sans, it appeared Sans was winning. Six turned toward Adonis with a goofy smile, which faded when he saw the greasy mess that was the bottom of the paper bag holding the potatoes. He dropped the three of diamonds pressed against his brow, letting it flutter to the ground.

"What happened?"

Adonis walked up to the table and set the bag on it before taking off his scarf and coat in a frenzy. "I was at the Storehouse, and Mainstay was having dinner with Bambi. Something weird was going on, so I followed him, and—"

"Don't care. What. Happened. To. The. Potatoes?" Six asked. He opened the top of the bag and looked inside. A hiccup caught in his throat. He overturned the bag and dumped the soiled, mushy mess onto the table. He reached into the pile and pulled out a small, soggy bandage.

"It was an accident," said Adonis.

Six shook his head and closed his eyes.

"I'm sorry! I'll pay you back."

Six put a finger to his lips and then spoke softly. "Did you at least get the green chile sauce?"

Adonis' mouth hung open. "It was an—"

"Accident, yes, I know," finished Six. "That's what I'm going to tell the Keepers who find me cackling over your twisted corpse in the street in about seventeen seconds."

He crossed himself, blew a kiss at the potatoes, and lunged for Adonis. He chased him around the room, at a slight disadvantage due to his level of intoxication and Adonis' smaller size in the enclosed area. Succulents toppled over when Adonis bumped an end table. Six nearly grabbed him then, but his coordination was off and he caught his foot on the edge of the rug, sending him to splay out flat on his stomach. He recovered and leapt over the cracked leather couch to cut Adonis off when Sans stepped in. He stood in front of Adonis' path and stonewalled, making Adonis slam into his chest and bounce back a foot. Six went in for the kill, but Sans held up a hand to stop him.

"What happened with Mainstay?" Sans asked.

Adonis rubbed his nose where it had collided with Sans' chest and caught his breath. "He met with Thallium."

"So what? You think that was worth this *travesty*?" Six pointed at the table and the pile of potato bits.

"They met in the alley. It was super shady. Thallium was firing him."

"From his position in the Body?" Sans asked.

"No. Something else. It had to do with Hallund. Mainstay complained about being told off, and Thallium agreed to pay him one last time. He's setting up a meeting for Mainstay and some person Friday night at the southeast wall."

"Who is he meeting?" Sans asked.

"I don't know, but he seemed desperate, almost panicky about it."

Sans turned to Six. "We need to bring Gavel into this."

Six stuck his nose in Adonis' face. "You're sure of what you saw? If we tell Gavel and this turns out to be nothing, he'll be full-on fuming. You know he's from Kino? In Kino, they disembowel you for questioning your superiors. He'll skin your heels."

Adonis squeaked. "But he left Kino."

"Nobody knows how—you try to leave Kino, Kino erases you. Another reason to be afraid of him. Which is why I'll say it again." He tugged at Adonis' collar. "Are you sure you saw what you saw?"

Adonis swallowed hard before nodding. "I'm sure."

"Fine." He let go of Adonis. "Then we'll tell him." A couple of tears pooled at the edges of Six's eyes as he stared at the mess of potatoes. "It better be worth it."

The isolation unit in the inner chamber made Wren feel trapped and exposed at the same time. She stood in the middle of the box, still unsure of what to do with her arms or where to look even after forty-eight hours of being in and out of it. The pain in her chest made her hunch over.

"We've been at this for days," said Caster. He stood just on the other side of the glass, staring into the box with his arms crossed. He called back up to the observation booth, his words muffled and hollow-sounding to Wren's ears. "She died. I think she deserves some time off, don't you? She can barely stand."

Eydis' voice came back over the speaker system. "Her heart is fine, and her ribs are nearly mended—you were there when I expedited her healing with a tonic."

"Yeah, speaking of which, how have I never heard of that treatment before? Seems, I don't know, almost miraculous," said Caster, leaving the 'miraculous' part out there to hang. "Do we have any other similar technology I should know about?"

Eydis looked down at him demurely. "No, sir, nothing you need to know about."

Caster snorted. "Uh huh."

"Let's begin," said Eydis. "Now, Wren—"

"At least let her out of the damn box," Caster interrupted. He started to run his hands over the seams of the booth, searching for the catch to open it.

Eydis' voice came back over the speakers. "We don't know what kind of power she has yet. The purpose of the unit is to keep her ability contained as we test it—we've been through this. This is for our protection, not her punishment. Please stand back. You're interfering with the baseline reading."

"She'll just be in there longer if you keep delaying our work," said Thallium. He sat on one of the recliners nearby, foot tapping furiously against the floor as he watched Wren in the booth. She'd gotten used to his presence, but the intensity of his stare still unnerved her.

Caster didn't turn as he responded. "Have you slept recently, Principal? You're wired as hell."

Thallium stopped tapping his foot. "We're making history here. You don't seem to understand what's at stake."

Caster rolled his eyes. "The same thing that's always at stake with you, Dad. Same as what mattered to the Valcin before you—domination."

"You know full well this is bigger than that. This won't only increase our reach and ensure the future of our city. It will start us on the path to recovery, real recovery of everything humanity has lost. It won't just be small villages and towns looking to us—it will be the world."

Caster turned toward his father and clapped loudly. "Inspiring! Really, just fantastic. Can't wait to hear that speech when you give it from the balcony of the Main House. I may cry."

Eydis broke the tension by speaking. "We have a good reading. Are you ready to try a test run now, Wren?"

"I'm ready," Wren said quickly, tiring of the bickering in addition to being physically worn out.

Caster turned back to the box and Thallium's foot went off tapping again.

"The platform is ready to receive any energy you put off. You've been doing very well, particularly during those few attempts yesterday morning where we picked up spikes of activity. My suspicion is that you were more relaxed shortly after waking and that that level of brain activity is more conducive to using your ability," Eydis said. "I suggest not pushing yourself too hard. All you need to do is let out what's already within you."

"But *how* do I do that? You still haven't told me," said Wren. Her voice echoed back off the glass.

"That's because we're in uncharted territory, little one. I don't know how, but perhaps consider this—how do you walk? How do you blink or breathe?"

"That's different."

"It's not. You learned how to walk, and now you don't have

to think about it. You blink sixteen times every minute, but you don't have to consciously move your eyelids to do so. Your lungs keep taking in and pushing out air, usually beyond your awareness. Letting your energy out should be no different. It's an equal part of you, natural for your body. Think about doing it and it'll become like breathing."

Caster shook his head. "You're basically saying 'if you believe it, you can achieve it.' You can't be serious."

"That's a bit of an oversimplification, but if you—"

Thallium cut Eydis off. "Start the test. We're running out of time."

"How are we running out of time? You're the Principal— it's not like you have to answer to somebody for being behind an imaginary schedule. Why are you in such a hurry?" asked Caster.

"That's none of your concern, Scout. Unless you've decided to get back to your real work of learning how to run this city."

Caster started, "What's that supposed to—"

"Enough. Please," said Wren. With every retort, the box seemed to be getting smaller. "I need to focus."

The men turned to watch her, and her mouth went dry.

"Hold on," said Caster. He ran over to a table covered in various tools and replacement parts that Eydis had used to revitalize the lab when they'd first started coming here daily. He rummaged through a big box, throwing smaller, empty boxes to the ground until he found what he wanted. He came back to the isolation unit with a bulb of twisted glass.

"Open the door of the unit, Eydis. Please," said Caster. "That is, if you really do want my help down here."

Eydis smiled at him kindly. "Of course." She pressed some button on the console, and the door popped open with a quiet hiss.

Caster held the bulb out to Wren. "It looks different, but it's the same thing Freddy had. Remember?"

She nodded and took it.

He closed the panel. "Focus on that. Make it light up like Freddy did. Don't overthink it."

She exhaled and held the bulb in front of her. She thought about how Freddy had wound the little crank on the side of the box faster and faster to make the light come to life. But then she remembered the way the bulb had popped and gone dark, and fear crept in—what if she couldn't do this? What if she couldn't do what they thought she could, and then she became worthless? Would they send her back into the Open alone, and take away the mercy that had been granted to Survivor in exchange for Wren's participation in this bizarre endeavor?

Caster must have picked up on her anxiety. "Hey," he said, "I'm here. Also," he whispered loudly, "looks like you *are* overthinking it." He stuck his tongue out at her.

She returned the gesture and relaxed a bit. No thinking. No thinking. No thinking.

After what felt like an eternity, the bulb started to illuminate. Dim at first, but as she let her mind wander, it burst into bright light and hummed with energy. Her eyes grew wide.

"Nothing to it, huh?" said Caster.

"That's wonderful!" said Eydis.

"Yeah, it's great. We can light a small bathroom now," said Thallium. He turned and looked up at the observation booth. "Move to stage two."

From the distance between them, Wren couldn't see the exact details on Eydis' face, but she slouched over the console as if she were fatigued. "Keep the bulb going, Wren, but also send as much energy as you can into the box. Imagine it pouring through your feet into the platform like water from a cup."

"I don't know how much more I have," Wren said.

"Doesn't matter. Just see what happens," Caster said.

She shook her limbs out and tried to go to the same calm headspace as before as she closed her eyes. She thought about her time with Alma and the kids, but then the heat of fire came to her mind and she tensed. She thought of Biter, the taste of fruit, her sister's odd sense of humor—everything that had soothed her in the past. None of it worked. She opened her eyes to see Caster standing across from her, and he started making silly faces, crossing his eyes and pretending to hang himself. She laughed and felt the tension begin to dissipate.

A charge buzzed through her, starting at her chest and flowing down to her feet. It was tangible, like the stretch and pull of her arms and legs when she'd climbed trees as a child. It expanded and contracted, flowed slower and faster, just by her thinking one way or the other. She thought big and let it fill her up, zooming down to her feet, which tingled with the sensation. It felt strangely good, akin to the release of fear through a scream. She lost herself in the thrill.

"You can stop now, Wren." Eydis' voice broke her trance.

She let the tingling fade away, and it receded back into her chest and settled down there to sleep.

"How did I do?"

Caster stared over her head up at the big screen behind the isolation box, his mouth slightly open. Thallium clapped hard once and whooped as he sprinted for the stairs leading to the observation booth. Wren made a tight spin in the box and looked at the screen.

She recognized the stretch of Diameter projected on it as the Trading Center. Several booths were already open for business. It was dawn, but the sun hadn't come over the wall yet. People stood still in the street with their necks craned upward, staring at something out of view. The image zoomed out, going far above ground level, to reveal the towering streetlamps blazing with life, casting pools of yellow down on Diameter and the people frozen there in shock. The view zoomed out still further to show streetlamps lit up all over The Disc. The power lines draped over the city from their source above the lab like veins, connecting the lamps and feeding them energy not seen for hundreds of years.

"You did that," breathed Caster.

On screen, the streetlamps dimmed and then went dark once more. The people in the streets turned to each other and began chattering. In the lab, Thallium picked Eydis up around her middle and whirled her around in the observation booth. Then he released her and went back to celebrating on his own, punching things around the room.

"Come up here. Both of you," said Eydis, beaming down at them through the huge window.

The door of the isolation unit unlocked, and Caster opened it wide. Wren stepped out and set the lightbulb on one of the recliners as they passed it on their way to the stairs. They went into the booth.

"That was..." Eydis paused, the first time Wren had ever seen her struggle for words. "Incredible." She wrapped her arms around Wren. "I'm so proud of you."

"Yes, yes, we're all chuffed," said Thallium. He punched Caster playfully in the chest. "Now it's time to take this gift on the road!"

"Already? But why?" sputtered Caster.

Thallium ignored him and spoke to Wren. "You're the future, my girl. A miracle! We can't keep you all to ourselves." He took her hand and kissed it.

Caster put his arm between Thallium and Wren, making him release her hand. "Why the rush?" he asked again, through his teeth this time.

The joy on Thallium's face dimmed. His tone felt eerily serious as he addressed his son. "If you want specifics, then come home. Get back to work running this place with me. Then you'll have the need to know."

Caster pursed his lips, giving no answer one way or the other.

"Regardless of the nitty gritty," said Thallium with the same exuberance as before, turning back to it with dizzying suddenness, "I've waited far too long for this day. My father died without seeing it. Now that it's finally here, there's no point in screwing around. Wren," he gave her a small bow and the strangeness of it made Wren do a double take, "you're now an ambassador of The Disc. Congratulations!"

"Wait," said Wren slowly. "I'm not free?"

Thallium raised an eyebrow at her. "Free? You've been free this whole time. It's your sister that's my prisoner. However, you've just begun to really work with us. We're only getting started. Do you have somewhere you'd rather be?"

Feeling the comfortable weight of her belly still full from breakfast, how her skin was beginning to change from cracking to smooth, and the way Caster's arm brushed against hers as he shifted his weight between his feet, she had to admit that no, there wasn't anywhere she'd rather be. But Survivor would rather be anywhere else.

"No, I don't want to leave," Wren said. She drew herself up and squared her shoulders. "But I know my sister does. I'm committed to seeing this through, doing what you ask. Please let her go."

"Hmm." Thallium clicked his tongue as he thought. "Tell you what, let's see how this first outing goes and then discuss her release upon your return. Is that fair?" He held out his hand to her.

Wren considered the offer, not moving except to glance up

sidelong at Caster. His jaw was tight as he glared at Thallium, but then he seemed to sense her gaze and looked back at her.

"It's up to you. Not him," he jerked his head toward Thallium, "not me, not Survivor. Whatever you decide, I'll be with you all the way."

Without thinking, she stretched up and kissed him on the cheek as she'd done in her dream days prior. He looked surprised, and as she backed away from him, she realized Thallium and Eydis had similar expressions on their faces. The kiss must have been inappropriate, but she wasn't sure why. She'd always expressed love through touch with her family, the people she trusted the most. But perhaps that was what had surprised them—not the kiss itself, but what it meant. She ignored the embarrassment trying to cripple her and addressed Thallium, finally shaking his hand. "Yes. That's fair."

"Of course it is!" He released her and turned to Eydis. "My dear, please put together a proper traveling party for our ambassador. A couple of bodyguards and a medical officer should do it. Maybe old guy, Ark."

"I'll be leading the escort group. I want to put my own men together," said Caster.

"Will you now?" Thallium beamed. "That's wonderful, son. Truly. I'm glad you're finally embracing this mission."

"If Wren's sticking around, so am I."

"Marvelous. You'll leave for Dearborn tomorrow morning."

"Dearborn?" said Caster. "They're tiny, just a couple hundred people."

"We have a connection in Dearborn, if you'll remember. One with a well-respected name. If we get him on board, other communities nearby will follow suit. Or have you forgotten your old friend?"

Caster's slow, forceful exhale showed he hadn't forgotten, and made Wren wonder if 'friend' might not be completely accurate. "Dearborn. Fine. I'll get my men together," said Caster. "Come on," he said to Wren.

Eydis stopped Wren with a gentle touch on her shoulder and leaned in close by her ear. "Be careful. This is just the beginning—come back safe. We have more work to do here."

Wren met her eyes, nodded slowly, and then followed Caster out of the booth.

They thought the silence and the dark were punishments. They put her in here for trying to escape, but the dark was a companion, a presence like the feel of the sun or the cool of the night, keeping her company from the outside in. She opened her mouth and let the darkness spill in. She swished it around, rubbing it in the cracks between her teeth and the soft place beneath her tongue before relaxing her jaw and letting it drip back out over her lips. Silence didn't torment, either. It kissed her ears that still throbbed from the voices of the herd, the babble of the other prisoners screaming for justice or threatening to kill themselves, as if that were a means to revenge. Darkness and silence, her good doctor and nurse, were the punishments she hadn't dared hope for. The three of them sat together on the cold floor and thought about revenge, real revenge, where people died and she was the reason.

She'd probably start with their leader. Whoever this Principal was, he needed to go. Then maybe his family, definitely the men who'd brought them here, especially the fat one.

But she could only dream about it. There was no getting out of here—she'd tried. The door was thick, heavy, and triple bolted. Sometimes the most basic security was the most effective. They'd bandaged the wounds on her legs, but she'd removed the cloth. To amuse herself, she ran her index finger around the edges of the burns, sloughing off the ring of crusty skin that proceeded to immediately ooze and reform after she finished. Pain was cleansing.

She wondered if Wren was facing some similar sort of punishment for the escape attempt. She hoped she was. It was her fault they'd been caught, and a little discomfort might do a better job of showing her she couldn't trust these people than Survivor's insistence alone. Wren deserved discomfort. She deserved to be alone, to know the feeling of truly being abandoned even with warm bodies and faces all around. Then she'd realize they were better off together, away from this herd held in by a wall. Once they were away from the sheep and their bleating and their stench, Wren would see clearly again.

The people in the street had looked at Survivor with the panic of prey staring at a predator they'd thought extinct. They had no idea about life on the outside. They'd never felt true fear, never had it walk into their room in the night and tried to beat it back with a stick, only to hear it laughing in response. She knew it intimately. It hung above her even now. The Gentleman was nowhere in sight, but he was out there all the same. Out there and furious. And he knew exactly where she was.

She was trapped, doomed to wait for him to bust in and get her, which he would eventually resort to. All she had to do was wait. She scraped at a thicker part of the scab near her knee, and her breath caught when it separated from her flesh.

As if on cue, a slot just wide enough for a pair of eyes to look through opened toward the top of the door across from her. She forced herself to stand and prepare for a fight, ignoring the protest from the wounds on her legs, which shot pain through her muscles all the way up her back. The door opened, letting some of the darkness get shoved out by the light of the round, ornate lantern held in the hand of her visitor. It was a woman.

Survivor relaxed her stance slightly and shielded her eyes against the brightness. "Do you mind? I'm trying to think about what I did. I'm almost near tears. You're ruining it."

The visitor closed the door behind her and came within a few feet of Survivor. The circle of light emitted by the lantern fell half on the floor, half vertically up the leg of the visitor. The woman's feet were bare, and a silvery dress fell below her knees. She raised the lantern. The light climbed up Survivor's toes to her torso, showing every mud, blood, and urine stain, and the light stopped on Survivor's face, sending shooting pain through her eyes to the back of her skull. She squinted past it and slapped the lantern away.

"Can't look for free. Definitely can't touch for free."

"You're a mess. A total mess," the woman said. Her voice was rich honey on bread.

"Well, fuck you too."

The woman pulled the lantern closer to herself to illuminate her own face. It had the creamy finish of someone who lived indoors and slept well. Her eyes were pools of gold, and the blond hair falling past her shoulders had a tinge of red.

"You're a mess, but it's definitely you," said the visitor.

"I think you have the wrong cell. I don't know you, lady," scoffed Survivor.

"No, you wouldn't. But I know you."

"Is this some psychological tactic to make me lose my mind? Won't work. Crazy doesn't disturb the already crazy." She sneered at the woman for good measure.

The woman blew right past the nonverbal threat. "What's the first thing you remember? Your first *real* memory."

This was getting annoying now. She was pushing it. "None of your fucking business."

"Humor an old woman, please," said Eydis.

Survivor held her mouth shut. Maybe silence would make

it clear the woman was wasting her time. In spite of herself, Survivor found her mind shooting back to that day in the desert when she was a child, starving and alone, when The Gentleman appeared to whisk her away.

"Very well," the woman continued. "How about I answer for you? Your first memory isn't until you were ten years old. Am I close?"

The woman looked at Survivor with such familiar fondness that it made her stomach turn. And the bitch just wouldn't stop talking. She had to give them credit at The Disc—they knew how to torture.

"No idea," replied Survivor. "Don't know how old I am, don't care. You're wasting my valuable alone time. Get out."

The woman gave a delicate little sigh. "I see you're not ready to know your past yet. When you are, I'll be happy to discuss it with you. Come find me." She put the lantern on the floor and took a red and white tube out of her dress pocket and approached Survivor, who tensed to spring. The lady held up her hands. "For your legs." She squeezed a globule of clear ointment out of the tube. She bent down and applied it to Survivor's wounds, and Survivor nearly kicked her when the ointment met her skin and sizzled like it had hit a frying pan.

"What did you do?" hissed Survivor, bent over and clutching at her knee.

"Give it a minute," said the woman as she put the tube back in her dress pocket. As soon as the words left her mouth, the sizzling stopped. Survivor examined her legs to find the wounds completely closed, scabs turned soft and pink. They itched furiously, but when she tested her weight on both legs, the pain was gone.

"My name is Eydis," the woman said. "I apologize for not visiting you sooner."

Survivor looked at her with new curiosity. "Who are you, exactly?"

"The Principal's assistant."

Survivor immediately grabbed her by the throat, but not so tight that she couldn't speak. "You've been hurting my sister. Poking her like an animal."

Eydis didn't look nearly as scared as she should have, instead responding calmly and quietly, face smooth. "It's a good deal more sophisticated than that, I assure you. All of our work has been done with Wren's permission. And now, it's finished. She's awake."

"What does that mean?"

"Her abilities are restored. The part of herself that had been caged is free again."

Caged? Free? Whatever they'd done, it had changed Wren. It was clear from how she acted in the street, the way she'd tossed their relationship, their life together, aside so easily. Now they'd somehow taken it a step further. What the hell had they done? "I want to see her."

"Sadly, that's not possible."

"It is if I break your neck and leave." She increased the pressure enough to make Eydis swallow against her palm.

"Then you wouldn't have the information I have to offer. You'd be going out blind with no way to get through the wall."

She was right. Escaping on her own hadn't gone well last time she tried. Survivor released her and went back to her spot on the floor, which was still warm. "Why the hell are you here? If this visit doesn't have a purpose, I'll go back to my beauty sleep and absolute silence."

"I'm afraid that's not possible, either." The woman sat gracefully with her legs to one side and her opposite arm out to support her weight. "It would seem our Principal has no use of you now that Wren has decided she prefers life here, even if that means it's without you."

That stabbed into Survivor's gut and twisted. "Then I guess you're here to take me to be executed? Is that it?"

"Not quite. The Principal met with an associate of his recently, someone I'm guessing is connected to you. The Gentleman?"

It felt as if all the air had been sucked out of the room, out of Survivor's lungs. She grabbed her knees and fought for breath.

"Based on your reaction, it looks like my hypothesis was correct," Eydis continued. "The Principal has not shared details of the arrangement, and it would seem suspicious of me to push for more information when I'm at his service rather than he at mine—I'd like to keep him thinking I'm his servant for the time being. But he requested I arrange for your release into the hands of The Gentleman this very evening."

A rush of urgency took hold of Survivor, flooding her with options. Throttle this woman and run with no supplies and no idea where The Gentleman was outside? Appeal to her humanity and deceive her into letting her go? Break that lantern to pieces and kill herself with a sharp bit? She settled her mind, found her breath, and simply replied, "I'm not going back. Just kill me if it's all the same to your leader."

"It's not. There's a political history between The Disc and The Gentleman's clan that goes back several decades. Similar trades have been made before—a commodity in exchange for peace. The Principal has no choice but to give you over to avoid war. I, however, do have a choice. As do you."

"Do I now? Is it to kill you, the Principal, and take my sister back? Because that's the one I like."

"Perhaps in time, you can accomplish some of that. However, the more pressing matter is your escape. I can either order Keepers in here with the push of a button," she reached with her free hand to the black bracelet on her other wrist and held her finger over the button there, "and have you turned over to The Gentleman as I was ordered to do. Or you can agree to do something for me, and I'll release you myself now."

Survivor's laugh bounced around the walls of the small cell. "You're going to betray your leader?"

"He's not my leader, he's a means to an end; I need his resources. I'll keep tolerating him for now. But there are other things that need to be set in motion. Do you know the town Hallund?"

"I've heard of it."

"It's southeast of here. It's a farming town, far smaller and simpler than this city but full of strong men and women and quite profitable. Thallium recently sent a man to poison their water, a man I believe you've met before. Mainstay? He only has one hand now."

Survivor kept the growl in her chest to a quiet purr. "So?"

"I need you to take him to the town he poisoned so that they can deal with him. Motivate him to confess."

"Just leave without Wren? No."

"But Wren's already leaving."

Survivor's eyebrows shot up, and she quickly tried to conceal her shock. "When?"

"Tomorrow morning. Traveling to a town in the south called Dearborn. Here in The Disc, we have some power from solar cells that I maintain, big versions of this one here." She moved her hand from the bracelet to the lantern and tapped a little blue-black rectangle sitting on top of it. "We're lucky. Outside The Disc, smaller settlements have far less. They burn what little coal or wood there is left to keep warm. Some have small generators, but many have never seen electricity. The Principal is making your sister and a select group of escorts show off her newfound ability to produce energy."

"Produce energy? What the hell does that mean?"

"It means she's extremely valuable. Humans would kill each other to use her. The Principal believes it won't come to that, that she'll be an incentive for others to join him and give him their loyalty. He believes if it were to come to war, Wren's ability would end it swiftly with minimal bloodshed. He can't see the inevitable—men *will* die over her. He will likely be one of them."

A little thrill ran through Survivor at that thought. "You don't seem too upset about all that death."

Eydis gave a thoughtful smile, both sweet and condescending, and said nothing.

"If you let me out of here," Survivor said, "I'll get my sister back. You know that, right?"

"I'm counting on it. I care about her a great deal, and you'll need to warn her—after you deliver Mainstay to Hallund and he confesses, news will spread fast about The Disc's role in Hallund's demise. Find Wren in Dearborn and get her out before the town grows suspicious of her, then bring her back to The Disc."

Survivor snorted. "Fuck that. What's to stop me from taking Wren and disappearing into the Open?"

"Nothing but Wren herself, I'd imagine. But I'll leave that between the two of you. Do we have a deal? Because every minute that ticks by gets you closer to being handed over as a sacrifice to the Marauders." She stroked her black bracelet.

Survivor thought it over, but it didn't take long to determine this was her only option. She'd escape The Gentleman, get revenge on Mainstay for trying to have her killed in prison, and show Wren that going with her back into the Open was the safest option for them both. "Fine. Deal. Where can I find the fat one, Mainstay?"

"He's making a deal with a merchant tonight at three o'clock. Southeast section of the wall. The merchant will be there early to scope out the meeting place. Get what you need from both of them." She stood in one fluid motion and took something from her pocket—a vial containing dark magenta liquid with "R6" adorning the outside. "Take this with you to Hallund, in case their people don't believe he's guilty of contaminating their water."

Survivor rose and took it. As she went to open the top, Eydis stopped her.

"That can kill five thousand people, if conditions are right. It will absolutely kill you if you ingest it. Keep it closed at all times."

Survivor held it away from her and slightly up, trying to fathom that kind of power to kill. She fought the urge to open the vial anyway and see if it tasted salty or sweet.

"There are two tunnels that lead under the east side of the wall," Eydis continued, "on either side of the Main House in case of an evacuation, far away from the Main Gate, near which The Gentleman and his men are encamped. I will leave the tunnel south of the Main House open for you. It's always locked and therefore unguarded. You'll be able to walk right through, or drive, if you can find a vehicle."

"Or you could be lying and The Gentleman is waiting for me on the other side of that wall."

"You'll be risking capture either way. I can lead you to him in chains or you can take your chance to evade him as a free woman. Which would you prefer?"

The lady made a good point. "Fine."

Eydis nodded once. "Good. I've left a sack with basic

supplies just outside the door here. Good luck." She turned to leave.

Survivor called after her. "I don't give a shit about your town or your plan. You can't control me, not now or ever."

Eydis turned back and lifted the lamp so that Survivor could see her eyes. "I learned that long ago," she said wistfully. She walked out, and her light bobbed up and down in the dark passage until it disappeared.

Survivor let the darkness lick her skin for a while longer, rotating her hands and arms in the air. Then she pressed her lips to the wall before walking through the door. She closed it behind her so the darkness wouldn't get too warm.

CHAPTER ELEVEN

ASHA AND WREN HAD BOTH TRIED TO SIT BY CASTER, BUT he'd taken the seat across from Asha, putting Wren in the middle. Asha grumbled about heating up water for tea as she stood again. Wren looked around Asha's home, at the love stuck in every corner. She could see it in the cleanliness of the surfaces and the way pretty things hung on the walls.

"Is that a new cross?" said Caster into the quiet. He pointed above the fireplace at a specific "T" made of pounded sheet metal edged with a vine pattern.

"Anniversary present from Gav," said Asha. She stared at Wren as if weighing her worth. Her gaze wasn't angry, but its power still made Wren shuffle in the hard seat.

The kettle over the fire whistled, and Asha turned her attention to it. She scooped a spoonful of dried green leaves from a square tin into the cups in front of them and then poured steaming water on top. Wren sniffed. It was slightly spicy and made her nose tingle.

Asha put a plate down between them, covered in little

round discs of something tan and sticky. She popped one in her mouth and talked around it. "No cobbler this time."

"Again, I'm sorry," he said.

Asha rolled her eyes.

"Anyway, the reason we're here," he turned to Wren, "is to tell Asha what's going on with you."

Wren chewed on the inside of her cheek. "You mean what I can do?"

"Exactly."

"Why?"

"Because she's smart. Mean, but smart."

Asha kicked him under the table.

He winked at her. "And because the three of us need to start working together. Right, Ash?"

Asha sighed. "Right."

"Why don't you tell her about what happened earlier, Wren? With the lamps?"

Wren reached for one of the little discs on the plate. "I turned on the lamps in the street."

"What do you mean, *you* turned them on?" said Asha.

"I let out some energy, and they turned on. They're really bright." She took a bite of the disc—it was sweet and slightly bitter, soft and stringy. It stuck to the roof of her mouth.

"Holy shit. That was you? Was it just this block?"

Wren smacked her lips as the sugar dissolved. "Every block."

Asha sat back in her chair. "My God."

"This is yummy," said Wren, reaching for another disc.

Caster chuckled. "Go slow. That's a lot of sugar."

"How is this possible?" Asha continued.

"I'm special," said Wren. "My genetic marker." She ate another disc.

"A genetic marker? Is that what Eydis called it?"

Wren nodded.

"I don't know," said Asha. "I'm not buying it."

Caster took a swallow from his mug before speaking. "What do you mean? What else could it be?"

"Humans have a history of mutating, it's true. Your hair," she nodded at Wren, "is a classic example of that. Red hair didn't exist for thousands of years until a mutation formed, but the foundation for that change was already there. Hair changed color, it didn't spontaneously appear. This is different. And abilities like this don't just appear."

"Maybe they do sometimes," said Caster. "The Fall put more radiation into the world than ever before. Only now are women starting to have completely healthy babies again. Lymphoma is at an all-time low. Maybe we're seeing the positive effects of the radiation. Positive mutations."

"Like Sans? Do you consider the Harbingers to be a positive effect? Because I think he would disagree with that. Besides, we don't *know* that radiation caused the Harbinger mutation, it's just the easiest answer. The harder answer that I believe we need to consider is that all of these anomalies—Harbingers, Wren's ability, your healing—are not the results of evolution, but of man playing God."

That idea was left to hang in the air as Asha took a sip of tea.

"As for you two," she waggled a finger between them, "the common denominator between you is Thallium."

"Look, right now, I'm less concerned about where Wren's abilities came from and more concerned with Thallium's plans for her," said Caster.

"What plans?" asked Asha.

"We're going on a trip," said Wren. She took a drink, and the spicy tea washed the remaining sugar from her mouth.

Caster cut in. "Thallium wants to use her as leverage over the surrounding territories."

Asha shook her head. "This has been Thallium's goal all along—use her for profit."

Wren had lived twenty-one years in the Open with no power. It had been simple and, for the most part, happy, at least when she was with her family. Here in The Disc, people had just a little bit of power and yearned for more, as if their lives were lacking. And with this talk of using it to manipulate other people who didn't have it, Wren wondered if the world would be better off without it entirely. "Why does everyone want power?" she asked, more to herself than looking for a real answer.

"It's not just power," said Caster. "It's the ability to heat homes during the winter and keep our people from dying of hypothermia, to grow crops in a climate-controlled space so we'll never starve, to power weapons that make Marauders look like angry children with twigs. It's everything."

"It just seems dangerous," said Wren. As she said it, she felt a flutter in her chest and recognized it as the energy within her, familiar now after flexing it in the lab so many times. It thrilled her to feel it there waiting to be used whenever she needed it when it was wanted by so many who had none of their own. Perhaps that was the appeal and the danger—how she liked the way that power felt.

"It is dangerous," said Asha, "in the wrong hands. Thallium's hands are the wrong hands. He won't just give that kind of power away; he'll dole it out in meager doses to those who come to him on their knees."

The contents of Wren's stomach sloshed around. She put down the uneaten treat still in her hand. The sweetness was making her sick. She realized she'd been stuffing herself on sweetness, on sugar and chicken and nice dresses. Survivor was right. If she ever saw her again, she'd tell her so.

"Clearly," continued Asha, "we have to stop him, and we need to work together."

"How can we stop him?" said Wren. She kept to herself the thought that stopping him meant going against him, the man who had clothed and fed her even though it was for his own gain. Something about that felt foolish and wrong, like biting the hand that had pulled her out of the Open.

"By removing him from power. Peacefully," said Caster.

As he sat there, saying something so complicated with such simplicity, Wren couldn't help but admire him. He'd always been kind to her, and the way he looked at her—as if she were a star in an otherwise black sky—made her aware that there was an entire part of herself that she hadn't known existed. She wanted desperately to give in to the excitement, the vulnerability of being alone with him and simply talking. She would be happy doing only that for a long time and wondered if he would be, too.

But up until now, he'd seemed unsure of himself, of his role in his own story. Reluctant to lay claim to anything, including his own title as future leader of a people he chose to love even when they were unloving. As he talked about removing his father from power with plain and simple certainty, she saw a glimpse of the leader he could be. Decisive, strong, merciful. She hoped he could see it, too.

"What if he refuses? Won't he fight?" she asked.

"He absolutely will," said Asha. "But maybe there's a way we can avoid that. At least, Caster wants to avoid it. I could go either way." She snickered.

Caster glared at her, and she shrugged. Then he turned to Wren. "I know I'm asking you to risk everything. My father has his Keepers, and I'd say the vast majority of The Disc is loyal to him because he continues to keep them safe and fed, even if he does enjoy luxuries they don't. But I see him reaching beyond his own walls and that frankly terrifies me.

"I know that when he fixates on something, he obsesses until he gets it. With you at his disposal, I'm not sure he'll ever be satisfied with what he has. I don't want you or my people to suffer for his greed. But I want to know what *you* want."

Wren looked between the two of them, at Caster's scars and Asha's tired eyes, with no idea how to respond. She'd never been asked what she wanted. She'd never had options other than to fight to live another day or to give up. "I just know I don't want people to get hurt because of me and what I can do."

"The best way to avoid that is by getting away from Thallium, but if you run, he will follow you," said Asha. "He'll find you eventually. Which is why we have to get him to step down and let Caster take his place. To convince him to do that, he has to see that the surrounding territories back Caster. Then we'll have to show the people of The Disc that Caster will care for them better than Thallium. If we get allegiance from within and without the walls, Thallium should step down. He would be a fool not to."

"And how would I help you do all that?" asked Wren.

"When we go to Dearborn tomorrow, we're not going to offer your power in exchange for their loyalty to The Disc. We're going to offer it freely and tell them it's against Thallium's wishes to do so. They'll be the first to back me on the outside," said Caster. He took a deep breath. "At least, that's the plan."

Survivor's voice echoed in Wren's ears. *They're going to get you killed. It's too risky. Don't be so stupid—I taught you better, and so did Alma!*

Alma. Her constant warnings about The Disc came to mind, as did the vision of her as the monster from her dreams guarding the purple orb. With talks of greed and rebellion, she began to see a glimpse of why Alma had tried to keep her ability hidden from her. She wondered how much Alma had really known about it, and the thought disturbed her so much that she pushed it away.

She nodded. "I'll help."

"Thank you," said Caster.

"Fantastic," said Asha, "I need a drink." She downed what was left in her cup.

"Me too," said Caster. Asha slapped him hard on the ear. He rubbed at it. "Then we leave for Dearborn tomorrow to talk to Gray."

"That kid you used to hang out with when you traveled with Thallium during the summer?" asked Asha. "Didn't you hate him?"

"It was mutual. But he's grown up a lot since then, and I have too."

Asha stifled a snort.

"I've met a couple of his men," Caster continued with a glare at Asha. "They're young, but he's trained them well. We'll need them. You up for the trip, medical officer?"

Asha stared into her empty mug. "I'll tell Gavel when he gets home."

"*What* will you tell him, exactly?" asked Caster.

Asha continued to stare in her cup, as if she were searching for the answer at the leaf-covered bottom. "Something generic yet convincing, I hope."

"That'll do." Caster stood to leave. "I need to take Wren back. The more sleep we can all get tonight, the better."

He went for the coat rack by the door.

Asha stood as Wren did and got close as if to hug her, lowering her voice so Caster wouldn't hear. "This is dangerous.

We have to keep this a secret—you can't tell anyone. You understand that, right?"

"Yes."

"You trust us?"

Wren looked over at Caster, who held her red cloak open for her. "I trust him."

Asha smiled the first real smile since Wren had met her. "Good answer."

Gavel laid on his stomach on top of the wall, looking through his night scope at a section of The Disc thirty-five feet below. He shifted closer to the inside edge of the wall, and the rough brickwork tugged at his clothes. Only the main gate area was made entirely of steel, containing defense systems and circuitry the Principal's android had designed. The rest was just brick and mortar covered in an outer steel façade.

Gavel squinted into his scope. For all the money the scope had cost him, he could barely make anything out through the murky green lens and decided it was more toy than tool. He knew their surroundings by memory, at least—mostly storage buildings containing tools and raw materials for construction. There were no lamps here. They weren't worth the fuel it would take to burn them in an unpopulated area. A guard shack stood just north of their current position, more than likely unmanned. This area wasn't deemed a high value target for thieves, nor a hotspot for unruly drunks and general misconduct. And yet, something felt off here, and Gavel was fairly certain spying on one of his own men was responsible for the churning of his stomach.

"I don't like this," he said finally, shifting his weight between his elbows. The cold of the breeze from the Open behind them had begun to seep into the back of his oilskin duster.

"Sorry, sir, but we thought we had to tell you," said Adonis. He lay prone a couple of feet away, peering through a scope of his own.

Gavel set his scope aside and picked up his flashlight. He flashed it twice to his left and received the same double flash back several yards away at ground level. He repeated the action to his right, and again received a double flash in return. "Nothing. You're sure it's the southeast wall?"

"That's what Thallium said. We're early. It's five till three. Maybe they're not here yet."

Gavel rubbed his eyes and then looked through the scope again, stretching his vision to the upper limit of focus in the dark. If something moved at this time of night with any source of light, they'd probably see it, but if the meet went down in total darkness, the odds of them seeing it were about the same as spotting someone dressed in tan clothes moving slowly a half-mile away in the desert. He felt blind without his Scout, but Caster was attending to the Principal, about to embark on a mission for him. Gavel would have to do this without his senses.

"I don't like this," Gavel said again.

"Mainstay's been acting weird. Not showing up for training, keeping to himself. Plus, with how he was talking outside the Storehouse, Thallium's definitely up to some shady shit." Adonis choked out the last word as if he realized at the last second that it was sedition.

Gavel turned and leveled his gaze at the young Grunt, who squirmed under its intensity. "We don't *know* anything. Until we do, we presume innocence. Understood?"

"Yes, sir." Adonis turned away and shoved his scope back

against his eye a little too eagerly, hitting the fragile bone underneath and wincing.

They kept on the lookout for a bit longer before a triple flash came from their right, further south at ground level near the wall. The two got up immediately, stowed their scopes, and crouched as they jogged along the top of the wall, which was no more than eight feet wide. They reached a service ladder, and Gavel went down first with Adonis close behind. As Gavel's feet touched the ground, Six approached them, creeping close to the wall in the dark, his flashlight dangling at his hip to give off just enough light for the company to see each other as they conversed.

"Spotted Mainstay about a block away, coming from the north. Must be heading for that respite shack near this section of the wall."

Adonis dropped from the ladder and landed by him. "Those are tiny, only big enough for two guards to sit. We can't get anywhere close."

"We can get close enough to observe." Sans' voice behind Adonis made him jump.

"Stop doing that!" said Adonis.

Six stepped up and held out a fist to Sans. "Nice one."

Sans bumped his fist, but the action was more reflexive than celebratory.

"There's a tool shed across from the shack," continued Six, "but it's pretty small. One of us could watch from there. It'd be close enough to see, maybe hear if the wind stays calm. If we get any closer, they might bolt."

"I'll take the shed," said Gavel. "Sans, watch the perimeter. Make wide passes and make sure nobody else is out here."

Sans didn't respond. Gavel thought he was carrying himself tighter than usual, with tension in his posture that was usually so nondescript.

"Thief, are you feeling well?" he asked.

It was a question Gavel didn't have to ask him often, but the entire Body knew the meaning.

Sans rolled his shoulders. "I'm well, sir."

"Good. You two," Gavel turned to Six and Adonis, "back up on the wall, behind the shed."

"Sir, we won't be able to help you from up there," said Six.

"I don't expect to need help. We're here to observe, not intervene. If there is something going on, I'll confront Mainstay tomorrow with the evidence. He'll get to tell his side of things and share what kind of work he's doing for the Principal. We do not go on the offensive tonight. Now go."

"Yes, sir," said his men.

They split off, and Gavel made a wide berth around the block, coming at the tool shed from the south side since Mainstay was approaching from the north. He reached the shed and untied the bottom of the sheet of thick plastic covering the window. He took the bow off his back and slipped inside before lowering and retying the sheet carefully behind him so that it didn't slap against the wood frame. The shed was square, squat, and dark. He covered the end of his flashlight before turning it on, getting just enough light to ensure he didn't run into the bags of unmixed concrete, wheelbarrows, and trowels used to fix cracks and weak spots in the wall.

He picked his way between the tools and supplies to the window facing the respite shack across a narrow path. The plastic was torn in places and generally worn out from wind and tossed dirt. He stuck two fingers through one of the rips and widened it a couple of inches, enough to give him a clear view of the shack without being seen. There was no door on the shack, only a square hole through which to enter. It was no more than a large box with a couple of windows cut out of the front. Respite shacks were for shade and slight protection from the wind, not luxury.

Mainstay came around the corner and onto the path. Even though it was dark and he wore a hood, his short stature and gait gave him away. He looked around one last time before approaching the shack. When he was satisfied he was alone, he went up to the shack and knocked on it twice. A cloaked figure emerged and set down a lantern, turned so far down that it let out only a tiny circle of light. Mainstay backed up several feet.

"Where's Frederick? I do business with him," he said angrily.

The figure held out a small, cloth bag tied closed with twine. Mainstay took a step forward, but then stopped himself.

"Who are you? Did he send you?" he pushed.

The figure nodded, undid the top of the bag, and held out a rolled cigarette.

Mainstay tapped his foot as he thought. "No. Where's Frederick? I need to see him."

The figure continued to hold out the bag and cigarette in one hand while using the other to sweep back a fold of the cloak. An ample chest was revealed, and the woman stuck her leg out of her cloak and pointed her toes to show the shape of her thigh.

"Both? But..." His tone changed to one of epiphany. "Thallium. Is this a gift from him? All is forgiven?"

The woman nodded again.

He laughed, though it sounded more like a giggle. As he went up to the woman, she stuck the cigarette in between his lips. He reached for her, but she kept him back and lit the cigarette with a disposable lighter. He inhaled deeply, and before long, he was struggling to stay standing. He stumbled and laughed, reaching toward the stars and then stomping on the ground as if there were bugs underfoot. In what appeared to be one last moment of clarity, he threw himself toward the woman, hands groping at the air.

She grabbed him by the collar and threw back the hood of her cloak. With her free hand, she flicked the lighter to life near her face. It was the violent outlier.

"How the minds of men stumble. You fell for my tits again." She made a show of licking her lips. "I'm ready for the other hand now."

She picked up the lantern and started pulling him along. He shrieked. Gavel punched the plastic sheet until the ropes attaching it to the windowsill snapped, and then leapt out onto the path. He drew his bow.

"Stop!" he said.

Survivor grabbed Mainstay around the neck, put a knife to it, and continued walking them backward. Mainstay's eyes were wild, spinning around and seeing things nobody else could see.

"Hey, it's the Dark Wonder," said Survivor, smiling to reveal her broken teeth. "Sorry, but I'm in a hurry. We'll play some other time."

Gavel's index finger touched the familiar spot near the corner of his mouth as he drew his bowstring back, and he fought the urge to let his shot fly at her right eye. "What did you give him?"

"Nothing he hasn't had before." They neared a main street connected to the path running in front of the shack. "If you follow me, he's dead." She pulled Mainstay into a jog and turned right, heading east.

Gavel ran into the street and tried to line up a shot, but she was pulling Mainstay along in a clumsy run behind her, using him as a shield. Gavel backed off the tension on the bow.

The sound of shoes on gravel broke the quiet as Six and

Adonis sprinted toward him from the direction of the wall. "What happened?" Six asked.

"The outlier. Wren's sister. She took him."

"He didn't fight back?"

"He's drugged. I couldn't take her out—didn't have a clear line of sight. Six, check the shack."

Six did as he was told, grabbing the lantern Survivor had abandoned on his way to the respite shack.

"We've got to stop them!" Adonis started to take off, but Gavel grabbed his collar.

"She would have killed him already if she wanted to. She wants him for something. Let her get some distance from us, then we'll surprise her. There's no way she can get through the wall." He shouldered his bow. "Sans!" he said, just slightly louder than normal talking volume.

Sans reappeared, running from between two buildings across the street. "Sir?"

"Survivor was here in ambush. How did we miss her?" Gavel asked.

Sans' lip pulled up into a snarl. "I don't know, sir. She's clever. I believe she's good at covering her tracks."

"She'd have to be with where she's from," said Gavel. He cursed under his breath. If Caster had been with them, they would've seen this coming. "No more mistakes," Gavel continued, clapping Sans on the arm. "I want you to pick up her trail and—"

"Gavel!" Six called from inside the respite shack.

The three men went over to see what was wrong and poked their heads inside the shack. Six shined his flashlight inside. On his face and gagged was a beaten and tied-up Frederick Hawthorn de Bourgh. Six squatted next to him and pulled out the gag.

"What was this meeting about?" said Gavel.

Freddy coughed a glob of blood onto his chin and shifted to a sitting position. "A favor for Thallium. The Soldier's been doing some work for him."

"What kind of work?"

"I'm sure I have no idea," Freddy said as Six cut the rope from around his ankles. "Those details don't matter to me. Thallium paid me for my goods, and then I provided those goods to the Soldier. That's all I know."

"What goods were you selling?"

"This customer has an affinity for Sally-D."

"You deal in *salvia*? Talk about risky," said Adonis.

"Not when the Principal lets me deal it in small amounts. Comes up from a place south of here, somewhere he's been before. Shipments are infrequent and tiny—the smaller the supply, the higher the prices, and Thallium gets a cut. It's economics. What you gentlemen should be more worried about is your friend. He just took a substantial hit from the most potent fortified leaves I've personally tried. He won't be able to pick his nose without assistance, much less defend himself, for the next few hours, especially if she convinces him to keep taking more of the drug."

"Did the outlier do this to you?" asked Gavel.

"No, I tied myself up and then ran into a doorknob repeatedly." His hands fell into his lap as Six cut the rope off his wrists.

"What does she want?" asked Gavel.

He felt around his quickly swelling eye. "If I were to place a wager, I'd assume she's getting out of here. She made me give her directions to Hallund and then took the keys to my SUV. Logic would say she's proceeding to the vehicle port now to get it, since I told her exactly where it is."

"Coward," said Six.

Freddy glowered up at him. "She threatened to cut off

certain appendages that I value, and I had the distinct feeling that she wasn't bluffing. Believe me, it's worth losing my vehicle."

"The SUV won't do her any good. She can't get through the front gate," said Gavel.

"That's what *I* said. She didn't seem overly concerned." He tried to stand but fell back hard on his tailbone instead. Adonis reached in and helped him to his feet. Freddy raised his swollen chin high and straightened the lapels of his rabbit fur coat. "Now, if you'll excuse me, this evening is pretty well botched, and I've grown weary of it."

"You aren't leaving. Not yet," said Gavel.

"I'm here on the Principal's business, and a vicious she-devil attacked me and his associate. You wish to detain me on what grounds?"

Gavel hesitated.

"That's what I thought." Freddy hobbled out of the shack and toward the street.

Six walked up to Gavel. "Sir? He could tell Thallium. Then our investigation's blown."

"He's legally in the right," said Gavel.

"With all due respect, so fucking what, sir?"

Gavel looked between the faces of his men and Freddy shuffling across the street. Whatever was going on with the Principal and Mainstay demanded investigation, as much as Gavel's gut roiled at the thought of betraying his ruler. God willing, they'd discover that Thallium's actions had reasonable explanations. But if Freddy told Thallium about their involvement and he happened to be guilty, he'd stop them from finding the truth. He finally nodded at Sans, who set off after Freddy.

"What's the plan, boss?" asked Six.

"You're going with Caster to Dearborn in the morning?" said Gavel.

"Yeah. He asked me and Adonis to come. Said they shouldn't need a Thief, so Sans isn't going."

Gavel nodded. "Then Sans, Frederick, and I are going to Hallund."

The Gentleman squeezed his right hand shut over two pecan shells, cracking them together and splitting them open. He then picked through the shell debris, grabbed the tender nuts, and ate them together before repeating the procedure. The pain in his hand at the effort was great, but he let it wash over him, using it to focus his mind—meditation through pain.

He, Fen, Beo, and a handful of his Marauders waited in the half-light and silence of the early morning on top of a small mesa on the east side of The Disc. The Gentleman stood hunched over a telescope on a tripod, pointed at the wall. He swept it casually back and forth between two points with his free hand.

It was nearly dawn on the day Thallium was supposed to give up his prisoner—just over six hours before the last possible moment to give up his prisoner, to be precise. But The Gentleman wasn't at the front gate as he should have been. He'd gone around the back, camping a mile out on the east side of the city so he could have a good view of the two tunnels he knew had been there since the days of Thallium's father. He'd left several of his men outside the front gate in case Thallium made good on his word and met the deadline, but after the way he'd about thrown a hissy fit during their meeting, The Gentleman got the sense that he didn't intend to be a man of his word.

If The Gentleman were right, and he usually was when it

came to reading people, Thallium would get a hell of a spanking for reneging on their deal.

Aside from The Gentleman, there were eight other clan leaders within three hundred miles of The Disc. The relationship between them was tenuous, but what The Gentleman had told Thallium was true: as The Disc and other territories grew, the clan leaders had come to realize—under The Gentleman's urging, of course—that they either had to be willing to work together or die one by one when the folks they preyed on as a way of life became too strong. That time was coming, and if Thallium was cocksure enough to try to get one of his prisoners out and hide her elsewhere rather than turn her over to her rightful Master, then that time would be nigh indeed.

He continued to sweep the telescope between the two exit points.

"Master," Fen's voice behind him interrupted his focus, "please sit and rest. I'll take over for a while."

The Gentleman tossed shell fragments over his shoulder. Fen sputtered—must have taken some pieces to the face. The Gentleman didn't look up from the telescope. "Nah, that's all right."

"It's possible he'll just hold on to her inside, isn't it?" Fen continued, this time off to The Gentleman's left, out of the line of fire. "If he doesn't believe we're capable of getting through the wall, why would he move her?"

"You could be right. We've been watching for days, and he hasn't had the gumption to move her yet. But I wouldn't put anything past the Valcins. Self-entitled varmints. We have to be prepared for all manner of shenanigans. Understand?"

"Yes, sir. Can I get you another coat? Are you warm enough?"

"I'm fine. I'm not some old sack of bones. Not yet."

Dirt crunched as Fen slowly retreated.

In the days and nights he'd spent waiting and watching outside the city, The Gentleman had imagined countless versions of his reunion with Survivor, what he would say, how he'd say it. But in the end, he'd determined it was best not to rehearse such things. Doing so would interfere with speaking from the heart, and what was said in the moment would ring more authentic than the perfect, practiced words.

A tiny sliver of light at the bottom of the south tunnel appeared. It was a dull blue glow, and it grew bigger as the door rose. It was stark enough compared to the gray morning light that he didn't need the telescope to see it—his men had started chattering because they'd spotted it just the same. But the telescope did provide a clear view of the woman driving a vehicle out of the tunnel, a woman with tangled black hair, fierce eyes, and a scowl that could cut glass.

"Well, ain't that something?" The Gentleman said.

"Is it her?" Fen asked excitedly over the quiet muttering of the others.

"Sure enough. But you said she had a new family—a sister. She's alone."

Survivor laid on the accelerator, going straight east and then seeming to curve ever so slightly to the south, as if to give The Disc a wide berth.

"I don't know, Master. They seemed close. But can't we take Survivor now? She's the traitor." Anger had seeped into Fen's voice, the righteous outrage of a brother scorned.

"Hmm. No. That won't teach her the lesson she needs. We'll follow her. If she's as close to the redhead as you say she was, they won't stay apart for long. We'll get them both together." The Gentleman stole one last glance at Survivor. Her hands were wrapped tightly around the wheel, and her gaze was fierce and focused. She clearly had a particular destination in mind.

He stood straight finally and stretched his back, then turned to the cluster of men and women waiting with restless postures.

"Pack it up. Be quiet about it, and stay hidden. Don't want to tip her off."

They scattered to their work, all except for Beo, who stood there while people shuffled around him gathering supplies and loading up vehicles. Beo moved to one end of the mesa and stared down at the vehicle, so close to the edge that a stiff breeze might have blown him off.

The Gentleman stepped up next to him. "Your sister's coming home. You excited?"

Beo's face was inscrutable, but The Gentleman saw a flicker of eagerness there underneath the marks of honor.

"Yep," The Gentleman sighed. "Me too."

Asha tucked a few extra clean bandages into the top of her backpack before pulling the drawstring tight. She considered making the bed, but then thought better of it. She'd been the only one sleeping in it last night, and the heavy blankets were barely disturbed. Her leather boots felt tighter than she remembered, but she hadn't traveled in several years and it was a wonder they fit at all. She tucked the laces of the right one into the top of the boot beneath her knee, and then lowered the leg of her tan linen pants to cover it. A noise in the kitchen—the slam of a cabinet door—caught her attention. She shouldered the pack and left the bedroom.

Gavel stood in the kitchen with his back to her, rummaging through the pantry. His bow lay on the table next to his full quiver, poncho, and canteen. She dropped her backpack on the table from several feet above. It slammed down, making

Gavel's gear clatter. He started but didn't turn. Must have been due to years of conditioning telling him that his wife was furious and he should postpone the onslaught as long as possible.

"Didn't mean to wake you," he said to the pantry.

"I was already up. I'm on my way out."

He turned at that and took in the sight of her in travel attire.

"Out where?"

"I could ask you the same thing about where you were last night."

"I was working. Training my men."

"In the middle of the night?"

He walked up to the table and shrugged. "Night training." He reached for the drawstrings of her backpack, but she pulled the bag away and swung it over her shoulder before he could look inside.

"Where are you going?" he said.

"Caster asked me to go with Wren and his group to Dearborn as their medical officer. Should be gone for a few days."

"Medical officer? Isn't that Ark's job? Why would Caster ask you to go?"

She always told Gavel the truth, with a few notable exceptions. It was a habit so strong that it often got her into trouble, such as when she spoke her mind about Thallium. She knew she'd be terrible at lying to him now, so she forced herself to glare at him, substituting anger for deceit. "Ark's getting up there, you know? He's not as fit as he used to be. I should be the one doing these kinds of things now. Are you trying to tell me I can't go?"

He studied her. "Of course not. But I'm wondering why you're only telling me about this now."

She amped up the glare. "Caster came by last night to ask

me to go. You got home about ten seconds ago. When exactly was I supposed to tell you?"

He broke his stare, cleared his throat, and went back to the pantry. She let out a silent breath of relief that he hadn't discerned her fib. He grabbed a sack of raisins and a round loaf of bread, tied them in cheesecloth, and put them in his pack on the floor.

"Where are *you* going?" she asked. "You aren't due out for another patrol yet."

He shouldered the pack and went for his bow, examining the string rather than meeting her eyes. "On walkabout."

"Walkabout? What's that supposed to mean?"

He put the canteen on his belt and wrapped his scarf around his neck. "I just mean nowhere in particular. Doing some wilderness training with Sans. He's interested in becoming the Head of his own Body. We need to cover a few things before he takes the test."

"Silent Sans, the loyal follower, wants to be a Head?"

He threw his hands up. "That's what I said."

She stuck out her hip and fought the urge to cross her arms.

"I should be back about when you are." He walked around the table and leaned in for a kiss. He waited for her to take the bait. She kissed him once on the lips, like a little girl told to kiss and make up. He went for the front door. On his way out, he paused. "Be careful." He closed the door behind him.

She kicked the leg of the kitchen table. "You too."

What asshole decided it was a good idea to combine metal, wheels, and magic to make something move fast enough to kill the one driving it? Survivor drove the merchant's SUV toward

Hallund, her already tangled hair turning into a convoluted series of knots as it whipped around her face.

Mainstay was curled up in the front seat, examining the straps crossed over his torso and the buckle connecting them as if they were chains or snakes, something to be feared. His nose dripped, but he didn't care to wipe it.

The vehicle rocked them back and forth as bugs splattered on the tiny windshield. Driving in general disturbed her, stirring memories she didn't want to dwell on. But it was so much faster than walking, and the wailing mess of a man next to her could not have possibly gone on foot.

The last time she'd been in a vehicle was over ten years ago. She'd grown up riding in them, and being in the SUV now sent her mind back to that time before she could stop it. Her earliest memory grabbed hold—the day she'd met The Gentleman. She'd been unable to completely shake it since Eydis asked her about it.

TWENTY YEARS EARLIER

She stood hunched over, sucking on the pulp of a barrel cactus, her hands bleeding from breaking past the spines. And then there he was, standing on the short bank of sand next to her. He seemed so out of place, in the dirt in his white brimmed hat and jacket. A turquoise handkerchief poked out of his front pocket. She thought she was hallucinating until he held his hand out to her.

"Why hello there, darlin'. You look hungry. Are you hungry?" he asked.

Holy hell yes, she was hungry. It had been days since she'd eaten anything more substantial than a handful of prickly pears. But she just watched him, still sucking on cactus, unmoving.

"Why, you can't be more'n ten? Eleven?"

She stayed silent. She didn't know the answer. Her childhood existed in her memory as only bits and pieces—a flash of a pink teddy bear, an incessant beep that she still heard in the quiet of the night, pain. Always pain.

"Ah, well. Never mind," said the man. "Point is, you could use someone to look after you. Would you like to come with me? I've got a family close to here, just in the shade of that outcropping of rock over yonder." He took his hat off and swept the air with it toward the land behind her. "Well, whaddaya say?"

He was middle-aged, handsome, with a big dimple in his left cheek. A constant smile of brilliant teeth. She went with him.

He didn't let his "family" anywhere near her—mostly big men with strange markings on their skin and pieces of metal and bone poking out of their flesh. Some drank black liquor and tossed dice, others stretched big sheets of skin over drum shells. They watched her pass into the camp that day in silence, nodding to The Gentleman. He took her straight to his tent—a sprawling canvas structure filled with blankets and pillows, a sitting area where ginger tea and flatbread sat out waiting for him. She ate her fill and then he washed her in his big copper tub, gently scrubbing the grit from her skin while he sang "All the Pretty Little Horses," careful not to get lavender soap in her eyes as he rinsed her hair. He named her Angel.

That was the way it was for the next two years. She followed him around, more pet than child, and he would dote on her, adorning her in lacy dresses and giving her stuffed toys, sharing with her the red and white peppermints stashed in his left pants pocket. She rode next to him in his dune buggy when they traveled; he let her sit on his lap and steer sometimes. He'd make her wait with his most trusted man in the dune buggy when they resupplied—Reskin, a towering man with one ear and a dead-eyed stare that could make anyone's hair stand on end. They played pick-up sticks, catching the beating of drums and faint screams carried on a breeze from the next dune over.

Sometimes, The Gentleman's men brought back women, rarely a kid, all disheveled and petrified. At the time, Survivor figured they were like she had been when The Gentleman found her—desperate and dying, still needing to adjust to this new family. The women and children in the camp mostly stayed together during the day. They did chores, set up and tore down camp. When Survivor tried to join them, they'd let her, all the while watching her out of the corners of their eyes, confused, on guard.

One day, she woke to blood on her sheets, going up the back of her underwear. The Gentleman came to her bed to bring her dried fruit for breakfast and found her trying to scrub it from her sheets, terrified she was dying. He squatted down to her eye level, and his constant smile dropped to a sad line.

"It's all right, darlin'. You'll be fine." And yet, he studied her face as if she were dead, already gone. He kissed her forehead, left the fruit, and walked away, mournfully singing, "Blacks and bays, dapples and grays, dancing through the sky."

Everything changed.

He kicked her out of his tent and took away her nice clothes, replacing them with a plain cotton dress more suited to labor. She was told to stay with the women and children. The newer women—those with tenderness and physical strength left in their bodies—took pity on her and taught her how to set up tents and hang laundry on a line. One of the women was blond and willowy and drew Survivor under her watch, a fierce mother hawk.

The first night in the women's tent, they slept in a heap together, older women on the outside, snuggling against the backs of younger women, who held the boys and girls as they slept. Survivor had wrapped her arms around a boy with poofy red hair and big gaps in his teeth. Little Beo. He breathed rapidly, chest heaving as his feet did little kicks. She hugged him tighter, and he relaxed against her.

The tent opened, blinding light from a lantern shining across the sleeping group. The blond woman behind Survivor whispered in her ear. "Close your eyes and don't move. They like it when you move." She did as she was told.

There was a scuffle as women were pulled to their feet around Survivor. A hand tugged at Survivor's elbow, and she squeezed her eyes shut tighter. The blond woman removed the man's hand and begged him to take her instead. Survivor only opened her eyes when the blond woman's plea was cut off—the man had slit her throat. She slumped to the ground and bled out on the scratchy blanket, drowning on her blood. Reskin stood over her with red dripping from his blade.

He dropped to his heels and pulled Survivor up by her elbow. "You have to press hard." He put the bloody knife in her hand and drew her into a crouch between his legs, his hand over hers as he drew the knife across the woman's already slashed neck. The last of the light faded from the woman's eyes and she went limp. Survivor vomited next to her corpse. "Firm and deep," said Reskin. "You'll learn."

He stood and pulled Survivor up with him, leaving the red-headed boy to shiver alone on the floor with those who weren't taken. He carried her out of the tent and into his.

Hate took root in her that night, growing whenever they would force her to be bait for traveling parties, suckering them in to help the wounded young girl before the Marauders ambushed them. And it grew still more every time she saw The

Gentleman with his new "Angel," the girl under his care that would be replaced after a couple of years, whenever she reached womanhood. They wore her old dresses, had her old name. She had no name anymore. Didn't want one, and nobody offered to give her one. Every time she caught Beo crying for his daddy in the dark, the roots of hate stretched further into her until they became the structure holding her together.

PRESENT DAY

"Please, please, please," said Mainstay as he uncurled slightly in the front seat of the SUV. Apparently, his mind had melted and left him with a one-word vocabulary. Before, he'd screamed for mercy, for himself to wake up, for the warmth to come back. He'd begged someone named Bambi for forgiveness.

He dropped the salvia joint onto the seat, scorching a hole into the fabric. She picked it up and shoved it between his lips. "Please what? Please go faster?"

She laid on the gas, and they soared over a rise, landed hard on the vehicle's nose on the other side, and kept going.

He took a long pull from the joint and cried louder.

She was beginning to like this driving thing.

Freddy's workshop was a tall garage with a thick, wooden workbench stretching all along the back wall. The bench was covered in a heap of tools. Bizarre inventions of metal bits and gears sat plunked here and there, some poised as if Freddy had gotten distracted and stopped mid-task to move on to something else. Chains and cables hung from the ceiling, so low in places that one had to duck beneath them. Together, it all added up to barely contained chaos, organized in a manner known only to Freddy.

Near the workbench was a vehicle currently shrouded in a vinyl cover. Sans reached for it.

"Do you mind?" asked Freddy. He brushed Sans' hand away from the cover. "This is a sophisticated piece of equipment. One that's being unveiled prematurely, I might remind you."

He pulled the cover back in a great whoosh, tossing dust upward. A car, or something that vaguely resembled a car, sat there. It was a hulking mass of scrap metal, PVC pipe, and mismatched tires—small in the front, almost comically large in the back.

Freddy stepped back, holding the cover in both hands to his chin as he beamed. "Isn't she glorious?"

"Does it drive?" asked Gavel from where he watched them in the doorway of the garage. Sans and Freddy turned at his voice. He walked over and tossed his stuff on a pile of supplies in the dirt near the vehicle.

Freddy dropped the cover and spluttered in Gavel's face, "Does it—How dare—"

Sans pushed Freddy back with a sideswipe of his arm, knocking him against the driver's side panel of the car. Freddy composed himself, brushing off the bright red vest over his bare chest. "Of course she drives. I just haven't finished detailing her yet. This is my masterpiece, an achievement of modern engineering. I may love my SUV, but this is my *child*. Can you put your love for your child into words, sir?"

Gavel tapped his hand against the roll bar stretching over the center of the vehicle, mounted across the seats. "How fast can it go?"

"Plenty fast, I assure you. Though I don't suggest pushing it far over forty—never know when a dune will sneak up on you and flip you bumper over bumper." He stroked along the edge of the front wheel well on the driver's side. "As you're taking my baby hostage in exchange for my silence, I suggest you treat her well and bring her back in one piece. There's plenty of fuel for your journey in the tank, just one more rare commodity you're robbing me of. Toodles." He turned to leave.

"You're coming with us," said Gavel.

Freddy stretched up onto one foot and spun around on his toes. "Excuse me?"

"We need a third man. You're also a liability to leave here."

"No, no, no, no, no. I'm not going an ungodly amount of miles across the blazing desert to confront the lady who nearly cut my balls off. That's not happening."

"To be clear, Scavenger, I'm not requesting."

"But I—I'm injured!" He framed his bandaged face with his hands.

"You still have one good eye, and that's enough to drive," said Gavel. He grabbed a bundle of sand-colored cloth from the top of his pack and threw it at him. "Get changed."

Freddy sifted through the tan poncho, khaki cargo pants, and a long-sleeved white shirt. "You expect me to wear this?" He held the bundle away from him like a dirty sock.

"Bright red and fringe would make you a moving target for Marauders. We're taking a big enough risk by driving. We leave in five. Put it on," said Gavel.

Freddy began putting on the clothes, cringing as he inserted his limbs into the fabric like he was wading through human waste.

Sans got close to Gavel, speaking softly. "I requested immediate exit on your behalf for a training exercise. The gatekeeper wasn't fully awake when I called. She didn't put up a fight."

"She didn't say anything about a gate breach this morning?"

He shook his head once. "I don't know how the outlier did it."

Gavel picked his bags up and went for the boot locker soldered to the back of the car. "We'll ask her when we find her. Let's go. I want to be gone before sunrise. The Principal will be watching Caster's group; we can't cross their path. Pack it up."

The shining walls surrounding The Disc were still visible in the distance as Caster's travel party marched toward Dearborn. The silver glint reminded anyone looking back that they were always within reach, and their actions wouldn't go unnoticed. Caster tucked the tops of the tattered tan rags he wore over his coat into his collar and focused on the journey ahead, struggling not to think about what had happened earlier that morning.

Caster had been standing in his old room in the Main House before the sun rose. He was there to pick up Wren to join the group leaving for Dearborn, but he'd decided to take a detour to stop by his room and gather some miscellaneous items he'd left when he abandoned his father's home. A small book of poems by Heaney with a faded blue cover, his favorite pocketknife, and a journal filled with his charcoal sketches. He'd flipped through the journal until he found one he'd done of his mom when he was maybe seventeen, of her sitting in a chair in his bedroom, staring out the window. He was wondering what she was thinking when Thallium spoke from the door of the room.

"Planning on expanding my library into this room. Unless you're intending to use it again, of course."

Caster closed the journal and tucked it in the inside pocket of his coat. He turned to face his father. "The fireplace in here would suit a library well."

Thallium leaned against the doorframe, a shadow of sharp angles backlit by the bright light in the hallway. "I want to thank you for your help these past few days. I truly don't believe Wren's restoration would have been possible without you. I hope we can work together more often."

Caster headed for the door. "I'll help Wren whenever she needs it." As he sidestepped around his father, Thallium spoke, his voice barely above a whisper.

"I'm aware that you lost two parents the day Reina died. I can't say I would have done things differently, but I can admit I should have eased up on you when you were grieving. You didn't deserve those scars."

Caster stood there, half in and half out of his old room, inches from his father. He cleared his throat. "Yeah. Yeah, I did lose two. But I wouldn't have done things differently, either."

"I miss her. Every day."

Caster left at that, nearly running down the hall to Wren's room. His father's vulnerability disturbed him not because it was likely a farce, but because there was a chance it wasn't. And he had no idea what to do with that.

He turned his attention to the journey ahead. The fact remained that Thallium needed to be unseated, peacefully if at all possible. Caster knew too well the Principal's unpredictable moods and how they affected those around him. The people of The Disc were at risk of becoming collateral damage. If things went well in Dearborn, it would be the first step in gaining enough outside influence to force Thallium out of power.

The group traveling to Dearborn was fairly small: Caster, Wren, Six, Asha, and Adonis. It was large enough to not be considered an easy target, but also not so large as to draw attention. That was exactly the way Caster preferred it. His father would have preferred they leave in glorious procession, fifty men with banners emblazoned with the Valcin crest waving.

Caster had refused, and Thallium had been in such a good mood about Wren's restoration that he hadn't put up a fight.

They'd been walking for a little over three hours. When they started out at dawn, the temperature had been in the low 80s. Now, with the mid-morning sun beginning to flex its muscles, it had reached 103. It would continue to climb like a snail on a wall, determined to crawl a good deal higher before it called it a day.

Few words had been exchanged since the gate opened. Adonis asked about their route to Dearborn, Asha made sure Wren was plenty hydrated, and Six cracked a joke about the reproductive behavior of scorpions. At one point, Wren had tried asking Caster about Thallium's relationship with Eydis, but he'd dismissed her; after cutting her off, he caught her eyes and tilted his head up as if stretching his neck. Wren followed the gesture and saw the drone flying twenty feet above, its orange eyes blinking occasionally. After another hour of near silence, the drone suddenly stopped, hitting a boundary they couldn't see. For the next ten minutes, Wren glanced over her shoulder every twenty steps to see the drone still hovering, suspended but no longer moving forward. Finally, Caster spoke to her.

"Sorry about earlier."

She opened her mouth to reply when Six jogged up between them.

"Holy 1984!" he shouted. "How much range do those things have now? I thought it was limited to five miles."

"I'm guessing Eydis made a few improvements at the request of my father," said Caster

"Oh, the great and powerful Thall," said Six. He elbowed Wren in the ribs. "How would you like to have *that* for a father-in-law? Seems to me you'd be better off going for a man without family ties, one who's quick with a blade, maybe of Italian-

Mexican-Greek descent." He pushed his dark hair back and twirled a gold- and black-handled stiletto between his fingers.

"What's a father-in-law?" asked Wren.

"That's enough," said Caster. He shoved Six in the back.

"Fine," said Six, turning to Caster. "All right, man. You got us all the way out here, the butt crack of the desert. Tell me we aren't really journeying to sell Wren's wares to the highest bidder."

"Of course not," said Asha from behind them. "But we need Thallium to think that's exactly what we're doing."

Six turned and walked backward, facing Asha and shooting finger guns at her. "When I heard you were coming, I had a feeling there was more to this merry band than running the Principal's errands so he doesn't get sand in his goatee. I know it's none of my business—Gavel's my C.O. and all—but what did he think about you venturing into the wild with no intention of following our supreme leader's orders?"

She adjusted the weight of her pack. "Never thought I'd say this, but you're *right*, pretty boy. It's none of your business."

Adonis, stooped over from the weight of the packs and bedrolls on his back as he walked next to Asha, adjusted the thin tan shawl draped over his head and down the back of his neck. "Wait, we aren't going to Dearborn?"

"We're going to Dearborn to show them what Wren's capable of, and to offer it to them because it would help them," said Caster.

"Then we *are* doing what the Principal said," said Adonis.

"No. We're seeking their support of a Disc without Thallium," said Asha.

Six stopped walking backward, nearly making Adonis slam into his chest and fall on his ass. "You're planning a revolution."

Everyone else stopped. Caster handed his canteen to Wren, who took a sip. "Not exactly," he said.

"Dearborn is a town of laboring men and women—traders, primarily of textiles," said Asha. "But they're protected by a group of soldiers. Not high in number, but they'd make solid allies. It's a relatively safe place to feel out the feasibility of removing Thallium from office with the support of surrounding territories."

"Remove Thallium and replace him with who?" said Six. All eyes turned to Caster, who was taking a gulp from his canteen.

He lowered the canteen and screwed the lid back on. "Me, at least initially. Maybe an elected council after that. Whatever we determine is best."

"Psh. To our people, that's the same as saying they'll be ruled by coyotes in top hats. It doesn't compute, bro. It'll be you or some other douchebag," said Six.

"Not my primary concern right now," said Caster. "Let's focus on the immediate. We need support outside The Disc to dissuade Thallium from putting up a fight. There are too many Keepers and Bodies in The Disc loyal to him for us to make a move. Outside assistance is crucial. And Wren's agreed to offer her talent in exchange for that assistance."

Wren nodded.

Six shook his head. "That's a hell of a lot to wager on an outlier. No offense, sweetie." He patted her on the head and a scowl formed at the edges of her mouth. "Thallium's been in power for almost two decades, foaming at the mouth for more, and nobody outside our walls has done diddly jack about it. You really think that this girl's newfound, unpredictable, mysterious hocus pocus of an ability is going to tip the scale? What if she's not strong enough?"

"I can do this," said Wren. Everyone stared at her. She pulled her scarf down from her mouth. "My sister and I lived outside your walls, without your food and weapons our whole lives. I'm strong enough." Her hands and hair had taken on white-purple auras, emitting a low humming sound that died out after she finished speaking.

"Atta girl!" Asha shouted, throwing her fist up in the air and making Adonis jump.

Six grinned and started bouncing on the balls of his feet. "Remarkable. Onward!" He took off at an easy jog and started whistling. The notes became indistinct as he put some distance between himself and the group.

The glow around Wren's hair and hands dimmed and then retreated into her, like the sun shaded by a cloud. She shook her hands out. As she put her scarf back on, she saw Caster watching her out of the corner of his eye.

"What?" she asked.

He suddenly looked far off into the distance. "I was just thinking that we better pick up the pace. I want to be there well before dark, and we've got about eighteen miles to go. Right, Ash?"

She walked past him, half-heartedly trying not to smile. "Uh huh."

Wren and Adonis fell into step next to Asha. Caster watched Wren. Her sleek figure was dressed in cream fabric that brushed the ground and made it look as if she were floating through this world rather than living in it. She was a paradox, an enigma of strength and meekness, grown woman and naiveté, a puzzle he was afraid to figure out and terrified of failing to solve. She was different, set apart from anyone he'd known before by her hope and her strength. He had to keep her safe. With one final glance back and an automatic check of their surroundings, he followed several paces behind the party.

PART IV

TO WAR

CHAPTER TWELVE

GAVEL HAD BEEN ON A MOTORIZED VEHICLE FEWER TIMES than he'd swum, and they lived in the desert. After several hours of riding in the front seat next to Freddy, his stomach curdled. He felt shaky and spread thin, as if his brain had fallen out of his ear on the dirt a few miles back and was sloshing forward, trying to catch up. Freddy whistled behind the wheel. His sour mood had turned giddy at the opportunity to see what his vehicle—his "lady fair"—could do. He steered toward a dune up ahead and clipped it enough to give him a big smile as the car lurched a couple feet. Gavel looked back at Sans in the seat strapped above the boot locker, facing backward to look at the ground they were leaving behind. He tapped him on the shoulder and spun his hand in a tight circle. Sans nodded, and the two switched seats. At least this way, if Gavel puked, Freddy and Sans probably wouldn't notice.

He strapped himself into the backseat. As they clipped another dune, he was vaguely aware of Freddy yee-hawing while he pitched forward and dry heaved. He felt a tap on his elbow. He turned, and Sans tucked something into his hand—

dried ginger root. Sans put his fingertips to his mouth and then turned back to face the windshield. Gavel popped the ginger and let it rehydrate with saliva before chewing it like gum. Spicy juice trickled down his throat, and his stomach calmed a bit. It was hard to get anything past Sans, but in this case, Gavel was glad he'd noticed his discomfort. Of all his men, Sans was the least likely to mention it to anyone.

Now that he wasn't on the verge of losing his meager breakfast, he pulled his scope from the inside pocket of his poncho. Sand, clumps of cacti, heat waves, and the horizontal line of blue and tan where the sky met the earth were the only things around. The sun's position said that it was high noon. At this rate, they'd reach Hallund in about two hours. Which meant they had two more hours to risk in open terrain. Freddy's vehicle was surprisingly quiet, but Marauders looking for a target would see it.

Gavel spent those final hours alternating between looking through the scope, chewing his ginger, and thinking about how he'd left things with Asha. Lying to her was the most unnatural thing he'd done. One of the best parts of their relationship was how they never held back, never lied to patch something over; he loved her fire, and she knew exactly how to deal with his coldness. It might not have been the most peaceful dynamic, but twenty-eight years of marriage showed it worked. Once she found out he was cruising around, risking his life, and betraying the ruler he'd often defended at the expense of her respect, she'd unleash hell. Somehow, the idea of being charged with treason or being attacked by Marauders sounded a little less daunting by comparison.

Freddy gave a shrill whistle that made Gavel turn in the restraints to look ahead of the vehicle. Sitting just a mile out was Hallund, a gray and white blotch on the tan landscape. It was about a quarter of the size of The Disc, a square grouping of awnings and massive tents built for permanence rather than convenience. In the center of town, covered by draperies of opaque plastic sheets to protect against the harsh desert, and surrounded by guards for protection against predators, was the core of their economy—fields of hardy crops.

The people of Hallund were farmers, primarily of nopales, but also okra, hot peppers, and soybeans. Their work made them strong, tan, and dismissive of luxury and architecture designed for form over function. The only thing about their town that could be considered impressive from a distance was their watch tower, a tall rectangle of steel beams and PVC pipe with a covered room at the top to house a lookout 24/7. Gavel turned his attention to the tower now. He pulled a blue and white checkered strip of fabric from his pocket and held it high overhead to flap in the wind. The emblem was widely recognized as a request for peaceful entry and a meeting with a town's representative. Through his scope, he saw a similar banner held out of the watchtower, showing assent to their request.

As they reached the boundary of the town, Freddy slowed the car to a stop. Standing between the two posts that functioned as their main gate was a short figure in an orange robe. She looked on and waited for them, her posture stiff and slightly hunched. Gavel recognized the figure as Derma, an old woman who presided as an elder over Hallund with two other individuals. She clasped her hands at her stomach and wore a black bandana over her nose and mouth. Her white hair, in tiny cornrows, gave away her age along with her skin, worn and wrinkled like wet leather.

At her elbows were two men, stout boxes of muscles, with black braids going down the center of their otherwise clean-shaven heads. They wore identical black bandanas across their faces.

Freddy took in the sight of them and slid down in the driver's seat, trying to fit in the floorboard. "They look rather stressed. I'll bring the car around when we're ready to go, shall I?"

Gavel hopped down from the backseat. "Get out."

He did, with a great deal of sulking.

Sans walked around the car and came up next to Gavel. Tiny trails of red snuck into the whites of his eyes as he met Gavel's gaze. He held his kanabō in a ready stance. Something was wrong here.

Gavel shook his head. "Stay alert. They're scared. We need to find out why." He shouldered his bow and led them over to Derma. He bowed to her and her men.

"What's your purpose here, fighter?" said Derma. Her voice croaked with the cadence of a woman who might have had a lovely alto tone many years ago but had since inhaled enough dirt and heat to make her a gravely baritone.

"High Elder," said Gavel, "one of my men was taken by an escaped prisoner of The Disc. We tracked the prisoner here. We request entry to recapture her and take back our man."

"You mean the wild woman," said Derma. "She's gone. Left the man with us."

"Then we intend to take him back."

She stuck out her tongue and ran it futilely along her cracked lips. After a good deal of licking and thinking, she pointed a bony finger partially obscured by her orange sleeve at him. "Leave your weapons."

Sans took half a step forward, but Gavel stopped him with a glance. Gavel took off his bow and walked to the boot locker on the back of the car. Freddy followed right away, but Sans walked more slowly, as if he had to concentrate on each step.

"It's all right," said Gavel softly to Sans as he stowed his bow and quiver.

"We'll see," replied the Thief. His kanabō wouldn't fit in the boot locker, so he stuck it in a gap between the locker and the rear of the car. The grimace on his face made it look as if he were stowing away his right arm instead.

They returned to Derma.

Gavel held up his hands. "When did your policy change to forbid honest men from protecting themselves?"

She smacked her lips once. "Step forward."

The three men stepped up and one of the big guys patted each of them down. Gavel and Sans were allowed to pass, but they stopped Freddy. The guard took a metal cylinder the size of a small can of soup out of his pants' pocket, and then held it up and examined it with confusion.

"Here, allow me to show you," said Freddy. He pointed to the side of the cylinder where a little needle danced in a bead of water until it pointed north. "I have a poor sense of direction." He looked down and scuffed the dirt with his boot.

The guard looked to Derma, who without another word turned to lead the way into town. Freddy took the compass back and slipped it into his pocket, leaving his hand to hang there by his hip.

Gavel walked in front with Derma while the guards followed close behind Sans and Freddy. As they entered the town, solemn glares over the edges of black bandanas greeted them. Workers shambled through the streets pushing wheelbarrows of thick green cactus pads topped with red fruit, children hit rocks with sticks, and a few men sat on stools under the edges of their tents as they sipped hot beer. People touched their hands to their brows as Derma passed, and she returned the gesture. She hocked back phlegm, lifted the edge of her mask, and spat on the side of the road.

Gavel leaned down to speak to her. "I had heard a sickness appeared here. Did you lose many people?"

"We're *still* losing people. More sick every day. We have so much work to do. Too few to do it now." She tugged the corner of the bandana dangling over her chin. "These make people feel better, but they don't do much."

"Then the sickness isn't airborne?"

She shook her head. "Caught through touch. Fluid exchange. The masks make people remember to be careful."

"I'm sorry. Do you know where it came from?"

She spat again and mumbled something indistinct before answering. "We know." She pointed up ahead. "Your friend is in there."

He followed her gesture to see a large building made of plywood with a black plastic roof. "I don't recognize that building. Is it new?"

"Yes, new," she said.

Heaped at the base of the building near the door were mounds of riches: coins, silver sets, opalescent stones, even cocoa and unopened wine bottles. A young boy around five or six—a little wisp of a kid—walked up and set a string of hematite beads on top of one of the mounds. He saw Derma and Gavel's group coming, kissed the wall of the building, and dashed off in between the tents.

Sans began to breathe heavily, and Gavel looked back to see him squeezing his eyes shut. He reached back and thumped him on the chest. Sans opened his eyes, now the pale pink that hinted his Harbinger side wanted to emerge. He mouthed "something's not right" to Gavel, who shook his head once to command him to stand down. Sans was correct, but there was nothing to do about it now. A cold rush of adrenaline started under the skin at the base of Gavel's skull. He fought the warning and tried to keep from reflexively going for the bow that wasn't there.

Derma stepped up to the building. The door had a thick

bar across the outside, though it wasn't currently locked. She gently pulled the door open and entered, signaling for Gavel to follow.

He entered to see thin beams of sunlight falling into the shack from slits cut high up in the walls. The inside of the walls were concrete, which belied the delicate plywood on the outside. The stench of sour, rotten flesh hung in the air, riding on the backs of the heat and the dust. Light streamed down on piles of bodies, over fifty men, women, and children stacked neatly on the floor with their arms and legs crossed. Most had their eyes open, and streams of blood turned black were crusted to their cheeks, chins, and temples.

Derma stopped walking after everyone was inside and one of the guards closed the door behind them. "The end comes rampaging on the infected, and they burst forth from this world as the fluids burst from their bodies like sores popping." She pointed at a body lying alone in the middle of the aisle running between the piles of corpses. Gavel stooped down.

It was Mainstay. His face was rigid, his muscles twisted, as if he'd gone through a violent death rattle before life finally left him. Rivulets of blood, still glossy and fresh, dripped out of his orifices and onto the floor around him.

Gavel stood and took two quick steps back.

"You recognize this sickness," croaked Derma into the half-darkness. "It's an old enemy, a demon from your past. Yes?"

Images of Reina came to mind, struggling for breath after Asha helped her sip water while Caster floated by the bedside, a ghost of a young man who was dying alongside her. He swallowed hard. "What did you do to him?"

Derma walked around Gavel to stand between her two guards, leering at him as she passed. "The wild woman told us he knew where the sickness came from. She said he'd talk and that we could have him. She gave us the source." She took a vial filled with pink liquid from the depths of her sleeve and held it out like a jewel.

"I don't understand," said Gavel.

"We've been given death." She tucked the vial away. "The wild woman left, and we brought the man here. When he saw the faces, he screamed more. He saw demons, too. We held him over the corpses, next to their faces like lovers, until he talked. He poisoned our water with the pink sickness under orders from your ruler. We let him taste our water. It's faster that way."

The guards grew twitchy and Sans side-stepped closer to Gavel. Freddy threw his elbow up to cover his nose and mouth.

Gavel's stomach turned with this revelation. It wasn't definitive proof that Thallium was behind the murders of innocent people, but it was damn close. All his loyalty could be to a corrupt man. Again. He felt the fool.

"Even if this is all true, *we* aren't here under orders. Release us, or you risk starting a war," said Gavel.

"War?" Derma laughed, a noise like air shoved through sludge. "We're already at war. Our messengers travel now to our allies to tell them of your ruler's treachery. Of *your* treachery. On sand bikes, they'll be there before nightfall. The woman made sure we sent one to Dearborn." The wrinkles around her eyes deepened as she grinned.

Fear gripped Gavel by the throat. Asha and Caster were walking into a trap.

"Stand aside!" he shouted, genuine panic driving him now.

"Not many know this, but our people have a warrior's spirit. To keep your crop alive, you have to be willing to kill threats to it. You can give our living dead the warrior's death they want. They get bored in here, waiting to die."

As she spoke, twenty people, men and women, moved from the shadows along the concrete walls of the building. They were pale, some already bleeding from their eyes or the corners of their mouths. They held crude staffs and sharp-edged shovels up as if they'd been waiting for an opportunity to use them.

"Derma, these people are innocent," said Gavel. His tone was even, matter-of-fact. "I don't want to kill them."

"Kill them?" she said. "They're already dead."

The guards opened the door, let Derma out, and then rushed after her. Freddy darted for the door as they were shutting it, but three infected men moved to block his path. He backpedaled to Sans and Gavel, and the three of them stood back to back as the mob, weak with fatigue but strong with determination, circled in closer.

Freddy took the compass from his pocket and hit a tiny button on the bottom. A rod shot out of the cylinder, sparking and buzzing with electricity. A man lunged for him, and he jabbed the rod into the middle of his chest. Buzzz-ZOT! The man flew back and smacked so hard into the concrete wall that a sprinkling of dirt fell from the plastic ceiling.

"HaHA! It works!" said Freddy.

"Then use it!" Gavel shouted. "Sans, now!"

Sans' breath turned heavy, as if he were lifting weights with his lungs. Then he threw his head back, opened his arms, and roared. His eyes glowed crimson in the half light as a switch flipped inside, releasing his Harbinger strength. He charged and plowed through the group closest to him, and before Gavel could blink, he had taken one of their machetes and was lopping off heads in a blur.

Gavel wrapped his scarf around all but his eyes and made a mad dash for the door. Sans bellowed and struck down the infected as the buzzz-ZOT and concurrent flash of Freddy's death stick lit the place up like a thunderstorm. Gavel threw his weight against the door, but it held from the other side. As he wound up for another run at it, something pulled his leg out from under him. He fell to the ground, smacking the back of his head hard against the dirt. Four figures loomed over him, pale and dripping, as his vision began to blur.

The hottest part of the day was beginning to subside, and Wren was grateful for it. Whenever she and Survivor traveled, they rested in the hottest part of the afternoon. They weren't alone in this practice. It was so common that ill-intentioned people in the Open exploited it. Survivor had told her several years ago that it was one of the preferred times for Marauders and even pettier thieves to attack travelers—when they were exhausted and their heads swam in the fuzziness of 120 degree heat.

Caster didn't let them rest that afternoon, claiming that he wanted to reach Dearborn before dark. Wren knew he wasn't lying, but reaching Dearborn before dark would have been possible even with a brief rest. However, the tension in his shoulders and the way his gaze constantly roamed over far off things she couldn't see stayed any protest she might have voiced.

Finally, breaking through the waves of heat in front of them, Dearborn showed itself on the horizon. If it hadn't been for the tapestries of blue, purple, red, and gold hanging from poles as bright advertisements for their goods, Wren probably wouldn't have been able to spot it. It was obvious the town was small even from this distance, and something about it attracted her. The tapestries were bright and welcoming. There was no wall around the town, just more poles with bright flags at their apexes to show where their territory began.

"Have you been to any town other than The Disc?" Caster's question drew her out of her stare.

"No," she said. "Just the Open."

"Every town is unique, with its own way of doing things. Types of leadership vary, what people trade, and how they view outsiders. Dearborn is relatively tame compared to some, but they are suspicious of new people. It's only logical, but I want to warn you before we get there."

Six jogged up and interrupted their conversation. "What's the plan, boss? We go in, say we've got the deal of the century for them, and then somehow slip in that we're on a mission to overthrow the most powerful man in this corner of the world?"

"Your job is to be silent and look intimidating. Think you can handle that?" said Caster.

"Psh. The intimidating part, I got. The silent part?" He wobbled his hand from side to side.

They reached a boundary line of tapestry poles. A beaten path on the other side led into town. Caster stopped at the edge and held up his hand. The group stopped behind him.

"Are you going to attack us, Gray? Or welcome us in?" said Caster.

A slow-building laugh sounded behind a long, gold tapestry just inside town. A man stepped out from behind it, resting a strange bow loaded with a small arrow on his shoulder. He chewed on a splinter of wood. He was neither tall nor short, with a wave of black hair and dark circles under his eyes.

"Want to tell me what you're doing here, Caster? Might help me decide," said Gray. He smiled around the splinter to reveal his pointed canines.

"I was hoping to discuss some business with you."

"Sounds harmless enough." He hung his bow from the strap on his shoulder, letting it fall against the back of his hole-riddled cotton shirt. He whistled, and three more people emerged from behind tapestries. Two were women—twins—though it was hard to tell at first glance. One had a high black ponytail stretching down her back, and the other's hair was short, cut in choppy spikes stabbing away from her face. Their eyes and how they communicated to one another through them alone gave them away as sisters. The other was a guy with a baby face, tangled brown hair, and bulging biceps. Gray looked to be near Caster's age, but the others seemed younger, not quite adults yet.

Caster walked up to Gray. "Quit smoking?"

Gray rolled the splinter to the other corner of his mouth. "Again, yeah. A humbling endeavor."

"Pretty sure 'humble' didn't used to be in your vocabulary."

"Not yours, either."

An energy passed between the two men, and Wren wasn't sure if it was good or bad. They stared each other down, as if bracing for a punch to be thrown, until Caster finally held out his hand. Gray's pointy smile broke out again, and he shook Caster's hand heartily.

"Come in out of the sun," Gray said. "Let's catch up so I can see if you're still an asshole." He turned and started down the path leading into town.

The group followed, passing through swatches of shade beneath the flapping tapestries. They were even more beautiful up close. Intricate knot designs and stitching bordered bright centers. Some had words in languages Wren couldn't read, others had animals. One featured a fierce-looking bird—a roadrunner, she realized—on top of brilliant yellow.

"We'll go through the hub, if you don't mind," Gray said over his shoulder. "It's faster."

They walked through more tents until they came to a huge awning. Beneath the structure, sitting in circles with needles and thread and spinning wheels, were elderly women and a few men. Clothes, banners, and other textiles rippled in the breeze, hanging half-finished on big structures with levers that added another strand with each pull. Others sewed by hand over their laps. A couple of large boxes—blue with handles on top—whirred off to the side, connected via a system of wires snaking along the ground to over twenty machines, all in use. Power somehow flowed between them to make the machines plunge needles down over and over in constant percussion as their users pulled fabric through.

As Gray led the group between the circles of workers, he patted his people on their shoulders and leaned down to kiss the hand of one tiny lady sporting a high bun. She smiled a gummy smile. A few of the workers glanced over at the strangers, but more out of reflex than interest. Their focus was on one another and their tasks, and they didn't appear too worried about these foreigners marching through their midst. Wren got the sense that that wouldn't have been the case if Gray weren't present.

They reached the end of the shade structure and came out on the other side to a striking white building. It was made of brick, with narrow arched windows and a bronze bell at the top of a point. Gray opened the heavy wood door, and they all filed in. It was cooler inside. Wooden benches sat in rows leading up to an open space with a table draped in deep indigo cloth, on which sat two cups and a cross. Gray put his bow down on the closest bench, and Wren realized it could be fired with a pull of a trigger. Gray bent over a basin of water near the door, washed his hands and face, and then stood back from the basin.

"Been a while since you've been to church I'd bet, Caster." Gray chuckled to himself and shook the water from his face. "Now, what's this business you want to discuss?" He wiped his hands on his pants.

Caster took his pack off, and the group followed suit, laying their gear near one of the front benches and then gathering in a loose cluster—Caster's people framing him as he stood opposite Gray and his fighters.

"How much gas do you have left in your stock to run those generators out there?" asked Caster.

Gray raised a sharp eyebrow. "Not enough. What's your point?"

"When that's gone, your production and export will slow to a crawl. You won't be able to trade to feed your people. All your sheep will produce wool you can't use, except to spin yarn you can't knit fast enough."

"Yes. And your point is?"

"You've protected these people since you were a kid. You've trained your fighters to do the same. Thieves and Marauders are threats to them, certainly, but what if you could protect against the threat of losing their livelihood?"

Gray sat on a bench and stretched a leg along it. "How would I do that?"

"Bring in one of your dead batteries, and I'll show you."

Gray smirked. "Jeb, go grab Little Blue."

The big, baby-faced guy left and returned shortly with a faded blue box with outlets dotting its surface. He plopped it down on the ground between Gray and Caster.

Caster held a hand out to Wren standing next to him. "This is Wren."

She waved at Gray.

"Pretty ladies always make the best salespeople," said Gray to Wren. "Good to meet you. Sounds like you're going to make me quite the offer. Wow me."

She picked Little Blue up, surprised by the weight, and held it in front of her in both hands. She forced her tired, hot muscles to relax, and that flutter started in her chest and moved down her arms. Her hands began to glow, low and purple, and then a little green light on the battery came to life.

The baby-faced guy, Jeb, backed away as if she'd just performed witchcraft. The twins exchanged a complex series of looks expressing a range of emotion, primarily shock. But Gray's reaction was far more reserved.

"How 'bout that?" said Gray. He got up and took the battery from her. He tossed it to Jeb, who held it away from him like it was alive and might bite.

Asha went up to Wren and took hold of the inside of her wrist as she stared at her watch.

"There must be quite the story explaining how that," said Gray as he waved a hand in a big circle directed at Wren, "is even possible. But frankly, I'm more interested in the price tag. How much cash would this cost me?"

Caster shook his head. "No cash."

Gray gnawed on the splinter. "Then what?"

"Nothing. Wren will charge all of your dead batteries so you don't have to rely on limited fuel to provide for your people."

"Uh huh. Where's the catch, old buddy?"

"No catch. My father wanted me to come here and make you pay with your fealty for it. I'd rather give it to you for free."

"Oh ho, I'm sure daddy won't like that. You're disobeying his orders now? Aren't you a little old for a rebellious stage?"

"Thallium's reach is outgrowing what's reasonable. He wants to rule over you and every other town and village we know about. My blood or not, he needs to be stopped."

Gray's eyes got big. After a pause, he burst out laughing. His fighters laughed with him. "*Your* father. The man I watched you worship every time he and my uncles socialized? You want to go *against* him. I don't buy it. You want to catch me on record saying I want to take him down, is that it? Then you can finally make good on the threat you made to have me hanged when we were teenagers because I beat you when we sparred?"

"You only beat me once. And you cheated."

Gray showed his canines again. "There are no rules when you're street fighting." He reached over and poked Adonis in the ribs. "The Bastard of the Desert couldn't handle a little dust in his eyes at your age."

Adonis snickered.

Gray sidled up to Adonis and whispered conspiratorially. "Did you know I gave him that nickname? He was always so sensitive about the circumstances of his conception, which of course meant I had to spread it all over the area. Funny how some things stick, isn't it?"

"I think it's kinda cool," said Adonis.

"Hear that, old buddy?" Gray addressed Caster again. "The youth of today think you're cool."

"Stop stalling. Are you with us or not?" replied Caster dryly.

"Look," continued Gray, "I want to believe you when you say you've outgrown your father. I know personally that such a thing is possible—my uncles used to lead this place without mercy, treating their people like slaves and running them hard until they died and were replaced. Up until I killed them last year."

"Then the rumors are true," said Caster. "I was going to say I'm sorry for your loss, but it looks like that would ring a bit hollow."

Gray shrugged one shoulder. "I didn't *want* to kill them. They left me no other option. I say this to acknowledge that, even though we've had our tiffs over the years, I'd like to believe you're not the self-entitled pretty boy I remember."

"Time will tell," said Caster.

Gray slowly bobbed his head, examining Caster and his traveling companions. "Time will tell," he echoed.

A young girl burst into the chapel, face smeared with dirt. She marched up to Gray, pigtails bouncing, as she wiped her filthy hands on her pink shorts. Gray knelt next to her, and she whispered something in his ear. He looked past her to the door and stood.

"Let's finish this discussion later. I'm sure you're all tired, and something urgent has just come up. Macey," he turned to the twin with the ponytail, "please get our guests some supper. They'll be staying the night. We can pick up where we left off in the morning, don't you think?" He shook Caster's hand, picked up his weapon, and left. The pigtail girl ran out after him.

Through one of the skinny windows, Wren caught a glimpse of Gray walking away next to a tall man with a dark braid down the middle of his shaved head.

"Are we concerned?" said Six under his breath.

"I trust Gray," said Caster.

"Too bad it's not mutual," muttered Six out of one side of his mouth. He then waltzed over and offered to help Macey carry a tray full of bowls of drinking water almost in the same breath he used to ask her how old she was.

Caster took Wren's hand and squeezed it. "You did great."

Her stomach filled with a strange swimming sensation, and she let his hand go. As he went to help Adonis set up space to sleep, she tried to keep herself from staring at him, and her gaze shifted again to the window. Standing there, glaring at her, was the little pigtail girl, her nose smushed against the glass.

CHAPTER THIRTEEN

Hot silence, broken only by the panting of his men and the sizzling of Freddy's death stick, filled Gavel's ears. He propped himself up using one of the dead men's shovels, trying to take only shallow breaths despite what Derma said about the sickness not being airborne.

"Sans," he coughed. "Get the door."

The mouth-breathing killer that was currently Sans shoved his way through the bodies, pushing them aside with his feet.

"They're victims too. They deserve respect," said Gavel. He started to slide off the end of the shovel, but Freddy caught him and took his arm over his shoulder.

Sans moved the not-yet-cold limbs more gently. As he approached the door, a peep hole opened from the outside. One of Derma's men peered in, apparently sent to see how things had turned out. Sans put one hand to the handle, the other to the center hinge, and snapped them off. Then he shoved with both hands on the center of the door. It fell forward, slammed into the guard's face, and knocked him on his back. Sans walked across the fallen door, trapping the guard underneath like an ant under a thumb.

Freddy pulled Gavel's arm tighter over his shoulders, and they walked out together after Sans, the bright sun accosting their eyes. Close by with Derma stood six women and men armed with scythes, rakes, and their fists. Sans stomped toward them, his eyes completely red, the irises gone. He trembled, letting out shaky breaths and glaring at the group gathered just across from the building now overflowing with death.

"Red eyes! He's infected!" shouted one of Derma's guards.

They fled, some screaming to nearby civilians that an infected was on the loose. Derma backed away, keeping her attention on Sans, until she butted up against a rusting metal plow. She managed to put a hand over the bandana on her face before Sans grabbed her around the throat and shoved her against the plow.

As he squeezed and she began to turn blue, Gavel's approaching voice made his hand stop. "Put her down."

Sans grunted, gave his head a quick shake, and obeyed. She gasped. He turned away from her, and his eyes grew clearer, turning from crimson to candy apple red, through shades of pink until the irises returned and the whites shone with calm clarity.

"He's a Harbinger. Not sick," Gavel told her. Then he pulled his scarf, a tangled mess stained with blood, from around his head and threw it to the ground. His face was clean, but his clothes and those of his companions would have to be changed as soon as possible, the soiled ones burned. He reached up to touch the wound on the back of his skull, checking the damage. He and Freddy joined Sans and stared down at Derma. Gavel pointed back to the scarf on the ground. "That was a gift from my wife. I liked that scarf."

"Yeah!" said Freddy. "He *liked* that scarf!" He jabbed the death stick toward Derma.

If Gavel ever rolled his eyes, he would have then. He took his arm back from Freddy and bent down close to Derma's face. "My intention in coming here was to get my man back, not go to war with you. I'm sorry for what he did to your people, truly. His actions and those of our Principal will be called into question." He held out his hand. "Can I have your word that any further conflict between our people will not erupt until we've had a chance to investigate?"

She ripped off her mask and spat in Gavel's hand. "War is a boulder on a hill. Ours is already tumbling down the side. You can't stop it."

He wiped her spit off on his poncho. "I'll tell our Principal your stance." He grabbed her wrist and pulled her arm straight out. She winced, preparing for the blow, but he only reached into her sleeve. He withdrew the vial of magenta liquid and released her. "This evidence doesn't belong to you."

He dropped the vial into a pouch on his belt before putting his arm over Freddy's shoulder again, and the three of them retreated down the path to the town's front entrance. Civilian eyes peered through tent flaps, and the sound of crunching dirt started to grow louder several yards behind them as Derma's men found their courage.

"Walk faster, Freddy," said Gavel.

They made it to the buggy, and as Freddy headed for the front seat, Gavel stopped him.

"Take off your clothes," he said.

Freddy pretended to be bashful. "I didn't know you felt that way."

Sans, already stripped to his underwear, spoke close behind Freddy, making him start and squeak. "Now. And wash your hands, then your face."

Sans placed fresh clothes from the boot locker on the ground nearby for Gavel and made sure he could manage changing on his own before continuing to clean himself up. Four men appeared near the gate and watched them, and Gavel changed more quickly. The men seemed to be trying to decide if attacking was worth the gamble.

Once he and his men were clean, their soiled clothes in a pile on the dirt, Gavel got settled in the buggy's front seat. The four men started to inch closer, but Sans took his kanabō and stood astride the back seat, resting the weapon on his shoulder as he stared at them. They hesitated.

Gavel pointed to the pile of clothes and called out, "Burn it. Please."

"And yourselves too, preferably!" Freddy brandished his death stick at them before jumping into the driver's seat and starting the engine. They backed up, gaining speed, and then Freddy whipped the car around. Their tires kicked a cloud of dust toward Hallund as they took off.

"We're going to Dearborn. Immediately," said Gavel.

"Not back home?" asked Freddy.

"We have people in Dearborn. And they're in danger. Can this thing go faster?"

Freddy snorted. "*Fast* is the epitome of understatement to describe my lady fair." He caught a glimpse of Gavel's vacant expression. "Yes, much faster." He laid on the gas and shifted gear.

Gavel braced himself against the dash. Sans continued to watch Hallund to make sure they weren't being followed while Freddy focused on not crashing. Gavel's impulse was to grab his scope and check their surroundings, but he settled for taking a quick look around. He blinked past the motion sickness that crept into his gut. The lurching of the car and the danger in Dearborn overwhelmed his desire to follow protocol. Right now, he had one job, and that was to reach his wife and son before it was too late.

It stank of old people and sheep shit. Survivor couldn't figure out what it was at first, the strange mix of dusty feet and excrement. The old musk managed to overtake the shit smell when she broke the lock on one of the trunks under the covered area of the town, in the aisle between the circles of chairs and tables topped with weird devices shaped like crooked arms. When she opened the trunk, the smell billowed out. She wrinkled her nose and pawed through the garments inside. In spite of the odor, the fabric was soft and nice to touch. She stretched and tugged it roughly between her hands. It was durable, too. She swung her pack around and stuffed a few shirts and skirts into it, or at least what she assumed were shirts and skirts in the dark.

Why would they leave these treasures unguarded? Idiots. They were too busy guarding their borders, so trusting of their ability to keep unwanted people out that they thought it impossible for someone to slip past them. It hadn't been hard.

Eydis had said Wren was here. And the messenger Hallund had sent to warn Dearborn of Thallium's treachery had been easy to follow. She'd left the SUV about a quarter mile outside of town, stuck in a ditch, its rear wheels spinning like the twitching of something recently dead; turned out it wasn't "all-terrain" as its tires had advertised. She ran the rest of the way to Dearborn, then snuck past their perimeter guard. She had spotted Wren that afternoon, standing inside the white building, looking through a window with Caster, an all too complacent expression on her face.

Wren had lost her instincts, forgotten all of Survivor's

lessons. *Trust no one. Never allow yourself to be used. Do what I say to stay alive.* Since they'd left the cave, a lesson had fallen out of her head for every step they took. It had cost them their freedom, and if Survivor let it continue, it would cost Wren her life. It was a life Survivor had promised Alma she'd protect. She would keep that promise, even if it meant taking Wren against her will.

Here, in this stinking backwater town, was her chance. No walls, none of Thallium's lackeys. Just Thallium's son and a few of his idiot friends. All of which would sleep tonight, and then in the dark, Survivor would take her sister back.

In the meantime, Survivor intended to see what she could scrounge from this sad little village. She planned on grabbing Wren just before midnight. They'd go north. Far north. Wren enjoyed going north, said it always felt easier than going south, somehow cooler. Since Survivor had time to spare, maybe she'd check the old ones' food stores or the quality of their well water next.

A hodgepodge of candles sat in clusters in the sanctuary at the opposite end of the chapel. They were of varying heights and colors, some dripping delicate tendrils of wax to the floor, others adding their little drips to thick ropes of wax that reminded Wren of the rock formations in the cave she and Survivor used to call home. The fire that Survivor had constantly kept burning in the cave to cast curtains of orange on the wall was echoed in this grouping of tiny flames. Burning together, each waving whenever they felt the urge, they cast low light around the room, bright enough to see by but soft enough to allow sleep.

Her left side was getting sore, and from this angle, she was

looking straight across at a snoring and drooling Six. He'd
insisted on sleeping across from her, casting the occasional
eyebrow raise and taking his shirt off before he tucked his
blanket up just beneath his chest as he rolled up on his side to
face her. She'd blinked at him several times before closing her
eyes, willing her body to sleep. When she'd opened them again,
he was slumped down onto his pillow, snoring and cuddling
with his blanket.

She rolled onto her back. Except for the noise of Six's snoring, it was quiet. The occasional breeze kissed the outside of the
chapel, but it was gentle, not the howling she was used to.
Everyone had fallen asleep easily. Asha went to bed first while
the boys stayed up and, with the exception of Caster, drank
something bitter from a flask Six brought. They gave Wren a
taste, and it turned the part of her tongue it touched numb. She
lay down after that, close to Asha, but her mind wouldn't let
her rest.

A soft noise came from her right. She turned onto her side
to see Caster lying on a bench with his head propped up on his
bedroll as he read a book with a faded blue cover. *Death of a
Naturalist* was inscribed in gold on the front. He held it close to
a candle sitting on a stool next to the bench. As he turned
another page, his gaze shifted to the bunch of sleeping people
on the floor, as if to do a quick headcount to make sure they
were all where they were supposed to be.

He saw she was awake and waggled a few fingers at her,
casting shadows on the wall behind him that caught her eye.
He followed her gaze, then let his book rest open on his chest
and curled the fingers of his right hand, leaving just the pointer
and middle fingers to stand at attention. Wren looked at the
wall and saw he'd made a rabbit. He made it hop up and down
until he got her to smile. He let his hands fall back to his book.
They looked at each other with tired eyes until something near

the door caught his attention. He sat up and turned his ear toward the door.

"Someone's coming. Alone," he said softly into the quiet.

A moment later, the door of the chapel started to creak open.

He tossed the book onto the bench and shot to his feet. His hand fell to the knife at his hip. Wren sat up as he picked his way through the sleepers to hide behind the door. The door opened a couple of feet, just wide enough for Survivor to slip in.

Wren shoved her blankets off, jumped over Asha, and ran to her sister before Caster could come out from behind the door. She nearly hugged her but then held back, remembering how they'd left things. "What are you doing here? Did Thallium let you go?"

"No. His assistant did."

"Eydis? But why?"

Survivor went for her arm in response. "It's time to go. I have plenty of supplies for us." She adjusted the new drawstring bag hanging over her shoulder nearly down to her feet. "Now."

As she turned to lead them back through the door, she bumped hard into Caster.

"Move," she growled.

"Let her go," he said. His tone was strained, as if there was so much more he wanted to say but didn't.

Wren wiggled her arm out of Survivor's grasp. "I'm glad you're here, but I'm not leaving."

Survivor tugged at her own hair in frustration. "We don't have time for this. We can argue outside of town. Come with me." She drew in a slow breath. "Please."

As Wren was about to respond, Caster turned toward the cracked doorway, listening again. "What the hell?"

He left them standing there in suspense until the door opened wider and Gavel ran in with Sans and a badly beaten Frederick Hawthorn de Bourgh close behind.

Freddy spotted Survivor as he entered and skidded to an abrupt stop. "You!" he shouted. Sans elbowed him in the ribs, and he lowered his voice to an angry whisper. "You ruined my business, you fiend!"

She pointed at her eye. "I'm surprised you're not more upset about your face."

He darted halfway behind Sans, less than subtly hiding. "How dare you!"

Caster closed the door and addressed Gavel. "What are you doing here?"

"You're all right? Gray hasn't hurt you?" said Gavel.

"Hurt us? No, why would he do that?"

Gavel started to respond, but then he spotted Survivor, who stood off alone in the space as if she didn't want to even pretend she was associated with any of them. "You murdered my Soldier," said Gavel, his tone deadly flat.

"Actually, the good people of the little farming village did that. I just inspired them to," Survivor replied.

"What happened? Mainstay's dead?" said Caster.

"Clap e-binds on that criminal!" Freddy exclaimed, letting the volume of his voice get away from him again. He grabbed the e-binds from Gavel's belt and threw them toward Caster. They fell short, landing with a dull thump on the dirt. Survivor bared her teeth at him, and he ducked back behind Sans.

An abrupt snort came from Six as he started awake mid-snore. He leapt up in his silk underwear, silver and shining like the walls of The Disc, and took in what was happening. Adonis slept nearby, and Six kicked him lazily in the gut, making him cough and wake. "Get up. We have a situation here."

Freddy peeked out from behind Sans.

Six saw him. "Huh. You're still alive." He tugged on his pants and spoke through a yawn to Adonis. "I owe you a batch of potato cakes."

"I loathe you," spat Freddy.

Gavel shushed everyone. "There's no time for this now. We'll sort through it soon enough." He crossed to where Asha still slept amidst the pandemonium. He leaned down and brushed a bundle of curls back from the side of her face. She stirred and opened her eyes.

"Hey, baby."

She sat up. "What's going on?"

"We need to go."

"What's going on?" she asked again, the rest of the sleep fading from her voice.

"We came from Hallund. They're not happy with Thallium, and they sent a messenger here to tell your hosts that they should kill you."

Her eyes narrowed. "Why were you in Hallund? Hallund isn't 'wilderness training,' last time I checked."

He sighed. "Fine. We weren't training. We had reason to suspect that Thallium was connected to treachery there and went to investigate." He stood and reached a hand down to her. "We need to leave."

She slapped his hand away and jumped up. "I cannot believe you lied to me."

"We're going to do this now? Really?"

"Uh oh," said Six. "Someone's in trouble. Better back up." He shooed Adonis to safety.

"You said it was just training. Walkabout, my ass!" She threw her canteen at him, but he batted it away, knocking the cap off and spilling a twisting stream of water as the canteen spun and fell. She stooped down to grab one of her boots next to her sleeping area and then held it aloft, as if trying to decide which of Gavel's vital parts to aim for.

"Never mind backing up. This is too good," said Six. He crossed his arms and settled in to watch.

"What did you find in Hallund?" Caster broke in.

"Evidence that suggests Thallium contaminated their water," said Gavel.

"*Thallium* contaminated their water?" said Caster.

"So it seems. He supposedly ordered Mainstay to do it," said Gavel, careful not to take his eyes off his wife. He withdrew a tiny bottle from the pouch on his hip and held it aloft. "He used this." A bolt of recognition shot through Wren—she'd seen dozens of those vials her first day in the lab. "Rubedo. Same thing that killed Reina. Thallium seems to have somehow weaponized it."

Caster stared at the vial. His face was inscrutable. It seemed like he was present only in body, and his mind and spirit had shot off in opposite directions.

"This strain...it's terrifying," continued Gavel. "Even now, people in Hallund keep turning up sick. And the deaths are," he searched for the right word, "violent." He tucked the vial back in his pouch and held his hands open toward his wife. "I have to find the truth here, even if it is that Thallium's guilty."

Asha's initial anger at her husband dissipated. She dropped the boot and busied herself putting it on, a tiny smile on her face.

Finally, Caster spoke. "We need Gray and his men even more than before. We have to convince them to join our fight."

"What do you mean, our fight?" said Gavel. "You're here on Thallium's orders."

"That's what he thinks. We're here to lend Wren's power to assist them in the hopes they'll support us when we remove Thallium from office," said Caster.

Haughtiness snuck into Gavel's expression at that. "Just a quick trip as a favor to Caster, huh hon?"

Asha cleared her throat and started gathering her stuff.

Gavel marched up to her, his voice low and monotone. "You're biting my head off for lying about investigating a crime the Principal might be involved in, while you're here planning a coup."

"Well I guess we need to work on our communication!" she blurted in his face.

Caster looked around the chapel, searching for something. The high beams near the roof were shrouded in darkness, the windows showing only the black of night. "What kind of resistance did you meet getting in here?"

Sans responded. "None."

A silence fell in the chapel, heavier than the weight of hundreds of voices shouting. It weighed down the benches and stopped the travelers where they stood.

"Trap. Get out," said Caster.

Everyone started to move for their things until Gray's voice rang out from outside the building, carried on the still night air to them. "Caster, old buddy. I think we need to talk."

Dots of red appeared over each of their hearts except for Caster. Six batted at the one on his chest as if to swipe it away. When it didn't move, he got frustrated and grabbed at it.

"Be still," said Gray. "My people here have some retro weapons. Very twenty-first century. They might be old, but they're pretty good shots. The windows they're aiming through are narrow. That's why they have orders to fire if any one of you runs for it. Might not get all of you, but at least the slower ones."

"Gray, what happened in Hallund wasn't us," shouted Caster.

"I'm going to come in and we can have a chat about it. How about that?"

They all stood silent and unmoving, waiting for Gray to appear. Finally, he pushed the door wide open and stepped inside, his bow aimed at Caster. He gave an exaggerated sigh. "How is it that I know your father better than you do? You really believe that he's only interested in Wren for her ability to provide power?"

"To manipulate the surrounding territories to his advantage?" Caster replied. "Absolutely."

"Come on, think bigger. What are the limitations on the power she generates? Do you have any idea? What other forms can it take? You aren't out advertising a resource for sale. You're out warning everyone nearby that you have a weapon more powerful than any other in existence."

A flash of realization danced across Caster's features, but he replied, "You're wrong."

"Your father just used biological warfare on a few hundred men, women, and children as a simple field test."

Gavel spoke up. "There's not enough proof to know—"

Gray ignored him. "Is it so far a stretch that, now that he's found a cleaner method of world domination, he'd want to take it out for a spin? She could erupt at any second. Get out, now."

"We don't even know if she's capable of that," said Asha, putting a hand on Wren's shoulder. "And as much as I despise Thallium, I know he would never send Caster into harm's way knowingly. He sent us here to bribe your loyalty, not take you and his son out with a mystical female weapon."

The flutter in Wren's chest started up. She felt it begin to pulse there, faster and more deeply, as if it liked the designation Asha had just given it.

"Thallium wanted to bring people to their knees," Gray accused. "Instead, he's brought them up in arms. Everyone nearby will hear what he did. I'll tell them. You came here hoping to gather manpower against your father? Mission accomplished. You had better run home to daddy before that manpower catches up with you."

"Please, Gray," Caster tried one last time. He held his hand to his heart. "We mean you no harm."

Gray continued aiming at him. "Look, Caster. We're old friends, and you're a moron. It's for those two reasons that I'm letting you all leave here alive. Get out now. I won't ask again."

Nobody moved. The dots on Asha and Six began to waver a bit, as if their controllers were starting to get nervous. Gray kept holding his weapon on Caster, and the pulsing in Wren's chest grew larger, filling her up before she even realized what was happening. Purple light emanated from her, growing brighter and brighter as she felt it consume her inside.

Everyone turned their heads in her direction, and their eyes went wide, their mouths falling slightly open.

"Wren?" Caster said calmly. "Are you okay?"

Heat began to pour off of her in waves. Gray retrained his bow on her.

"Wren, take a deep breath," Asha called over gently. "It's all right, sweetheart."

Wren shouted at Gray in a panic. "Make your people stand down."

"Not a chance," he replied.

The light turned white, and she felt the power within her slipping beyond her reach, growing still bigger and bigger like it would never stop. "Now! Do it now! Please!"

Gray hesitated only another moment, then he lowered his weapon and released an ear-splitting, shrill whistle. The red dots on their chests disappeared.

Everyone froze. The power within her froze too, not growing nor shrinking for what felt like an eternity. She took shaky breaths and willed it to recede by consciously relaxing each of her limbs to gain better control. When it finally withdrew into her chest to rest, she bent over at the waist and put her weight on her knees.

Caster lunged for her. "Are you all right?" He wrapped his arms around her and took on her weight, stroking the back of her hair.

She backed out of his embrace and looked up at him. "No."

Gray called over from the doorway. "That look peaceful to you, Caster?" He took the splinter from his mouth and threw it on the ground. "Get out."

CHAPTER FOURTEEN

IT WAS BELOW FREEZING, AND WHILE IT HAD BEEN PLENTY tolerable under blankets in the building in Dearborn, out on the exposed earth a mile from the little town, the cold weaseled its way into sleeves and pressed up against bare skin and settled there to rest. Gray had let them gather their things but didn't offer any materials to construct a shelter against the nighttime desert. They had no dome or tent. They hadn't needed one for the two-day trip to a settlement, and it hadn't been worth the weight of hauling just in case of an emergency.

The group did have light for such an emergency, however. They cracked and shook small plastic sticks, which illuminated with a green glow, and they lashed them to the sides of their feet. The light allowed them to see each other and where they were walking well enough, but it was dim and close to the ground to avoid attracting unwanted attention. Freddy drove the buggy at a crawl next to the group, keeping the lights off, as Sans stood on top of the backseat and watched their surroundings through Gavel's night scope. Caster held up a hand once they'd passed the mile mark, and everyone came to a stop.

Asha whispered, "We need to keep moving. It's the best way to stay warm." The wind was so slight that the night made her plea audible to all. The grand Open suddenly felt intimate.

"We shouldn't keep moving if we don't know where we're going. We need to discuss this," said Caster.

Asha looked at Wren, who stood next to her sister, shivering.

"Fine," said Asha. "But buddy up, people. Body heat is the next best thing to movement if we're going to make it through this without hypothermia. Try not to sit directly on the ground. It'll steal your heat faster than you think."

She walked over to Gavel, and they put their packs on the ground next to one another. He sat on his pack and opened his big arms to her. She sat on her own pack and draped his arms over her shoulders like a new coat.

"We won't be here long enough to need each other's heat, because Wren and I are leaving," Survivor announced.

Wren just stood there, teeth chattering and unsure of what to do until Caster came up. He sat on his pack and put his knees up, waving her down to join him. She did so and hooked her elbows around his knees as he covered her arms with his. A dull growl came from Survivor's general vicinity.

Freddy got out of the buggy and stood next to Six. He slowly opened his arms.

"I would rather my limbs fall off. All of them," said Six.

Freddy let his arms drop.

Six started to go for Sans, but he already had Adonis in a bear hug.

"Damn it," muttered Six.

As he turned back, Freddy's arms were wide open again.

"No means no!" Six walked in place and tightened his coat.

"The way I see it," Caster addressed the group, "we don't

have many options. We have to go back to The Disc if we want to find out the truth about my father. The best way to do that is to get him to trust me and have him show me what he's been up to."

"Your family, your problem. Not ours," said Survivor, pacing like an animal stalking prey.

"You made it Wren's problem when you got her brought to The Disc. If it weren't for your crimes, she'd still be tucked away somewhere in the Open," said Caster.

Survivor didn't seem to have a response to that. She ignored it entirely. "Go back and tell Thallium Wren's dead. Wren, untangle yourself and say goodbye."

Caster scooted a bit closer against Wren. "You're just going to take her? Have you asked her what she wants?"

"My guess is she wants to live. With me, she will," said Survivor.

"If you want her to live, then she needs to return to The Disc," said Asha, talking past the slight chatter of her teeth. "She has an ability we know nothing about. Nothing. I was a fool not to protest this venture when we have no idea what she's capable of, other than producing energy. The how, the why, the limits of that ability are all unknowns. And unknowns in the medical world have another term—risks. Look at what just happened in Dearborn. If she comes back to The Disc, I can do some diagnostic—"

"She's not yours to keep in a cage and prod when you're feeling bored," growled Survivor.

Asha leapt out of Gavel's arms and took an imposing stride toward Survivor. "Grow the fuck up. You can't help her and you know it. All you know is how to end life, not how to preserve it."

Survivor grinned. "You're partly right. I'd be happy to show you how well I end life."

Asha held her ground, and it appeared as though she wasn't afraid to see Survivor try.

"Even aside from Wren's medical needs," Caster cut in, "nobody out here trusts us. Gray and his people will make sure of that. We'll have no resources available to us, no allies. Unless we can convince the territories otherwise."

"Brother, no offense," said Six. "But your reputation in the wide world is as Thallium's loving heir and a playboy. That's how Gray still thinks of you. Nobody out here knows who you really are, and you can't convince them on your own. That will take time."

"Well, I'm not going back," said Freddy. "I failed the Principal and now I'm a liability—I saw Hallund and I will continue seeing it every night in my dreams until I die an old, disgustingly wealthy inventor, crushed by the pressure of having to top my previous creations. My public will mourn me."

"Shut up, Freddy. Nobody cares what you do. Stop talking," said Six.

"I care," mumbled Freddy, putting his hands in his pockets.

A tense quiet settled on the group. Even Survivor let it continue, a smug smile on her face, as if she enjoyed watching the others struggle to find a solution to an insurmountable situation.

Adonis finally broke the silence. "Maybe Freddy's right. We shouldn't go back. It's not like we can convince the people Thallium's evil—they love him. He's royalty. He's untouchable."

"Adonis makes a good point," Gavel said, and the young boy beamed when he heard those words come from his leader. "It would be incredibly dangerous to start a rebellion in such a climate. But I believe we'll need the people of The Disc on our side if it turns out that Thallium is guilty and needs to be taken out of power."

Asha coughed out, "*If*. You and your ifs."

"Yes, *if*," Gavel continued. "We need more evidence before I can determine the correct path forward. Evidence that's in The Disc, not out here."

"Then go back. All of you," said Survivor. "Your ruler is an asshole, you can't help Wren when you don't even understand what's happening to her, and your people hate us. She's safer out here." Survivor turned to Caster. "Admit it. You can't protect her."

Wren felt Caster's body tense against her back.

"Yes, she's in danger if we go back," he replied. "But in the Open, she'll die. You'll both die. You were damn near close when I found you the first time."

Survivor paced faster and muttered to herself.

The terror Wren had experienced in the church in Dearborn came back to her. It had felt like her power was going to consume her and everything it viewed as a threat—and all she could do was watch it happen. "I'm going with Survivor," she said into the darkness.

"What?" said Caster.

"If there's even a chance that Gray's right, that I'm a weapon, then I can't go back with you. People will die. Maybe you. I won't risk it."

"We don't know you're capable of that."

"I feel it," she said, looking at the ground. She was thankful Caster was at her back so she didn't have to meet his eyes. "Deep in my chest, the hidden places of my mind. It wants to get out." Her hands radiated purple under Caster's. "When we were back in that church with a weapon aimed at you, it nearly did."

He wrapped his arms around her tighter, not shying away

from the light emanating from her. "Next time, I won't be able to stop it," she said.

"Then we learn to control it," said Asha, her tone utterly confident as she returned to her spot with Gavel.

"Together," said Caster.

Wren's voice caught, and she swallowed past it. The flutter in her chest waved at her playfully. "I don't think I can," she whispered.

Survivor marched over and held her hand out to Wren. "It's time." The feel of her palm was rough and familiar, as was her forceful pull upward.

Caster stood with her and took hold of her other hand. "Please. Don't do this."

She turned her head sideways toward him. The amount of vulnerability she saw in his expression nearly made her let go of Survivor's hand, but she held fast. "You once told me I'm strong. I'm starting to believe you. Thank you." She let go of him.

She reached for her pack. The group watched in silence as the two sisters started to leave, only to have Survivor stop mid-step and stare into the black void of the Open, her head tilted slightly to the side.

"What is it?" asked Wren.

"Shh," Survivor hissed.

"Someone's coming." Caster's words made Wren spin around. His gaze was far out on the horizon, his head tilted similarly to Survivor's. His eyes grew wide. "Vehicles."

Then they all heard it. The rattle in the distance of dirt being kicked up, engines whirring.

And drums. A pounding, slow and deep, off in the distance.

Survivor turned to Wren, honest-to-God fear in her eyes. "He found me."

"Marauders!" said Caster. "Everyone, circle up now! Women and children in the center!"

Everyone obeyed except for Freddy, who squealed like an idiot and froze in place next to the buggy.

"Goddammit! Move your ass!" said Six. He slapped Freddy in the back of the head, and he snapped out of it.

Survivor joined the cluster of women, sticking close by Wren as she peered in the direction of the noise to see familiar torches lighting up a half mile away—bursts of nauseating yellow in the dark. They were blinding, and grew even more so as they got closer, fast. The sound of howling, the noises of beasts through human throats, came from the direction of the lights. The drums grew louder, their beat faster, the booming of skins stretched across massive wooden frames.

Gavel whispered something to Asha, who closed her eyes and nodded. He kissed her hard and then gave her a little shove toward the center of the group, tucked in with the others behind the men. He jogged up to Caster, who stood between their group and the incoming Marauders as if he believed he could stop what was coming.

"Don't do anything stupid, son," Gavel said, holding out his hand.

Caster took his hand and hugged him. "Yes, boss." He pulled away. "Look after your bride."

Gavel nodded and fell back to stand in front of Asha.

Nearby, Adonis breathed hard and heavy, like he was trying to find courage but failing. Caster turned to him. "In the middle. Now, Grunt."

"What?" said Adonis. "I want to fight!"

Sans broke rank and came up to him, and the red of his eyes

made Survivor do a double take. His chest heaved as he replied to the kid. "Not tonight."

Their attackers got closer, the drums beat louder, and Adonis gave in. He slid into the group, cramming himself in near Wren and Asha. Caster turned to face those in the middle of the circle. "They probably want the buggy. Stay quiet." He eyed Survivor. "Can you do that?"

She looked toward the lights. "He wants me."

"What?"

"The Marauder you're about to meet. You can't bargain with him. This isn't some random raid. He's here for me, and you're all collateral. If you want to live, you'll have to fight." She moved closer to him, out of earshot from Wren, who stared at the oncoming lights with silent resolve from between Asha and Adonis' shoulders. "He'll hurt Wren to hurt me."

Caster opened his mouth to speak, but before he could ask anything, the howling grew loud enough to drown out everything else. He shouted at her over the noise. "Hide."

She joined the others, trying to block Wren from view with her body. Hiding was futile, but it would give her a chance to evaluate their numbers, to form a plan.

The Marauders closed in. At least ten voices melded together in a lilting song of high- and low-pitched cries. The light got brighter, blinding them and illuminating their faces in great streaks of yellow confusion. Caster stepped up, separate from the group, his stance wide and confident.

For a half a second as she took in his profile, Survivor understood Wren's fascination with the man. He was an idiot with a death wish, clearly, but he looked nice as he waited to be murdered.

Survivor reached back and pulled Wren's hood further over her face, tucking flyaway pieces of hair behind her ears within its depths. "You're going to get through this. Stay with the group, out of sight."

"What? Where are you going?"

She pulled her own hood up. "To my Master."

Three vehicles, large by the sound of their engines, drove in circles around them, shining down torchlight backlit by big mirrors, creating a carousel of flashing beams, dirt, and noise. The faces of the drivers and passengers, even the exact shape of the vehicles themselves, were indiscernible in the commotion.

The vehicles came to a stop, but their passengers continued to howl. Then someone stepped out onto the hood of one of the vehicles and jumped to the ground with a heavy thud, into the light of the nearest torch. The howling stopped instantly.

Straight out of her nightmares he leapt. Just barely more than five feet tall, dressed in khaki slacks, a button-up shirt, and a blue suit jacket. A paisley silk pocket square poked out of his breast pocket. Salt and pepper hair showed beneath his white panama hat, which he pushed up just slightly, enough to give him a good view of the group.

He pointed to Sans. "That one. See the eyes? Harbinger. Take him down."

Sans erupted in anger, but before he could take two steps, a giant dart shot through the air and stuck in the middle of his chest. The dart was attached to a thin, curled silver cable that disappeared in the darkness by the Marauder's vehicles. Electricity spun down the cable and exited through the dart into Sans' chest, dropping him to the ground. He convulsed there until The Gentleman drew his hand across his neck. The current stopped.

Fen, bald and sickly, with those yellowed eyes that were much too excited, came out from the shadows. He held a car battery—a jerry-rigged weapon. Cables stretched from it to the dart stuck in Sans' chest. He put a foot on Sans' shoulder and tugged hard on the dart. The wound it had made pooled and spilled over with blood.

"Son of a—" Six started to exclaim from where he stood just to the side and slightly in front of Survivor.

"We don't want a fight," said Caster. "Take our vehicle and we'll be on our way."

The Gentleman took off his hat and waved it at Caster. "Now, son. Why don't you just set a spell? We have business to discuss." His drawl made it seem as if he were dragging his words through mud. "I'm The Gentleman. Pleased to meet you."

"We won't fight you," Caster said again. He took his bowie knife from his belt and dropped it on the ground. "I insist you take the buggy."

"Now, now, now," The Gentleman continued, with all the leisure of a man sitting down to a drink, "I have no interest in your vehicle, adorable as it is. What is that, a straight-four engine?"

Freddy grumbled quietly somewhere behind Wren.

"Anywho, we have some business to attend to. You're Thallium's boy. Pleased to finally meet you formally." The Gentleman put his hat back on and stuck his hand out.

Caster hesitated to take it.

The Gentleman pulled his hand back, apparently ignoring the slight. "I saw you once, long ago, having a fine time with your daddy at the rat races in Ranlock. Thallium and I go way back, so far back that I knew *his* daddy. We have an arrangement that's kept me off your doorstep for decades, an arrangement that he recently broke. I warned him what would happen if he kept my daughter from me."

"What are you talking about?" asked Caster.

"Never you mind, son. As much as I appreciate you trying

to defend your kind here, this ain't about you." He called back
to his men. "Restrain him."

Two Marauders came out of the shadows behind The
Gentleman and descended upon Caster, but he didn't fight.
They put his hands behind his back and bound them with rope.

Asha's cursing on Survivor's right made her ears ring. "Get
away from him, motherfuckers!"

Gavel stood in front of her and kept her back.

Once Caster was bound, the Marauders each held one of
his shoulders.

"Now then, we can chat in just a bit, Valcin Jr.," said The
Gentleman. He bowed low to Caster. "But first, I have a family
reunion to attend to. Ain't that right, Angel?" He stared right
past Six's shoulder, picking Survivor out from the crowd easily.
"That hood don't keep you from me, child. Take it off. Go on."

Survivor started to move, but Wren wrapped her arm
around her waist, the soft purple glow growing stronger from
her hands. As much as she wanted to, Survivor couldn't glare at
her for risk of drawing attention to her.

"Let go," Survivor whispered without moving her lips,
never breaking eye contact with The Gentleman.

Wren's grip tightened.

Survivor pushed against the surprisingly firm hold Wren
had around her hips and whispered, "Please, sister."

Wren finally released her. Survivor didn't look back as she
shouldered her way out of the circle and walked halfway to
The Gentleman, each step scraping purposefully against the
compacted desert ground. When she stopped, she threw her
hood back and looked straight toward one of the yellow spot-
lights. Give him a good look, why not?

The Gentleman smiled, white teeth gleaming. "There she
is. Much better. Looks like life in the Open has been kind to

you. Got yourself a whole posse now. Men, women, children."
He whistled.

Survivor's mouth had gone dry. She salvaged what saliva
was left and swallowed before speaking. "These people are
morons. Cattle, like the rest of them. I used them to get out of
The Disc and was going to rob them tonight before leaving."

"That right? Old habits die hard, don't they?"

"My habits are fine the way they are."

"Um hmm, um hmm." He held the lapels of his jacket and
looked her over. "My, my, it's good to see you." He spoke louder
then so even his men near the vehicles could hear him. "For
those of you who don't know, this lady here was the finest killer
I've ever known, except Reskin, may he rest in peace. Though I
suppose you were even better than him, weren't you? Or does it
count if you murdered him in his sleep?"

He had no idea what he was talking about, but she
preferred to keep him ignorant about what had happened with
Reskin. It was none of his business. "Doesn't seem to matter."

"No, I suppose not. But what does matter is what you did
afterward. You ran. What do you have to say for yourself?"

She held her tongue.

He let go of his lapels and burst with rage. "Speak, woman!
You left like a goddamn thief in the night. Left your FAMILY!"

"You were never my family."

"That's right. You got a new family now. A sister, isn't that
right Fen? A lovely redhead, tall slip of a thing?"

Fen pointed toward Wren, and Survivor's heart hammered,
but she kept it from showing on her face.

"There, Master," said Fen with a giggle.

The Gentleman sighed. "Don't just point, go get her why
don't you?"

Fen dashed toward the travelers and groped for Wren
between Six and Adonis' shoulders. The boys drew their

weapons, and just as Six was about to stab Fen through a yellow eye, The Gentleman called out. "Stand down! Or I'll have your fearless prince skinned."

Caster held his tongue as the Marauder on his left, a huge man with eyebrows threaded with bone fragments, punched him in the liver, sending him to his knees.

"Stop!" said Wren to her companions. She slid between them and walked up to stand next to Survivor.

"Well," said The Gentleman, "ain't she just lovely. What's your name darlin'?"

"Wren," she said simply.

Survivor's worst fear turned into reality before her as her past and present collided. As The Gentleman walked around Wren, examining her, Survivor bit the inside of her cheek until she tasted blood to keep from screaming.

The Gentleman finished his examination and retook his place in front of Survivor and Wren. "Reminds me of someone, another pet you once had. Surprised you haven't abandoned her like you did him."

"Fuck you," Survivor spat.

"I'm just stating facts here, Angel. But Beo was better off without you, became a man of purpose, of drive."

"You took his soul," said Survivor.

"Took it? He gave it to me!" He sucked on his teeth and called into the darkness. "Beo! Get over here!"

Survivor's breath caught when a man stepped from the circle of darkness into the light. He stood with hunched shoulders next to The Gentleman, but even so, he towered above him. She saw the child he had been, the one she used to wrap her arms around every night so that he could sleep. He still had his same dimples, same hairless chin. But his eyes were lifeless now. The exuberant joy that even the horrors of murder and torture hadn't taken was now gone. Scarification wandered all over his face, down his neck to disappear under his shirt. His once tousled red hair was chopped short and ragged.

"Look at him. Strong, confident. And his accomplishments?" The Gentleman waved his hand in front of Beo's face. "There for all to see and admire."

A visceral rage struck Survivor. She'd never stopped wondering if Beo were alive, as much as she tried to forget how she'd betrayed him. She'd left him and now here he was, far worse than dead. "Get away from him!"

At the sound of her voice, Beo's expression softened. He blinked, and suddenly, there was the boy she knew. It was like he was waking up as he shook his head gently from side to side.

"He's been living in luxury since you left," said The Gentleman. "You did him a favor."

"Beo," Survivor choked out. She studied him, this ghost come back to haunt her, a ghost she'd made.

He looked at her with unbridled delight when she said his name. He opened his mouth to speak, but The Gentleman cut him off with an upward box of his right ear. Beo cupped it with his palm and hunched over, eyes downcast in shame.

"Boy, take hold of pretty little Wren here," said The Gentleman. "Gently, now."

Beo moved around Wren and held her arms behind her back.

"Take me instead!" came Caster's plea from several feet behind them. The same Marauder that had punched him elbowed him in the gut this time. He doubled over but talked through the pain. "I'm valuable. My father would pay you for me. Take me and let the others go."

"Mighty noble of you, son. Mighty noble indeed," said The Gentleman. "But just so we're clear, I ain't shopping for a better offer. This debt I'm owed must be collected." He walked closer to Survivor, lowering his voice. "You knew the cost when you left us." He gave a curt nod to Beo, who pushed Wren to her knees.

Survivor said plainly, "That woman is valuable to Thallium. She's his property. Is killing her to punish me worth a war?"

He chuckled. "Come to think of it, yes, it is. Seeing as how Thallium already started one by going back on his word and not handing you over. He chose this war."

Time was short now. Survivor spoke in a rush. "If you kill her, you risk killing us all."

The Gentleman raised an eyebrow. "Is that right?"

"She's more powerful than you can imagine."

"Hmm. As much as I'd love to hear the meaning behind your cryptic words, you know me—ever the pragmatist. Sounds like she's a threat I need to eliminate. Beo? Do oblige."

Beo held a knife to her throat, a knife Survivor recognized from a lifetime ago.

Panic, wild and snarling, burst from Survivor. "But you have me! There's no need for this. Just take me back!"

"Aw, sugar," sighed The Gentleman. "She means that much to you, eh?"

"No, don't," said Wren to her sister. She swallowed against the blade, and a drop of blood fell as it split her skin. "You're not his. You're better. You've saved me enough."

"You idiot," said Survivor, a small crack in her voice. "I never saved you; you saved me."

The Gentleman clutched at his heart dramatically. "Just precious, really. Beo? Kill her."

Beo hesitated.

The Gentleman spoke slower, the tone he took before he lashed underperforming members of the clan. "Beo, I said kill her, boy. Do it now!"

Just then, a painful grunt came from Caster behind them,

followed by a quick series of thuds, flesh on flesh. Survivor looked back to see the Marauders who'd held him reeling, more from shock than injury. And then in three great strides Caster reached Wren and snatched the knife away from her throat. All futile, but Survivor respected him for trying. She respected him even as the spear came out of his stomach. The Marauder stabbed it in with a horrible pop and ripped it back out immediately with an extra firm tug. Caster lurched forward and collapsed to the ground in front of Wren.

Asha wailed.

Wren dove next to Caster. She turned him from his front to his back and put pressure on his wound, which coated her hands with his slick blood, so warm in the cold of the night that it sent steam up to caress her face.

The Gentleman walked to Caster's other side, across from Wren, careful to pull up his slacks just a bit before he dropped down into a squat. "Hate to do that, but it was coming anyway, darlin'." He reached over and touched her chin. "His daddy broke his word. Told me he'd hand your dear sister over, and instead I find her mucking around out here with you lot. That boy was dead no matter what. Least this way he got to be the hero."

Caster reached up to wipe the blood from Wren's neck with the sleeve of his coat. The rope he'd slipped out of still dangled from one of his wrists.

"I'm so sorry," she said, unable to keep the tears from falling.

He removed one of her hands from his gut and pulled it to his lips, kissing the back of it lightly. "I'm not."

The purple aura around Wren's hands grew brighter, illu-

minating Caster's midsection. She took her hands off of him.
Power and heat surged in her core, wanting to break free.

"What the hell is this?" The Gentleman stood and started
backing away.

Survivor started to laugh. "I warned you, *Father*."

The light grew brighter, and Wren rose to her feet. Heat
started to pour off of her as the light moved up her arms,
consuming her body piece by piece.

She let it.

The Gentleman continued his slow retreat and then
screamed to the shadows. "Kill her now! Kill them all!"

Like insects swarming, the Marauders descended upon the
group of travelers, but none were bold enough to brave Wren's
heat. She stood there, pulsating with anger and a darkness that
had a glimpse of freedom and intended to use it. The fight
around her lit up in pale purple.

A trio of Marauders went for Gavel, who struggled to keep
them off, and Asha jumped onto one of their backs, stabbing at
the base of his skull with a pair of small scissors. A man grabbed
Adonis around the waist as if to carry him off, but Six sent a
throwing knife through the Marauder's eye. A monstrous man
covered in bone piercings sprinted toward unconscious Sans on
the ground, axe raised to strike, and Freddy ran with a buzzing
rod to intercept him.

So occupied were the Marauders with the fray that they
didn't notice Survivor charge at The Gentleman. Beo leapt in
between them, and Survivor halted.

"Please, don't. Beo," she said.

The Gentleman sidestepped so that Survivor could see
him. "I told you, he's family. A family protects its father." He
clapped Beo on the arm. "Son, she abandoned you. Now you
can have your revenge. It's far overdue. Take it."

Beo drew the same knife he'd pressed to Wren's throat moments before and held it down by his thigh.

"If you have to, then do it. I understand. I deserve it," said Survivor.

"You do," Beo said, his tone plain and simple. "But he deserves it more." He tossed her the knife, which she deftly caught. Beo then slammed his shoulder into the The Gentleman's chest so hard he fell to the ground, where he lay helpless on his back. Survivor was on him in a flash, and before he could even flail, she'd straddled his torso and cut his throat.

As he lay bleeding out, Survivor tossed his hat away. She kissed his forehead and stroked his hair as she sang, "Go to sleep, my little baby. When you wake, you shall have all the pretty little horses."

He sputtered and finally his eyes grew dim as blood soaked his blue suit.

As she watched her sister kill, her friends fight for their lives, and Caster lying unmoving on the ground, the dam of Wren's control finally burst.

She threw her arms up, her spine arching back unnaturally far until she stared up at the constellations, crystal clear and watching her. A brilliant flash of white and purple enveloped her and burst outward with a CRACK, sending out a shockwave like a dying star. The force blew out the torches, metal clashed as vehicles turned over, and profiles of men whose screams were lost in the subsequent BOOM flashed white. The light disappeared as fast as it had come, leaving the stars to shine down onto the eerie quiet. Wren fell back as the energy, hot and pulsing, receded into her body.

She faded in and out of consciousness with no idea how much time was passing. A series of noises and images and pieces of sentences told her she at least wasn't dead.

"Oh my God," said Asha. "Their heads. They're..."

Someone vomited.

It grew brighter. Dawn? Wren opened her eyes. Asha leaned over her as wind whipped their hair around. Wren was vaguely aware of the sensation of moving, and moving fast. Asha touched her neck and cheeks.

"She's burning up. Her pulse is weak," said Asha.

Wren closed her eyes, then Survivor's voice floated over from Wren's left. "I told you, Eydis can't be trusted. She's up to something even Thallium doesn't know about."

Asha's voice replied, "She's the only one who can save her, so that's where we're going."

More darkness, then Asha's angry shout roused Wren. "— still burning up! Can't you make this shitbox go faster!"

Then she heard Caster's voice, felt his breath at her ear. "You're doing great. You'll be fine."

He was alive.

She searched for him, but sleep took her again, she didn't know for how long. Then Survivor stood over her, backlit by bright blue sky. They'd stopped moving. Survivor's expression was hard, her face still smudged with remnants of the blood of others.

"I can't go with you. Too dangerous," she said.

"Go. We need to get her through the gate." Caster's voice.

Survivor kissed her forehead. "I'll be close. Stay alive. I promised Alma." She disappeared.

Wren tried to lift her head. The gatekeeper's blue hologram face hovered above the group of travelers.

"We need to see the Principal and Eydis. Now," said Caster. Wren realized he was holding her.

"You have not been properly cleared."

"Bitch, open the gate!" yelled Six. Wren's head lolled to the side to see him and Adonis holding a groggy Sans between them. "You can fucking cavity search us, but open the door!"

Loud gears turned, and metal groaned as the gate unlocked. Sweat and veiled panic covered Caster's face as he adjusted her weight between his arms. "Almost there. Hold on."

The sensation of running consumed her as everything faded to black.

Noonday sun came in through the slanted window in Thallium's study, and dust particles hung in the air, suspended by hope. Caster sat in one of the leather chairs, clasped hands under his chin. He didn't know how long he'd been sitting, and part of him wanted to stay seated indefinitely with his eyes unfocused, turning the shining dust to diamonds. The study door opened, and a gust of air stirred up the dust. Thallium walked in.

"Eydis got her stable," he said.

Caster closed his eyes and rubbed the bridge of his nose, exhaling in relief. He cleared his throat before speaking.

"When can I see her?"

"She's unconscious," said Thallium. "She won't be seeing anyone for a while."

Caster leveled his eyes at his father, who was already staring at him. "How long is a while?"

"As long as it takes for her to recover. I'm sure you can understand that." Thallium walked over to the bookcase by the opposing chair and stopped himself mid-reach for the water pitcher. He walked to his desk instead, took a round bottle of Sangre del Sol out of the top drawer, and set two short glasses out.

"None for me," said Caster.

Thallium poured the drink anyway, thick and red. He took the glasses, handed one to Caster, and sat across from his son.

"I heard you were injured. Badly," said Thallium.

Caster could still feel the sharp pain in his gut, the way the spear had ripped through his organs. And the blood, so much of it flowing out freely. He'd just started to go cold all over and shake uncontrollably when the pain stopped, the flow stopped, and then time seemed to stop when Wren's power erupted into the night. He should be dead. Beyond repair, without a doubt, dead. And while he intended to find out why he wasn't, Thallium didn't need to know about any of it.

He shook his head as casually as he could manage. "Not badly. Just a flesh wound. I'm fine, clearly."

Thallium studied him for a moment, but then shrugged. "Good, I'm glad. On to the next issue, then. What to do about Hallund. Gavel said they couldn't be reasoned with?"

"No. They're convinced that you were behind their water contamination and the death of dozens of their people, and that you intend to do the same to nearby communities."

The Principal tsked and took a sip of his drink. "Some people just believe what they want to believe. Can't change that."

"I was told the sickness in Hallund looks like rubedo," said Caster.

His father returned the statement with a neutral "hmm."

Caster swirled the alcohol in his glass. It smelled strangely sweet, but he recalled it had an edge that burned like fire all the way down. He set it, untouched, on the table.

Thallium eyed the glass. "That's an extremely rare vintage."

"I remember."

Thallium smirked. "You've done well. You were handed a difficult situation and you dealt with it with aplomb. How do you think I should respond to this misunderstanding with Hallund?"

"We need to go out again, once Wren has recovered, and deny the claims. Let me go to the surrounding towns and convince them they need what you're offering. Earn their trust back."

"Is that so?"

"These are people we trade with, people our economy relies on. We can't afford a war." He slid to the edge of his chair. "Let me go talk to them."

Thallium took another sip. He held the glass up and looked through it, examining its clarity. "Why don't you ask me what you're waiting to ask, son."

"Fine. Did you poison the water in Hallund?"

The Principal set his drink down on the bookcase. "Yes."

His admission shocked Caster far more than the idea that he'd committed the crime. "And you what? Expect me to do nothing in response?"

"I expect you to allow me to explain why. I had Eydis modify rubedo. She made it stable in water, increased its virulence, and extended the incubation period. The plan was to use it to frighten surrounding territories enough for us to take their land and resources without a fight.

"I'm not a fool—we made a treatment. We were going to give them that treatment, and they would thank us for it. They'd *worship* us for it.

"Hallund was a trial run. When I learned of the havoc the virus had wreaked, I quelled the entire initiative. It was too powerful. All of the rubedo has been destroyed."

Caster didn't respond.

Thallium leaned back and opened his arms wide to rest them on the arms of his chair. "I was trying to save the many at the expense of the few who got sick. It was a mistake. I'm sorry."

The muscles in Caster's arms, tired as they were, screamed

to kill Thallium where he sat and pose him in that ridiculous chair for all of eternity. He hadn't truly believed his father had been capable of something like this. Thallium was prideful and greedy, but he'd kept his people safe, had protected their way of life. Given them a way of life to begin with. But to discover that Thallium's greed had driven him to resort to mass murder? As his son, it was hard for Caster to swallow.

"Sorry? You're sorry?" Caster said, his jaw tight.

"Yes, son. I'm sorry. It can't be undone, but I wish it could. I'll have to live with that mistake, as I live with many others." Thallium stared at him, the dust hung in the sun, and Caster shifted against the leather. Thallium retrieved his drink. "I would like to work with you. You're more important to me than any territory or legacy. Can you forgive me? Or will we have to part ways for good?"

Caster stayed silent, keeping his father in suspense. He didn't have the support he needed to subvert Thallium's position. Soon, everyone in the outlands would believe Caster had been out doing Thallium's dirty work in Dearborn. The people of The Disc, including Thallium's formidable personal security force, were none the wiser to their Principal's treachery. And then there was Wren—Thallium had her again, and this time, he'd locked her up tight.

If Caster were to stop his father, he couldn't do it by openly opposing him. Not yet. For now, he'd have to stick close to him, once again become his confidant and his ally. He just prayed he could do it convincingly.

"You were doing what you thought was right. I can see that," said Caster finally.

Relief touched Thallium's brow as it unknitted. "Thank you. Truly."

Caster stood and went to look at the bookcase behind Thallium's desk, hoping that keeping his attention on something else would make him sound more casual. "What's your next move, then?"

"An excellent question. We face opposition from all sides beyond our walls. I'm sure we've already lost any semblance of amicable relationship between us and nearby villages. And I have it on good authority that the Marauder clans are more unified than we thought—they will likely seek revenge for the demise of one of their Masters."

Caster spotted a small paperback copy of *The Hobbit* on a shelf and grabbed it. He kept his smile to himself as he thumbed through it. "You believe we need to prepare for war?"

"I already am. I've also locked down The Disc. Nobody in or out, all trade ceased."

Caster tucked the book into his back pocket. "Lockdown? You want our enemies to have time to band together outside our walls? But we trade in the winter with the farming communities, we need outside plants to make medicine. It's a death sentence for our people."

Thallium rose and crossed the rug to Caster, his confidence not lessened by being just shorter than his son. "Nobody will trade with us anyway, not until we can smooth things over."

"How do you intend to do that?"

"With Wren, of course. Now that we know she's capable of more than turning on some streetlamps. People will have to stand down once we discover how to harness that power."

The weight of that statement sunk in slowly, so disgusted and heartbroken was Caster by what it meant. "You're making her into a weapon."

"Making? She *is* a weapon, son. Her display in the Open with the Marauders has made that clear." He patted Caster on his cheek. "Not to worry—she's in good hands with Eydis."

"I'd like to see her."

"As I said, she's unconscious. Who knows for how long.

You'll have to wait. I'll tell you when you can see her. In the meantime, let's keep you occupied with other tasks, shall we?" He lowered his voice even though they weren't in danger of being overheard. "Someone released Wren's outlier sister without my permission. She could not have escaped on her own. I want whoever it was found. And if there's one person among my forces willing to betray me, for some outlier scum no less, then there are others who would do the same. I want them routed like the rats they are, and I want you to do it."

Everything in Caster screamed at him to punch his father squarely in the jaw, to unleash all the anger and the fear on his flesh. Instead, he held out his hand. "I'll do it. We can't afford threats from outside and from within."

Thallium shook his hand firmly. "Spoken like a true leader. Good luck."

Caster broke the handshake. "I need to go debrief my men, if that's all right."

"Certainly. Shall I have Prady bring your things to the Main House? Since we'll be working together again. And when Wren wakes, you won't have to go far to see her."

"You've changed your mind about turning my room into a library then?"

Thallium smiled. "For now."

Caster gave him a bow and then met Asha and Six on the other side of the security fence beyond the study door. They fell into step next to him, speed walking down the hallway to the stairs. Once they were out of earshot of the Keepers, Asha spoke.

"Is she..." she trailed off.

"She'll make it," said Caster.

"Good," said Six. "When do we head back out? The sooner the better to recruit..." He stopped talking and looked around as if they were being watched, which in most of the Main House and government buildings, they were. Or potentially being listened to by the Operator. "...more people to defend The Disc."

"We're on full lockdown. Effective immediately," said Caster.

"What? For how long?" said Asha.

"Until he's finished weaponizing Wren and we've found the inside threat to Thallium."

"Son of a bitch," said Asha, clearly not caring one iota about who might hear her.

"Well," Six said through the side of his mouth, "that should be interesting."

"Get everyone together. We're meeting," said Caster.

"Tonight?" asked Asha.

"Tonight."

Wren woke to the feeling of soft sheets on top of her and a cold metal table beneath her. The lab was empty except for her and Eydis, who sat nearby at a mobile desk unit, typing away. Numbers and graphs moved and changed on the computer screen.

"What happened?" she asked.

Eydis stood and went to her and examined a small, white band around her wrist with a square display. She pressed a button on the band and studied it. "Good morning. How are you feeling?"

"Tired."

Eydis went back to the computer and typed in a series of numbers.

Wren raised her head just enough to make sure they were alone. "Where's Caster? Are the others alive?"

"They're fine." She returned and slipped the sheets off of Wren, folding them and setting them at her feet. "You've been here for a little over a week. I had to keep you asleep so you could heal. Here." She held her hands out.

Wren took her hands and pulled herself up to sit. She wore white panties and a band across her chest, both made out of smooth, tight material. "What are we doing now?"

Eydis helped her stand and guided her to the isolation unit in the middle of the lab. She opened the door. "We need to make you stronger. I'd like to run some tests. May I?"

Wren thought about it, took in Eydis' soft smile, and nodded. She stepped into the box, and Eydis closed the door behind her, locking it.

Eydis swept her hair back to put an earpiece in place. "Can you hear me?" Her voice came over the speaker system, perfectly audible in the box.

Wren nodded.

Eydis studied her from inches away, separated only by the glass. "You're even more beautiful than I imagined you'd be. I wanted to tell you when you came back, but Thallium thinks I have no concept of beauty, and I intend to keep him thinking such thoughts." She tapped the glass with her nail. "You got my hair. The others didn't get my hair, but you did. It's even a prettier shade."

"Your what?"

Cold, green fluid, thick like nectar, started to flow in from the bottom of the box, interrupting Wren's train of thought. It rose slowly but steadily, climbing past her ankles, raising goose bumps on her skin. She stretched out her arms and pressed against the opposing walls of the box, pulling her legs up.

"It's easier when he thinks I'm not human," said Eydis. "Otherwise, he'd start asking questions and become fixated on achieving eternal life. He'd open me up and dig around to see how I work." She smiled wistfully as she opened her hand against the glass, as if this were a reunion long overdue. "Of course, I like to think I'm not human anymore. I'm something else entirely, as are you."

The fluid continued to slowly rise, nearly at Wren's toes that she'd pulled halfway up the box. "I don't understand! What is happening?" Panic started to take her. The power in her chest responded by swelling to life, sending purple light to her hands and feet.

"Calm down," Eydis said tenderly. "The fluid is perfectly harmless, a breathable compound that will allow for more protection from your abilities. Those abilities are beautiful, staggering, and hardly a random genetic trait—I put them there intentionally before you were born, or more appropriately, made. You were the first successful Carrier. I gave you and your siblings that designation because you all carry the hope of a better future in your bodies. A future where greed and complacency are no more."

Wren lost her grip and splashed down into the fluid, which had risen just beneath her breasts. She started to float in it. It was terribly cold, and shivers racked her body. She banged against the glass with her fists. "I don't remember any of this! You're lying!"

"I know—I'm sorry those first years of your life were robbed from you. My assistant at the time stole you and the other Carriers and took you from me. Before she did, she wiped your memories with a very old device. Risky and reckless. But she did it out of misguided love, and I suppose we can't blame her intentions."

Wren tried to think past what was happening in the box and force herself to process what Eydis had just said. "Alma? She worked for you?"

Eydis nodded. "I still miss her sometimes—it gets lonely

down here without an assistant. But Bug has shown potential. I'll give her a try. That way, you won't be alone down here even when I have to leave."

The fluid sloshed gently around Wren's neck. "Please, let me go." The power in her chest swelled, and the purple turned the green fluid in the box an ugly black.

"Not yet, little one. Not until you're ready. I'm going to help you control this power, harness it. And then," Eydis whispered fervently, "we'll use it."

The purple light turned white hot and exploded from Wren, but instead of shattering the box and freeing her as she'd expected, it petered out and sent streams of tiny bubbles through the liquid to tickle Wren's skin.

Eydis kissed her palm and touched it to the glass again as the fluid rose past Wren's head, drowning out her scream as the world around her turned cold.

DEAR READER...

I'm thrilled you're here!

You've already done so much by reading my book, but I'm going to ask you, from my heart, to do one more thing—**please review *First Carrier*.**

I sure hope you loved it, but regardless, please leave a review online wherever you purchased the book. Reviews are extremely powerful for us authors, and it just takes a quick minute for you to make a difference in someone's career.

Finally, I want to hear from YOU! Have questions or comments about *First Carrier*? Text me! No, really. Text me at 505-433-1727.

Thank you!

Madeleine

ALSO BY MADELEINE MOZLEY

Book two of The Disc Chronicles coming 2021!

Want more now? You can get *Replicate*, a collection of short stories featuring Wren, Survivor, and Caster ten years before the events in *First Carrier*. Here's the best part—you can get *Replicate* for FREE.

Go to Madeleine's website MadeleineMozley.com and sign up for her mailing list—you'll receive *Replicate* in your inbox to download in the e-book format of your choice right away. Plus, you'll be in the know about what's going on with book two!

CREDITS

All of these beautiful people had a hand in bringing this book into the world. Madeleine would like to thank...

David Mozley: The first reader of *First Carrier*, my brainstorming partner, and this book's biggest champion. Without him, this book would not exist.

Josiah Davis: Editor and encourager, who helped pull me out of the trap of the endless revision cycle.

James Schlavin: Creator of the coolest cover art of all time, who didn't settle for the wrong shade of red.

Sheri Coen: Beta reader, proofreader, and the best mom in this world and any other.

Killian Coen: Weapons and combat advisor, and a badass brother.

Melissa Blakely: Beta reader, proofreader, and whiskey-sharer.

Kelsey Miller: Space expert who provided a sanity check on the cosmic happenings behind the world of *First Carrier*.

Ben Clifford: Medical guru who made sure I (and all the

other writers in his life) know how the human heart actually functions.

Tracy Jones: Design advisor who looked at approximately 2.3 million fonts with me.

James L. Rubart: Expert in back cover copy who helped make the blurb for *First Carrier* sing.

ACKNOWLEDGMENTS

None of us live this crazy writing life alone. All of the below individuals inspire and challenge Madeleine. She'd like to thank...

The Author of Life, who wrote the ultimate story long ago. I write because of You.

David, my better half, for your endless support of me and my writing, and for not letting me quit. I love you.

My extraordinary kiddos, who are far and away the most wonderful pieces of art I'll ever make. You inspire me daily.

Mom, for constantly loving me and my writing, and for sharing your passion for reading with me from the day I was born.

Dad, for understanding my writing style and thinking I could have written *Breaking Bad*.

Meemo, for helping me turn my childish thoughts into a poem called *Black*, and for the endless grammar lessons. I treasure them all.

Rachelle, for being an incredible writer and even better sister, and for letting me text you rants about publishing.

Thomas Umstattd Jr. and his Novel Marketing Podcast, for the fantastic information I continue to consume ravenously.

The fine folks at Rust is Gold and Flying Star, for letting me sit and type away for hours—your coffee warms my soul.

Everyone who reads my work. You give it life by doing so.

ABOUT THE AUTHOR

Madeleine Mozley is a desert-dwelling word fiend. She lives in New Mexico with her husband, two kids, and three fur babies. Her desire to put green chile into everything she cooks can't be contained.

If you'd like to connect with Madeleine, you may:
- Visit her website MadeleineMozley.com.
- Email her at MadeleineMozley@gmail.com.
- Find her on Instagram and Goodreads.